Alex Keegan has worked for the RAF, in direct selling and as a computer consultant. He gave up a sixty-thousand-pound salary to take a degree in psychology and sociobiology. He took up writing seriously after being involved in the Clapham Rail Disaster and now lives in Southampton with his wife and their two young children. A committed runner, he is a UK top-thirty veteran sprinter.

Alex Keegan's second novel, *Vulture*, is also available from Headline.

Also by Alex Keegan

Vulture

Cuckoo

A Caz Flood Mystery

Alex Keegan

First published in 1994
by HEADLINE BOOK PUBLISHING

First published in paperback in 1995
by HEADLINE BOOK PUBLISHING

10 9 8 7 6 5 4 3 2

All characters in this publication are fictitious and any resemblance to real persons, living or dead, is purely coincidental.

ISBN 0 7472 4685 8

Printed and bound in Great Britain by
Cox & Wyman Ltd, Reading, Berks

HEADLINE BOOK PUBLISHING
A division of Hodder Headline PLC
338 Euston Road
London NW1 3BH

Dedicating a first novel is not to be undertaken lightly, but in my case the task is easy. There are people to whom I'm deeply grateful for their criticisms and advice: these are led by Caroline Oakley, my editor, and David O'Leary, my agent. There are people who steered me right on technical matters; these include some anonymous police-women and men and Brian Lane who explained a little bit of forensics to me.

But at least as important are those people who kept pushing, who kept encouraging when 'unpublished' to me was the heaviest word in the English language; my own family of course, Debbie, Toby, Clare, but more so the ones that had made it but never pretended it was easy, Barnaby Conrad, Barbara Large, Ian St James, Merric Davidson, Louise Doughty and lastly, Steve Harris who didn't wave his four published books but his two box-files of rejections!

I'd particularly like to thank 'Betty' who got me started again but in the end there is only one person to whom this book could be dedicated.

There is a real Caz Flood. All I ever borrowed was the name, and that with permission, and absolutely nothing in this story relates to her. But the real Caz is a bobby too, still in uniform, cheeky, chirpy but, most of all, brave. Throughout the year this book took to write, Caz Flood was off sick, recovering from a beating that she and two colleagues, one male, another female, took from a gang of under-sixteens in a peaceful seaside town a long way from Brighton. The real Caz Flood would be happy to run as fast as my Caz but she would probably say, 'It's a bit tricky at the moment!' There's no one else I could dedicate this book to, so, for all good coppers, particularly you, Caz.

Cheers, mate!

One

Cold Monday morning, six o'clock. November. Brighton sea-front had to be grey, windswept and damp. It was, but as far as Caz Flood was concerned, it was the only place, the perfect place to be. Yesterday she had been a beat copper, a woodentop, today she was a DC, a detective constable, and nothing, but absolutely nothing, could stop her now.

She sat on the stairs in white bikini briefs, her eyes flashing. Today! Yes! And now four quick miles to run before breakfast! She pulled on a pair of cushioned white socks and knee-length Lycra leggings, then her club shirt, bright enough to hail a passing ship, and finally she slipped into a pair of lightweight Asics trainers before creeping down the stairs and out the door. At the last moment she grabbed a pair of white cotton running gloves, her only concession to the day.

Her flat was in a side-street, an easy downhill to the front. She moved lightly on the balls of her feet, almost a dancer as she jogged towards the sea. The cold had hit her like a fist in the face when she opened the door, but already she was sharp and excited, the wind making her more alive, her face lit up by its edge. She wore no bra – the one thing running cost her was her boobs – and she could feel her skin bristling as her body-heat began to rise. In a minute she wouldn't feel the cold and in two more she would be warm enough to push for two quick miles. She felt glorious. Finally but definitely, her world had taken shape. It had taken her six hard years since university, but this was where she had aimed to be, in her own place, earning decent money, fit, independent, in the right job and now, moving up.

She ran east, towards the old Dolphinarium, passing bay-windowed guest-houses, increasing her leg speed until she was running at six minutes a mile. On Tuesdays and Thursdays she did the middle part of her run the hard way, on the shingle beach for strength, but today she could glory in speed. The street-lights were still on and would be for another ten minutes, but their yellow wash was already fading in the red-orange early morning light breaking over the rooftops.

At the Dolphinarium she crossed the road, pushing up the gentle hill for two minutes before turning back. A few cars were out now, cruising like animals on the dewed road, but she was running very hard, straight along the front, and hardly saw them. A panda car rolled by slowly, tooted once, then kept pace with her. She ignored it until she reached her mile marker, then turned her head as she slowed. She was grinning, hardly out of breath as she said good morning. The driver was a ten-year PC just starting to get fat. He spoke, saying that her tights fitted very well. Smiling at him with near-perfect teeth, she told him to piss off.

'Oh dear, above us mortals now are we, Detective?' the driver said.

'No, Harry,' she said, 'just the ones who can't take no for an answer!'

His radio was squawking and he grinned, 'OK, Blondie, have a good one anyway.' He pulled away quickly. She could see him answering the call as he U-turned back towards town.

'This is a *great* job,' she thought, 'even if nobody on the force knows what a new man is!'

She jogged slowly to her stopping point, stretched absent-mindedly, then crossed at a pelican just below her street. Now it was light.

Her next-door neighbour was Mrs Lettice. She was outside her door in a candlewick dressing-gown, collecting her milk. Caz danced towards her, flicking out her arms and legs, the music to Rocky in her head.

'Morning Mrs L! Lovely day!'

'Isn't,' Mrs Lettice said, 'too cold to be out gallivanting.'

'Got to stay fit Mrs L!'

'Nonsense, child.' She shook her head. 'I'm ninety-two years old and I've never done a day's exercise in my life!' Then she was gone, shuffling slowly away towards her little kitchen, muttering as if their conversation continued.

Caz smiled at her disappearing back, then grabbed black railing and skipped up her own flat steps. She was still smiling as she took her door key off her wrist. Deep in her head, a policeman's question was trying to be heard, but it faded feebly, unable to compete with either the hot juices of her run or her excitement. She pulled a blue band from her pony-tail as she walked down the hall and flicked her long hair away from her neck. At the bottom of the stairs she let out a delicious animal noise and ran to the top landing two steps at a time.

She shampooed in the shower, using the suds washing over her body to roll back the good sweat of her run. Before she had stepped under the water, she had expertly fly-kicked her running clothes into the laundry baskets, club kit left, socks and knickers to the right. Two nil! Ready in the bedroom were her work clothes, more soft white socks and pants, a T-shirt screaming 'Seize the Day!', a pair of 501s and fresh trainers. She would top-out with her Hard Rock Café jacket, the most expensive piece of clothing she had ever owned. Not a single item was navy-blue.

Breakfast was Marks & Sparks' freshly squeezed orange juice and a couple of slices of toast. There was no milk left in the fridge for coffee. She didn't take a delivery – some mornings she might not be there – but Mrs Lettice was good for a half-bottle in emergencies.

'Run out again, have we?'

''Fraid so, Mrs L.'

'Well, I've got plenty spare. I just took six pints from Mr B.'s front door.'

'What?'

'Mr B. He hasn't taken his milk in. He must be away.'

'Do I know him?'

'Mr Burnley? I don't think so. He's a nice young man. About your age. I think he works in an office. One of those credit card companies.'

'Well, thank him for the milk, anyway!'

Over coffee, Caz tried to place Mr Burnley but decided she hadn't even briefly met him. She had seen the uncollected bottles of milk earlier, but had only registered it unconsciously. These days the old 'message to a burglar' was far less common, because foraging druggies usually took any bottles still left out after eight o'clock. It was still stupid not to cancel the milk, though. Some people just couldn't be told.

She cleaned her teeth, then looked up to see herself bright in the mirror. Her clenched fist came up in a small victory salute. This was it – it was time to go to work. She stared at the green eyes in the glass as they locked on to hers. She saw her reflection say, 'Go for it, DC Flood!'

Two

Mrs Lettice was waiting for her as she left the flat.

'Miss Flood?' The old dear looked suddenly frail.

'What's up, Mrs L?'

'I just wondered, could you . . . ?'

Caz glanced at her watch.

'I'm sorry. It's Mr B. I wonder, could you . . . ?'

'Is he back Mrs L?'

'Oh no. I don't know. It's just . . .' she pointed down to the basement. 'His front door key is in the lock. See there? Should I just take it out?'

'Would you like me to, Mrs L?'

'Oh, would you? Thank you, Miss Flood.' She was visibly relieved. Caz smiled. 'I'll be back in just a tick, Mrs L.' She went down the steps.

The basement well was spare and neat, a winter-emptied window-box freshly forked and the stone-slabbed floor recently swept. The windows were clean, the curtains drawn. The door was original and had been repainted that summer.

Leaving a house-key in the lock wasn't that rare a mistake and Caz thought nothing of it. She took the key to give to Mrs Lettice and briefly peeked through the door-light into the gloom behind, seeing nothing. She was about to turn away when she smelt fruit. Not fruit but sweet. Not sweet but something sticking in her nose and mouth. Some memory made her stomach juices lurch.

'Mrs Lettice,' she said heavily, 'would you stay there please. I'll just check everything is OK. I might be a little while. Do not come down.'

The door opened with a schlatt! of wood and a rush of the sweetness went by her as if something was trying to escape. She went in, leaving the door open and calling a useless, 'Hello?'

She pushed a light switch with a leather elbow to show a rich blue carpet, candy-striped walls split by a gleaming white dado rail and just one picture, a water-colour of the Sussex Downs. Despite what she was expecting to find, she heard herself whispering, 'Nice.'

The first door on the right, richly white, opened on to a small living room with a black Habitat suite and one tall fitted bookcase. Low in one corner was a quality rack stereo and nearby were scattered compact discs. She saw a George Michael, some re-mixed blues and a Jimi Hendrix. A small red light showed mains power. The CD player was on 'pause', eighteen seconds into track three. The wall-to-wall carpet was a lush, indeterminate pastel, and a large black cushion splashed with angular colour lay against the sofa's edge, strategically placed between the loudspeakers. Ah, Caz thought, this is where we feel the blues. It was a sexy flat. She tried to picture Mr Burnley. She saw him as dark and probably handsome. She could see him drinking late night wine and talking softly. She could imagine lying there.

A curved archway went through to a galley kitchen. The oven door was swung down and the remains of a pizza sat stale on two white plates. A stoppered half-empty bottle of Australian Chardonnay was next to the fridge but had never been put inside.

There was only one other door, that to the bedroom and the en-suite bathroom. Caz could feel the presence of what had to be the other side.

The smell was no worse and she felt it should be, but she knew that she would have to open the door. She turned away to take a deep breath, then, with a tissue held between her damp hand and its cold brass, she pushed down the door's long latch. The smell took her full in the face, the deep, sweet perfume of blood.

The bedroom was as whole and confident as the rest of the flat, very masculine despite its soft colours. November sun slashed in through a break in the curtains, across the velvet bedhead, across the pale blue cotton pillows and across the sheets. Sheets that were once simple blue but were now dark with the life-blood of whoever lay huddled beneath.

She should now be on the radio, calling it in. As first on the spot she would be IC, the officer in charge, in total control until formally relieved by at least a DI and 'scene of crimes'. If the Chief Constable wanted a look at the body he couldn't get past her. That was how it worked. Everything logged, nothing touched, no one there without a reason.

She wasn't shocked by blood or death. One year in 'traffic' with all its senseless carnage had removed the last sensibilities she might once have had. She wasn't afraid. It was more that she was chilled by the realities of mortality. She knew, against everything, that she had to lift the sheets and confirm the death of Mr Burnley.

She had no real excuse. She wanted to look for no other reason except raw curiosity. She took the sheet between a finger and thumb, lifting it gently away from the head. Against the victim's back the sheet had been welded brown by his blood and would not move without considerable force. She could see little below the neckline, but the grey-blue of the man's face told her there was no possibility of a pulse. Burnley was very dead. She shivered in the room's sudden cold. 'And you liked George Michael too . . .' she whispered to him, vaguely and sadly, as if to a friend. Carefully she replaced the sheets as she had found them and left.

Harry, the driver of the panda, was the first to arrive and the first to be refused access to the basement by DC Flood. She put him straight. 'You know better than that, Harry. How about you get Mrs Lettice inside and sat down with a nice cup of tea?' She was happy with power.

Within an hour the street was the scene of a circus, the road closed off to all but residents, with uniforms at both ends, two squad cars slewed across the road and two unmarked cars up on the pavement across from the dead man's flat. An ambulance had been sent away until they were ready to move the body. The back garden was tiny but six men were already working it on their hands and knees, dressed in white paper dungarees.

DI MacInnes, Bob Moore (a sergeant), and two DCs she knew only as Saint & Greavsie were assigned to the team, as, to her delight, was she.

'You were going t' be with me anyway, Flood. Welcome aboard.'

She was almost at attention as she said, 'Thank you, Sir!'

'Don't be such a tart!' MacInnes said. 'You touch anything, Flood?'

'In my report, Sir: the light switches, the door handle, the front door.'

'The body?'

'Just for signs of life, Sir.'

'Are you being funny, lass? There was blood everywhere!'

'I mean, I just took a look at his face, Sir, before I called in.'

'And he looked dead, right?'

'Yes, Sir!'

MacInnes turned to his sergeant. 'Get Saint & Greavsie to start door-to-door, working out from here. We'll have to wait for forensics before we can sort out the stiff. Leave the old lady for Flood, she knows her.'

'I'll . . . pop upstairs then, Sergeant?' Caz offered.

'You do that, Flood.'

As she was leaving, glad to be heading for the cool day, Moore grunted something about women at the sharp end. MacInnes snapped back. 'She kept her bottle, Bob. There's a few PCs who wouldn't have.' He coughed to clear his throat, 'Now, where the fuck is forensics?'

* * *

Mrs Lettice was coping well, even if suddenly she looked every one of her years. Harry Deans was an old hand, and had started by telling her that Mr Burnley, Mr B., was ill, then very ill, then, while she sat with tea, more than just very ill.

'I'm afraid Mr Burnley has died, Mrs Lettice.'

'But I've got his milk,' she replied.

Caz was very gentle with Mrs Lettice once Harry Deans had gone. She seemed terribly frail now and when she answered Caz's soft questions, she spoke slowly, her voice little more than a whisper. It was obvious that she knew very little. She had never known Mr Burnley to have anyone home, she said, but he had often played his music. It was modern stuff, she explained, quite loud.

In a dormitory street where hardly anybody knew anybody, she was fairly well informed, but, she explained carefully, Mr Burnley was not a neighbour she had shared much time with.

'I've taken the odd parcel for him,' she added, 'and things like the milk, I help with that . . .' She sipped her tea. 'We spoke a little in the summer when he had a week off. He was quite a nice young man.'

Thinking of those rooms, Caz imagined that she was probably right.

She asked softly, 'Who lives upstairs, Mrs L?'

'Upstairs? It's empty. A young couple had it but they got into trouble with their mortgage. They moved out in July. It was repossessed.'

'Can you remember their name?'

Once again Mrs Lettice looked very old.

'Oh dear, oh dear . . . I . . .'

Caz touched her blue-skinned hand.

'Don't worry, Mrs L. I can find out from the building society.'

'Oh, thank you,' the old woman said, 'sometimes I . . .'

Three

They were at the nick before eight the following morning. The squad and three drafted-in uniforms waited in a yellow-walled room for DI MacInnes and Sergeant Moore. At the back of the room was a Kinderman slide-projector on a tall stand. One of the uniforms, a tall and awkward PC called Tingle, was edgy and nervous, desperately needing a cigarette.

Greavsie had decided his quick movements and too-loud voice were out of order. He made a sudden grab for the boy, 'What'd'you think, lads? Think we should 'ang Billy out the window for a quick drag?'

'Sod off, Greavsie!' the PC said quickly. He was bigger than Greaves but unsure of his situation. 'You drink, I smoke, all right?'

'Oh, that's personal, Billy,' the older man hissed and made a grab for the other's groin, coming away instead with his real target, the cigarette pack, which flew sideways to another copper.

'Give us me smokes, you bastards!' the young man shouted, half chasing, half pleading as his cigarettes curved from hand to hand. Greaves was laughing as they finally landed with Caz Flood. 'Caz?' Billy said. He walked slowly towards the offered box. 'Caz?' She held his eyes and hers read love and sympathy. He reached out his hand, genuinely grateful. Caz was smiling sweetly.

'Filthy habit!' she said, still smiling, and tossed the pack through the open window.

The boy looked hurt, but before he could react, the DI entered with Sergeant Moore. 'Listen up!' Moore said, and passed a rack of slides to the PC near the projector, 'DI MacInnes!'

Then MacInnes spoke. 'OK, lads. We've got ourselves a nasty little murder. Someone do the lights.'

'Inkerman Terrace,' the DI began. Caz's street appeared on the white wall. 'Straightforward bedsit land. Main crime problem is burglaries. Little bit of low-level drug use, coke and grass. We've even heard that someone's resurrected LSD. Nothing unusual.'

The projector clacked.

'Number 42. The old dear is a Mrs Lettice. Top floor is unoccupied.

'Basement flat. The victim bought it just before the last property boom. Very clean, well-decorated, decent stuff.

'Front room. Nothing at all unusual. CD was still on.

'Kitchen. There were two plates out.'

There was a shot of the pizza. 'Mushrooms, peppers and onion. Our body was vegetarian.

'The bedroom. Apart from the obvious, no signs of a struggle.'

Another click-clack. The heaped bed.

Another, the dark crown of Mr B.

'Sheets were stuck to the victim's back.' Another click.

'There was a lot of blood but so far, only in the bed.' Burnley's torso, wickedly striped. 'This looks horrible, but forensic say it didn't kill him. This did.' (A blue pointed puncture in the abdomen.)

'Or this did . . .' (A blood-crusted close-up of savagely slashed genitalia.)

'The anus was attacked too. We're not sure yet exactly which wound killed him.'

'George Burnley. Twenty-nine. Sales Exec. for American Express. No record. Solid, white Protestant. Not bad looking. We think he worked out. There were a couple of fitness magazines. There was a joint in the kitchen. Parents are dead. Has a sister in the Midlands.

'Door-to-door has shown up nothing yet. No one knows which way he leaned, but this looks a lot like the boyfriend did it. There were semen stains in the bed. We heard ten minutes ago that only one set belonged to Burnley. Lights!'

MacInnes' face was alive, dark eyes burning. This was the look he was famous for. He liked to catch killers. Someone had once told Caz that MacInnes had never had an 'unsolved'. He hated killers too much to let them go. 'Any questions?'

She wanted to say something, but his dark face made her hesitate. He looked menacing, shifting his weight as if ready to bite her the moment she spoke. 'Sir? As you know I was first into the flat . . .'

MacInnes nodded.

'Well, Sir, for what it's worth, I didn't think it was a gay bloke's pad.'

'What the hell does *that* mean, Flood?'

'Well, Sir . . . well, the place felt sexy.'

'That's it, Flood?'

She felt ludicrous and tiny. 'Yes, Sir, I just thought . . .'

'God spare us from DCs who think!' He looked up at the ceiling as a few in the room laughed, then quieted them all. 'OK, OK, Sergeant Moore will take over for now.' He moved to leave, then spoke lightly to Caz. 'Have a word in my office when you're finished.'

Moore stepped forward. 'Right, you lot. I want to catch this bastard before the trick cyclists move in. We want all the usual stuff.' He was pointing as he spoke. 'Talk to the taxi-firms. I want every call that went within a mile of the street. We continue door-to-door. Saint, Greavsie, you can do the gay clubs, see if anyone recognises our stiff. Flood, you talk to Amex, see who really knew him. Anything big comes up, hit my office straight away with it. Otherwise we are back here for five tonight. OK, now sod off and do some work. Let's find out who Burnley *really* was.'

DI MacInnes had his office three doors away. Caz tapped and went straight in. He was looking at a very thin file: George Burnley's.

MacInnes remained eyes down, reading the file. She waited, thinking he looked small. Caz knew his upbringing had been a quiet one on the borders, but he still looked like a Glasgow-born rough. Her two guvnors were chalk 'n cheese. Bob Moore was jovial and two stone overweight; the DI was skinny enough to have a thyroid problem. He spoke.

'What, exactly, were you trying to say in there, Flood?'

'I thought you might be interested in a woman's perspective, Sir.'

'You're not a woman now, Flood. You're a copper!'

'As a copper then, Sir, I could *feel* things in that flat.'

'Like what?'

'Like it was somehow sexy, Sir. I felt good in there. I felt as if me and Burnley might have been close had I ever met him. I can't justify it, Sir, but I know I'm right.'

'We're not talking about women's intuition, are we, Constable?'

'No more than you've broken cases on a hunch, Sir.'

'Oh, not any more, Flood.'

'Sir?'

'We don't have hunches any more, Flood. We have computers.' He waved at her. 'Sit down a minute.

'This town is a melting-pot and a flesh-pot, you know that. We've got an active gay community but they've always co-operated with the force. In twelve months we've had three murders of gays but given the type of town this is, the murder-rate isn't abnormal. Every one turned out to be a straightforward "domestic" and we wrapped each one up in a month. They call this town "Bohemian". I've never known what that means, but the shopping's good and I like it.'

He stared at her intently. 'This isn't just a domestic, Detective, even if it is the boyfriend. Whoever killed Burnley did so much damage to his arse we can't even *tell* if he ever had anal intercourse.

'I want this shit as soon as possible, Flood. The bastard is really sick. You've seen the pictures. I just hope to God this is a one-off.' He tried to look kindly, 'I've no hassle with you putting in your four-penn'orth, girl, but this time I think you're wrong. Be careful what you say and when you say it. If you really think something that's a bit off the edge, you come to me or Sergeant Moore.'

He waved a gnarled hand at her, suggesting she should leave, then he spoke again as she stood. 'You know what Bob Moore thinks of women coppers, Flood?'

'Everyone does, Sir.'

'Prove him wrong then, Constable!'

'Yes, Sir!'

Now he was smiling. 'Well, piss off then!'

Four

Amex House was just off Brighton's Grand Parade, a walk across the road from the nick in John Street, the smooth white of its eight storeys broken up by dramatic dark blue glass. The rear of the building overlooked the golden domes of the refurbished Brighton Pavilion but from the seventh floor up the front offices would have a pleasant view of the sea. Reception was crisp and efficient, overseen by a uniformed security guard who for once actually looked as if he would be able to handle most situations. She was suitably impressed.

The personnel officer was a Valerie Thomas, and Caz was surprised when a clean-cut smooth-looking male emerged to offer his hand.

'Detective Constable Flood?'

Slightly flustered, Caz said she was expecting a Miss Thomas.

'I'm afraid that's me!' the man said. He had a mid-Atlantic accent and smiled with doctored teeth. 'There's an interview room just there.' His arm brushed past her pointing to a pine-coloured door. 'Tea or coffee?'

Thomas was armed with a small file and carried a Toshiba lap-top computer. She followed the arm and led their way into a tight little room which felt like a railway carriage.

'I'm sorry about the room, Officer. It was a bit short notice. Please sit down. I share my office with my secretary, so I thought . . .'

'The room's absolutely fine, Mr Thomas.'

'Oh, Valerie, please!'

'Valerie?' She laid on the question as thickly as she could.

'I should carry a special card explaining. It was all my mother's fault. Her first big love was some young Russian she met in Finland or somewhere. I ended up being called Valeri, no "e". My Dad wasn't at all impressed and he added the "e" on at the register office.' He was laughing at himself, light blue eyes shining wet.

'School must've been tough.'

'Wigan!' he said with a twinkle.

'Yeah, tough,' she said.

'It was worse in Liverpool!'

'Liverpool?'

'Mam and Dad split up and we went there. She worked for a while in a factory for a big flour company. It's pulled down now.'

'Why didn't you change your name?'

'Pride! In the early days I had to fight for it, then it became a matter of principle. I thought I was looking after the name for my mother.'

'Is she still in Liverpool?'

'Yeah, she remarried. A bloke called Tom, used to be an engineering officer on ship. I think she's got a thing about sailors!'

Drinks arrived. A silver tray, real cups and saucers.

'Good Grief!' Caz said, goggling at the formality. Valerie laughed and threw back his head. It was a nice laugh. He touched his light brown hair.

'I used to wear this long,' he said, still smiling. 'When I had it cut my Mum nearly cried. She said I looked just like him.' He went quiet for a moment, then his face softened. He was remembering something.

'So you,' he said, 'do you have a first name?'

'Detective?' she offered. He just looked at her. 'Caz,' she said. He still just looked. She gave in. 'But my warrant card says Katherine.'

'But not after Catherine the Great?'

'Not as far as I know,' she said. She decided she liked him. She poured, milk second, and they drank tea. She finally brought up George Burnley. The nick had so far managed to sit on 'cause of death' and Valerie asked her how he had died.

'In suspicious circumstances,' she replied.

Giving her a vaguely scolding look, Valerie opened his Toshiba. He flicked a switch. 'Be just a second,' he said.

'Slow boot up, noisy hard disc but a great machine,' she smiled at him, 'gas plasma mono screen. I'm surprised you haven't got colour.'

'I'm trying,' he said, 'but even the American Express Company can recognise a recession.'

'Hundred-meg hard disc?' she asked.

'Yeah. And four megabytes of ram.'

'Three eight six or four eight six?'

'Three eight six two five DX.'

'Pretty quick then?'

'Quick enough!' He typed px and pressed the Enter key. 'I've got a Paradox database on here. I've got basic information on everyone in the building but I've linked it into all the social and sports clubs. So what do you want to know?'

'Everything unofficial,' she said.

Valerie Thomas turned the computer away from the window light and towards her. She looked at the screen inside the opened lid. 'OK. George Burnley, no middle name, age thirty.'

'We have him as twenty-nine.'

'No, he's thirty. Look, date of birth, sixth of November.'

'That's today.'

'Well he won't be having a party!'

'I guess not,' Caz said slowly.

'OK,' Valerie continued. 'Now, let's see. Went on the ski-trip last year, played soccer for the department a couple of times, and he was on the squash ladder, ten places above me.'

'What about holidays, that sort of thing?'

'Took a week off at Christmas, two weeks off in February – that'll be the ski-trip – and a couple of days in August. Can you see all right?'

'It's OK.' She moved her chair closer.

'Company car: BMW 316i, J-reg. No bumps.'

'Anything else?'

'Departmental. Let's see. His boss is Reg Smith. Gave Burnley a pretty good performance rating. He was probably on for promotion.'

'Any problems. Anything unusual?'

'Not according to the Tosh.'

'Does that mean no?'

'Probably, but not definitely. That's the reason for the paper.' He exited the programme and shut down. He smiled again. 'Just be patient. Some things don't go on computer.'

As he opened the file he explained. 'I used to work for one of the big five banks. Say some money goes astray or a customer complains that a deposit is under-recorded.'

'Yes . . .'

'Well, naturally enough, the bank's inspectors have to investigate the problem. They interview anyone and everyone who could be involved and they try damn hard to prove the thing one way or the other. Bank workers are no more and no less honest than anyone else. We get bad ones just like you can get bad coppers. If we find a definite culprit we get rid, that's obvious. Nearly always they avoid a criminal prosecution. It's better for the image to keep it quiet.'

She hadn't realised how close their faces were. He smelt of Cacherel. 'Very often it's not possible to isolate an alleged offence and find an offender. Sometimes a problem may be narrowed down to a small group of individuals but we can't pinpoint *the* one.'

'So what do you do?'

'We record every investigation, and if someone is under suspicion, we log the fact. It probably sounds like Big Brother but it's exactly the opposite. A dishonest bank-teller creates an atmosphere of distrust. If someone's name pops up regularly, we can find ways to test his or her honesty. What we try to do is *remove* suspicion. The best inspectors are like good coppers, they can smell villainy even when they can't prove it.'

'So you log all your unsolved cases on computer?'

'Definitely not!' he said. She asked him why.

'Ah, that's *because* of Big Brother!'

'You're losing me.'

'The Data Protection Act!' His face lit up. 'These days all employees have the right to see any item of information recorded about them *if* that information is held on computer. If we suspect, say, Joe Bloggs of quietly milking a few hundred accounts and we enter that on a computer, we're in dead trouble because now Bloggs can come along whenever he likes and demand a print-out of everything we know about him!'

For the second time that morning she said, 'Good Grief!'

'So we have to put paper between computer systems. That way we stay inside the law.'

'Go on.'

'Well, let's say Joe Bloggs *is* under suspicion. All we need is to write somewhere on the computer file "refer to manual file so-and-so". The manual file is confidential and *not* covered by the DP act.'

'OK, but how do you cross-check or look for patterns?'

'On the computer! On another system.'

'How?'

'Simple. On the "open" file – the one Bloggs is allowed to read – we say "refer to manual file X". In the paper file we can put down that we're suspicious about certain activities and refer to a second database which contains all the unsolveds. Bloggs is now a number but we know it's Bloggs.' She was leaning forward, a little too interested. 'The systems are passworded elbows-deep. If anyone broke in we'd be fined fifty grand and the programmer would be on his bike!'

Caz was suddenly excited, the thought that Burnley might have been involved in some amazingly complex scam and had been killed by Mr Big flashing through her head.

Thomas sensed her rising interest and cooled it. 'In George Burnley's case I don't think we're going to find anything too exciting. He's got an asterisk here, under comments, that's almost certainly trivial. Let's take a look.' He opened the file, tilting it from her and pausing for effect.

'Well?' she said.

'Very undramatic, I'm afraid, Miss Flood – it is Miss, isn't it?' Caz failed to respond. 'It seems that George took an extra day off in August without informing his boss, no big deal, and got picked up twice over expenses for getting petrol out of area.'

'Christ! Is Amex that tight?'

'Not at all. Not normally. George probably pissed off his boss when he skipped school in August. One of his off-the-patch credit-card slips was for the day he had off. Unlucky coincidence, I'd guess.'

'For a minute there I thought I was on to the Brinks-Matt bullion.'

'Sorry, Caz. Maybe next time, eh?'

'Maybe.' She looked a little sad. 'Where did he get the petrol?'

He smiled. 'Let's see.' He shuffled some paper. 'Some place called Grigglesham Foster. Can't say I've heard of it.'

'It's between Guildford and Petersfield. There's a good pub there.'

'Well, there's a Texaco garage as well. George Burnley spent twenty quid at it, twice.'

'Not enough to get killed for though, is it?'

'What is?' Thomas said.

Valerie took her upstairs to see Reg Smith, a soft-mannered, portly little man, in his early fifties and balding. He left her with him, but only after whispering, 'I'll give you a ring.' To Smith he said, 'Morning, Reg. This is Detective-constable Flood.'

Smith was visibly shocked and looked as if he had been crying. As he stood and held out his hand towards Caz, his movements were slow and over-controlled. He looked tired, clinically depressed.

'It's George's birthday you know. We'd all bought him a card.'

'It must be very difficult . . .'

'He was a good lad. A good worker. Everybody liked him.'

'I'm sure. What about his social life? Mates? Girlfriends?'

'He was very chatty with the secretaries but he was on the road a fair bit. You'd have to ask them.'

'What about hobbies? Sports? What did he do with his holidays?'

Smith looked distracted, vaguely interested in the slow-motion world outside his office. She prompted him again. 'Mr Smith? Holidays?'

Without looking at her he said, 'No idea.'

'I understood he went skiing in February.'

'Oh yes. I couldn't go . . . Bad back . . .'

She waited a few seconds. 'Er, Mr Smith, I doubt that it's important, but you were concerned about Mr Burnley's expenses earlier this year. Is that right?'

'Oh, that was nothing really, just a storm in a tea-cup. George was a day late back after a long weekend, I ended up missing a deadline, and he got his wrists slapped.'

She could see his face filling, tears threatening in his pale eyes.

'You don't think that was, why George . . . do you?' he asked. 'George wouldn't have killed himself over—'

She interrupted. 'No, Mr Smith, Mr Burnley didn't kill himself. Mr Burnley was *murdered*. We are just trying to get some background on him. We just want to know what kind of person he was, who his friends were, what he did in his spare time.'

'Oh,' he said softly. She could see him adjusting, his guilt lessened.

'I'd like to know what was different in July. Valerie Thomas said that George was in line for promotion. Why the admonishment?'

Smith coughed and sat up. 'It was really nothing. George worked bloody hard and obviously was going places. I just presumed he'd be promoted.' He moved again. 'In July he went through a funny patch, only a few weeks. You know, late in, slapdash reporting. It was so out of character I had to pull him up.'

'Was he under some kind of pressure? Was he worried?'

'No. That was just the point. He was unbelievably cocky. A bit *too* chatty with the girls. I don't know exactly, he was just over the top.'

'Tell me about the odd day off.'

'Ah well, that's a good example,' Smith said. He was perking up now. 'Who hasn't been "sick" once in a while? I needed George in that day and he let me down. I challenged him about it but I wasn't really mad. He was usually so conscientious that I put it down to a one-off occasion, girl trouble or something. It was his attitude that made me angry. Normally he was so keen. Suddenly work seemed to be a bit of a joke to him and so was I. So I slapped his wrists.'

'And after that? Was he OK?'

'Yes. He settled down well and was just like he was before.'

'Could it have been drugs?'

'No, I don't think so. He wasn't spaced out or moody. He was just a bit high but it wasn't speed or anything like that. I'm not naïve, detective. My son and daughter are at university and I've seen enough variation on the eyeball to know when someone's on drugs. I'd bet my career George wasn't. It was something else.'

'But you don't know what.'

'Not the faintest idea,' he said. By now he was managing to smile.

The secretaries added little. They'd all liked him, he was good-looking and friendly and most of them had had lunch-time drinks with him at some time. 'Never tried to chat any of us up though,' a girl called Janet said, and another one said, 'More's the pity!'

'Do you think he had a girlfriend?'she asked.

'Well, he never said he did.'

She pretended to laugh when she asked about boyfriends.

'George? Blokes? Nah, can't believe that. Nah.'

They were girls and they were nearly sure. She was a woman and she knew. George Burnley was straight. Dead, but straight.

She stood up, thanked the girls, took a look out over the sea, then left. In the lift she thought about George Burnley, DI MacInnes and Valerie Thomas. The security guard in reception gave her a half salute. She turned her collar up as she ducked back into the day.

Five

Door-to-door had been painful. Hardly anyone was in and those that were knew no one other than their immediate neighbours; and in many cases, their knowledge didn't even spread that far. The lads had resorted to leaving notes asking residents to ring the nick. Once upon a time they would have worked straight through but now overtime was rationed out, even for murders. Burnley's photo was recognised by only two people. Neither had seen him with a partner, male or female.

'So, so far the lot of you have picked up nowt?' Sergeant Moore said. He looked for Caz, 'Unless we count the fact that Burnley fiddled his expenses!' He wanted to stare her down, but she flashed back, seething. MacInnes stepped in. 'Well, we do have something. Forensics have come back on the semen in the bed. Some was Burnley's, but there's a confirmed other, unknown. For now it's sample B., for Boyfriend.'

'OK, we need to hit the clubs again tonight but there's no overtime.' The room groaned. 'OK, OK, I know it's tough, but you'll all get brownie points if we crack this one. We've got better pictures now, from the sister. We need to find out where Georgie trawled.'

A DC suggested that maybe Burnley was a cottager. The DI grunted acknowledgement. 'OK, we check the usual public toilets, but go easy on the punters, we don't want them going cold on us. Posters on the doors might help, but try to keep the sweets sweet, ay, lads? And let's try the muscle shops and the Health Clubs. Burnley was well worked out. He must have trained somewhere.'

They were in at half-seven the following day. MacInnes had decided he wanted them on the streets before nine o'clock. Saint & Greavsie had pulled a blank in the clubs, their only bite turning out to be from a guy who fancied Saint. Now Greaves couldn't leave it alone.

'Well, they can always tell, you know, mate. How long is it you been divorced, now?' Saint raised the finger and hunched down into his coat.

The lads were rabbiting. A few looked red-eyed, as if they'd put in a bit extra. Sergeant Moore came in, conversations continuing.

'OK, what we got?' he shouted, hushing the rumble. 'Anything?'

They had one hit. Burnley had used a mixed health club called 'Trim' for nearly two years, and had just paid for a month's trial at a new glossy place called 'Lean 'n Mean!' The payment would have come up once they'd analysed Burnley's bank account but the DC with the news had one chalked up by the boss anyway.

'Everyone says he was an OK bloke. A bit quiet. Bit serious. Used to like to train late on when the club was quieter. Worked out for an hour and then 'ad a swim three or four times a week.'

'What about boyfriends?' Moore asked.

'Nowt, Sarge,' the DC said. 'Apparently this place "Trim" is known as a bit of a pulling place for young birds. Not really poof territory.'

'What about the new club?'

'Hasn't got a reputation yet. Very fancy. All stainless-steel, rock music and mirrors. They had his photo on file, but no one really knew him. He'd been there twice last week.'

'Good lad, anyway,' Moore said.

There was a knock on the door and a young uniform opened it. In walked a WPC carrying a large, white-faced board. There were a few of the usual ribald remarks, but the DI told everyone to 'shut it!'

The young PC, Billy Tingle, straightened out an aluminium easel and the WPC lifted the board on to its metal pegs, smiled briefly at Billy, and left the room.

'Inkerman Street,' MacInnes said firmly. 'The Xs are the doors we've got answers at. I want all Xs this time tomorrow. The board stays in here. I want to see the crosses going on soonest. Let's stop pissing about and get ourselves this nutcase.'

'Caz Flood?' MacInnes spoke as if he couldn't see her. 'DC Flood, we need to know who lived in the flat upstairs and we've drawn a blank with the electoral roll. Get on to that, will you? Start out by talking to the building society.'

'OK, boys and girls, off you go then!' Moore said.

They filed out, Greavsie with his hand on Saint's backside. Most of the guys were laughing but Caz fumed. Moore had taken the piss and the DI had treated her like she was straight out of police college! Arrogant bastards!

She was embarrassed to realise that she didn't know which building society's sign was pinned to the wall eight feet from her bedroom. She dared not ask. Instead she left, looking purposeful, apparently en route to the society's office, but first driving past the end of her street and quietly taking in the name.

She arrived at the Nationwide's offices after miserably struggling to find a parking place for her MG. A nearby shop had sold her a strange new time ticket to place on the dash. It began to rain so she grabbed a black Goretex running-top from the back seat. She was wet when she entered and the junior who first spoke to her was not impressed. She needed to snap at him and flash her warrant card before he produced the deputy manager. When he arrived she was still feeling aggressive.

'Detective-constable Flood!' she barked, flashing the card again.

'And how can I help you, *Detective*?' The manager rolled his hands together and almost bowed to her, his head slightly to the side.

'We need to trace a former mortgagor of yours.'

'Address?'

'Inkerman Street, 42b. We believe it was repossessed, but we'd like to contact the previous owners.'

'To help with your enquiries . . .' he smarmed. Her neck bristled and she simply stared. 'Er, right. Hmmm, let's see. When exactly was the house repossessed?'

They waived confidentiality on a need-to-know basis. The couple had been in trouble for just over a year before they'd posted the keys through the office door with a brief apology. His name was Trevor Jones, she was Jenny Wilkinson. There was no forwarding address but someone had scribbled in one corner 'try St Mary's, Soton?' According to their file, Wilkinson was a secretary for a solicitor in Hove, and Jones worked for a shop selling up-market hi-fi equipment. Both of them had moved on.

'What does this mean?' she asked, pointing at the scribble.

'I'm not sure,' the manager said, 'it looks like Jim Green's writing.'

She raised her eyebrows.

'James Green is our new business manager. He's off at the moment, presumed sick. I tried to ring him a few times this morning but his phone was engaged. If you need to speak to him I can give you his address.'

'Yes . . . Please . . .' She was writing in her notebook, distracted. 'And the names and addresses where Jones and Wilkinson worked.'

'No problem. I'll get one of the girls to do a photocopy now.'

'Too tough for a man, is it?' she said half-heartedly.

'Oh, Detective,' he said, 'that is quite funny.'

'I wasn't joking,' Flood said but he was already shouting to a young secretary who came high-heeling towards him across the office.

'Mandy, this is Detective Flood. She needs this file photocopied now.' The girl left and he turned back towards Caz with an almost sickening grin, 'You can't keep a dog, Constable, *and* bark yourself, can you?'

The clerk was already at the Xerox giggling to a friend and nodding their way. Caz sighed, this wasn't one up for women's lib.

Caz considered the options. She could drive out to Hove to speak to the solicitors or take a walk in the rain to Pearson's Hi-fi where Jones had worked. She decided on the third option: trying Jim Green. The scribbled note might mean that he knew where they were anyway.

Green's place was in Onderman Road, six parallel streets away from her own, a through road lined with tall buildings and ending on the promenade. If it were late at night she could've thought she was arriving home, but by daylight, even in the rain, she could see it was one step – and about fifteen thousand pounds – up from Inkerman Terrace.

Green had the ground floor flat, actually raised above street-level and access was through a heavy communal door with stained glass. To the left of the entrance were three weather-pitted intercom grilles, and the bottom name accompanying them said simply 'Jim G!'

She rang and heard nothing. She rang again. Nothing. She could feel the rain curling from her ears and twisting down inside her Goretex where she was almost warm. Her Levi's were already well damp. Once more she rang Green's bell, the middle bell and the one for the top floor, leaning on for a longer blast and gently cursing the weather. One of the grilles crackled, a woman's voice. 'Hello,' it said, 'is that the council?'

'Police, Ma'am,' Flood answered. 'I wonder if I could have a word.'

'You're not the council, then? I thought you'd come about the smell.'

The grille crackled again, 'First Floor!' and the door buzzed as the speaker released the security lock. 'Give it a good push,' the woman said, 'the door sticks when it's been raining!' Caz pushed once. Hard.

As soon as the door was open she knew. She turned towards the sea, trying not retch, but it was as if the smell had disgusting fingers in her face and down her throat. She grabbed for a hanky but it was too late. Her hand was still in her pocket as she gagged and suddenly she was heaving. She threw up into the basement, her vomit splattering off a silvered dustbin lid and against a wall.

Caz had to spit her mouth clean before she could call it in. When MacInnes and Brown arrived she was soaking, her head back, facing the rain, letting it wash over her, her exposed hair lank and matted and wet.

'Jesus, Flood!' MacInnes said. 'Are you all right?' He passed her a moulded paper face mask. 'Here take this. What're you doin' – killing off yer old lovers?'

A panda pulled up, the driver in too much of a hurry. It skidded into the kerb with a thud. MacInnes spoke to Sergeant Moore, 'Bob, if that's Harry Deans, he should have a sledge-hammer in his boot. Get him up here straight away.'

Bob Moore was the heaviest of the three men, and he ended up with the hammer. Green's door was inset in an alcove, awkward to swing at and tougher than expected. Moore was sweating and getting angry. He removed his mask for extra air, but the smell reached out for him. He gagged, swore at the stench and rained blows on the door. Eventually, one clean strike burst the lock. Suddenly they were in.

They did not have to look far for Green. He was at the end of the hall facing them, sat on an open wooden commode and naked except for a pair of pink socks. His throat had been cut and his head tied to the tall chair's back to keep it from falling forward. The flat was wickedly warm. Even their masks didn't protect them completely from the smell of his body.

Six

'George Burnley was killed between ten on Friday night and the early hours of Saturday morning. Jim Green, we think, died some time after midnight. The room where Burnley was found was cold, but Green's central heating was on high. Both killings appear to have a strong sexual motive and marks to the victims' backs are virtually identical.'

Trevor Jones's photograph, front and profile clicked on to the wall.

'This man,' MacInnes looked up at the face, 'is in the frame.'

Tension in the room broke slightly, low voices beginning like a sudden rush of air.

'Trevor John Jones, born Cardiff nineteen sixty-three. Had a flat above Burnley's until the twenty-eighth of July this year. Jim Green was his mortgage advisor. A little bit of form, got six months suspended in nineteen eighty-four for receiving goods and was bound over in eighty-six for assault.

'The charge in nineteen eighty-six was over the Cherry affair. Jones was one of four lads on a stag party who stumbled into the Green Cherry public house. When they realised it was a gay pub, things got a bit out of hand. There was a heavy ruck and Jones and the others got a bad pasting, but not before Jones had done some pretty serious damage to one of the regulars. Apparently, he used an ashtray on a guy until he was dragged off. Someone then glassed Jones's face quite badly. In court his brief argued that the whole incident was unfortunate and unprovable and hadn't his client suffered enough already?

'He was bound over for twelve months.'

Sergeant Moore took over from the DI. 'Jones has, or had, a common-law wife, Jenny Wilkinson. She worked in Hove, Jones sold stereos at Pearson's in the town centre. We've nothing definite on where they might be now but we think they may have moved to the St Mary's district of Southampton.'

DC Greaves stood up. 'We've still got nothing concrete on Burnley's "persuasion" but Jim Green is known to us. He was done for an indecent act in a public place three years ago. He was a trainee accountant with a chain of chemists before he worked for the Nationwide and was known as Poof in Boots. He had a scatological fetish. Collected all sorts of strange gear, including the chair he was found in.'

The DI again. 'Green showed evidence of having sex before he died. There was a definite presence of semen in the expected places. Forensics will be coming back with a DQ-Alpha and a DNA fingerprint on the body fluids but we can presume that the semen isn't his.'

Now Moore spoke, 'What we've got is a known homosexual dead and a second victim as yet unproven. We've a suspect linked to both bodies who we know must have had a grudge against queers. We need to find Trevor Jones and pull him in before there's another death. DC Saint, Greavsie and PC Tingle will be travelling to Southampton this morning with me. DI MacInnes and DC Flood will visit Pearson's Hi-fi and the solicitor's. The rest of you carry on with the door-to-door. Go to it!'

MacInnes had the use of an unmarked Sierra 2.0i, which was parked underneath John Street Police Station. He had told Caz she would be driving after he had asked her who she wanted to interview first.

'I think we should try the solicitor's, Sir! The Wilkinson woman might have kept in touch with one of the other girls.'

'So doesn't the same follow for Jones?'

'Doubt it, Sir. If he was doing a runner, he'd be a bit more careful. He wouldn't want to leave a trail.'

They exited the car park, and turned left to roll down Williams Street. MacInnes asked why did she think the woman wouldn't be so careful?

'It's Jones that's doing the runner, Sir. And social networks are more important to females. Even if Wilkinson was trying not to be found, she might well want to keep in touch with an old friend.'

'Social networks?' MacInnes said wryly.

'Mates,' Caz replied.

They drove out to Hove, parked in the High Street and walked a short way, turning into a new precinct made of brown brick. Bugle, Street & Hammond had the whole of the copper-windowed first floor, above a card shop and only a minute away from the nearest Burger King. As they entered, Caz wanted to ask who would be speaking for them but MacInnes pre-empted her, telling her that this was her pitch.

Inside the first door was a bare room with a high counter and a single bell, first line of defence against salesmen. She rang the bell and a tiny girl popped almost instantly into view. She was like an elf and had dazzling, naturally red hair which made a flood of curls around her face.

'Good Morning!' the girl said, bright-eyed like a rabbit. 'Can I help you?' Caz flipped out her warrant card. 'Oh,' the girl gasped, 'the POLICE!'

They were led by an older woman through neat, grey-carpeted offices to the principal's rooms. The redheaded receptionist was dancing in front of two typists, obviously passing on the news of their visit. The woman knocked at a heavy mahogany door and immediately entered, announcing them. Inside, sitting behind a wonderfully expensive desk, was a huge square man with surprisingly long white hair. He smiled as they entered, but when he realised that DC Flood was female he quickly moved to offer her a chair like a head waiter. Caz smiled involuntarily. She thought he looked like Father Christmas.

'I'm Bugle,' he said, sitting himself back down, 'Street is retired and Oliver Hammond is dead.'

Flood and DI MacInnes briefly connected eye-to-eye, thinking the same question.

'I'm eighty-two,' Bugle grinned, 'but still sharp as a button.'

'I'm sure, Sir,' Caz said. 'We just have a few questions.'

'Fire away, Miss,' the old man said.

'It's about a former employee of your firm, Sir, a Miss Wilkinson.'

'Jenny Wilkinson, you mean. She left us Friday August seventh.'

Caz began to write in her notebook, 'You did say the seventh of August, Sir? Are you sure?'

'I'm not senile, Madam.'

'Of course not, Sir, but it was a little while ago . . .'

Bugle pressed an intercom button. There was a short, barked, 'Yes, Mr Bugle?' and he requested the file. 'Jenny Wilkinson worked with me a lot,' he explained. 'My wife died last year, and Jenny was a great help. I can assure you, she left on August the seventh.'

The older woman came in without knocking, a light blue file in her hand. She placed it quietly on the leathered desk and tapped it once. 'Mrs Wilkinson's file,' she said flatly, and left.

Bugle spoke again, looking through half-moon glasses at the file and speaking matter-of-factly, like a doctor reading a patient's record. 'Jenny joined us on April the third 1991. She left on August the seventh 1992. She was a first-class girl. I gave her an excellent reference . . .'

'A reference, Sir!' Flood interrupted. 'To which firm?'

'To none, Detective, I'm afraid. Jenny asked if we could give her a testimonial to take away when she left. We were happy to do that.'

'Is there anything else you can tell us?'

'Not really. I gave her a farewell bonus and I was sorry to see her go, but other than that, there is little I can say.' He paused. 'If you want to know about her friends, that sort of thing, I suggest that you speak to Mrs Packer. She brought in the file.'

Caz stood up with MacInnes and shook the old man's hand.

'Would you be kind enough to order some tea for me?' he said. 'Have young Sally bring it in. She's the pretty little thing with the red hair.'

Mrs Packer directed them towards the typing pool. Two of the girls had left in the time since Mrs Wilkinson's departure, but these two, she explained, had known Mrs Wilkinson quite well.

'Old bag always called Jenny "Mrs",' the first girl said as soon as Packer had left. 'She knew she lived with Trevor, but she couldn't admit she was single. Like something out of the fifties, she is!'

'Did you know Jenny well?'

'We were good mates. Used to go to Mac's for lunch quite often.'

'Have you heard from her since she left?'

The girl hesitated then said, 'No.'

Caz decided on a quick lie. 'Look, Jenny's not in any trouble with us, er . . .'

'Miss Brent, Diana,' the girl said.

'Jenny isn't in any trouble with the law, Miss Brent . . . but we have reason to be concerned about her . . . well-being . . .' she glanced towards the DI for support but MacInnes pointedly looked away. She continued. 'We need to contact Jenny urgently for her own safety.'

'It's not that nutter of an ex-boyfriend, is it?' Diana asked.

'I'm afraid I'm not at liberty to tell you anything more, Diana, but . . .' She let the 'but' hang in the air.

'It is, isn't it? The bastard's still going round frightening people!'

'As I said, I'm not at liberty to say anything.'

'Oh it's all right, Miss, really. We can keep things dead Q-T here!'

'I'm sure,' Caz said, smiling, 'Can you tell us anything? Anything that might help us find her?'

'I don't really know,' the girl said. 'When they lost their 'ouse . . .' She turned to her mate and added, 'That was really awful, wasn't it?' The other girl nodded. 'When they lost their 'ouse, when they had to hand their flat over – Jenny stayed for a week with me and Trevor rented a room off of some Paki in Southampton. Jenny wasn't happy because the place was on the edge of the red-light district and a couple of times some pervy kerb-crawler tried to pick her up.'

'Do you have an address?'

'No, but about a month ago I got a phone call from Jenny and she said she'd moved. She said her and Trevor were sharing a big four-bedroomed house with another couple. She was really happy. There was a little park outside and she was half-way between a big new pizza place and a McDonald's!'

'Anything else?'

'No, I don't think so.'

'Did she say anything at all about work? Did she say anything else about where she lived?'

'Trevor couldn't get any work, she said that. She stacked shelves in a supermarket for a little while but when she phoned me she'd jacked it in. She said she was startin' a new job.'

'Where?'

'Don't know. I asked her where but the pips went and she never said.'

'So far so good, Flood. Do you want to let Sergeant Moore know?'

'Not yet, Sir. It might be worth trying Pearson's.'

'Down to you, Constable.'

'Yes, Sir.' They were approaching Brighton's city centre and the one-way system of the Old Steine. She was thinking. 'Sir, Green had traced Jones and Wilkinson to Southampton . . .'

'We presume.'

'What d'you mean, Sir?'

'For all we know, Jones or Wilkinson may have contacted *him*.'

'Why?' They were approaching John Street.

'I don't know *why*, Caz. I'm just keeping an open mind.'

'Yes, Sir!' she said, swinging down the ramp into the nick's car park.

'Don't hit anything while you're parking, either, Flood!'

'Sir!' she said.

The old bugger had called her Caz! It gave her a glorious thrill.

She parked twice as fast as necessary, reversing in perfectly next to the Chief Inspector's Scorpio. MacInnes winced. 'Would you like to come round to Pearson's with me, Sir?' she asked. 'Or would you like a brief rest up before we drive to Southampton?'

'Don't push it, Flood,' the DI said. 'Just keep doing your job!'

They were about to walk up the ramp together when someone called after the DI. A young detective jogged up to tell him that a package was in from forensics and that one of the uniforms on house-to-house had radioed in to say that a woman might have called on Burnley late on the Friday night.

'Get round to Pearson's now, Flood, and check it out. Back here quick as you like, OK?' MacInnes said. With that he turned and paced quickly across the underground car park. She noticed he had strangely short strides, almost like a bird.

The hi-fi shop was a dead-end. The wages were so poor that, since June, they'd had a complete change of staff. The new manager, trying to be helpful, had promised the names and addresses of those that might have known Jones but they would come from head office and it would take at least a day. She got away quickly.

MacInnes called her in before she had taken off her coat. 'DQ-Alpha's back on the Green body. Same "fingerprint" as Burnley's bed,' he said, still high on the information. 'The bed was full of it, too, so we know that both Green and Burnley had the same visitor.' He was irrepressibly pleased. 'As soon as we pick up Trevor Jones he'll be dead to rights. This DNA fingerprinting is as tight as a squirrel's arse!'

'There's was nothing doing at Pearson's, Sir.'

'Well, we half expected that.'

'Might get something back tomorrow from their head office.'

'OK, OK.' He couldn't sit down. 'Get control to contact Sergeant Moore and the others. I need to speak to him. And there's a PC coming in says one of your neighbours saw Burnley with a woman about ten o'clock on Friday night. Shouldn't matter now, but speak to him anyway.'

'Are we going to Southampton, Sir?'

'Soonest, Flood. I want Jones before the newspapers decide we've got our own Hannibal Lecter! Speak to your PC and we're away!'

'Who is it, Sir, the PC?' Caz asked, exasperated.

'How the hell should I know, Flood?' MacInnes shouted. 'I only work 'ere! Ask the bloody station sergeant!'

The desk sergeant put her straight. 'Sergeant Moore and the boys aren't on our radio-channel now. They'll have got in touch with Southampton Central and switched to channel twenty-four as soon as they were on their patch. You know the rules, Flood, stay on the local wavelength in case you need to call in for help. We'll bell the Southampton desk. They'll radio Moore and get him to ring in.'

'DI MacInnes says soonest, Sarge. He's like a cat on a hot tin roof.'

'That's his problem. You want to speak to PC Berry now?'

'Please, Sarge.'

'He's in the canteen.'

Nick Berry was in a corner when she found him, sitting with a WPC and half-way through demolishing a steak-and-kidney pie. She knew Nick, and had worked with the WPC. As she sat down she pinched a mouthful of her tea. 'Hi, Julie,' she said, 'you getting them in, chuck?'

Nick wasn't an earth-shaker but he was efficient, and he quickly related his news. An old dear, three doors down from Burnley's flat, had told him she knew Burnley, and that on Friday night he had stopped outside her window with a woman. He took out his notebook.

'Mrs Ralph,' he read, 'the woman was thirty to forty years old and was wearing a long grey mackintosh with a hood.'

'How old is Mrs Ralph?'

'Sixty-six.'

'Sixty-six! That's sharp observation for an old-age pensioner.'

'She's an ex-copper!' Berry said intently. The WPC was back waiting with the three mugs. He glanced up. 'Oh, sorry, luv,' he said, waving at the table as he continued, 'no, I'd say she was a pretty sharp lady. I'd say she knew what she was talking about, and there's not much wrong with her eyesight. We're supposed to be looking for a bloke, I know, and this woman might just be some friend, but she has to be worth talking to. If she went to his flat she might have seen something.'

'Thanks, Nick. Let me have a copy of her statement as soon as you can, will you? Fold it up and leave it in my tray. Meanwhile, ask the lads to check if anyone else saw a woman in the street that night, but for Christ's sake don't be too leading with the questions!'

'No problem!'

'Hey, you did all right, Nicky,' Caz said, then to Julie she smiled and said, 'look after our Nick, Jools, he's a bit precious.'

Julie's brown eyes flicked towards the PC for the briefest of seconds. 'Nick?' she said. 'What, *this* Nick? You've got to be joking!'

'Yeah, I am, Jools,' Caz agreed, as she stood up, 'only joking.'

She was smiling vaguely as she left. Julie was leaning low towards Nick, whispering. She had had to move the teas to get close enough.

The DI was still jumpy and wouldn't wait for her report before they set off for Southampton.

'I've already had words with their DCI. He was ready to call

Winchester and bring in the IRU! I told him we hadn't found our man yet and that we would be being a bit previous.'

'But if Jones has killed two people, Sir, and pretty violently, won't we *have* to pull in Instant Response?'

'Yes, and they'll love it too. You know what they're like, they'll all be tooled up and probably bring in dogs. No, let's wait 'till we know at least *roughly* where our man is.' He looked up, 'Are you going to sit behind this effing lorry all the way to Portsmouth?'

By the time they had passed Chichester, MacInnes had told her that Moore and the others had been pulled out to wait. 'There's a few streets of three-storeyed four-bedroomed houses between St Mary's and Ocean Village and there's a Pizza restaurant there. If you take a look at the map, those houses sound a lot like the ones we're looking for.'

'In the boom, they were going for a hundred and fifty grand, now they're not moving at eighty-five. Bob Moore's already spoken to the nearest estate agent. He says that quite a few of the houses have been rented out. Oh, and get this,' – as Caz swung out to pass another lorry – 'there's a little park out at the back of these houses . . .'

'So that's it then! Do we call out the Instant Response Unit now, Sir?'

'I'm just doing it, Flood.' He grabbed the handset.

Seven

The Ocean Village marina and shopping centre was busy. There was no legal parking anywhere. Caz parked the Sierra badly up on a kerb, stuck a 'POLICE' sign on the dash and chased quickly after MacInnes.

The lads were waiting in the Deep Pan Pizza Co. The restaurant was quietish with two or three couples eating. The DI had already flashed his warrant card by the time Caz caught him up and they were directed to a booth where Saint & Greavsie sat opposite Sergeant Moore. All three were finishing off pizzas and Saint and Greavsie were sipping halves of Carlsberg. MacInnes sat with them but Flood was forced to sit at a table immediately across the aisle.

'OK, Bob,' MacInnes asked. 'What we got?'

'There are four streets half a mile from here; all the houses are three or four bedroom jobs. We've got six addresses that we know are rented, but this one looks favourite.' He tossed an estate agent's sales material, two pages of clipped-together A4 and a colour photo.

'We asked after our man on the off-chance, but no go. According to the estate agent, three of the houses are occupied by families but the one you've got there is rented by someone called Black. One of the agent's girls went round there last month and there was someone else staying there with them. Black said it was an old mate who'd just dropped in. The address is on the details. We don't think there's anyone in and Tingle is obbing the house from the Escort.'

'Sounds like we got time to eat, then,' MacInnes said.

MacInnes ordered an anchovy pizza, Caz had garlic bread and salad. He finally decided to ask her about Nick Berry's witness, suggesting that she told him and the lads what she'd found out.

Caz felt uncomfortable but knew she had to speak. She coughed.

'It may not be very important now, but PC Berry has an eye-witness, a Mrs Ralph, who says she saw Burnley with a woman in her thirties just after ten p.m. the night he was murdered. The statement should stand up. Ralph is sixty-odd but Berry told me she's an ex-copper!'

'You're not still trying to convince us that Burnley was straight, are you, Flood?' This was Bob Moore, almost friendly, but a low sneer lurking.

'You *know* what I think, Sarge,' she retorted. 'You know what I said. Nick Berry brought this in. I'm just doing my job.' She caught MacInnes' look but didn't know what it meant.

'Well, if we can find this woman, she may be able to give a fix on Jones,' Moore said neutrally. 'If we can place him at the flat . . .'

'Shouldn't need to, Bob,' MacInnes said. 'Both semen samples gave us a good DQ-Alpha and we'll be getting DNA. When we catch the sod, the forensic should be enough to bury him.'

'What's the score, Sir?' Greavsie asked. 'Are we bringing in the Instant Response Unit?' MacInnes said yes, and Greaves added thoughtfully, 'I did Jones in '84. He came in like a lamb then. I know he had that bundle in the Cherry, but I don't think he'd take us on.'

'It doesn't matter,' the DI said. 'We go in with IRU back-up. Dogs won't hurt. For all we know, Jones may be right round the twist.'

Billy Tingle was parked fifty yards from the house. Caz walked with the DI towards his car. They carried two plastic folders and looked like canvassers. As they drew close, Tingle visibly stiffened.

'Not keepin' you awake, are we?' MacInnes said.

'No, Sir. 'Course not, Sir.'

'Anything happening?'

'Not a dickie-bird, Sir. I think I've seen two people all morning. Kids dropping leaflets through letter-boxes.'

'OK, Constable. Look, Flood will stay with you now. You'll look like a couple. Stay on your toes.'

Flood opened the driver's door. Billy Tingle looked at her once then squeezed across the seats. The DI was already walking away.

'Billy!' she said. 'You've been bloody smoking!'

'For Christ's sake, Caz!' Billy answered. 'I've been out of my skull with boredom *and* I'm frozen solid. Give us a break!'

'OK! OK!' Caz said. 'But keep the packet in your pocket from now on.'

She undid her jacket. There was a rustle of paper as she pulled out a bag from her waistband.

'What's that?' Tingle asked.

'This . . .' Caz spoke deliberately, as if giving a statement, 'is a small gift that I had just purchased for my nephew. I was concerned for my personal safety and grabbed it to defend myself.' She took a short riding crop from the paper bag and flexed it once.

'What's wrong with yer truncheon?' Billy said.

'Oh nothing, Billy, d'you want to swap mine for yours?'

'Er, no . . .'

'Exactly! A WPC's truncheon is tiny! Come on, Billy! We both know what the book says – "the truncheon is not the first line of defence" – but it's nice to have one just the same. That thing you've got has a bit of a whack. Mine has to fit in a handbag. It's pathetic! It wouldn't be seen dead in Linford Christie's shorts!

'This,' Caz said, slipping the whip up her jacket sleeve, 'is back-up.'

'Your funeral,' Billy muttered.

'That, Billy, is just what I'm trying to avoid.'

When DI MacInnes had called in for Instant Response, the senior officer responsible for Southampton control had a number of options. The Immediate Response Vehicle meant guns, a squad car authorised to carry weapons safely locked up but ready for an almost instant call-out. Dispatching the IRV needed approval by the assistant chief constable.

What MacInnes wanted was help in arresting a probably dangerous man. For that, dogs could be used. The inspector called in a unit. If the suspect was indoors then he would call in a specialist House-entry Team, very possibly armed and probably sent in with dogs.

About two miles from PC Tingle and Caz, in the white, fifties-styled architecture of the Southampton Civic Centre, two vans were parked up, waiting. A House-Entry Team had not been called out. Routine policy was to apprehend the suspect before he entered a building. If he got inside, they would contain the situation and then call out the HET.

'So I reckon we're a bit spare here, Billy,' Caz decided. 'MacInnes and Saint are that way, I guess, just round the corner of Mark Street. Sergeant Moore is with Greavsie in that side-street just over there. All we can do from here is frighten Jones off. Where's the phone?'

MacInnes answered.

'I'm moving with Billy behind the houses, Sir. Less likely to frighten our man off that way.' She started the engine, waiting for the bollocking, but MacInnes simply said, 'OK, Flood, do it now!'

She was just into first gear and barely moving when Sergeant Moore's warning came. 'Car coming! Looks like our man!'

A light-blue Vauxhall Astra turned into the street, the driver pulling over to stop outside the target house. The passenger door opened and Trevor Jones stepped out: short, hard, a grey facial scar. The two other cars were screaming into the street from both ends.

'Oh shit!' Billy mouthed as Jones reacted, running away from their car and straight towards MacInnes' Sierra. Caz slammed on the brakes and leapt from the Escort as Saint bounced his car up the kerb and slewed in front of Jones.

'Fuck you!' Jones shouted, and jumped on to the Sierra's bonnet and over the roof. Caz could see MacInnes's white eyes as she followed by the same route, her trainers treading down the windscreen wipers and leaving footprints on the black car-top.

'Yer nicked, Jones!' she shouted, trying to undo her jacket. Jones didn't look back but he raised the finger to her. She managed to release her radio. 'He's a runner!' she shouted, 'Going left! Out of Mark Street!' Jones was sprinting, quick on his feet. She paced herself, keeping him in sight.

'Left again!' She missed the street sign. 'Right! Looks like he's heading towards town centre! No left! That's left, left! We're going past a vegetable wholesaler's! Left again! We're passing Habitat! He's running down towards the waterfront! Oh, Fuck!' She bumped into the side of a passing car. 'Sorry! Right! Right! He's gone right! He's disappeared into some sort of excavation! Lower High Street! I'm still with him! The little shit! He's gone inside!' She ducked under a wet awning, sniffing the air. 'Christ!' she shouted. 'It stinks in 'ere!'

The excavation was surrounded by a high plywood fence and covered by canvas to keep out the worst of the rain. The ground was wet and slippery, a mix of mud, red brick-dust and patches of gravel. All around her dripped, and there was the smell of decay. She could see, but she would have liked her torch.

'Give it up, Trevor,' she called, half hearing her echo, 'there're about six cars half a minute away from us.'

'Get fucked, Mrs!' came the reply.

She shouted something formal and jogged quickly towards the voice. Then she called to tell Jones that her shoes were getting muddy and that was making her mad. 'Come on, Trev,' she sighed, 'give it a rest!'

Then suddenly she was on him. They were in a long dug-out room with five-foot walls and a muddy floor. He was at the far end and knew he was trapped.

'Trevorrr . . .'

He turned to face her.

'Come on, Trevor,' she said. His eyes were white with passion. He looked full into her face. One hand was in front of him.

'I don't want to 'urt you, luv. I've never 'it a woman.'

She grinned, 'It's not a problem, Trevor.'

'I ain't coming in!'

'Well, that's a shame, Trevor.' She took the riding crop from her jacket.

'Cos if you won't give up, and my boss is up there' – she pointed with the whip – 'what can I do?' She was moving slowly towards him.

She smiled again, 'You ever been whacked with one of these, Trev?'

He tensed as if ready to go past her. He looked hard and fit but he was very badly scared. She flicked the riding crop against the wall. 'Hurts like fuck this does, Trevor, believe me.' She stared, looking for warning of sudden movement, 'You really don't want to try it.'

'Trevor?' She waited. She could hear the water drips again.

'Trev?' She could smell him. He was trying to decide.

'You don't even want to *think* about it, Trevor.' She flexed the whip again, listening for the others arriving. Then, above her, she heard the thud of a chest against the wooden fence. Greavsie.

'You all right, Caz?'

'Yeah, I'm fine,' she shouted. Her eyes didn't move from Jones's face.

'Me and Trevor are just coming out.

'You turn round now, Trevor,' she said slowly. 'Lean against the wall.

'No problems down here!' she shouted again. 'None at all!'

Eight

They went back to Brighton police station in a convoy of three cars. Caz drove DI MacInnes, Saint and Greavsie followed in another Sierra with the prisoner, and Moore and Tingle trailed them in an Escort.

Once handcuffed, Jones had been surprisingly calm and had tried to tell them it had all been a mistake. He had thought they were heavies from Worthing calling in a debt that he couldn't repay. He'd run without thinking and had only given up when he had realised Flood was a woman. 'I never 'eard of an arm-breaker in a skirt. Soon as I realised you was a tart I knew you was the law so I came quietly.'

They had pushed him into the back of the second unmarked Sierra, followed by Saint. 'You'd be better to rest it now, Jonesey,' Greaves had said. 'Tell us all about it when we get to Brighton.'

Driving, Caz felt incredibly tired. She'd been shaking soon after the arrest, but now all the adrenaline had left her and she felt wasted and sick. She drove in silence.

'The cock-up was down to me, Flood,' MacInnes said. 'You *were* in the wrong place and I should have had the dog vans close up.' He let her drive for a moment. 'Jones turning up like that was just bad luck, but we got away with it. You did OK.' She was still silent.

'It's been a bit of a tough week for you, hasn't it?' he said.

'I can take it, Sir,' she finally replied. 'It's what I want to do.'

It was gloomy late afternoon when they turned into the car park under the police station. Jones was bundled upstairs, booked in and stuck in one of the cells. There were messages for most of them. Caz had received one from American Express.

They were all jaded from the last few days' activity, and Jones needed to be interviewed, so MacInnes and Moore briefly conferred. The DI left and Moore turned to the rest of the team. 'We're gonna sweat Jonesey for an hour, then Greaves and me will interview him. Saint, Tingle and Flood, do your reports, then piss off home.' He could see protest rising in Caz's face. When he spoke again it was for her, even though his eyes covered all the team. 'You've *all* done well, but right now you need a rest. Now the boss is going to do his usual and start on Jones at eight o'clock.'

'The usual?' Caz asked Greaves as they checked their messages.

'It's tradition. He'll kip for an hour, shave, take a shower, and then get dressed in clean clothes. That way he goes into the prisoner on top of his form. He keeps everything here at the nick, even another blue suit.'

'And it works, does it?'

'Too right! You know MacInnes's record. He's the best there is.'

She walked to her desk, the nick's buzz still warming her. A few office PCs were leaving and a few called her name. She was reading a note and raised her hand to the voices behind her. The note said, 'Save my life, ring this number before six! Val.'

She sat down heavily, shoved old paperwork away with both hands, took a deep breath, and pulled an empty arrest report from a drawer. Then she picked up the phone. Even as it rang, she was writing. It was two minutes to six.

'Valerie Thomas!' His voice. She was trying to picture his face.

'It's DC Flood . . .' She paused. 'Caz.'

'I'm glad you called,' he said.

'I'm pretty busy, Valerie.'

'Is this a bad time? I could ring again.'

'Yes. Er, no,' Caz replied. 'No. I'm just a bit . . .'

'Tired?'

'Something like that,' she said. She was filling in a report and making small mistakes. 'Yeah.'

'What you need is someone to cook you a really nice meal,' he said. He was annoyingly cheerful. 'I know someone who'll volunteer.'

'Val, I'm knackered. It's not a good time . . .'

'Is that a No?'

'Yes. No. I'll be lousy company.'

'I know,' he said, 'we've met already, remember? What time?'

'Can you give me a lift home?' she asked. He said yes. 'OK, I'll be outside your offices after seven.'

'After seven.'

'Yes, soon as I can.'

He rang off without saying goodbye. He was nearly as sharp as her. He had rung off before she could change her mind.

Her arrest report was boring. The bare facts: '*the suspect attempted to evade arrest by running from the scene, initially in a northerly direction*', she felt missed a little of the passion. '*. . . causing slight damage to a police vehicle*' didn't quite capture the look on the lads' faces as Trevor Jones had legged it over the bonnet of the Sierra, and '*I proceeded to pursue the fleeing suspect and eventually apprehended him*', she decided wasn't quite breathless enough to do justice to the afternoon's excitement.

She lied when she wrote of Trevor's arrest. The suspect '*then gave up without a struggle once confronted by myself*'. There was no mention of the riding crop. When she had emerged with Jones, the leather was in her waistband, running down the small of her back. She wrote further, indicating the minor accidental damage done to a thirteenth-century merchant's house, and added that a letter of apology should be sent in due course to the archaeologists working the site. She finished and had enough time to freshen up in the loos, but when she set off to meet Thomas at ten-past seven, she felt like a dog.

* * *

It was raining again when she left the police station. She had no umbrella so she leaned forward, collar-up, and scurried quickly towards Amex House and shelter. While she waited, she noticed a silver-blue Daimler-Jaguar with original trim, parked fifteen feet away, its engine running. It was beautiful, a mid-sixties model still with the original wire-wheels. She wasn't an aficionado but she knew it had a 2.5-litre V8 engine and that the wheels had been made in India.

It was Valerie. He wound the window down and leaned across the seat, calling to her, 'If I was a gentleman I'd come and get you, but there's no point in both of us getting wet! Come on, get in!'

She felt a flutter in her heart – for the car, not for him – and dashed across. As she swept into its rich refurbished leather, she suddenly felt guilty. 'Oh hell, Val,' she said, 'I'm covered in mud! I am sorry.'

He laughed as he said he didn't mind, then asked would she like him to drive along the sea-front? The Daimler's heater was blowing hot air along the floor and she curled her knees towards him on the bench seat, waiting for the warmth to get through to her. She felt odd.

'Tell me you're not rich,' she said. 'I don't like rich men.'

'I'm not rich,' he said. He didn't look at her, 'But I *am* lucky.'

'This car is gorgeous, Valerie.'

'Oh I know,' he said. He pointed to a tiny package above the walnut dash. 'For you, a little present.' She took it, a small paper bag. Inside was a packet of Lucozade tablets. 'For energy,' he explained. He was grinning. 'Well, you said you were tired.'

'You don't know how tired,' she said slowly. She suddenly wanted to cry. 'It's been a tough few days.'

'I tried to get hold of you at John Street but you were never available. I didn't leave a message until today.'

'I've been working hard.'

'Are you good at your job?'

'I'm a detective, I have to be.'

* * *

Her arm was on the top of the seat, her cheekbone resting lightly on her shoulder. The ends of her fingers were close to his upper arm and she moved just enough for them to occasionally brush his suit. Rain drifted in waves against the windscreen as the tiny wiper blades ticked left and right. He had begun to play a tape and someone (Nina Simone?) was singing 'Summertime'. Her brain sent a message to her face to smile but it was too late. Her last thought before falling asleep was about Valerie Thomas. She tried to make herself think 'bastard'.

She knew she could do without this.

Nine

She woke slowly into a dim world that made little sense. A tiny clock with glowing luminous hands was about two feet from her face. She felt warm and safe. There was a faint musty smell of drying water.

When she woke again she saw the small clock in the dashboard, the Daimler's large steering-wheel, the pale green lights of the stereo. She heard a blues riff, very, very low. Above her, cars schlapped past in the wet and also above her, (her head was in his lap), Valerie dozed, upright, his head back against the door, one arm across her shoulder for comfort or for warmth. The time came into focus. Ten-past-ten!

'Oh Jeez!' She stared at the clock, the time slowly registering. She felt painfully stiff. Carefully she tried to rise. 'Valerie? Are you awake?'

'Almost,' he said.

She was now upright. 'Hey I'm really, *really* sorry.'

He was smiling with his eyes. 'How was it for you?' he said.

They were parked somewhere high above the sea, amber lights below them. She asked where they were and he said, 'In the warm.'

Then he said he would take her home. She thought he sounded sad. They didn't speak again until they reached the outskirts of town.

'I live just off the promenade,' she told him, 'Inkerman Terrace.'

Before he could say something she added that yes, she had found George Burnley. He kept his eye on the road but she sensed him thinking hard.

'Look,' she said softly – she was trying to make a decision – 'are we still on for this meal? I know it's late but I really do need to eat something.' He seemed to be concentrating on his driving. She tried again. 'It might not be exactly what you want right now, but I could do with company.'

'It's not a problem,' he said. He was staring ahead. She still felt sad.

Val parked and they walked together up the steps. She took his arm. It had stopped raining but the air was still moist and the street-lights sparkled. She took one last look at the night before closing the door.

She led Valerie up crimson-carpeted stairs to her upstairs lounge. That was fitted with a blue-grey Berber carpet, a low mahogany table her father had made for her, and one massive sofa. The rest of the room was space except for a NAD monitor stereo and a ludicrous pile of soft toys in one corner.

'They're my piggies,' she said before he could ask.

Off the lounge was the kitchen. She directed him there.

'I eat absolutely anything, including dead animals,' she told him. 'I'll stick a CD on but then I've just got to have a bath.'

She darted from the room and water started rushing off-stage. Then she returned to look through the compact discs. She shouted through to the kitchen, 'What music d'you like?' She could smell onions. His head popped round the door. He was wearing a pinnie, totally unfazed. 'Something soothing,' he said. 'How about Phil Collins?'

'Dire Straits?' she suggested.

'Great!' he said, 'but if you put "Brothers in Arms" on, I'm going!'

'Love over Gold?'

'Fine,' he said, 'and I prefer red wine.'

'There's a rack of cheap stuff in the kitchen,' she told him, 'that'll do for cooking. I'll be back in a sec. The better stuff is in my bedroom.' She left him a bottle of Chianti Classico Riserva and an opener.

She preferred showers but tonight she needed a bath. Her calves still felt tight after the afternoon's running. She poured a little bath oil into the tap-fall, watched it foam, then turned off the taps and climbed in. The aroma of Valerie's cooking drifted across the hall, through her pastel bedroom and in through the open bathroom door. She turned her head towards it, sniffing the air.

She could hear 'Telegraph Road' drifting through from the lounge. There was a man in her kitchen opening a nice bottle of wine, and something in there smelt wonderful. She lay back in the pink water and flexed her toes, relieving her tight muscles, trying to feel good. Valerie Thomas made her feel safe. He made her feel warm. Worse, he made her feel comfortable. She wasn't certain how much she liked 'comfortable'. She had a sudden glimpse of a secure, loved future and she wasn't sure if she should want it.

She was a copper. She was an athlete. Being either required a cutting edge; neither allowed any weakness. She'd seen too many runners and too many good coppers go soft. Once they'd found a serious partner, they couldn't go the extra mile. Without enough anger they couldn't do the hours or take the pain. That couldn't, that wouldn't, happen to her; where she was going was far too important. Being a real copper took commitment. Maybe that was why so many of the good ones ended up with broken marriages. It wasn't just the danger and the lousy hours; the job got your soul. All a lover ever got was your heart and your body.

'Telegraph Road' was fourteen minutes, fifteen seconds long. She had promised herself she'd be drinking a glass of Chianti before it finished. She got out of the bath shaking her head; towelled quickly and, forsaking underpants, slipped into a pair of soft navy sweatsuit trousers. As she pulled on the matching top, she remembered waking in his lap. By leaving her hair damp she made it back to the kitchen with a minute to spare. He was finishing a bolognese and she went straight to him to kiss his face. She had decided she could take the risk.

He had still had the wooden spoon in his hand and bolognese sauce on his lips. The heel of his hand was at the nape of her neck as he held their contact and he turned his face slowly, their cheeks sliding together until he could get his mouth on hers. She could taste him but, as they kissed, she felt or heard a cry come from between them. She didn't know if the sound was his or hers.

They kissed like returning lovers, his tiny touches all over her face, thank-yous all unsaid, on her lips, her nose, her eyes and in her hair. She had the dizzy sensation that they'd known each other in some past life and she wanted to tell him. The meat sauce steamed around them. He pushed her slowly away, a hand on each cheekbone but she made him work at it, her face still turned up to him, ridiculously eager. 'The dinner!' he said.

He diverted her by asking for a glass of wine, calming her down. The square kitchen table had been laid out, even as far as a lit candle and red tissue napkins. When she came to him again, he pointed like a schoolmaster and she sat down.

'It's with rice, I'm afraid,' he said, 'I couldn't find any pasta.'

'Oh really?' Caz said grinning. 'Not even that *huge* jar?' There was spaghetti looming over him three-foot high, inches from his face.

'Oops!' he said. He served, ordering her to like it.

His jacket was somewhere in the front room and he'd removed his tie. Through his pale blue shirt she imagined she could feel his shape, muscled but on a light skeleton, a miler not a sprinter.

'What d'you do?' she said. 'I mean, for a hobby, in your spare time?'

'All sorts,' he said. 'I work out, I run a little bit, I swim twice a week. The car takes a bit of work and I like to spend time at vintage car auctions. If I can get an oldish motor that's a little under-priced, I'll buy it, restore it and then sell it, but I don't do it for the money, I just like to bring them back to life. If I sell on and make a little bit of money, I can do it again. I guess if I was rich I'd keep every one, but if I was rich' – he looked up – 'you wouldn't like me.'

'You've got orange lips!' she said.

He pretended not to hear. 'I used to own my own micro-light.

That's a hang-glider with an engine. I had to sell it to a friend to finance the Jaguar, but I still get up once or twice a month. It's so different up there.'

'I used to fly with my Dad,' Caz offered. 'He used to teach ATC kids and he could fiddle me rides.'

'Any kind of flying is great, but micro-lighting actually puts you *in* the sky. It's like the difference between driving a car on holiday and touring on a motor-bike. On the bike you're *part* of the scenery.'

'Pirsig,' she said.

He said, 'What?'

'Pirsig. *Zen and the Art of Motor-cycle Maintenance*.'

'Are you winding me up?'

'No, really,' she said. 'It's a book. It was a cult bestseller. This guy went all over the States on his motor-bike with his son riding pillion. He said what you just said, you have to be *in* the scenery, not just in a box travelling through it.'

'Oh,' he said. 'So what do you do, Detective?'

'Mainly I run. I love it.'

'That all?'

'No, not all. I do a bit of aerobics, not the dance-your-eyeballs-out stuff, but more for the stretching. Runners are notoriously stiff.'

'And?'

'What d'you mean "and"?'

'What do you do for enjoyment?'

'I told you, I run!'

'Nobody *enjoys* running.'

'*I* do!'

'So what else?'

'Well, I read a bit. I did psychology at university and I was pretty heavily into genetics and sociobiology, that sort of thing.'

He looked deliberately blank, so Caz elaborated.

'Looking at humans as animals or gene-carriers. Explaining their behaviour in terms of their evolution. It's fascinating.'

He was smiling but she continued. 'It's like right now, we have exchanged ritual feeding signals, and I've danced and postured to inhibit your aggressive tendencies.'

'What!'

'We can't help it!'

'What aggressive tendencies?' Val protested. 'I'm not aggressive.'

'Of course you are. No joke intended, but it's in your genes. As I say, you can't help it. You're a male mammal. You're territorial, explosive, dominant and possessive. Even if you'd read every "New Man" book ever written, you'd still be a man.'

'You pompous bugger!'

'No, I'm not. Not even a bit. I just understand how the world really is. I believe in women's rights and loving and caring and sharing and trust and all the other "wonderful" ideals there are, but in the end a man wants to make babies with almost anyone who'll let him and a woman wants to be safe. We are *built* that way. You and I are in *conflict*. Every man–woman relationship is a negotiation, a subtle contract. Men are dangerous. Women get pregnant. We're different!'

'Of course we're different!'

'I don't just mean we *look* different, or that we've got different bits.' She took a sudden swig of her wine. 'I mean we have different drives, we have different places to go, different things to protect.'

He picked up the wine to pour, but she caught his wrist and stopped him. 'All of us, we're trapped. We're wrapped up in rules of behaviour. We break those rules at our peril. I'm not supposed to say "I want you" and straight away leap into bed with you.'

'It's OK by me!' Val said quickly.

'Oh yes, I'm sure! We both know it's going to happen but *you* expect to seduce *me*. Most men freak out if a woman makes the running. Forget the bullshit, they simply don't expect it. Males were built to court and bully. Females learned to deflect and survive. That's the way it is. Right across the animal world the golden rule has always been "don't get left holding the baby". It just happens that boys manage it more often.'

He took her staying hand and held it, pouring with the other. 'Yes, but surely with contraception, the pill et cetera . . . ?'

'Oh, you mean that just because my head knows I can't get pregnant, all the rules that have been built into my body over millions of years just somehow go out of the window?'

'Something like that.'

She was drinking again, another quick gulp. 'Well, they do, they don't. Women have always wanted sex, they're no different to men. But they have to be more aware of the occasional side-effect, you know, like a nine-month pregnancy or the sixteen-odd years afterwards! We've had these bodies for ten million years or so, the pill for thirty. We can do it whenever we like now, just like a man, but our genes only *half* want to. They ain't heard of the pill and they scream when they see a willie.'

'Do you?' he said.

'What?'

'Scream when you see a willie?'

'Of course not, I'm a nurse.'

'Are you?'

'No but I couldn't think of anything else to say. Our genes say "make him court you a little bit. That way he won't clear off as soon as he's got you pregnant". When we do it any other way we're wobbling.'

'You're talking too loud,' Valerie said, 'and you're drinking too fast.'

'That's your fault, you've got me excited.'

'You sure it's not the bolognese?'

'Oh, it is,' she said, 'definitely. D'you want some more of this?' She waved the bottle. He nodded and she emptied it into his glass.

'So where does love fit in then?' Valerie said.

'Ah love,' she sighed, 'the bloody armistice. Another time, maybe.'

She looked slowly into her glass, turning it slowly, watching the red wine tilt towards the rim. They were both thinking of someone, of something else. She was suddenly aware of the night, of the rain, and of the cold outside.

'Let's get pissed together,' she said. 'Put something bluesy on.' She left to get another Chianti from the bedroom, and came back to Aretha Franklin singing 'Drinking Again'. He was sitting on the floor next to the sofa with a fat-bellied fluffy pink pig on his knees.

'That's Vincent,' she said. 'He sleeps with me. When I'm away I think he bonks Victoria. That's her over there. She's a tart.'

She stroked his hair, a huge black pain welling up in her. They both knew they wouldn't make love tonight. She wanted to cry again. A cork popped and he poured some more wine. She touched his face.

'You're a nice bloke, Val. Why do I think this is going to hurt us?'

'Love usually does,' he said.

Ten

He must have put her to bed. She woke cuddling pink Vincent, his tiny brown eyes close to her face, oversized belly snuggled into her neck. She was struggling to remember. It had been raining, Trevor Jones was locked up, Valerie had cooked, they had done two bottles of red.

She rolled from her side and on to her back. She could feel her knees, a sure sign she'd been drinking red wine. Gently she flexed her toes. Did he go home? Surely she didn't let him drive? She pulled her left leg up and across her body, the knee towards her right shoulder. He would be in the lounge. She stretched the right leg, feeling the line of muscle across her hip. On the sofa.

The folded leg now vertically up towards the shoulder, same side. She was slowly coming alive. Valerie. Valerie. The other leg, tightening and loosening like a leopard. Now the arms crossed over her chest, pulling at each shoulder, tight, loose, tight. Now hold it. Now release. He must have put her to bed.

She reached out from the midline of the double bed, her fingertips just catching the webbed edge of the mattress beneath the sheet. Now she was a taut crucifix watched by pink Vincent. Some thought about the night washed through her. She ran hands down the definite line of her ribs and over a tight stomach. Valerie? Her hands continued, fingers like whiskers, the base of each thumb pressing at the lift of her sex, the right knuckle forcing a central path.

She stretched again, a pelvic tilt pushing her body heat into her cupped right hand as she held herself. The light brown of her secret warmth felt secure and delicious. She remembered. Valerie *had* cared enough. He must have slept on the sofa. Damn, a decent man.

She sat up, forsaking the duvet. Her shoulders prickled. She stretched towards each ankle in turn, head down towards the knee, her hamstring extending. Each nerve in her body was slowly wakening, like bird-song beginning well before first light. She was becoming alive.

The digital display on her clock radio showed a red 5:05. Normally the rude buzz that started her day would happen at five forty-five. She could roll back into her nest, pull Vincent towards her and lightly sleep, or do the same and day-dream. She could rise early and run a little further, or even skip the run and wallow in a soft, deep bath. Lastly, she could walk naked through to Valerie, bite his hard shoulders, or draw neat white nails up his back, before slipping underneath his body on the sofa. She compromised. With her still right hand cupping her deeper heat, she slipped back under the bedclothes. Her eyes closed and she lay quietly, thinking of him. She could see his back; every red, finger-nailed line and every clean, delicious bite. Vincent looked away to watch the clock. She rose five minutes before the alarm.

When she went to him she was in running kit bright enough to hurt his eyes. She served him coffee on a tray with separate milk and sugar but did not make the drink up. She didn't know him that well.

'I'll be thirty minutes,' she said. 'Why don't you steal my bed?'

The streets were greasy with a thickened dew that had almost become a frost. She trod carefully until she reached Kingsway, and then turned away towards the piers. Here the extra heat of the hotels and passing traffic had dried the street and she moved slightly quicker than her usual warm-up pace, striding out past the Brighton Centre and the Grand Hotel.

When she reached the Old Steine, she swung left towards the Pavilion then crossed the road and pushed up the shallow slope of St James Street before swinging left again and cutting uphill towards

Amex House. The building's smooth white reflected the last of the street lights and she thought it looked like an anglicised pagoda. Then she thought, 'Why did I run this way? To see where he worked again, or to go past the nick?' Somewhere deep in the station, Trevor Jones would be locked in his cell. If he was managing any sleep it would a restless one. She remembered the look in his face when she had cornered him. Her fear had reflected his but she had had time and help on her side. She hadn't felt she was in front of a murderer, and in the end she had out-psyched him.

She ran smoothly down Edward Street towards the Grand Parade, trying to recall Trevor's face. No matter how hard she tried, she couldn't see the face of a killer and she wondered exactly what the DI had seen that she hadn't. Something deep in her felt wrong and she began to run hard, forcing the feeling away with pain. She ran back towards Valerie.

Valerie was in her bed when she got back, listening to 'Today' and reading her copy of *The Selfish Gene*. He was sitting up next to Vincent, looking dreadfully right. 'This is good stuff,' he said, waving the book.

'You're listening to Radio Four!' she squeaked sarcastically.

'The best radio there is!' he answered. 'Anyway, I only switched it on.'

She went to him, relegated Vincent to the floor, then grabbed both Valerie's hands, their fingers linked. She kissed him briefly, and said he could borrow the Dawkins book. She smiled, 'And thanks for last night.'

'Thanks?' he said. 'For what exactly? You were dead from the neck up. No doubt it would have been much the same from the waist down!'

'What!' She would have liked to slap him and tell him he was a sod, but he held her fingers as she tried to pull away.

'I know,' he said. 'It was tough but I coped. Victoria was very understanding.'

Caz put the back of her hand to her forehead. 'Oh no! Not

Victoria! Vincent will be devastated !' She picked up her piggy and held it as she warned Val, 'You have to be careful what you say in front of Vincey, he's very sensitive.'

Valerie looked at her. She dripped sweat. Her green eyes shone. Their eyes locked together and they stared at each other. She blinked first.

'I want to take you away,' he said softly, 'I *need* to take you away.'

'When?' she said.

'Now,' he said.

She told him that Saturday would be much more sensible.

She left him so she could be first in the bathroom. While she showered with the head on 'pulse', letting the hot water beat her to death, she heard Led Zeppelin being played in the lounge. Endorphins were sailing through her courtesy of the run. She felt long, lithe and powerful.

Valerie had put the CD on in the middle tracks, and she could hear 'Kashmir' building; like Ravel's *Bolero* but even sexier. She was used to walking round the flat undressed, but she came out in a towelling robe. He was in the lounge, doing sit-ups in his boxer shorts, his feet under the sofa, holding the movements in the middle third, his elbows splayed. He was even leaner than she had expected.

'I hope your back's flat!' she said. He merely grunted.

She made tea and toast and poured them both fresh orange juice.

'There's a new toothbrush for you in the bathroom,' she told him, 'and there's a clean towel on the bed.' Then she thought for a moment, 'Aren't you going to be a bit seedy at work today?'

'I would be,' he said, 'but I'll nip home once I've checked in. My flat is only a hundred yards away from Amex.'

'And everyone will presume you've been out on the tiles all night.'

He laughed. 'Well, a man has a reputation to maintain . . .'

'And a lady?' she said.

'Yours is ruined, I'm afraid.'

Suddenly she felt uncomfortable. She was aware of seconds drifting away on a stream of small-talk. Start time at the nick was eight-thirty but she liked to be in before eight. Unless she rushed she was going to be late. Curtly, she told him. He said they would be gone in ten minutes.

She dressed quickly, white underneath, a white 'Fruit of the Loom' T-shirt, navy trousers and a double-breasted dark blazer. Office wear, everything practical. The shoes were flat-heeled to spare her Achilles tendons, and they laced up.

She was slipping back into the work groove and began to think of the lads, Sergeant Moore, the DI. She wondered about Trevor Jones. Had he been charged yet?

'Are you ready, Val?' she shouted. There was an edge to her voice.

'A minute,' he said, then appeared immediately, his shirt open-necked and his tie in his hand. 'Nope, not even that. You ready?'

They went down to his car and this time he opened her door from outside. He tried to tell her she looked great but an anxiety was building up in her and her shoulders stiffened.

'Val, can we get off? The time?'

He went round, got in and started the Daimler.

'Look, Val,' she said, searching for the right words, 'I'm sorry. This is my first week as a detective and I'm a bit uptight . . .' They were moving away. 'I just need a while. I need to find my feet . . .'

'I didn't know there was a problem,' he said.

Valerie dropped her off in Kingswood Road, at the back of the police station. She touched his hand briefly and said, 'I'll ring you,' before she slipped out of the door; then she strode away, head up, past the departing traffic wardens and a few uniformed officers checking their pandas. She did not look back, but felt the Daimler and Valerie quietly drift away.

As she walked through the doors the nick's smell came to her again, like a loved pet, artificial, oddly clean. There was a sense of echo, of long corridors, of clanged doors, of shouted abuse. She was walking quickly towards the squad room, deep into the nick's heart and she could feel her neck hairs tingle as she braced herself for the day.

It was five past eight and Trevor Jones would have had his breakfast by now. DI MacInnes, dressed in his usual blue suit, would be at work already; Sergeant Moore would be outside, parking his Sierra; Saint & Greavsie were probably in the canteen right now cracking awful jokes and grabbing a quick tea before their shift.

It was good to be back. She felt as if she'd been out a month.

Eleven

DI MacInnes and Sergeant Moore came into the room on the stroke of eight-thirty. Neither of them looked particularly happy. The easel was up and Inkerman Terrace's missing X's were arrowed.

Moore spoke.

'OK, lads, Caz. As the Indian Chief said, there's good news and bad news. Bad news is, Jones has an alibi for last weekend. He says he went night fishing with a bunch of mates. Southampton has already had a word with a couple of 'em, and it looks like the alibi will hold.'

There was a murmur of disappointment.

'Good news is we don't have to let him go. Jones was so worried about being in the frame for the murders that he rolled over on a couple of our outstanding burglaries, and Southampton think they can have him for four or five on their patch.'

MacInnes continued, 'Thanks, Bob. So, it's back to the blankets, lads, soonest. We need the rest of these door-to-doors, and we'd better talk to our Mrs Ralph again. If some woman really was talking to George Burnley the night he died, she might be of some help.

'We're getting a few more plain-clothes and two more uniforms from Worthing. They can work with PC Tingle and PC Brown on Onderman Road. We should have the victims' bank statements first thing this ay-em so let's try and see where they spent their money. We've been promised their credit card slips but they're a bit slow in coming. What we need to find is some link between these guys, other than the fact that they were both benders. Maybe they worked out together at the same gym or they frequented the same club.'

Moore took it up again. 'Saint & Greavsie can go back to do the clubs. We've got a pretty good picture of Jim Green and it won't hurt to push Burnley's face past the punters one more time. The DI and myself will be taking another look at the crime scene – see if a connection comes up there. We'll be taking DC Flood along for the ride.'

There was a cough. A couple of chairs shifted and someone at the back asked about Saturday afternoon. 'What do you think?' Moore said.

'Bang goes another weekend!' Saint muttered from behind Caz, 'I was supposed to be taking my kids to watch the Albion!'

'Well, you should say thank you to the DI, then,' Greaves said, grinning. 'He's got you off the hook!'

Caz was thinking about Valerie. The meeting was breaking up and the lads dispersed from around her. Revisiting the scene of crime would be useful, and she guessed that while the killer was still out there her love life would have to go on hold. She supposed it would wait.

'OK, Flood, let's go,' Moore dangled the Sierra's keys in front of her.

'Right, Sarge!' she answered. 'Burnley's first?'

Moore drove the Sierra out from the nick's second car park, swung it left down the hill and moved out into the traffic on the Grand Parade. The men were discussing the arrest of Trevor Jones and his interrogation the previous night. Caz sat quietly on her own in the back. The sergeant was arguing that Trevor Jones was a bad 'un anyway and it was good to see him banged up. MacInnes shook his head. He needed to make a point.

'Maybe so, Bob, but, with hindsight, I'd say we were a bit too keen. Everything fell together a little too easily. Right at the beginning we said this wasn't just a domestic, we should've remembered that. When Flood here kept popping up with bodies, I think we got a little excited. We had a connection between Jones and the victims, but so what? He knew 'em both? So did Mrs Lettice! Jones was scarred once upon a time after a ruck in a gay pub? What about his mates? I think I was just a bit too keen to put my murder suit on. Maybe my age is beginning to show.'

'We're all allowed one a year, Tom . . .'

'Aye, I guess so.'

'Maybe Flood did it!' Moore said.

'Connected to both deaths,' said the DI.

'Lived close. Opportunity.'

'*And* they were men. We got motive!'

'Probably got no alibi.'

'OK! OK!' Caz finally broke her silence. 'I confess! I confess! I went round to borrow some milk from George Burnley and he wouldn't lend me any, so I cut off his balls. I killed Green because he was good-looking and gay. The waste, I couldn't stand the waste.'

'Ah, so you are with us then, DC Flood?' It was the DI's first smile.

There was a PC on duty guarding Burnley's basement flat. In a normal age they could have placed a police seal on the door, but in one of the burglary capitals of the world that would mean nothing. The constable was fresh on, just over an hour into a four-hour shift. The duty was a lousy one and he was happy for any kind of company. Caz knew him vaguely.

'Hi, Jim. Mrs Lettice keeping you happy?'

'You what?' the PC said. 'I getta cup of tea and a biscuit every half an hour and she talks to me like I've only just arrived. I think she's potty!'

They opened up the flat. The smell was all but gone. The PC attempted to look inside but Sergeant Moore offered him a sickeningly cheesy smile before he shut the door in his face. 'So it's not just me then,' Caz thought.

Moore switched on the lounge light. The room felt stale. Caz tried to remember her first response to the room, to George Burnley.

'And you still say this decor is sexy, do you, Flood?' It was the DI.

'Yes, Sir.'

'Why exactly?'

'It isn't easy to explain, Sir.'

'*Try*, Flood.' She wasn't sure if he was angry or not.

'It's warm, Sir. It's simple, sensuous even. It's laid out for seduction. It feels like a honey-trap. You would have to lie just here, Sir, to listen to the music from the CD player. That's when he would have brought out the white wine and the glasses.'

'And that's it?'

'More or less, Sir. Sometimes attractiveness wears a badge but sometimes it just is. This is the second case.'

'Why couldn't it be a gay guy's knocking territory?'

'I don't know, Sir, but it isn't. It would feel different. I don't know why exactly. I think that maybe the honey-pot would be a different shape. You know, for a different kind of bee.'

'But you only think . . .' MacInnes said. He turned away.

Sergeant Moore knelt by the bookcase. The lower two feet were made up by a small cupboard. Inside were a couple of box-files and a sheaf of papers. He removed them and placed them in an evidence bag. 'These should keep us busy for a while,' he said.

The bookcase was filled, but with very little literature of an obviously gay nature. There were a couple of Jack Kerouac's and a paperback copy of *The Naked Lunch*, *Loot* and *Prick up Your Ears*, but this was all readable stuff, as likely to be owned by a gay as a straight. Burnley also looked as if he was into languages. There were three Spanish–English dictionaries as well as novels in both French and Spanish, a few amateur psychology books and, most surprisingly, two volumes on genetics that she recognised from her undergraduate days.

'Burnley certainly read a bit,' she offered.

'Probably bought his books by the yard,' Moore said.

'One thing that concerns me,' MacInnes said from the kitchen, 'is the absence of any signs of a struggle. Two reasonably sized men have been brutally killed in their own homes. The flats show no sign of a forced entry in either case, so the best guess is that both victims knew their killer.'

'They were killed during sex, maybe?' Moore said.

'Maybe,' MacInnes retorted. 'That could fit Burnley, but what about Jim Green? Green was definitely killed in the hall while he was in that chair. There was no blood anywhere else.'

'But he had sex with the killer?'

'Certainly, if the bed's anything to go by!'

'So in Green's case –' it was Caz interrupting – 'they must have decided on something a bit different, bondage or something like it. Green let himself be tied up, then he was killed?'

'Any better ideas?'

'No, Sir. Was there any evidence of bondage with Burnley?'

'There were marks, it's not impossible. We just don't know.'

They went through to Burnley's bedroom. The bed had been stripped for analysis, but a clear polythene sheet covered the mattress. The deadman's outline had been drawn on the cover with a black marker pen. The curtains had been opened to let light on to the death room. The windows, unlike those at the front of the flat, were grimy. MacInnes looked into the en-suite bathroom. It was immaculate.

'Too clean, Bob?' he asked.

'Difficult to say, Tom. The house was very neat.'

'So we still have nothing.'

'Forensics did a fine toothcomb on the bathroom. Came up with traces of Burnley's blood, could be a shaving cut. No way of knowing for sure.'

'So nothing.'

'And nothing to say he was gay either?' Caz said.

'Except for the way he died, small point,' said Moore.

'And the killer's semen,' MacInnes said.

Twelve

Green's place was different. Inside, the smell of death lingered, no longer emetic but nevertheless disgusting. Outside, in the road, a large mobile incident room had just been activated; it was large, white and dramatically striped.

'Fascinating hobby,' Moore said, looking round the flat.

'Takes all sorts, Bob,' MacInnes replied.

The lounge was significantly larger than Burnley's, and again was well decorated. The room was a light pink, slashed with a darker diagonal, and various prints were scattered opposite the window on the longest wall. She recognised an Ansel Adams landscape and another black-and-white print, this one of a bare-chested car mechanic holding the heavy wheel of a Chevvy effortlessly against a muscled thigh.

Beneath the prints, there was a white ceramic-framed park bench, and beneath this was bright white china; piss-pots and bed-pans from an age before disposable cardboard. The whiteness appealed to Caz.

'So how sexy is this place, Flood?' the DI said.

'It isn't,' she answered.

'Why not?'

'I don't know, Sir. You're asking me about feelings, about responses that I can't volunteer. I just am and this place just is. If something happens it happens.'

'So what happens?'

'Well, the place doesn't make me feel sexy, Sir, if that's what you're asking. It's interesting, but it isn't sexy. The, um, collection is somewhat unusual, but the way it looks – hard white on the royal carpet – I like it.'

'But it's not sexy?'

'No, Sir. I'd say interesting.'

Green had owned a nice stereo, a composite with a particularly fine heavyweight turntable. Next to his vertically stored record sleeves was a white glove and record cleaner. A careful man. An original fitment, over-painted white too many times, was in a corner, nearest the window. This had a cupboard containing a wad of elastic-banded receipts, some gay pornography, a number of mint postcards and a few board-games. Caz was removing them, passing them behind her for the Sergeant and the DI.

'You ever played Scrabble, Flood?' Moore asked. He made the word 'scrabble' sound dirty. She ignored him. The game was a travel set, each piece's corners designed to clip into the board. She removed the cover. Inside, the start of a game spread right from the centre's double letter square. Someone had started with 'CHILD' and this had been followed with 'ETERNITY'. 'LOOT' had then been added, making the cross words 'YO' and 'TO'.

'Yo?' Moore said. 'What the hell kind of word is that?'

'It's an exclamation,' Caz explained. 'Like in "Yo-ho". It scores.'

'But no scorepad,' MacInnes said casually.

'A shame,' Caz said, 'with such a good start.'

The DI began undoing the elastic band from around the receipts. He spoke to his sergeant.

'We're going to have to tie these two bodies together, Bob. I don't like coincidences and I hate the idea of a random killing even more.'

'We've already got the link through Jones.'

'If we presume Burnley knew his neighbour.'

'I know Trevor Jones said they didn't really know each other, but he was squeaky at the time. He'd've said almost anything.'

'Maybe, Bob, but they don't seem the same sort. I don't see them as mates unless Jones was Burnley's bit of rough.' He put the elastic band on his wrist and turned to Caz. 'How about you, Flood? Do you see our bodies as a couple? What do you see? From a woman's standpoint?'

'I'm not a woman, Sir, I'm a copper!' Caz flashed back, responding to his sarcasm, 'but the two victims are incredibly similar. They both worked in finance. They both lived alone. Their flats were quite close to each other, both of them were twenty-nine years old. They were both well-off, fit, good-looking blokes. They had reasonable taste and it seems they both liked their music – look at the stereo systems. Oh,' she paused, 'and they had a professional decorator, maybe the same one.'

'And they were both gay?' MacInnes added.

'No, Sir. Burnley was not gay.'

'Why do you think they had a professional in to do the decorating?' Moore asked.

'The quality of the finish. It was especially noticeable back at Burnley's. The decorator had gone right back to the original wood and the white was immaculate. An amateur can do it as well as that but it will take him for ever.' She pointed at the cupboard. 'That's a typical DIY man's finish, paint on rubbed-down paint until the shape underneath disappears.'

'I thought you said this place had been done by a pro?'

'Everything but the cupboard. The decorator probably asked for silly money to strip back the doors and Green told him to forget it.'

'And what time of day would *that* have been?' Moore said.

'The DI asked me what I *thought*, Sergeant.'

'Oh, yeah.'

'And I'd say there's a good chance we'll find a 1992 receipt for the work done in this room somewhere in that pile.'

'It might've been a pound-notes job.'

'I don't think so, Sarge. This one would be up-market.'

'Oh, for Christ's sake!'

'And I think he'll drive a Volvo, maybe a Range-Rover.'

'*What!!*' Moore said.

'This kind of decorator should be a bit of a poser. He wouldn't be seen dead in a van but he would need solid transport with a bit of room. If it's not a big solid motor, it'll be something flip like a mini-moke or even a deux-chevaux.'

Moore snapped. 'I think you're taking the piss now, Flood!'

MacInnes was smiling.

'Actually I'm not, Sarge,' she replied sensibly. Now *she* smiled. 'I'm profiling, using logical processes to build up a picture of a protagonist. The FBI developed the technique. They used it to catch serial killers. I'm using my analysis of the decorat*ing* to project the characteristics of the decorat*or*.'

'Sounds like bullshit to me.' Moore was aware that the DI was at best neutral. He went half-way, 'Still, at least you're thinking.'

'Thanks, Sarge.' She paused. Behind Moore, the DI was holding up a lilac card. She coughed. 'I see the company as, as . . . pink, no, not pink, lilac . . . and the name something like . . . something like uh . . .' She waited for the DI.

'Avocado?' MacInnes suggested.

She smiled, 'And if you like, Sarge, I could give you the decorator's phone number.' Moore was no longer amused.

'Yes, now where is he from? Not central Brighton?' She was shaking her head, looking at the DI. 'Not Hove? A little further out? I think maybe . . .' MacInnes mouthed a 'P'. 'I think maybe Patcham. Yes that's it! Avocado Design, Patcham Hill. Exactly the sort of place he'd live.'

'You must *want* to work late,' Moore said.

They left with two marked evidence bags, locked up and went into the incident van. Moore suggested coffee while the DI got updated. A woman constable brewed up for them and Caz could feel conflict; she had been promoted from tea-girl but her replacement was another female.

When MacInnes came off the phone he had nothing much to say.

Door-knocking had produced little new, in particular no one who could add to the sighting of the woman in Inkerman Terrace. It was beginning to look as if the witness might have made a mistake. There was a whisper that a DCI was about to come on to the case, and another rumour suggested that a superintendent was about to be brought in. Saint & Greavsie had been working well. Green had spent a trial month at 'Trim' almost a year ago, but then had moved on to a place called 'Muscle' which was, according to Greaves, 'A bit more his way, know what I mean?' Jones was now definitely in the clear after one of his alibis turned out to be a special constable.

The proprietor of the decorating company was called Jeremy. No one believed his surname, but when Caz rang their number she nevertheless asked for a Mr Avocado.

'This is he,' a voice said. It was lightweight and sweet.

'Mr Avocado? This is Detective Constable Flood of John's Street . . .'

'Er yes . . . ?'

'Good morning, Sir. We are investigating the death of Mr James Green of Onderman Road.'

'Jim.'

'Yes, Sir. We understand you did some decorating for Mr Green.'

'Interior Design.'

'We would like to talk to you about the deceased.'

'I'm sorry, why?'

'It's just routine, Sir, we will be talking to everyone that Mr Green might have dealt with in the last few months.'

'If that is the case, what do you require of me, Officer?'

'We will need to take a short statement.'

'Would you like me to come into the station?'

'Onderman Road, Sir. We have an incident van here. Could you . . . ?'

'Come in? Certainly. Would one o'clock be all right?'

'That would be excellent, Mr Avocado. Will you be driving or would you like us to send a car?'

'No, that will not be necessary,' the decorator said formally. 'I can drive myself there.'

She couldn't resist the question. 'I'll look out for you, Mr Avocado . . . What car will you be driving?'

'I'm afraid my wife has borrowed the Volvo, but she has a little Citroën. I will be driving that. It's pink.' As Caz thanked him and said goodbye, she punched the air, feeling ludicrously pleased with herself. She thought briefly about Valerie but decided she did not have time to call him.

Caz told the uniform guarding the end of the street to let the pink 2CV through the barrier. It arrived ten minutes early and parked close to the incident van, its large, cross-plyed wheels splaying as they turned in. As she stepped out on to the metalled steps to meet the decorator and saw the car, she immediately thought that the lead character in *Herbie* should have been a deux-chevaux and not a Beetle. In comparison with the sit-up-and-beg Citroën the Volkswagen was positively boring.

Jeremy Avocado surprised her. He was tall, tanned, and definitely not ugly, large-framed with tightly waved light-brown hair kept short. As he said hello, his handshake was firm and positive and he held her gaze with sharp hazel eyes. She had expected someone a bit limp-wristed, and was very slightly taken aback by the strength of his grip.

By the time they had entered the eight-by-eight interview room, she had recovered. She reintroduced herself to him and offered him tea. He smiled politely but said he never 'did' caffeine and that he was fine.

'You won't mind if I do?' she said. 'But I've been heavily into drugs since I was four.'

'Please feel free,' Avocado answered.

She felt a little dry, and took a mouthful of her earlier cup. It was lukewarm. When she looked up, Avocado was looking at her steadily, over folded fingers, a faint look of amusement on his face. She pinked very slightly and apologised. 'We must get on,' she said.

She hadn't expected such a strong, positively masculine man, nor had she expected a tight, to the point, understanding of the issues. He explained that he loved the total design jobs he occasionally did for the rich and famous, but more typically he did bread-and-butter work like Green's. Avocado was quick to suggest that she needed to know when he had first been contacted by Green, when the decorating had been done, and how much it had cost. From a small navy blue book he recalled that Green had contacted him by telephone (he gave a date and time in September), that he had been recommended, and that his charge of four hundred pounds per room was fractionally more than Green wanted to pay.

'I charged precisely one thousand pounds to do three rooms. I never discount, but we agreed I would leave the lounge cupboards and the windows for some future date.'

Caz grinned lightly and asked if leaving the cupboard had challenged his aesthetic sensibilities. Wasn't it a matter of principle?

'Look, my dear,' Avocado affected a perfect parody of the decorator queen, 'there's a recession out there . . .' He looked at his fingernails, 'Why, I'm surprised at you.'

She apologised. Did he know who had recommended him? 'Oh luv, I thought you would *never* ask.' He was continuing his camp role. 'Why it was George Burnley, of course.'

'George Burnley, Inkerman Terrace?'

'Well done, *Madame*, yours in one!'

'Jesus!' Caz whispered.

'And to save you a *little* time, Officer –' Avocado produced some Thomas Cook paperwork – 'I've just got back from Florida. A lovely little holiday. I was there three weeks with Grace and the kids.'

The WPC brought in fresh tea. She checked again, did he want anything, but he shook his head. She asked him, how was business?

'Fairly good. Not booming but steady. My last serious commission was a few years ago, but I get by. I have a little ad in the Yellow Pages, but a lot of my work comes by word of mouth.'

'So how well did Burnley know Green?'

'Oh, Jim and George? I don't think they were, er, "close". I think they probably knew each other from one of the clubs. I didn't ask.'

'Do casual acquaintances recommend you very often?'

'People talk. In a business like mine, personal recommendations are it.'

'So your fame spreads?'

'Oh, yes. A half-mention at a party here, a dropped hint there. We self-employed never really stop working. Good news travels as quickly as bad news: where to get good drugs, a different club, an interior designer who's just a little bit more interesting... Whatever, you know how it is.' He gave an odd, quick smile. 'I am a specialist. If you have a speciality the word spreads, you know. Ripples on a pond, my dear, ripples . . .'

Caz checked on his labourer: a real craftsman, according to Avocado. She would need to double-check, of course, but he was already in the clear. The boss and the paper-hanger took their holidays at the same time each year. 'His family flew to Miami on the same plane as us. Went on to Orlando, Disney and all that . . . Terrible place. Wouldn't be seen dead there myself. We always rent somewhere. Usually in the Keys.'

Jeremy Avocado was presumably puttering the Citroën back up the London Road towards Patcham's over-large council estate and turning off just in time to park outside his bijou cottage on the hill. Caz was wrapping up his statement and checking the finer points.

The decorator was close to being a star witness, an uncluttered mind getting straight to the point. He explained that in a previous incarnation his business had specialised in very expensive, one-off design projects, where every aspect of the room's design was his responsibility: the furniture, the decor, even the art on the walls.

The recession had hit hard and the big earners were not calling just now, but the smaller jobs were coming in steadily enough to pay his mortgage. Green, he explained, had paid cash, one hundred ten-pound notes, no VAT. By splitting the original company into two equal halves (the wife's company was called Grace Interiors), Avocado had managed to keep each just under the VAT threshold. When he did very well he would arrange for Tom, his tradesman, to receive monies direct. Jim Green had insisted that he did not want a receipt and Avocado had been just as insistent that he must supply one. As soon as it was written, Green destroyed it. Yes, Jeremy had thought it odd, but then it was none of his business really, was it? Three lines on the statement added, 'It is my recollection that the nine-hundred-and-fifty-pound bill for Mr Burnley's work was receipted and that this was also paid for in cash. That work was completed in late August and I have had no further contact with Mr Burnley.'

Caz noted the cash payments, another tiny similarity, but shunted the fact sideways as two evidence bags dropped with a thud on her desk. She looked up at a grinning Sergeant Moore. 'Detective,' Moore said, 'that should keep you going a while. Let us know what you come up with!'

She took on Burnley's box-files first, looking for the decorator's paperwork while categorising the separate letters and receipts. She broke the work down, first by separating credit-card slips from invoices, then these from letters and guarantees. The credit-card slips were then split into Visa, Master-Card and Amex, and these three piles divided up again into this year and 'previous'. She started on the Visa slips; there were thirty-three.

Burnley had bought petrol in Brighton, in Horsham and in Guildford, had eaten vegetarian pizzas at a favoured restaurant in the Lanes, bought CDs and books from the High Street chains, and had sent flowers to a Midlands address in May. Using Master-Card he had drawn cash regularly every month except July, and bought a designer shirt for fifty pounds in September. His Amex receipts were almost all for petrol, and there were three, not two, in Grigglesham Foster. His hi-fi system had cost more than fifteen hundred pounds, bought from Pearson's Audio of Brighton.

All the letters bar one were standard: bank statements, bills for the gas and electric, and one concerning poll-tax. The only personal note was a thank-you to Georgie from Sis. The flowers were wonderful. Most of the receipts tallied with a credit-card slip. Two that didn't suggested George had shared an evening meal in Armando's, the noisiest Italian restaurant in Brighton. She made a note that a follow-up would be needed, but she knew the place too well. The waiters at Armando's were quite mad. By ten-thirty any night most of them couldn't even remember their own names, let alone the faces of customers.

There were a few virtually untraceable receipts that looked as if they were from a pub, perhaps for lunch. Two looked to have similar writing and were dated, the dates corresponding with the petrol purchases made in Grigglesham. Follow-up Number two. There was no reference to Jeremy the decorator or Avocado Design or Grace Interiors. For whatever reason, George Burnley must have binned the documentary evidence. His beautiful flat might have been decorated by the wallpaper fairy.

It was well past three o'clock. Before starting on Jim Green's elastic-banded paperwork she thought she should ring Valerie. He answered on the second ring.

'Hi,' she said, 'it's me.'

'Is that Victoria? I said don't ring me here. If Caz finds out she'll—'

'Very funny, Valerie.'

'How are you?' he said, very softly.

'Better than I was. Look, I'm tied up but . . .'

'You can't make the weekend?'

'No,' she said. There was a distant strangled 'aarrgghhhh!!' 'But if you can cope with mixing business with pleasure, we could eat tonight.'

'Is this the best I'm going to get?'

'Tonight, yes.'

'OK, the deal stinks but I'll bite.'

'Armando's. In the Lanes. Do you know it?' He said yes. 'Meet me there at nine o'clock. I've got to ask a few questions, then I'm all yours.'

'I've got to too,' Val said.

She asked, 'Got to what?'

'To ask a few questions. If you have the time.'

Green was green and didn't own a car. There were no petrol receipts among his sorted slips, and the few trips he had made had been by bus or train. In May, June and July, Green had gone to London; he had travelled to Portsmouth twice and Guildford a couple of times. There was a single bus ticket, issued in Guildford and costing two pounds thirty.

Jim appeared to have had a more active social life, and his personal letters' pile was considerable. She put it aside. Most of the receipts in the pile were for everyday purchases and, like Burnley's, some were unattributable, the sort of pencil-scribbled notes received in station cafés or a pub. On a whim she compared the bills with the two from Burnley's 'Grigglesham' days off. On one she thought the writing was similar, on another, though there was no similarity, the sheet looked to have come from an identical pad.

She held the receipts up to the light then lowered them. An ordinary receipt book, but how commonplace was it? Had both bills been issued in the same pub and, even if they had, where was it? An optimistic instinct wanted the pub to be in Grigglesham Foster, and so tie Green and Burnley to the same area, but she knew that Burnley could have bought petrol in one place and eaten in another, even Brighton. If it was Grigglesham, at least the door-to-door wouldn't take too long. From memory she thought there were only about twenty houses in the village.

Green's personal letters all seemed to be long and detailed, as though he underwent some long-range catharsis with his correspondents. An old friend from York University argued with him about both pop music and homosexuality and another, female and gay, told him about free rock-climbing in the Peaks and wondered about children.

Caz realised she might need to speak to the other halves of these extended conversations, and the woman in her already felt the anguish and sadness her intrusion would probably cause. Another letter, again from the female mountaineering friend, agreed that having offspring was a long-term desire, 'even for her', and that maybe one day they could work something out. Her letters were bright, alive, occasionally flip and noticeably intelligent, but underneath there flowed a sub-current of sadness. Briefly, Caz felt heavily dark and a peculiar sympathy seemed to roll through her. She tried to remember a quotation she'd once read but it kept floating away from her. Something like: '*I can choose how to act on my thoughts but I cannot often choose what I think*.'

She could choose to fulfil her sexuality as she thought fit, but she had not chosen to feel as she felt. Presumably Jim Green was like her, and this northern woman was like her. They may have been 'happy to be gay', or even 'proud to be gay', they may have said that they *chose* to be gay, to live their lives honestly; but in the end, in the beginning they just *were*, and they reacted to what they were. Now Jim Green was dead and some northern lass was bereaved. When her biological clock ticked loudest, who would hear it now?

'You died, Flood?' It was Sergeant Moore. She looked up, amazed to see it was six-thirty. No, she hadn't, she said, but she did think she had a lead on the murders. Behind him was considerable activity: PCs reporting in from door-to-door, two DCs using phones, Saint at the photocopier and the DI behind Perspex, also on the phone.

'Christ, Sarge, when'd the bomb hit?'

'Five minutes ago. We've just got ourselves a third stiff and now we're getting a new Big Chief to tell us what we're doing wrong.'

'Who?'

'Detective *Chief* Superintendent Norman Blackside!' Moore said, very deliberately. 'Just made up, still shiny. I don't think the DI is very happy.'

'I didn't even know he'd been made up.'

'Nor did I. Apparently he was just about to transfer with the new rank. Chief constable's flavour of the month, isn't he? A real blue-eyed boy. Just got back from a secondment in the States and now they want him to wave a magic wand over this one for us hicks.'

'What's he like, Sarge? I heard he was a bit heavy-handed.'

'You could say that. He spent eighteen months doing a masters degree in Information Technology. Now he loves getting the troops to burn shoe-leather while a few DCs pump up computer terminals. I heard he thought the Ripper Case was a perfect example of policing.'

'But they caught Sutcliffe by accident in the end, didn't they?'

'Ah, but the net was closing in – ask Blackside.'

'Sounds like this is just the beginning.' She waved at the receipts.

'Tell me about it!' Moore said.

Caz asked him about the third body. Where was it? Was it definitely one of theirs? Who had found it?

'DC Greaves, lucky lad. He's still there now. Saint & Greaves came in about one o'clock – you were in with the decorator – and they picked up the list of employees from Pearson's. The manager before this one was a bloke called Beecham, single, thirty years old. Moved to Horsham when he jacked the job at Pearson's. Greavsie found him dead in bed, just like George Burnley. No cuts on the back, apparently, but Greavsie said it looked like someone had driven a JCB up his backside.'

'When did Beecham die? Does this put Jones back in the frame?'

'We don't know yet, but Jones is definitely out of it. He's been nicked for a burglary in Southampton that went down Friday last. The owners were out from just before nine o'clock and back just after eleven. Unless Clever Trevor had a helicopter, he's off the hook.'

'Who's the special who backed up his alibi?'

'Another Jones, no relation. He's OK. A gang of mates met up about eleven o'clock to go fishing off Town Quay. Apparently, Trevor turned up at ten-past eleven and stayed until gone four in the morning. We reckon he was setting up an alibi for the burglary.'

'It's one hell of a coincidence, though, Trevor Jones being connected. What's the odds against that happening by chance?'

'Slim, but it depends which way you look at it. Jones was a neighbour of Burnley, so any other connections are reasonable. Green helped him with his mortgage. We know he helped George Burnley as well. They're connections but they're not independent. If Green was involved in the sale of one part of a house, he's fairly likely to be involved in another. If Green buys a class stereo, he's likely to buy it from the best shop in town, and that's Pearson's Audio.'

'So did Burnley,' Caz said. 'He spent fifteen hundred quid there.'

'But all we've got is that the three moved in similar circles. They were young, single blokes.'

'And what, talked to each other? Made recommendations?'

'Yes, precisely.'

'That's one of the things that I've picked up, Sarge. Burnley and Green both had their flats decorated by Avocado, but he looks in the clear. He said that most of his new business was picked from recommends. He called it "ripples in the pond".'

'Well, we know nothing about this Beecham chap yet, except that he's dead. If he was one of Avocado's customers, maybe they were getting knocked off for using the wrong colour loo paper.'

'If he was, then I think we might start to get a bit paranoid.'

Caz looked past the sergeant to see the DI coming off the phone. Moore half turned, still talking to her. 'If Blackside's true to form he'll have the whole squad in tomorrow at seven o'clock sharp and it'll be twice as big by Monday. Either he's got a funny handshake, or his daughter's screwing the chief constable; Christ knows where he gets his numbers from.'

Caz groaned. She had a feeling this was going to be a bad weekend.

Thirteen

Armando's Ristorante was almost always full, but Caz was guaranteed a table. Once upon a time as a student, then as a young copper, opposite a male escort or in a group, occasionally alone, she had earned her certain booking through many years of faithful support. The food varied but the atmosphere was always something special, the waiters crazy, the music always intrusive, the smell of garlic thick enough to cut.

She had mentioned to Gabrielle ('you say Gabbry-ell-uh') that she would have to ask a few questions, but this was really a social visit. He laughed, rattled out something Italian, then chuckled down the phone.

'Ah! so this lucky man. When are you goin' to make me 'appy?'

'When you and Anita stop making babies, Gabrielle!' she told him.

'Ah, but you English always pick nits!' he said. The table was booked.

She had wanted to be there at eight forty-five, hoping to have finished her business before Valerie arrived, but she got there at five-past-nine to see him waiting in the entrance alcove. He was lit by ultra-violet light and his work shirt glowed . He kissed her but she thought the kiss less than certain. 'I thought you might not be coming,' he said.

She retaliated. 'Why shouldn't I? I'm working, remember?'

She could see Gabrielle in the gloom of the far end of the

restaurant. As she raised her eyes he raised two carafes of red, 'See, I am serving?' She waved acknowledgement.

They were given a table at the edge of a tiny dance-floor, their chairs side by side in a foot-deep arched recess. She saw this as a stroke of luck; she always sat with her back to the wall, facing the crowds, and she knew that many men wanted to face the room. Yes, she told Piero, she did want garlic bread, yes, she would like wine, but the gentleman might want to see the list. 'Oh, thank you!' Valerie said, faintly bemused.

'I've been in this place so many times before,' Caz explained to him. 'Armando knows me well and thinks I'm his grandchild, Gabrielle thinks I would be offended if he didn't chat me up, and the other waiters know me so well they no longer bother to bring a menu.'

'So what's good?'

'Any pizza, ask for it nice 'n juicy, any pasta. The steaks are a bit rich and the fish depends on the weather. If you like chicken you could try *petto di pollo cacciatora*; that's chicken cooked in a white wine with basil, tomato, mushrooms and onions; not bad. I don't choose any more. I let them do it for me. They ask me rich or poor? Running or not running?'

'You can explain if you want.'

'Rich means a steak or a nice piece of fish. Poor means I get pizza or pasta. If I'm racing on the Sunday I get the fish or the pasta.'

'So what is it now, Caz, rich or poor?'

'Neither. It's "working".'

'I was afraid you'd say that.'

'Which means pasta and enough wine to blur the edges but not enough to have any kind of hangover.'

'So how long have we got?'

'Maybe forever, but tonight, not long. They gave us a new Chief Super today and he wants us in tomorrow morning for six-thirty. I haven't seen the papers: did you know we've had *three* murders now?'

'No, I didn't.'

'Well, no doubt it'll be all over the tabloids tomorrow.'

'And what about tonight?'

'Well, I have to ask a few questions here.' She waved a small envelope at him. 'See if I can find out who George Burnley had his pizzas with. Then I need an early night. I'll be up at five o'clock running.'

Piero came back and Valerie ordered in Italian. '*Per piacere, petto di pollo cacciatora, e penne rigate alla ghiotta, grazie.*'

'*Vino?*'

'*Sì, Barbera D'Alba Odderro.*' Then he whispered to Caz, 'You're a sick woman, Detective!'

'I'm a dedicated professional!' she retorted. 'And you . . . are a fraud.'

'And I recommend the *Scallops St Jacques Provencale*,' he said. 'Can you come flying with me on Sunday?'

'Yes, no, probably,' she said. 'I'll know for sure tomorrow.'

She opened a grey envelope to reveal a sheaf of Burnley's photographs. 'I have to check on our man. Five minutes?' She felt guilty and touched Valerie's hand. He said it was no problem and she left him. She saw her favourite waiter and shouted

'*Ciao, Gabbry-elle-uh. Come stai? Mi dai due minuti?*'

The head waiter did give her time but didn't recognise Burnley. She asked Piero. Piero was hardly concentrating, but was sure he didn't know him. Caz left them with a photograph and the dates she was interested in, asking in Italian that they please try very hard to remember.

The kitchen clanged and clattered with activity, the pizza ovens dark and black, great cast-iron pots conjuring sauces, stainless surfaces wiped automatically by pudgy-fingered cooks. It stank of garlic and she dizzily sucked it all in. She loved the place. Michael, the chef, waved and called, '*Ah, Signora, mia bella!*' to her. She waved back with the hand full of photographs. He gestured 'come here', and she went.

'*Cosa stai cercando, mia cara?*' he asked.

Michael remembered. George Burnley did not like meat, he told her, and the friend he was with had complained about a meal one night. 'Sì, this man he was older, with a bald 'ead. He a little man like me but big like dis.' Michael tapped his huge belly. 'The man, he eat good food, lots of sauces. He like *zabbaglione*.'

Valerie had been impatient. When she got back most of the garlic bread was gone. He told her to eat some quickly so he could breathe on her. He winked. 'They really love you here, don't they?' His eyes were gleaming.

They drank the soft fruity wine and absorbed each other. Caz asked Valerie to tell her more about flying and when he did his face was alight with the joy of it, as if he were up there. 'You'll love it,' he said, 'you're just the sort of free spirit that should fly all the time.'

She asked about the cold; wouldn't the summer be better for flying? He told her no, that was one of the great misconceptions.

'What the weather is like on the ground bears no relation to what's going on up in the air. Flying is much, much tougher in the summer. We fly early in the morning or last thing in the evening, before the sky has had a chance to cook up, just like balloonists. The best and safest flying is in the winter. You just have to wrap up well, that's all.'

'I can take it,' she said, 'I've run winter cross-country!'

They ate their meals as if they were drifting. They said very little. Caz picked lazily at her creamy pasta as wild images blipped in and out of her consciousness. One moment it would just be his eyes, shining blue, then some imagined flying machine, then brown arms in a bed, the throb of the micro-light's engine, his face again, the tightness of his shoulders, clouds then buttocks, wings and feet, petrol then warm body fluids. She could stop it by just snapping to attention but it was delicious for as long as she allowed it to flow. She wallowed in it and warmth oozed down through her body. Then she heard him call, 'Hello?'

Their thighs were touching. He was whispering in her ear and sounded like dripping honey. 'Hello? Katherine?' He was soft, waiting for her, and she played with the images again. 'You shouldn't do that in public,' he said.

They lingered over cappuccinos, and she let him small-talk about his micro-light. He was like music; something in his voice wrapped her up and soothed her, like a mother bringing a candle up the stairs to light her dark. 'I really would like to fly with you,' she said quietly.

'But not tonight, right?' he answered.

She blessed him for knowing again. 'No, not tonight, Val. I'll get a taxi.'

In the distance, Gabrielle caught her eye, asking a question. She made a 'T' with her fingers, watched him bow 'Sì!' then go to the phone. She smiled as she watched the waiter's back. This place!

The staff knew her and they liked her. She loved them. In their own way they were her security, deep warmth, softness, the smell of her own quilt.

She could feel Valerie's leg against hers and could focus on any point where they touched. She wanted to run her hand across his quads to say, 'Yes,' but knew better than to do that tonight. Now it hadn't happened she was glad she had to wait. She wanted to swallow him live and she knew that would take time; she needed to eat him, to envelop him.

A primitive, deep part of her wanted him to quickly take her now, to rush her home, to let their passions tumble them headlong along some stream before they fell asleep. She wanted that to happen, to be bathed in his sweat; but something even more fundamental said, wait, this should not be rushed.

Fourteen

She had set her alarm clock for four fifty-five. The dream it interrupted had involved Valerie, Trevor Jones, and an indescribable flying machine. She had been trying to get closer to Valerie, scrabbling along the wings, greasy with an aromatic oil. Each time she reached out a naked arm for Valerie, Jones deflected it and his face filled the screen, his yellow teeth grinning at her. She woke exhausted. Her stomach was wet.

On her run she wore club kit, black shorts, red and white stripes down the singlet and lightweight black nylon leggings under the shorts. She wanted to hurt, so she pushed herself hard before she was fully warmed up. When she reached the pier she slowed, her chest burning, and walked down steps to the shingle edge of the sea.

There was very little wind up on the promenade, but at the water's edge it lifted a delicate spray from the waves, making a light, salty fog. She ran through that, hard, for four hundred metres at a time, the pebbles moving beneath her, sapping her strength. Her arms pumped and she felt hard and mean. On her third repetition she had the briefest vision of a cackling murderer and then another vision, her fingers pushing into his eyes. She was running too hard and slipped, her tiring legs unable to cope with the shingle's drag. She swore as she faltered and slid down into the wetted shale. She felt angry at Valerie. Angry because he was decent. She was damp and felt pathetic. She felt hate for some vague and distant evil rolling through her. Her anger grew. She wanted to squash it beneath her. She thought that her nemesis was the triple killer but something made her feel unconvinced. There was a smell of seaweed and, from somewhere, she heard seagulls' screams. Disgusted, she got up, determined to run until she was cleansed.

She started to run again. After five more surges through the shale the thoughts had been forced away. She was below her street and a light drizzle merged with the sea-spray, tinkling down on to her, light and cool. Her cheeks burned and the hurt faded as she let the day wash over her. Now she felt sated. Ravished. She could feel her heart, feel her muscles reaching out. There was a special, delicious tautness in her, a deep spring, deep down inside. She was whole. She could do anything.

When she arrived at John Street she looked immaculate. Her hair was tied back and her cheekbones were still flushed with power. She wore 501s, white Asics, a light blue cotton shirt with a button-down collar (no tie) and a brown leather waistcoat. She carried a Goretex jacket, rolled up like a baton in her fist. Her eyes sparkled.

They were due in at seven o'clock. She had parked her creaking MG at six-twenty-eight and was walking the nick's corridors at six-thirty. Tom MacInnes had been in for fifteen minutes, Bob Moore for ten. Norman Blackside had arrived before six.

They were gathered together just before seven-fifteen. The incident room had been moved up a floor and Blackside's Army was now billeted in a large seminar room with a cedar-panelled stage at one end and high slatted windows at the other. Ribs of pale light and shadow painted the stage and lit Bob Moore's face as he was speaking.

The same ripples of light and darkness were like water stains along one wall. The wall carried three large boards, studded with clinical shots of death in colour and black-and-white. Each tall board was named; George Burnley, Jim Green, and now, Peter Phillip Beecham.

Two more boards had been arranged alongside the others. They were stark; blank; white. Untitled. Empty. Sergeant Moore explained that they were the chief super's way of saying they needed to catch this bastard soon. Then they were told to listen up as Blackside entered.

When Norman Blackside had been a still-approachable DI he had been known as Garth. Before that, though no one remembered why, he had been called 'Chisel'. Now he was simply 'Blackside'.

He was a truly massive man, dark, thick-haired and dominating. His height and weight had led rugby teams for ten years until time had added inches to his muscle bulk and sheer pressure began to tell on his knees. He was deeply tanned, courtesy of two recent months working with the Los Angeles police and his slicked black hair shone with health. If he had been dressed in steel and astride a white charger he would have looked as real as he did now; taking the steps on to the stage in two strides and crossing to its centre in three more. Bob Moore retreated from him, deferent, a pack juvenile, fractionally bowed; his eyes down, submissive.

Blackside stood at the lectern and stared, waiting as the room quieted, his demand for absolute attention increasing as his shoulders lifted an inch. The babble had died to almost zero, just a whisper somewhere that Caz thought was near her. Blackside still did not speak. He was carrying a block of index cards in a huge fist and cracked them, edge down, once on the desk-top. The last sideways murmur instantly stopped. He still waited; a final test. Then he spoke. His voice was heavy and commanding.

'I–' he paused – 'am Detective Chief Superintendent Norman Blackside.' There was another breath's pause. 'And I do *not* fuckin' want to be here.' He looked deep into the room. 'I was supposed to be startin' at the Yard this mornin' and I *will* be there in six weeks' time. If I am still here at Christmas, next year is cancelled.' A chair scraped. Somebody coughed.

'We do *not* wait. We do *not* fuck around. We will have this bastard in December. By six o'clock tonight we will know what time the Mayor of Brighton shits. We will know everything about Burnley, everything about Jim Green, and absolutely every damn thing about Peter Phillip Beecham, deceased, in seventy-two hours. You may beat your wives and you may eat live babies, but you will get me this information. It will be logged. It will be checked by your superiors. It *will* be cross-referenced and we *will* find this nutter. Any questions?' There was no response from the floor. Blackside's striped face didn't move.

'Questions!' he said again, this time demanding an answer.

'Er, Sir.' It was Saint's voice. Caz had to stop herself turning as he stood up. 'DC Saint, John Street, Sir. Do we have a positive on Beecham yet?'

'Sar'n't Moore!'

Moore came forward, the start of his answer off-mike and unheard. '. . . Secretor.' He pulled the microphone towards his slightly red face. '. . . We're getting a rush on the DQ-Alpha and should hear tonight.'

'Thank you, Sergeant,' Saint said. Caz was embarrassed for him. A little tension had gone from the room. Someone asked a question about computers. Blackside answered him. Yes, they would be using 'Holmes'. Then he said that the killer's name and address was already written all over the three murders. 'Serial killers sign everything they do.'

'Are we saying that's what we've got now, Sir, a serial killer?' a man's voice at the back asked.

'It is not!' Blackside snapped. 'And if any of the papers mention the idea in the next forty-eight hours you're back in uniform.'

The replied 'Sir!' trailed into silence.

'That it?' Blackside said. He waited ten seconds, looking at the men. 'Sar'n't Moore?' He strode quickly right, signalling the sergeant to the mike as he left the stage. Bob Moore moved up to the microphone and took a deep breath, hushing the lads with his palms facing the room. Then Blackside was gone, one half of a double door clapping shut.

'OK, lads,' Moore said, 'it's new-broom time.'

Caz raised her hand.

'Yes, Flood?'

'Is DI MacInnes still involved, Sarge?'

'He's finishing a report for the Chief Super right now. Yes, he is.'

'Are we . . . ?'

'The same team? Yes. For now at least. We'll be going to Beecham's this morning.' He looked up, towards the back of the room. 'Right, I want DS Reid, DS Lucas and DS Lindsell to stay here. The rest of you take ten, grab a coffee, and be back in here five to eight latest.'

There was no movement. He clapped his hands. 'Come on, shift yer arses. Yer in Division One now!'

Fifteen

Caz concentrated on the road as she drove towards Horsham. Earlier, as she reversed Moore's Sierra, DI MacInnes had appeared in the basement car park, pushing open a steel door and letting it clang slowly behind him. She thought he looked smaller. Bob Moore was in the front passenger seat alongside her and the DI had slipped quickly into the back.

'Flood,' he'd said sharply, 'Bob.' It was sufficient to acknowledge them but terminal. He was to be left alone with his thoughts.

The car park had been slicked with rain water and oil, and as she left she managed to make the Sierra's wheels squeal. She glanced at the mirror. MacInnes hadn't noticed.

Bob Moore tapped the dash. 'Head for Gatwick. The stiff lived that side of Horsham. Small estate.'

She had managed to avoid door-to-door, at least for the morning. There were now nearly thirty coppers knocking doors, led by Lucas, Lindsell and Reid. Blackside had increased the width of the enquiry area and they were talking to all the taxi firms again. Billy Tingle and a WPC called Dibben were already drafted for the computer room and Tingle had been formally warned against smoking. It was small consolation to him that Moira Dibben was the best-looking WPC in Brighton. She hated smokers' breath with a passion.

The rain was at its most awkward; too light for full wipers but heavy enough to make visibility difficult between intermittent sweeps. Road dirt was smearing the glass with arcs of grey.

Peter Beecham's house was in a cul-de-sac on the edge of a new brown-bricked estate. The incident van was just outside the close. Rain and the passage of time had got rid of gawkers and only one curtain twitched as they drove up to Number Fourteen. The damp PC on the door insisted on seeing all three warrant cards even after Sergeant Moore had shown him his. 'And overshoes please, Sir!' he said to MacInnes. 'Orders from Forensic, Sir! Shoes're just inside the door.'

When they stepped into the nondescript hall and the equally ordinary lounge, they were wearing white plasticised paper bootees, isolating them from the crime scene. Dressed so, it was difficult for Caz to see either the DI or Sergeant Moore as voices from above.

'And the body, Sir?' she asked, very tentatively.

'In the main bedroom. Like the first two, no signs of a struggle.'

'No stab wounds either,' Moore said. For some reason he grinned. 'Just massive damage to his jacksie.'

'With?'

'Don't know yet, Flood. Forensic won't say.'

'And do we know if he's . . . ?'

'A woofter?' Moore said. 'What do you think, Flood?'

'Oh, I don't think anything, Sergeant,' Caz said. 'I try not to presume a thing. A good detective should always keep an open mind.'

'Abso-bollock-lutely!' Moore said.

Peter Beecham's life had ended in an extraordinary way, but his home suggested his journey there had been just the opposite. Grey carpet ran right through the small house, the lounge-diner, the tight stairs and the two small bedrooms. Even the kitchen floor was grey, this time with a fine pattern in the waterproof weave.

Throughout the house, the walls were bare magnolia, and there was just one picture, a Woolworth's print of a charging elephant. The kitchen was cluttered with plain white crockery, much of it in the sink, and the windowsill was lined with jars of Hornsea Pottery: Tea, Coffee, Sugar, Flour.

Upstairs was equally bland; the second bedroom empty except for an ironing board and an overflowing basket leaking shirts. Greaves had found Beecham sitting up in bed, propped between pillows with an opened volume of the *Encyclopaedia Britannica* on his lap. Beneath the bedroom window now there were another thirty volumes in two untidy stacks. Greavsies' size eleven footprint was on the top of one red leatherette cover, a footstep below the window through which he had broken in.

MacInnes was muttering, 'Bloody strange . . .'

'What's that, Tom?'

'A dead-ender like this, Bob, living in a dead-end house. Not a bloody book in the place but he's got thirty-odd volumes of *Britannica*. Doesn't that strike you as a bit odd?'

'Maybe he'd just bought them?' Moore suggested. 'Picked up a free draw ticket at the supermarket and ended up being hard-closed?'

'Worth checking out Flood?'

'I've already written it down, Sir!'

The bedroom wardrobes revealed nothing. There were two light grey suits and half a dozen blue shirts. On the floor were two pairs of Clark's shoes, highly polished black. There were no private letters, no receipts, no magazines or newspapers. Beecham's house was sterile, empty and cold.

Caz felt vaguely sad. She could imagine Peter Beecham sat downstairs, in front of the television eating Pot Noodles and watching the nine o'clock news. She was trying to imagine the book salesman's pitch.

'How much would you say a set of encyclopaedias costs?' she heard the DI say absent-mindedly to his sergeant. 'Five hundred quid? A grand?' Bob Moore thought at least fifteen hundred.

'Yet our man hasn't got a decent stereo, even though he could presumably have got one at a discount. He's got a cheap telly, MFI furniture, and yet he spends a grand or more buying books.'

'Maybe he likes reading,' Moore said.

'I doubt that. You'd expect to see *some* other evidence. One or two paperbacks at least.'

'If the books cost a thousand, Sir . . .' Flood was thinking. 'If they did . . .'

'What of it?' MacInnes said.

'That's what Burnley and Green spent on decorating, Sir. If we can find the *Britannica* rep and Beecham paid cash . . .'

'We've got what, exactly?'

'I'm not sure, Sir, but . . .'

'The rep's called Tomlinson,' Moore said flatly. He was holding up a white card. He grinned. 'Another one for your collection, Flood.'

She took the card from him. 'And don't find this one dead, for Christ's sake!'

Caz smiled thinly, 'I'll do what I can, Sergeant.'

Sixteen

Like women, men came in all shapes and sizes. She knew they came in good and bad varieties, some of them with more qualities than faults. On a good day she could see the better sides of Saint & Greavsie, and it wasn't even impossible to imagine Billy Tingle as a rounded-out thirty-year-old making one of her tribe tolerably happy.

But P. P. Tomlinson (BA) made her crawl. He was the kind of man that gave his sex a bad name. He smarmed. He presumed. He inferred. He leered and he lingered and flicked gross eyes to target points about her person. He was the office mauler; the date rapist; the man who bought blue movies involving animals.

His shirt was crisp and white and he wore a college tie with green, red and yellow stripes. His suit was newish but stained and his shoes, the great give-away, were dirty and scuffed. She knew she was being unprofessional but she instantly loathed him. She vaguely day-dreamed as they were speaking, hoping that something he said would allow him to be locked away one day. Like after visiting a particularly dirty home, she knew that she would want to shower as soon as she possibly could. She would itch and crawl now and for the rest of the day.

'It was a straightforward supermarket lead from Asda in Brighton as far as I can remember. I'd sold once before on his estate; they're mostly thirty-six monthly payment sales; there's not a lot of cash floating round.'

She shifted slightly, beginning to itch.

'I wasn't madly keen on travelling up to Horsham as he looked a bit of a no-hoper.' He grinned at Caz and her stomach heaved. 'But then I remembered the old adage, "throw enough shit at a wall, some of it sticks".'

She tried to pretend a smile.

'So I went to see him. A poky little place right? No decorating?'

'Yes.'

'Well, I went through my normal presentation. Laid out all our goodies as per the training course; set up the close and gave him a price.'

'And?'

'And I shut up, of course. First to speak loses. You should know that.' He waited a moment. 'Anyway, I was thinking about an alternative close like "cash-or-credit?" when he suddenly said, "I've got exactly one thousand pounds to spend, so if that's your best price . . ."

'I can get our basic set down to ten-fifty, so I rang the area manager and said I had an easy pick-up at a grand. The area manager said "tough". He said if I couldn't sell the fifty-quid difference, I couldn't sell at all.

'In the end Beecham paid a thousand and thirty and I arranged to pick up the other twenty at the end of the month. I don't suppose I will now.'

'And how were you paid?'

'Oh, cash, of course. That was the deal from the outset. Cash is *very* rare.'

'I'll need your telephone number,' she said. 'We may need to speak to you again.' He was grinning knowingly at her and she hated him for it. She desperately wanted an excuse to slap him down.

'Is that my home number or the office?' Tomlinson asked.

'We may need to speak to you at short notice.'

'I'll give you both,' he said. He was writing on the back of a business card when she asked him if he had ever had any other cash sales. He told her no.

'But I think we've had cash deals on the territory before. When I pulled this one, my area manager mentioned a couple we took about a year ago. We don't really like them all that much. There's profit in credit you know.'

'How can I find out?'

'Whether we've had pound-note deals?'

'And who the buyers were.'

'I can ask in the office this afternoon,' he said. 'Is that all right? I could phone you later.' Then he smiled and suggested that if he wanted to speak to her after hours he'd need her home phone number. She just managed a smile back and said she was ex-directory.

'You don't know what you're missing,' he said.

She told him she'd live with the loss.

Seventeen

Caz arrived back at the nick late enough to miss lunch, and had to make do with too-sweet hot chocolate from a machine in the mess room. Nothing was left in the food dispenser except a large pork pie which she ignored on health grounds. She went upstairs. Someone had Blu-tacked a notice to the murder-room door which read 'Army HQ'. She grinned.

DS Lindsell and DS Reid were standing over a high table, comparing notes. She said hello. DS Reid she didn't know well, but George Lindsell she did. He was an ex-runner, now well into his fifties, muscle on bone, ultra-thin, with tight grey hair and a runner's pinched face.

'DI says he'd like to see you as soon as you come in, Caz,' he said over his shoulder. 'And there's a couple of messages on your desk.'

'Thanks, Sarge,' she said, walking towards her corner. She could see three yellow Post-it notes stuck to her board. The notes made her think briefly of Valerie. She still had Sunday to arrange. Through a Perspex partition she saw Billy Tingle and Moira Dibben at their computers. Billy caught her eye and looked vaguely triumphant. When she looked at Moira, she thought she looked a little sad.

Valerie had left a sharp message. 'Six-thirty your house Sunday morning. Wear Hellies.' The other two were both from Jeremy Avocado asking her to ring. She pocketed two slips, glued back to back, and binned Avocado's second. Then she went downstairs to find DI MacInnes. As she passed the computer room, Billy waved to her with an ambiguous grin on his face.

MacInnes was on the phone. Through his window he raised his hand for her to wait. He looked animated; faintly pink. As the call appeared to be ending he waved her in. She opened the door. His Scots accent was as thick as she'd ever heard it. 'Ah wull, Suh. Ah'll tell huh meesel'.'

He put down the phone. 'Tek a seat, hen,' he said, breathing deeply. 'Well?'

She stiffened upright on her chair. 'We were right about Beecham, Sir. He spent just over a thousand pounds, all cash. Tomlinson said the estate was a bit dead-end and he never expected Beecham to have that kind of money. I think the money links the three victims.'

'You do, huh?'

'Don't you, Sir? Isn't the money too much of a coincidence?'

'No,' MacInnes said, 'not necessarily. Burnley spent nine hundred and fifty, Green spent a thousand, and this third chappy—'

'Beecham, Sir.'

'—Aye, Beecham. He spent a bit more than a thousand.'

'They're very close amounts, Sir.'

'But not the same. How many people d'you suppose have spent, say, between nine hundred and eleven hundred on *something* this week?'

'But they're not all dead, Sir! George Burnley bought a designer shirt for forty-nine pounds ninety-five the week he died and Pat Tomlinson told me that Beecham had exactly a thousand to spend. It *has* to be a link, Sir.'

'No. It *could* be a link.'

'And all three of them were the same age,' she heard herself trailing off pathetically.

'*Similar* age,' MacInnes said.

She sat still, defeated. 'I don't understand, Sir.'

'Do you ever touch this stuff, Flood?' MacInnes produced a half-bottle.

'Not straight, Sir, no.' He produced a bottle of ginger. There was a little flash of light in his eyes. She heard herself say, 'That'll be fine!'

He poured an over-sized measure into a plastic cup and passed it to her, his finger inside the rim. 'Cheers!' he said. She picked up the ginger to soften the whisky, poured too little and slugged it back in one. She felt her stomach burn before the liquid landed.

'Flood; Caz.' He was back to northern English. 'I think you have it, the instinct. Sometimes I think you're very much like me; well, like I was, once.' He waited, his eyes far off, thinking something dark and distant. 'I could get away with it, Caz, you can't.' He gestured at the half-bottle. She took it.

'I'm out of the Ark, Caz. People like me stay at the bottom of the greasy pole. There's no room for instinct now. I told you – we don't have hunches any more, we have computers. They keep telling me, information is the key. I keep locking bad people away but they tell me there's no need for my type any more. Jesus, Flood, we log every bloody thing we do and tape every bloody thing we say. If we fart during an interrogation it's considered harassment!'

'Sir?'

'Oh for God's sake, Flood, learn to keep yer head down. Even if you think you know better than your elders, keep shtumm! People like Norman Blackside will eat you alive if you rock their boat. People like him don't just live by the book, they bloody well wrote it!'

She looked across the desk at the DI. 'I hear you, Sir, but I'm not really sure I understand . . .'

'What I'm saying? I'm saying *hide*, Flood. I'm telling you t'hide yer light under a bushel. I'm saying keep yer pretty head down below the parapet but never, never stop thinkin' the way you do. Just don't tell anyone. Except maybe me.'

'And Sergeant Moore?'

'I said tell me.'

There was a long silence, then MacInnes spoke again. 'DCS Blackside asked for you by name, Flood. He needs another face in the computer room and it's you. I don't know why he came on to you so fast but he did. If I fight it you're out in the open and you're not ready yet, get some time in. Do the numbers for a while, Caz. Kiss a little arse.'

'But I'm a *detective*, Sir! I want to be outside . . .' She was lost for the right phrase, 'I need to be out in the field . . .'

'Catching killers?'

'Yes, Sir.'

'Then wait for the real war, Flood. If yer not in, you can't win.' He looked at her. He could see how close she was to tears. 'You're not quite ready yet, Caz. Not if you can still cry. Take this.' He passed her a note. 'That's where I'll be when ah'm no here.'

He let the room go silent again. Caz had bitten her finger hard to stop the first tear breaking. She took her second drink. 'They *are* connected, Sir; Burnley, Green and Beecham. I know it!'

'So do I, lass,' the DI said softly. 'I'm on *your* side, remember?'

Eighteen

When she rang Valerie he was in a meeting. She told his secretary to tell him that Caz Flood had rung and that it was about time they went flying. She was outside the computer room, hanging on for a few more miserable seconds before finally giving in to the inevitable. 'Valerie, where are you, you bastard?' she thought. 'I need you *now*, not in an hour.' She thought of him again and something incredibly primitive rolled down through her body. She had to consciously stop her pelvis from moving. It was her curse. She still wanted to be loved.

'Blackside's decided that this is my forté,' she told Billy. To Moira she said, 'He given up trying yet?' Moira's hand gesture was inconclusive.

She sat down in front of the computer. 'So it's us and Holmes, right?' she said. She punched the enter key. A directory of files scrolled up the screen and away. 'How's it going then, Billy? We found Peter Sutcliffe yet? Hannibal the Cannibal left his MO on the three stooges, has he?'

Tingle said nothing. He looked at the ranting DC, then slapped the pile of reports he was collating. He passed her an approximate third, his face expressionless, but his eyes with a flicker of victory in them.

'Oh, thank you, Billy,' she said, 'and thank you, Moira.' She turned back to the computer muttering, 'And thank *you*, DI MacInnes and thank *you*, Detective *Chief* Superintendent.' She turned to page one of seventeen inside the first of fifteen files just as the telephone rang. 'Tell him I'm in a meeting!' she said. She refused to look as Moira answered the call.

They ploughed deep into the door-to-door returns for the next three hours. Valerie rang twice more before five o'clock but she was still not available. Moira small-talked and even Billy relaxed, until at around four he could wait no longer and had to dive outside for a cigarette.

'I think you could get Billy to give up smoking with very little effort, Moira,' Caz laughed, 'but would it be worth it?'

'Oh, Billy's all right,' Moira answered, 'I could do worse.'

The phone rang. 'Are you in yet?' Moira said. She decided yes; Valerie had suffered enough.

'Thank you; one moment please.'

Caz took the phone. 'Valerie!'

'No, it's Patrick Tomlinson,' a voice said, '*Britannica*?'

'Oh, hello Mr Tomlinson.'

'I've got that information you wanted. About cash purchases?'

'Fire away.'

'Are you sure I couldn't persuade you to have a drink?'

She was certain. 'Is the Pope a Catholic?'

'Your loss.'

'Yeah, you've already told me.'

'OK, Detective. I've got three names for you: Brian Harvey, a Hove address, Arthur Dunn from Brighton, and a Mr J. Small from Peacehaven.'

'Thank you.'

Tomlinson's voice continued. 'They were all about the same time last year, so they're all due a call. We bring out a couple of books every year to keep our members' collections up to date.'

'Members?'

'Punters to you, darlin'. Clients.' She winced. 'When they buy a set of our encyclopaedias, we call them members.'

'How old were they?'

'Who?'

'Harvey, Dunn and Small.'

'No idea. I can find out, though.'

'Please . . .' Then she added as sweetly as she could, 'Patrick . . .'

'No problem,' she heard. 'But it might take a day or so.'

'Thank you, Patrick.'

'That it then?'

'Yes.' An idea rushed headlong in front of her. 'I mean no.'

'Yes or No?'

'Can you set up these re-visits for next week? Could you fix it so I could come along as a trainee?'

'With me?'

'With whoever's doing the call.'

'Me.'

'With you then.'

She said thank you before she put the phone down. She still felt slightly unclean as well as nervous. The idea of working even one evening with Tomlinson did not exactly fill her with the joys of spring, and keeping the appointments secret from the DI and the DCS was just asking for trouble. Then she decided, 'Sod them.' If they could farm her off, locked away with Tingle and Holmes, then she would just have to do a little overtime. If it came out she was out with a boyfriend. Where was the harm in that?

Talking to Pat Tomlinson might have made her itch but at least it had put activity between the instant of her demotion and now. It was nearly six o'clock. She was not quite so desperate to speak to Valerie, but she called him anyway. They arranged to meet at Amex House for seven.

The files beckoned and she turned, entering more flat police-speak into the Holmes database: Inkerman Terrace No. 23; single occupant; white female; Susan King; age thirty-five; away from scene of crime 2nd of November through to 7th. Ink. Terr. Sing Occ. Wh M. Jones, Keith. Poss saw M mid-to-late twenties near S-O-C; long blonde hair; long fawn coat; 9:30–10 PM on night of murder. 29 IT. SO. WF. O'Neill, Jane. Zero Info.

She typed quickly; words not data. Data, but not information. Good detectives should be looking for data which reduced uncertainty, nothing else. Facts for the sake of facts did no more than cloud the issue. Holmes would produce every commonality, tell them every overlap and tease out every coincidental fact. It was stupid enough to state that all three subjects were male (in case no one had noticed) but then it was clever enough to check for criminal records in the deceased and fingerprint matches at CRO. One of the problems with Holmes was that the mass of information on hand prevented the human detective from picking out which pieces of evidence were crucial, which suspects were more than just names with a record or accidental to the case. MacInnes was right, they were squeezing out instinct. It felt wrong. The computers stopped you thinking.

She thought briefly of Valerie and his lap-top computer. In many ways the Toshiba was just a well-organised book. Enter data, collate it, sort it, stack it, but it's still your data, still an extension of your brain. OK, so you could find things more quickly, but it was still only doing a human thing fast. Great clerks might design colour-code card-indexes and create their own categories but still they had their memory and the human's perverse ability to link across sets and play what-if? with their information.

It was when you fed data automatically and waited for the machine to tell you what it thought that you began to lose the sixth sense. She'd read the research papers on intuition; she knew there was no such thing as a hunch. 'Hunch' was just a word for a hypothesis based on information selected – teased out from everything known. It just happened to be an unconscious process. Coppers still had hunches but they were really just coming to conclusions using their long experience and *some* of what they knew. Sometimes they surprised themselves, sometimes they were wrong; but just because they couldn't *articulate* any of their reasons for thinking what they did didn't mean that there weren't reasons.

Her hands were moving automatically, touch-typing DCs'

shorthand into Holmes. She became aware that she had been typing so absently that she had no idea at all what she had done. It was like that awful scary feeling when you had driven somewhere and could not recall the journey. She saved, then made a print-out request, tabulated by house number. Down the right-hand side of the paper was a column almost completely filled with the bald statement 'zero info'. There were three places where the printer had not typed zilch. She read them. 'Male, possible fawn coat', 'Cream coat', and 'Macintosh, light-coloured'. She had typed all that without seeing it. She asked a wider question. Sightings? Times?

Holmes blinked and 'Please Wait . . .' flashed up on-screen. The printer started with a barrpp of the printer-head and the continuous paper began to spew out towards the floor.

Five sightings including Mrs Ralph's. Three of a man, one of a woman, one unsure. All saw someone in a light-coloured coat. Three said it was around ten o'clock, one said nine, one thought between nine-thirty and ten. One had suggested long blonde hair, the others had made no comment. No one had as yet seen anything near Jim Green's flat, and information was still coming in from Horsham.

'Well done, Mrs Ralph,' Caz said quietly.

It was suddenly seven-fifteen and she was alone. The outer office was in darkness and the light from her room was bright yellow, casting shadows across the day's debris and on to the floor. She looked up at the clock, down at the paper she had produced, and cursed.

Valerie's Daimler-Jaguar gleamed in the amber light reflecting off the Amex building. The engine was running. She came to the driver's side first, mouthing, 'I'm sorry!' to him and trying to see through the misted windscreen. She thought she saw a waved hand. 'Sorry!' she said again and scurried round to the other side. The door was locked. She tapped the window. After seconds the door clicked. She got in.

'I was asleep . . .' Valerie said slowly.

'I was late.'

'I never noticed,' he lied. She kissed him.

As the car dropped towards the Steine, she told Valerie she fancied a long drive. 'Is that all right with you?' she said meekly.

'Just say the word, boss.'

'Would you think Haslemere was too far?'

'I don't even know where that is!' he said.

'Between Guildford and Petersfield,' she told him, then she added too quickly, 'it would be a nice drive, Val, what, about thirty-five miles or so. We could talk a little bit, play some Billie Holiday . . .'

'Oh yeah?' he said. 'And have a drink in Grigglesham Foster, I suppose.'

'Oh, is that near there?' Caz said. There was drizzle on the windscreen.

'You bloody well *know* it is!'

'I really would like a long drive, Val.' She touched his arm.

'No problem,' he said, 'I just wanted to hear you say it.'

They drifted out of town, then turned off the A27 heading for Steyning and Storrington on the A283. Valerie had decided not to question their trip. He told her he had just finished reading her book, *The Selfish Gene*.

'It was a nice read. So I'm not me, right? Just a pre-set bundle of genes?'

'It's just a way of looking at heredity, Val. If we say *we* do things for a purpose, isn't that fair for other life-forms too? Dogs? Cats? Mice?'

'Course it is,' Valerie said, 'and maybe flies 'n fleas too. Maybe even bacteria and viruses. But *genes*?'

'Why not?' she said.

''Cos genes can't think!' He was driving easily, cruising at a steady fifty and enjoying the feel of the car. He said the explanations of behaviour were much more interesting. She asked him what in particular. 'Like, oh I don't know. Like the explanation of courtship, say, or ritual feeding. Like the explanation of jealousy.' A sign said Pulborough, five miles.

'Oh yes,' Caz said, 'jealousy's one of the easier things to explain.'

'Try me,' Val said.

'OK. Say two people, say you and me for example. Say we got together and made a baby. What can I know and you can *never* know?'

'I'm driving,' he said. 'You tell me.'

'I'll try again. You make love to a woman; she has a baby, whose is it?'

'Mine, of course!'

'How do you know? She might've had sex with someone else. So you can never be certain. But *she* knows who the *mother* is. Us girlies know we'll be left with the baby but at least we know it's ours. We can't avoid that forty weeks of gaining weight and we get more and more vulnerable the more pregnant we get. So we need to get ourselves a man. The father's OK, but any man'll do.'

'What!'

'Oops, your prejudices are showing, Valerie!'

'Go on.'

'You turn here,' she said. 'Take the A272 and head for Midhurst.' She paused. 'OK, a female mammal *knows* she is the mother of the child. She knows she needs help to bring up the child. Part of courtship is to try and get the old fellah to hang around more than he might otherwise want.'

'Yeah, but you said *any* man would do.'

'Of course. She has the child she aimed for. It's got her genes. She's got her insurance against time. If she can get some chap to invest his energy in the baby she's no worse off, *her* baby is being nurtured. It's the man who's missing out if he's investing his time in another man's genes.'

'What's this got to do with jealousy?'

'Well, forget any cocktail-party bullshit about jealousy being destructive or, "Let her free: if she loves you, she'll come back." Think of this – all other things being equal, the possessive male denies *other* males sexual access to his long-term partner. So he doesn't end up cuckolded. The laid-back guy, the liberated one, is more likely to end up looking after some other bloke's child. A man might even be happy doing that if he loves the woman but it *can't* be in his genes. It's a disadvantage not to be jealous.'

'OK,' Val replied, 'so if we were talking absolutely, if I'm right, a man's best strategy is to lock the female up to try to guarantee that his sperm is the only sperm that could impregnate her.'

'Absolutely!' Caz said. 'Remember, Val, we're talking bottom-line here. Men *do* do just that. They rarely lock them away physically but even that's been known. They use behavioural tricks to psychologically lock up their chosen breeding machine. Quote the girl who skips the office Christmas party because "Nigel doesn't like me going." That's classic caveman tactics. That kind of man only feels guilty because society has told him that jealousy is a bad thing.'

'OK, so why do women get jealous? If they know the baby's mother.'

'By comparison with men they don't, but a woman needs to know she can get some investment from the father. Her main concern is to try to ensure the continued maintenance of her child. A little dally on his part is not strictly as dangerous as her playing around.'

'So there's no problem with me having a bit on the side?'

'We're talking clinically, Val. If a man goes out bonking it doesn't matter all that much – remember we are talking basics here. But if some romeo started bringing a few babies home, *then* you would see *real* female jealousy. Then there would be direct competition for resources.'

'I only half see . . .'

'All male infidelity costs the female is a degree of security. That doesn't mean it doesn't piss her off just a bit. The cool lady loses out too – at least *some* of the male's resources are being spent elsewhere, but she still has her genetic representation being carried on.'

'We must be near Grigglesham,' Val said.

'Yes,' Caz was really enjoying herself. 'Men are at a far greater risk, so, on average, it will *pay* them to be quite possessive, even very possessive. Jealousy for woman has a much poorer return than for a man. Ipso facto, blokes are more jealous because it's a good strategy!'

'So why were you late tonight? Huh? Huh? Where were you?'

'Oh very good, Val.' They were slowing down.

'OK, I believe you,' he said, 'but jealousy still stinks.'

'That's a cultural fact,' Caz said, 'not a biological one. And we're there.'

Nineteen

There was a sign saying 'Please Drive Carefully Through Our Village', but no Ministry of Transport thirty mph-limit. Nevertheless, Valerie had slowed the Daimler down to a sedate twenty-five miles an hour, and they shhllapped through the houses, both of them with their windows down.

'God, I love the country!' Caz said.

'Like other people's pets,' Val answered.

'What?'

'The country. Like other people's pets. Like grand-children. They're great fun because you can give them back. The rural existence isn't all it's cracked up to be: high unemployment, low wages, poor services... It's nice to pop out and look at though.'

'Misery!' Caz said.

'Realist, more like,' he told her.

They passed a red public telephone box and two more houses. Ahead of them was a low-slung, bulging public house with a deep thatched roof and diamond-leaded windows. Across its front a long green and gold sign declared it to be the Drunken Preacher. 'Perrfick!!' Valerie said, swinging the car into the car park.

The Jaguar slipped in between a black Volvo estate and a white van displaying an electrician's logo. It was a busy Friday night and theirs was the last space. Through an open window they heard the soft murmur of voices, the tinkle of glass on glass and a sporting shout from the games room. 'Ah, this'll do nicely,' Caz said.

Valerie looked hard at her and made a face.

Inside, the lounge throbbed with life, small groups in its many-cornered bays surrounding low black tables covered in beer-mats and glasses. The low beams above them were hung with ancient brass and behind the bar a legion of staff pumped ale. There was a looping smell of sweet pipe tobacco which floated by, and a great round man held court to their far right, at least ten people listening to the tail end of his joke. He had badly cut sandy hair and his red face puffed out round bright blue eyes. As he hit the punchline, he rolled forward, slapping one of the crowd on the shoulders. 'Gearrgge!' someone said, 'yer a bliddy liar!'

'Ah know ah am,' George replied.

Valerie leaned close to her, his warm breath in her ear. What did she want to drink? She said she fancied a dry white wine. As he turned to the bar he touched her arm and she felt pleasure ripple through her. Then he was gone, lost in a sea of backs.

She had visions of having to remain on her feet after the long day but she managed to grab a pair of seats as a couple got up to leave. They had identical lilac and white anoraks and the same grey Rohan Bags trousers. When Valerie escaped from the crush by the bar she waved to him. He was standing like a waiter with the drinks in each hand and a bar menu tucked underneath his arm. He looked lost and his face brightened as he saw her. For the briefest second she saw him as a little boy.

'Thought you might like something to eat,' Valerie said. He tapped the vinyl menu on the table. 'I know I do.'

She chose chicken and chips in the basket, side-stepping the pies and avoiding the jumbo sausages. She called sausages 'bags of mystery'. The food list had been incredibly badly typed on an ancient portable typewriter with a dried-out cotton ribbon. It had extra spaces, an 'e' that dropped and an 'r' that was slightly high. Valerie ordered scampi.

The roving waitress had a badge that said 'Annie' and she was quick and sharp, not an awkward nineteen but a good thirty-plus.

She looked filled out and comfortable, married and maybe even happy.

''Bout five minutes, Miss!' she said. She placed a number seventeen on their table. By the bar there was a louder roar as George finished another joke. 'I wonder who the resident comic is,' Val said, dipping his head to get nearer her.

'Ahhrr, that'd be Geearrge . . .' Caz explained, 'bit of a char-r-racter, Gea-rge.'

She sipped the wine, cold and cheap but passable. Valerie appeared to be drinking Coke. Plus Southern Comfort, he assured her. She tried it and decided it tasted like cough mixture. He told her it was the easiest drink in the world; too easy, in fact. 'A bit dangerous really. Goes down a treat and sneaks up on you to get you badly drunk.'

He rarely bothered to get drunk, he told her. Getting mellow was a fairly common event but bad-drunk was rare. 'Except when I'm unlucky in love,' he said seriously. 'Then I can *really* self-abuse. I usually sit in the dark listening to Elton John's love songs and drink about a dozen of these.'

'I wouldn't have seen you as a brooder,' she said.

'Well you don't know me yet, do you?' he said flippantly. 'If I ever commit suicide, it'll be while Elton's singing "Blue Eyes" and they'll find an empty bottle of Southern Comfort by the sofa.'

'I could never imagine being that low,' she said sadly.

'What? On the sofa?'

'Low enough to kill myself.'

'I'd've said that once.'

'But?' she said. He looked away at nothing.

'I'm sorry,' she said.

'Forget it,' he said quietly. 'It's probably not the best time.'

Annie returned, calling out, 'Seven*teen*?' Valerie waved. She took two meals off a tray which carried six. 'One scampi, one chicken, one receipt! Than-*KEW*!' As she turned, she called out, 'Eight-*een*', the tray balanced effortlessly on her four spread fingers.

'Looks OK,' Val said.

'The food or the waitress?'

'The *food*, Caz. My ladies are waif-like and bony, like twelve-year-old boys.'

'Oh, thank *you*,' she said.

'No, I mean it. I'm attracted to the lightweight sporty type. My . . .'

He stopped suddenly and went quiet. She looked down at her drink. Then it came out in a rush. 'Her name was Kathy,' he said. 'We went to the same secondary school but we hated each other. Then we hung around together at university rather than be on our own. We dated other people, talked about our separate love lives, then one day we realised that what we really wanted was each other.' His one hand was balled into a tight fist. 'Kathy played hockey and she was very good. She probably could've played for England but she didn't want to go away. We were so damn comfortable together that we never argued. We were going to get married when she was twenty-five. I was going to be a rich executive and she was going to have babies and write cookery books.' His hand relaxed.

'We were so wrapped up in each other we hardly noticed the rest of the world. I was into a few dangerous sports but I had no personal ambitions. I just wanted to be with her. If it had happened, I think we would have ended up being Mr and Mrs Boring with at least four kids.' He went quiet again. Caz laid a hand gently on his forearm but didn't squeeze.

'She had an accident. Right after our final exams. Four of the girls were out celebrating and they went off the road coming back from a club. Kathy wasn't wearing a seat-belt and she went through the windscreen.'

'Oh, Val, I'm . . .'

'Oh, she wasn't *killed*, that would have been easy. She was cut terribly and she lost one side of her scalp. She was so pretty, Caz. I saw her for a while in the weeks after the crash but then she started to reject me. At first the doctors told me she would come round, but she got more and more hostile. We fought. When she came out of the hospital she went to her parents' home in the Wirrall. I went there once but it was so awful that her father asked me not to come back until she had got over the accident. That was six years ago.'

'Where is she now?'

'In Berkshire. Somewhere near Greenham Common. She disappeared for a while, turned up there during the peace sit-ins and then got a job working with handicapped kids. She sent a postcard to my mother about two years ago. She said the kids never saw her scars.'

Caz felt a hot, heavy weight in her stomach. 'And you still love her?'

'No, I don't think I do. Not any more. It's worse than that. When I get very low, I feel this terrible sensation of unfinished business.'

They sat quietly for a while; their bodies touching, people-watching; exchanging occasional comments. It was as if, after bad family news, they were waiting for the correct moment to tilt at happiness again. Valerie changed the subject. He guessed that George was a farmer and if not, a gamekeeper. He wondered why there were so many young women in his harem and decided it must be his aftershave.

Kathy's presence began to fade and Caz felt her confidence returning. She had slipped the food receipt away; from memory, pretty certain that it did not tie up with either Burnley's or Green's. It was in her Goretex jacket along with Val's note.

'So tell me about micro-lighting, Valerie. Will I be scared or excited?'

'You'll love it. I promise you.'

'Oh, Val, you're my hero!'

He puffed out his chest and flexed muscles. 'I know.'

'How big is it? Your micro-light?'

'Well, strictly it isn't mine any more, remember?'

'But how big?'

'About twenty foot wing-span and roughly ten foot front to back. The seat is in a capsule about six foot long that hangs underneath the wing.'

'It doesn't sound very big.'

'That's because it isn't.'

'But big enough, yes?'

'Definitely not, my dear. What do you think?'

'I think I've got to make a phone call,' she suddenly said, 'I am sorry.'

He looked pained. She explained, 'On the back of your note – I've only just remembered – I was supposed to ring someone this evening.'

'Be my guest . . .' Val said.

She dialled Patcham. An answerphone cut in. She swore, but waited for Avocado's message to finish so she could say she'd called. After the tone, she began to apologise. A voice interrupted.

'Miss Flood. This is Grace Avocado. Jeremy is in his office. Can you wait just a moment?' Caz said she could. In the background she heard the shout 'Honey! Phone!' There was an even more distant shout then Grace said, 'It's that detective. The one from Brighton!' After another fifteen seconds she heard Jeremy Avocado's voice.

'Thank you for calling me back, Miss Flood. I do appreciate it.'

'Not at all, Mr Avocado. How can I help you?'

'I think it is *I* who can help *you*. There's something I'd forgotten that I think you should know.' There was a pause. Avocado sounded excited. 'George Burnley and Jim Green. They're not the only ones who've died!'

'What? Would you repeat that? And slowly, Mr Avocado.'

'Yes, yes. Last year – no, sorry, it was the first week of January *this* year – I got a phone call from a chap called John Davies in Worthing . . .' Caz waited. She could hear Avocado's hurried breathing. 'Well, this Davies, he wanted a cash job, same as the other two.'

'Go on,' she said.

'Well, Davies wanted to haggle on the phone. I don't do that sort of thing, so I made an appointment.'

'And?'

'The day before the appointment I heard he'd died!'

'How do you know?'

'It was an accident, apparently. He got drunk and fell off his balcony. There was an inquest. The coroner said it was accidental death.'

'I see,' Caz said.

Avocado spoke again, faint excitement in his voice. 'Mr Davies wanted to spend between one thousand and eleven hundred pounds, just like the other two – those chaps that were murdered. Obviously I knew nothing about them then, so there was no connection to make. I just thought it was a bit of bad luck and gradually it sort of slipped from my mind. I've literally only just remembered Davies. I thought you ought to know.'

'You did right, Mr Avocado. Thank you.'

'Will I have to make another statement?'

'Probably. I'll check it out tomorrow.'

'Do you think it was an accident? Mr Davies?'

'I expect so. Don't worry about it. Someone will ring you tomorrow.'

She rang off and went back to Valerie. Her head was buzzing. He was looking down, watching his fingers tip-tapping the side of his glass.

'Hi!' she said. 'I'm all yours.'

'If only,' he replied.

Avocado's news had unleashed Detective Flood. For a few minutes she had managed to hang on to being Caz, but the policeman in her would not be denied. She looked again at the meal receipt while talking about her time at university. So detached was she that her answers – pure fact – were far more candid than she would otherwise have intended.

'Dost thou attend me?' Valerie asked. It was obvious he was annoyed.

'Not really, Val,' she said, trying to be gentle, 'I'm sorry. It's just that telephone call. More bad news.'

'Someone else killed?'

'I don't know. Perhaps.'

'And I presume you'll be working tomorrow?'

'Yes, Val. But I will be free on Sunday. We can go flying then.'

'OK. Let's talk about then. Be ready when I said—'

'Six-thirty sharp!' she said brightly.

'Right. Make sure you're wearing plenty of layers, vest and whatever. And at least two pairs of socks. If you've got silk underwear, wear it under a Helly-Hansen thermal. I'll provide a flying suit and boots and if you've got lightweight gloves – silk's perfect – bring those too. It's nice upstairs but it'll be fresh!'

'Will it be windy?'

'Probably, but that's no problem. If there's a steady blow, even a fairly strong one, we can allow for that. It's erratic winds, squalls, thermals and downdraughts that are the problem. The summer is the worst and any time after about ten in the morning, once the land has had a chance to cook up. I think I told you, that's why we go off at dawn and dusk when the air currents are a little bit more predictable.'

'So how big is the cabin? Is there a joy-stick and everything?'

'There isn't a cabin, Angel! There's just a single seat and that's slung underneath the wings. There's a bit of fibreglass called the pod and the seat sits in that. The wheels stick out of the pod bottom.'

'You keep saying seat singular. Where do I go – strapped to the wing?'

'Not exactly,' Val said. 'Let me show you.' He grabbed beer-mats to make a model. 'Look, here's the front. Here's the seat. You climb in first, open your legs and I sit there. There! It's very intimate: a bit like riding pillion on a motor-bike, but even closer.'

'Sounds cosy!'

'It is. It also keeps you a lot warmer.'

She thought a moment and then touched one of the mats. 'So the engine is here, right?'

'Wrong!' He made a pantomime shout. 'It's be-*hind* you!'

'Er, just how *far* behind me?'

'Oh, at least six inches!'

'So let me get this right,' she said, only half joking, 'I'm supposed to wear silk underwear, wrap myself around a man I only met a week ago, hang in a bucket from a couple of ten-foot wings with a propeller inches from my head and then *enjoy* myself?'

'You're very perceptive, detective . . .'

'Oh yes,' Caz said seriously, 'very.' She paused, thinking, then added tentatively, 'Val, I need to check a few things. I know you won't like it, but at least we're spending time together.'

'What things?' he said.

'Well, I need to know if this is the only pub in the village for a start, and I need to know where the garage is. While I'm at it I'd just like to check if there's anything here that might have caused George Burnley to visit.'

'So DC Flood is back, right?'

'Don't be cruel, Val. It's my job.' He looked grey but he said he was sorry.

The waitress Annie told them that Foster's Garage was the last building on the left going out of the village heading for Guildford. She also told them about the village's second pub. 'You must've come up the road from Midhurst, otherwise you'd've seen it. The Poacher's only a hundred yards from 'ere; jest round the next bend in the road. I used to work there. The wages are about the same as the Preacher, but you get much bigger tips in 'ere, 'specially on Friday nights. That's George Foster, over there, telling dirty jokes. The big chap.' Caz asked – was there much work in the village?

'It depends what y'mean,' Annie said. 'There's a few jobs on the estate farms but the pay's not much. I've got a sister works up at the clinic as a secretary but most of the villagers have to travel elsewhere for work.'

'I'm surprised there's a health clinic in such a small place.'

'Oh no, it's not that sort 'f clinic. I meant the private maternity place up at the hall, Grigglesham Hall.' She glanced behind her, worried that she was too long at one table, 'Look, ah'll 'ave t'go. Nice meeting you.'

'Thanks very much, Annie,' Caz said. She made a show of putting two pound coins out for the tip.

'Any time!' Annie said.

'Fancy a walk, Val?' Caz asked.

'Let me guess – you'd just love to see the Poacher . . .'

'It's just five minutes. You heard Annie, it's a hundred yards away.'

He looked into her face for a second with a look she couldn't read, then he shrugged his shoulders and quickly finished his drink.

From outside, the Poacher was probably the least attractive building in the village; the one that *didn't* get on to the picture postcards. Various tenants had tried: there were flower tubs outside, facing the road, and the cream front had been re-done that summer, but nothing was ever going to make a large stone shack into something lovely. As they went in she thought of silk purses and sow's ears. This was definitely a pig's ear of a place.

But inside it was a real pub. Whereas the Drunken Preacher would have delighted a tourist, the Poacher pleased the purist. While the Drunken Preacher catered for Peugeot 205 drivers and the nouveau rur-al, this place was where the beer came in jugs and was held in hardened hands. The walls were rough-plastered yellow, browned by hundreds of years of cigarette and pipe smoke. The floor was scrubbed pine, grey with age.

Behind the bar hung a row of pewter beer mugs, not for show but marked with the owners' names: John, Peter, Sam, Ted. There were few bottles of spirits: gin, whisky, rum, but nothing fancy; no Malibu, no Pernod, no crème de menthe. For food they did peanuts, crisps or the dish of the day. As the barman said, if they fancied it, they could 'ave Shep-urds Poi.

Valerie asked for a half of Grigglesham Real.

'And what'll the Miss be 'aving, Sir?'

'The same,' Caz said sharply. Miss indeed!

'Can I interest you in a bit of poi?' the barman said. He was holding a pad and pencil. 'There's still some of it left. The Mrs cooked it just this mornin'.'

'*Yes*!' Caz said quickly, her eyes fixed on his hands, 'just for one.'

'That'll be, Miss?' The pencil hovered. 'Miss?'

'Er – Thomas. Miss Thomas,' she said.

When they asked about the hall, the barman steered them towards an wispy-haired old codger supping Grigglesham Real at the end of the bar. 'You want t' speak t' old Tom 'ere. 'E'll put you right. Works in the grounds up there. Bin there for yurrs.'

Caz went over. Tom was still in overalls, dusty dark blue. 'Mainly I keeps the grass down,' he told her proudly, 'it's nearly all grass. I puts a few traps out 'cos the professor, him that runs the place – he doan like t'ave too many wild things clutterin' up 'is lawns.

'I got one of these big mowers,' he told her. 'Big as a tractor near on. I spends much of me day on that. The professor says keep the grass down between the road and the lake so it's nice t'look at.

'What, the 'all? It's a maternity place, innit? Rich foreign ladies pays a fortune to 'ave their babies there in style. They got more money th'n sense, I reckon. Anyway seems a bloody long way t' come just t' pop a sprog.'

'How d'you know they're foreign?' Caz said.

'Yer jokin'. They're dusky types, South American, I'd say, and Ayrabs. They wears dark glasses, 'n expensive clothes, 'n drive round them great long cars. You don't often see those kind of women round these parts.' He supped his ale. 'Drivers are always great big blokes with bulging suits.'

Valerie returned with another dark pint for Tom. The older man seemed pleased and turned to him. 'Oh, ta, mate! I was jest tellin' young Missus 'ere. We gets all sorts up at the manor. We gets royalty even. Princesses!'

'What about men, Tom?' Caz said.

'What y'mean? Like Princes?'

'Any kind of men.'

'Not 'ardly. There's me of course, an' there's the boss, George. Then there's the professor. There used t'be a young blond fellah working in one of the laberr-oratories but 'e's gone now.' He supped his pint.

'Anyone else?'

'Not regular. 'Ceptin' if you include the bodyguards, but they're jest lookin' after their bosses, ain't they?'

'And young men? Like my friend. Say in their late twenties, early thirties? Have you ever seen young men at Grigglesham Hall?'

'Only on Sundays,' the old man said, 'but not for quite a while now.'

Twenty

When they walked back towards Valerie's car she took his arm and leaned towards him. Valerie responded by crooking his and pulling her closer but she felt tension in his body as he acted out his part. She knew she couldn't blame him and she promised herself that come Sunday she would be a woman for him, not a copper.

Her day had started before five o'clock, and it was now nearly eleven, this on the back of the hardest week of her life. She knew that underneath she must be very tired, but she was still charged, buzzing with knowledge and the chase. There was something in this village, and she knew now that George Burnley had been there, more than casually, more than once. As if she had won a school-prize and wanted to hug her best friend, she now wanted Valerie, not for him alone but as a reward for her achievement. It made her feel vaguely guilty.

'On Sunday,' she was saying, 'I really will be all yours. Be patient with me, Val. I know I'm too keen at the moment, and I know I should relax, but it's very difficult. I'm shiny brand-new in plain-clothes and everyone is waiting for me to fall over. I can't do that. This is what I want to do.'

She squeezed tighter and pulled him closer, making walking awkward. He said nothing. 'Val, d'you understand? Just forgive me my first week?'

'I'll think about it,' he said, and when she looked up at him she almost believed he was joking. He grabbed her hand in the dark and kissed it. The kiss could have meant almost anything but they were together.

The white electrician's van was gone but the black Volvo remained, someone inside the Preacher making a full night of it. Valerie leaned past her to unlock her door. He let her slip into her seat and fasten her belt. Only then did he crouch, take both of her hands in his left and her chin in his right. As he looked into her eyes, it was as if he was searching for a clue. When he kissed her, it felt profound; not a prelude to sex. She felt odd and didn't know why. She tried to kiss him back but she was awkward, making contact high on his cheek near his eye. He grinned fractionally, pecked her and stood up. She felt painful loneliness from the second her door closed until he arrived at the other side, bright again.

'Right!' he said sharply, pointing at his tapes. 'What's yer fancy?'

'I get a choice?' she answered.

'Tonight, yes,' he said.

She dug out a relic, an old Animals cassette, and waited, listening to the hiss as they pulled away from the car park. They left quickly with Eric Burdon belting out 'Memphis Tennessee'.

They swished along small roads, high hedges snaking past the window as Valerie drove. She had her right hand laid loosely on his thigh, just to maintain contact. Then he began to sing: 'Club-a-Gogo', 'Road Runner', 'Don't Let Me Be Misunderstood'. She wanted to complain but couldn't; Valerie actually had a voice. Between tracks she laughed. 'You old rocker, you!'

They cut down through forests and on to the edge of the South Downs, on back roads so tiny that animal eyes flashed in the headlights, the Jaguar another animal gliding past them. They ended up in Arundel and found themselves on a wide open road heading east with other cars, faintly disappointed because the world was once again intruding.

Valerie turned off the A27 trunk road and headed towards Shoreham. Then he swung left for Hove. They drifted along the front, the sea silver to their right, passing black dockyards and cold grey beach huts until the buildings to their left were tall-storeyed like those of Inkerman Terrace.

'I'd like to stop over,' he said softly, 'but I'm desperately tired.'

'Stop. Please,' she said.

'Whatever,' he said.

They passed Onderman Road. It was just days since Caz had found Jim Green's body there. It was so distant and unreal that it didn't upset her. When they turned into Inkerman Terrace she sighed deeply, trying to be quiet. She now wanted Valerie so absolutely that she was terrified. When he had said 'whatever' she presumed he meant 'OK'. Suddenly she was frightened that he might say goodnight at her door. The Daimler pulled into her street slowly, the tyres phllapping as they tried to creep in unheard. She was nervous, and had pulled her hand away from him as they turned off the front. Now she was aware of her fingers, first a claw, then relaxed, then a fist. She tried to breathe deeply without making a noise but couldn't. She spoke in order to get air. 'I won't say coffee, but will you come in?'

'No Dire Straits?' he said.

'My collection is yours,' she told him.

'You mean now *I* get a choice?'

'Tonight, yes you do.' She knew she would dance naked on hot coals for him if he stayed. She would even let him play Abba's *Greatest Hits*.

'Let's get in,' he said, 'it's cold out here.'

As they stepped from the car she felt the sea's cool breath scarf itself quickly around her. The clouds had raced away and a three-parts moon lit the sea. She could smell ozone and seagull salt. Her shoulders tingled as she ran up the steps.

She struggled with the key for a second, glancing back at him because she was faintly embarrassed. When she turned, he was looking out towards the sea, his hands in his trouser pockets. She was thinking about 3-in-1 oil as the Chubb lock finally crunched clockwise; then she was through the door and into the warmth of her home.

The rich red of the hall carpet seemed luxurious, deep and warm, the house sensuous and inviting. After the chill of the evening, the heat from the central heating wrapped them up. It was one of those rare moments when she could feel the house actively welcoming her, like a child coming home after Christmas shopping to a bright front room and the smell of her mother's mince pies.

She pulled off her Asics and let the carpet stroke her feet as she climbed the stairs. Valerie had draped his suit jacket on the bulbed end of the banister and followed her. She was conscious of his eyes on her back.

Caz was far enough ahead to make it to the neutral territory of the kitchen. Automatically, she flicked on the full kettle even as she grabbed a re-corked bottle of Chianti. She tilted it towards him as he stood in the doorway, wordlessly suggesting 'Drink?' He held out a thumb and forefinger to indicate 'just a little one'. There was a half-roll of garlic bread on the kitchen surface. She used her eyebrows to offer him that. This time he touched his lips as a yes. Still no words.

She opened the microwave. The bread would need a minute. She pressed a button with her left hand, passing him his glass off-hand with her right. She felt him touch her as he took it. Still looking at the oven she picked up her own glass and sipped obviously at it, nodding her head.

With a ding! the microwave finished. She managed to open the door, pass the plate and drink more of her wine without once looking at him. Then she turned, shushed him into the lounge, leaned back to reach for the Chianti and followed.

They left the kitchen light on and the lounge's off. She sat in front of the TV, pressed the grey buttons on the NAD amplifier and the CD, pushed 'Open' and raised a hand behind her, waiting for a disc from Valerie.

When none came, she turned to look at him. He had his hand on the shelf of CDs but was just looking at her, in some way lost. She went to him and moved his hand to choose the music blind. His eyes never left her face and she had to guide his fingers over the CD cases. Finally, they selected a disc.

'Make love to me,' she said, then she turned and loaded the player.

'Make love to me, Valerie,' she said again. 'I need you inside me.'

He still hadn't spoken. As he moved into her she reached out to take the CD off 'pause'. She felt him just as Elton John began 'Blue Eyes'. They were finished long before the song and neither of them cared. They slept for an hour then rose and went to bed.

She woke at six wrapped around his back. He had isolated dark hairs on his shoulders and she had an almost uncontrollable urge to tweeze them out. To stop herself, she slipped from him and went to the loo.

She pushed the door slowly shut but in the early quiet the tiniest of creaks sounded as if they could wake the dead. When she clicked the lock she thought it echoed round the tiled room. She ran a shallow bath; slowly to make less noise, then squirted Matey into the water, making it ludicrously pink beneath the bubbles. When she bathed, she rolled water across her shoulders and down over her flat belly. As she lifted her pelvis to wash, she felt delicious and satisfied.

Valerie was still asleep when she clunked her way out and foot-stepped past him in a robe. She brewed some instant coffee, then sat in the lounge with her piggies, Elton John on subliminally low. She waited half an hour then, while 'Song for Guy' was playing, she went through to Valerie and kissed him awake. With his bright eyes and neat brown hair he was one of those sickening people who woke looking great. She pushed at his shoulder until he was flat on his back, then, with the robe opened, she moved astride him, grinning deliriously at him as she told him she wouldn't be running this morning.

'Anyway,' she laughed as she slipped on to him, 'I read somewhere that this is worth a five-mile jog.' He moved up to kiss her but she forced his shoulders back down.

'*You!*' she said absolutely. 'Don't *move!*'

Twenty-one

Valerie dropped Caz at John Street and she skipped brightly from his car to the front doors. Early for this extra shift would be nine o'clock. She walked in at eight.

The front desk was unmanned. She went straight past it, her footsteps echoing in a nick quieter than normal, walking immediately upstairs to Blackside's war room. It was still in darkness. She switched on the lights and went through to the computers.

'Holmes' was down, switched off for the night. She punched a wall switch and listened for the hard disk's chunter followed by the irregular beeps of the machine coming on line. As her terminal lit up she sat down and decided, for the exercise, to log on as Billy Tingle. The computer asked for his entry code. 'OK, Billy T,' she thought. 'What's your little secret?'

Some people were stupid enough to use their surname as a password; another very common choice was the word 'password' followed closely by 'Fred'. 'Sesame' and 'Secret' were other old favourites but Caz decided that Billy Tingle would be ruled by his groin. She decided to try 'Moira' first, instead of 'Dibben' and was given access immediately.

'Billy,' she said, 'you are bloody transparent.'

She logged off the computer and then came back on as DC Flood. The password she entered – zuccini – was a little tougher than Billy's. After a few seconds, Holmes blipped its hello. She asked about Grigglesham and got nothing. The surname Foster also returned nil. In 'last movements' there was no reference as yet to

George Burnley's meals or to any trips beyond Midhurst but the computer knew all about his membership of fitness clubs and how much he was paid by American Express.

On 'assailant' she had a three-way match. Two of the deaths had closely similar MOs, the third had common elements. The computer reminded her too that the assailant was male, probably twenty-five to forty-five, gay, and a type-A secretor with a strong DNA fingerprint. It did not know how not to be boring, so concluded by listing the separate instances of semen taken from bedding and repeated the fact that the same sperm was discovered at each crime-scene. After Caz's typing of the previous day, crossed with the input from Mrs Ralph, Holmes was estimating the assailant's colour of hair as blond with a forty-five per cent certainty rating. It was ninety per cent certain that he/she had worn a light-coloured coat. It concerned Caz that Holmes was treating a sighting as a likely perpetrator. Someone must have entered 'suspect' instead of possible witness. It was just as likely that the person in the fawn coat would turn out to be someone trawling for sex, a prostitute on a mission, or maybe (and far more likely) an innocent passer-by.

She was producing print-out at a phenomenal rate, yard upon yard of A3 sheets, most of it close to useless. The note in her pocket measured in inches, yet she instinctively knew that it was worth more than all these trees.

By nine o'clock, doors were opening, phones began to ring. She looked up as Greaves backed in carrying coffees spilling on to a tray. He spun and gave her a brief acknowledgement, pointing at the coffees. 'Want one?'

'Morning, Jim,' she said, coming through. 'Wet the bed, did we?'

'Oh, very funny, Flood!' She took a coffee. 'You're a bit keen, aren't you?' he asked. She told him she had come in because she was bored.

'I'm glad you're here, Jim. I need Burnley and Green's receipts.'

'Woffor?' he said. She told him she just needed to check something.

Jim unlocked a desk in his drawer and pulled out the rubber-banded paperwork in two separate polythene bags, each with the victim's ID. 'This what you want?'

'Yup!' Caz said. She asked him to witness as she checked through the paper piles. 'OK,' she said in a monotone, 'three grey-edged receipts, each approximately two inches by three, George Burnley.' Greavesie was nodding. He couldn't believe she was following the book. 'One receipt, grey-edged, two plain receipts, blue writing, two-by-three inches square.'

'Burnley?'

'Jim Green.'

'OK, got that. You gonna have them long?'

'Half an hour max, I reckon.'

'All right. I won't log it but it's in 'ere.' He pointed a finger at his head.

'Thanks, Jim.'

'No probs, Flood. Doan know why you bother though. If the DCS has marked you down, nuthin' is gonna happen for you on this one. Best just to keep out of the way and get blisters on yer fingers in there.'

'The data-entry room?' Caz said. 'Oh, I'm on top of *that*, Jim. I can do that standing on my head! This receipt stuff as well. I'm young enough *and* quick enough.'

The receipts felt hot in her hand and she went quickly out of the room. She wanted to play.

Caz went back into the computer room and sat down with Holmes. Then she brought out her receipts, spreading them on a table next to those from the evidence bags. The shepherd's pie she had bought last night had cost two pounds ninety-five, exactly the same price as the fish pie George Burnley had eaten in the Poacher. The receipts were from the same book.

She had thought one of the Green bills was a close match on a

Burnley, similar e's, f's and n's, same slope to the l's. Now she could see they didn't match – because Annie's neat hand had so obviously written on James Green's receipt: it was a perfect fit with her bill from last night. She punched the air.

So Green, at least, had been served by the waitress Annie, presumably in Grigglesham Foster. Burnley had eaten there once for certain, probably three times. There was a five-way match on the grey-edged pad, Burnley and Green had almost certainly eaten in the Poacher where last night she and Valerie had received one redundant plate of shepherd's pie. Bang!

The handwriting on Burnley's three Poacher receipts did not match. She could go back there and tie up the writing with the staff and maybe get lucky, but casual bar staff come and go; she might or might not get a hit. They had Green connected to Annie and the Poacher (unless she had worked elsewhere and used an identical pad), but she had a link from Green to Burnley if she could positively place Burnley in the Poacher. The pad was common to both men but there was no match on the handwriting or the menu items. She had to find out how rare or everyday the pad was. It was cheap, likely to be fairly widely distributed.

Caz laid the receipts out again, moving them round, looking for a pattern. She put Burnley's Fish Pie, Green's Lasagne and last night's Shepherd's Pie in a triangle. The same pad. Different writing. Probables.

Their scampi and chicken had been receipted on a different pad from Green's Lasagne receipt, but the writing was undeniably that of Annie. She picked up the second Burnley receipt and compared it again to this 'definite'. It really *was* similar but definitely not the same writer. Annie might have had a really bad night – maybe she was standing up when she wrote the receipt. No, she thought not. Similar writing, but not the same. She would need the experts to prove it, but she knew she was right. One triangle was strongly linked, the other one came with a dotted line. She needed more but she didn't know what.

Holmes beckoned so she pumped the space bar and brought the screen back to life. Under 'movements' she placed Burnley in Grigglesham and more specifically in the Poacher. She put Jim Green down as a contact of Annie Surname-unknown, and put him as probably in the village. When Holmes asked for the certainty level, she typed 99.99%.

There was a little more activity outside in the war room and she got up to go through for a little help. Greavsie was sitting close to the picture walls, typing up another door-to-door. She told him she needed to get into his drawers again. Then she said, 'I'll re-phrase that.

'Jim, do us a great big favour, would you?' she asked. 'Look after those receipts in there for two minutes?'

'You wanna type this for me?' Greaves said.

'Just two minutes, Jim?' she asked again.

She went to Greavsie's desk, found Green's bus ticket and checked it. It simply said 'Guildford Buses' and had the price. Where a date might have been was frayed and faded. She picked up the phone. Directories gave her a number. She dialled and listened to a distant ring. She waved to Greavsie. He was waving back, impatient. The ringing continued. She flicked the phone on to loudspeaker and replaced the receiver. The dark bring-bring attacked the room and someone shouted, 'Fer Christ's sake, Flood!' She gave him the finger, but of course she meant 'one minute'.

Greavsie looked a little pissed so she went through. 'You all right, Jim?'

'Yeah,' he said, 'I was playin' with yer jigsaw.'

'I'm trying to place Green and Burnley together in Grigglesham.'

'Which receipts are which?'

'That's Burnley. Burnley, Burnley, Green, Green, Green, me, me again.'

'Well, these two're the same writing.'

'Yes, Jim, I know.'

'Same as that one there.'

'What!'

'Look . . .' Greaves said, 'yer blind bat! The one 'ere with the grey edge – Lancashire Hot Pot – your one, chicken and whatever, and this one.' (It was Green's Lasagne.) 'They're all from the same person.'

'Oh, Jeez, Jim! Then that means Green and Burnley both ate in the Poacher and Annie has served both of them. I don't know how I missed it. Oh, thank you, Jim!'

'Who the bleedin' 'ell is Annie?'

'A waitress.'

'Oh,' he said. 'You gonna do my typing now?'

'No,' she said, 'I'm going to see the DI.'

'Well, turn that effin' phone off on yer way out.'

She was almost breathless, far too excited, and she didn't hear his last remark. She was just going through the war room's double-doors when someone shouted, 'Flood! The bloody phone!' She stopped and made a big show of changing direction, turning and making a parody of someone walking on tip-toe. Her finger was an inch from the button when the ringing stopped and a tinny voice answered, 'Guildford Blue Buses!'

She was surprised, 'Good morning,' she said, 'is that Guildford Blue Buses?'

'I jest said it was.'

'Oh . . . I'm ringing from Brighton, from John Street. I was wondering how far I could get from Guildford for two pounds thirty.'

'Are you bein' funny?'

'No.'

'Well then, it depends which route.'

'OK. Could you tell me if there's a bus from Guildford that goes through Grigglesham Foster? Probably the Midhurst bus?'

'Yeah, there is. Anyway, who are yer? What d'you wanna know for?'

Caz finally got it together. 'I am Detective Constable Flood. I'm ringing you from John Street police station, Brighton. I'd be grateful if you could tell me what it costs to travel from Guildford to Grigglesham.'

'One minnit, Officer.' It took three minutes. Then the voice came back. 'Two pounds forty.'

'How much?' she said.

'Two pounds . . .' the voice said deliberately, 'and forty pence.'

'Are you sure?'

'Of course I'm sure!'

Damn, she thought. She said thank you.

'There's not been some sort 'f complaint 'as there?' the birdy voice asked. 'A four per cent rise is less than inflation.'

'Four per cent? You've had a price increase? When was that?'

'October first. Trip would've cost you two-thirty before October!'

Her stomach leapt. Yee-hah!!! When she left the room she had to force herself to walk not run.

Twenty-two

The DI's office was down a flight of wide stairs flanked by cream walls. His door was ajar but he was not at his desk. Caz heard him opening a filing cabinet to the right. She knocked and stepped in.

'Sir . . .' She stopped suddenly, looking up at Norman Blackside's face. The DCS continued flicking through files. 'Flood, isn't it?'

'Sir!' she said loudly.

'Help you, can I?'

'I was looking for DI MacInnes, Sir.'

'I think he's in the Gents. Take a seat, he'll be back in a minute . . .' He pushed the drawer closed. 'The lass who collared Trevor Jones, yes?'

'I was closest when he gave himself up, yes, Sir.'

'I'd say it was a little bit more than that, wouldn't you, Constable? Don't sell yourself short, lass. There's plenty enough'll do that for you.'

'Sir.'

'You found George Burnley?'

'Monday last, yes, Sir.'

'And Green? Have you had counselling yet?'

'No, Sir. I haven't had the chance. After Burnley, there was Jim Green and now Beecham . . . my feet haven't touched the ground.'

'Get yourself counselled, Flood. Monday at the latest.'

'But I feel fine, Sir. Just a bit whacked.'

'It wasn't a suggestion Flood. I want you away from the sharp end for a while. It won't hurt you. Get yourself counselled, that's an order.'

'Sir!'

She heard the clipped step of the DI and one sharp rasp of his smoker's cough as he approached the office door. A hot flush of panic waved down through her and her hair-roots tingled. She hadn't been expecting to find the Chief Super there. What would she do when DI MacInnes came in? In the two or three seconds she had left, she flailed about for something casual to say, something to give her breathing space.

'You're going to be in Serious Crimes, aren't you, Sir?' she said to Blackside. 'When you go to the Yard?' MacInnes was in the doorway.

'Special Branch,' the DCS told her, glancing at his DI but ignoring him. 'Who said I was going to Serious Crimes?' She'd got her seconds.

'Er, no one, Sir. I think I just got mixed up. It's been a heck of a week.'

'You're stressed, Flood. You're tired. You get that counselling.'

'Yes, Sir,' she said. She stood up to acknowledge the DI. 'Good morning, Sir. I just heard from Guildford. If you remember we had a bus ticket in Green's belongings? The fare would have taken him to Grigglesham Foster. Oh, and I've spoken to Patrick Tomlinson, the encyclopaedia salesman. Peter Beecham had exactly a thousand pounds to spend.'

'Have you written it up yet?' MacInnes asked.

'No, Sir. I thought I'd let you know as soon as I could . . .'

'Well piss off and do it, Flood! I'll read your report.'

'Yes, Sir!' She looked chastised, about to turn away. 'Oh, Sir,' she said, 'Holmes has Mrs Ralph's sighting down as a suspect. Should we change that to pertinent witness? I think someone's had finger trouble, but I thought I'd clear the change before I made it.'

MacInnes was now with her. 'Do that, Flood, but log the override and give me a hard copy of what you've done by lunch-time. Be back here for twelve with the paperwork.'

She nodded politely to the DCS as MacInnes told her to get on her bike. Blackside was still by the open filing cabinet. As she strode away she saw him turn to MacInnes and speak.

The additional information from Avocado needed following up, and Caz made a mental note to contact the Coroner's Office and get a copy of John Davies's post mortem. She rang without thinking and got no answer. It was closed. They were civil servants, ESSO workers, every Saturday and Sunday off.

When DC Greaves came through with three more fat reports she was tapping her biro on the monitor screen. She grimaced at the work but he laughed and told her to get typing. She made another sad face, but inside she was smiling, flushed with the morning's double success. 'That thing with the receipts, Jim,' she said brightly. 'I owe you a pint.' Greaves left, still laughing; he was finishing early and was going to get to the game after all. She began to type.

By eleven-thirty she was looking for things to do. Greaves's reports were into Holmes and the latest door-to-doors were logged. She had written up her own work but had left out the news from Avocado and the possible leads from Patrick Tomlinson. She had decided that the Tomlinson stuff was too vague to log and she thought she would speak to the DI and see what he wanted to do about the Davies death.

She decided she would ring Valerie, so she asked Holmes for a series of standard reports. She selected 'print' and then picked up the telephone. It rang eight times before he answered. 'Hi,' she said quietly, 'it's me.'

'Is Detective Flood having a personal on the firm's time?'

'Sod off, Valerie,' she said sharply. There was no answer.

'Valerie?'

'Yes?'

'I – er . . .'

'Yes,' Valerie cut in. 'I'd love to be with you tonight,' he spoke in a rush. 'Yes, it *was* wonderful. Yes, of course I've never felt like this before. Yes, I *do* wish we were still in bed and we were still making love. No, I haven't any plans to do anything tonight and you're absolutely right, I think a romantic meal with you is a wonderful idea.' He pretended to gasp for air.

'Pardon?' she said.

'I said that was cruel this morning. I'm surprised you didn't want to handcuff me. It was . . .' she could hear the buzz of his word-filter working, 'OK.'

'Why thank-you Valerie. That's probably . . .'

'The nicest thing anyone's ever said to you?'

'Yes.'

'So six o'clock, then? Five?'

'Seven,' she said.

'Why so late?'

'I need to go for a long run.'

'I'll be sitting in my car outside your place at five to seven.'

'Fine. I'll be out five minutes later.'

'Bye, luv.' The phone went dead.

Holmes had just finished and MacInnes was in the doorway, leaning with his arms folded. It was ten to twelve. 'If Mohammed does not go to the mountain . . .'

'I'm sorry, Sir, I . . .'

'It's OK, Flood, I'm early. Let's do this over a pint.'

She grabbed her Goretex and went out of the room in front of him. They took the yellow back stairs and broke out into the car park.

The nearest pub was the Grapes and was popular with the force. They walked there but went into the lounge rather than share the bar with off-duty detectives. She sat down as MacInnes ordered two whiskies, both doubles, with a little water for him and a splash of ginger for her.

'Right,' he said as he came back. 'Who did it?'

She took beer-mats as food-bills and showed him that Burnley and Green had both eaten in the Poacher and had both probably been served by the waitress, Annie. There would have to be a follow-up to try to find out when, but Burnley could be tied to Grigglesham on three dates in July and August.

'That's about the same time as he began to behave oddly at work. I've spoken to his manager, Reginald Smith. He told us that, other than that, Burnley was exceptional and had never been any kind of problem.'

'And Green?'

'Well, all we know for definite is that he had a thousand pounds in cash to spend, the same as George Burnley and Peter Beecham.'

'That's interesting, but it does nothing at all for us, does it? We already know that the three men are connected. The same man killed them!'

'Yes, but we don't know why, Sir.'

'Unless they're all gay and this is some sort of nutter. A guilt murderer maybe?'

'You know what I think about Burnley, Sir. And, as yet, we've no evidence to show that Peter Beecham was a homosexual.'

'Well, he'd certainly had anal sex – we got a positive on the semen sample. It was B for boyfriend again.'

'Couldn't it have been rape, Sir?'

'Couldn't he just be gay?'

'Yes, Sir. He could be, but we have nothing direct, nothing else in his life to suggest that he was.'

'He lived alone.'

'So do I.'

'No known girl-friends.'

'He had no known boy-friends either, Sir!'

MacInnes took a taste of whisky, 'God, you're a little terrier, aren't you?'

'I'm just trying to keep an open mind, Sir. Is that so bad?'

'No, it's good. Just like you're keeping an open mind on Burnley.'

'That's different, Sir. That's a judgement call.'

'Instinct, you mean.'

'Maybe, Sir, but based on my personal experience, not insupportable.'

'OK, so you went to Peter Beecham's two-up two-down. Was that the home of a heterosexual?'

'I've no idea, Sir. It was miserable. The place had no soul. I got nothing at all there. I didn't pick up anything. I couldn't possibly say for sure.'

He was sipping again. 'OK, let's agree to differ on that one for now. What else is there?'

She told him about John Davies. 'And the Britannica salesman, Sir, Patrick Tomlinson? He has three names and addresses, all local, who had cash-money to spend in the last year. We're going to see them next week.'

'We?'

'Me and Tomlinson.'

'Flood!'

'You told me to keep my head below the firing line, Sir. If I log such a strange possibility and it proves to be a dead-end, I'm going to look pretty stupid. I'm going along as a trainee rep to suss them out. The addresses are almost certainly not leads. If they are, then we can send in someone officially. No one needs to know I was ever there.'

'You're walking a very thin line, Flood.'

'What would you have done in my place, Sir?'

'Same as you probably.'

'So, it's all right, then?'

'I never said that.'

'No you didn't, Sir. Then you don't know about this . . .'

'That goes without saying.'

'I have to do this, Sir. I can *feel* something, Sir. Everything is somehow tied up with these cash amounts and it all has something to do with Grigglesham Foster. I haven't got the faintest idea what, but I just *know*.'

'Careful, Flood. You're beginning to sound like me.'

'This bastard's *evil*, Sir. Sick. I really need to know we can get him.'

'And I don't?'

'No, Sir, of course you do. But it *does* feel personal. The idea that someone could have done that to Burnley so close to where I live. It . . . it . . . I don't know, but I just want this bastard so bad.'

'You can't get that involved, Caz. You have to stand back a bit.'

'Yes, Sir.'

'And you *will* need to go see the counsellor.'

'I don't really, Sir. I'm fine.'

'You might be, but you need to go because DCS Blackside has told you to.'

'But not next week. I don't want to be off this case.'

'Then lie a bit. Bullshit baffles brains, remember.'

'OK, Sir. I'll make an appointment.'

'You do that soonest, girl.' He stood up. They were having seconds.

'Yes, Sir.'

He stopped her as she went for her purse. 'Yer doin' all right, Flood, but ah'll get these.'

She finished at four; there was nothing left to do. Downstairs in her locker she had running kit and she went there to change. When she emerged she was in ankle-length Lycra leggings and a white Helly top. Her purse and keys were in a light-blue bumbag belted round her waist.

She ran easily down towards the sea, jogging on the balls of her feet at road-crossings, waiting for a gap in the traffic. It was natural for her to run past Valerie's flat and she was tempted to do otherwise, but she cruised down his street without a glance at his door.

The day was crisp and sharp, the first bit of sunshine for a week. She had less than an hour of light so decided to use it to the full. When she reached the road which rolled along the cliff-top parallel to the sea she turned towards Peacehaven and Roedean School. She had been running easily for ten minutes and was warmed up and loose. At a bench, she stopped briefly to stretch, then walked fifty metres to a small yellow X marked on the pavement. She took four deep breaths.

Her personal best for eight hundred metres was fractionally outside two minutes. When she pushed this one, her first four hundred (to a sprayed yellow Y) took sixty-six seconds, the next two hundred metres took thirty-six, and then lactic acid in her muscles began to burn. 'Elbows. Hands. Knees, Flood!!' she hissed in her head. 'Only one in front of you. Take the pain!! Elbows. Knees. Hands! Do it!' She could feel herself tightening up – her stride slightly shorter, the push of her trailing foot slightly less powerful. With fifty metres to go she was all-out and gone, running on nothing but guts. Without the adrenaline of competition she couldn't take the extreme of pain. Thirty-nine seconds! Two twenty-one for the half. Just OK. She spat on the floor.

She trotted through a mile in eight minutes, waiting for the hot spot below her throat to return to normal. By a bus shelter, she found another one of her marks, a small figure eight.

She went straight into this half-mile at seven-minute pace, speeding up at each tiny mark. Seven, stretch out. Six, think about knee lift, a little faster. Five, remember the arms front to back and not across the body, still faster. Four, keep the head up, think tall! Three, visualise the finish, go now! You're in front, break the girl with the finishing kick. Two – it hurts! Go! There's hot breath on your neck, flying spikes at your heels. Pass the water jump for the last time, hear the crowd, hear the England girl coming. The last bend, now she's on your shoulder, she is *not* better than you, you've taken out her finish. She is in the corner of your eye – ignore her, take another yard, seven hundred and eighty metres, is she still there? There is an 'F'on the road. Press your stop-watch, look at the judges. Two twenty-seven. You're still hard. Valerie hasn't got to you yet. You're still a fighter.

She jogged easily away from Brighton for another fifteen minutes, then turned back towards the city with the sea green and light below her to the left. When she reached her markers this time she opened up, but only enough to run two minutes forty seconds for each half mile; smooth, five-twenty miling.

She comfortably finished her seventy minutes of running at the bottom of Inkerman Terrace just as the street-lights began to glow. A vee of sweat showed at her neck and in the small of her back. Caz was complete again. Now she was looking forward to drinking tea and eating toast in a long and leisurely bath. She thought she would play Simply Red and wash her hair.

Twenty-three

She was in the bath for five-thirty and out for six. While she waited for Valerie she listened to Meatloaf and read Krebs & Davis's *On Ethology*. Her seat was cushions at the window and she shared them with Pink Vincent and a bottle of near-freezing Auslese, slurping the treacly wine and rolling it round inside her mouth.

The paper she was reading with Vincie was about strategies employed by subordinate mammals to attempt to get access to females. In a herd of deer the dominant stag was prepared to fight to maintain his right to every female. Because he was the strongest, biggest, and the cleverest stag, that made him 'attractive' in human terms. Attraction, according to the editors meant, 'I'd like my offspring to be as big and as strong as he.'

When it was impossible for individual stags to challenge the rutting leader of the pack, small coalitions would spring up spontaneously, and from these would emerge an apparent challenger who would 'dare' the leader and skirmish with him. Meanwhile, back at the ranch, the other coalition members were found to be at the female staff, desperately trying to maximise their genetic potential while their slightly stupid decoy took a bit of a hammering.

When first discovered, this unselfish behaviour gave sociobiologists a bit of a hard time, until someone realised that the young bucks in each coalition were related. The argument went something like, 'If I can't get sexual access to a female, I might as well take a risk and help my brother have a bonk – after all, we share half our genes. Two babies for my brother equals one for me. Half the hereditary loaf was infinitely better than none.' She read the paper, a famous one, and tittered when she read the punch line: 'We have called these younger males "sneaky fuckers".' The term was now established in the literature, much to the delight of students who felt obliged to mention it in every essay, from their first year right through to their final exam. She was still smiling when she heard the creak of his car arriving. It was ten to seven. Her overnight bag was near to her and she checked it for necessaries: toothbrush, knickers, warm gear for flying. She threw in the Krebs & Davis book, figuring that it might improve Valerie's arguments. After eight minutes she went out, feeling that she was being generous, going downstairs almost a full two minutes before the hour.

Valerie had bought a tiny posy of freesias for her which he had left on her seat. She pretended not to notice as she got in and went to sit on them. He squeaked as he grabbed them from underneath her and she made a rude comment about his being forward. He asked where they should go.

'I'd really like Armando's,' she said. 'It's where I'm most at home.'

'But it's bedlam,' he said, 'how can you have a romantic meal there?'

'By being together,' she said.

She was right. They left the car in the street outside Valerie's flat and walked down the hill to Armando's. There, they squeezed into a dark corner and immersed themselves in its garlic, noise and wine. Gabrielle found them, accused them of hiding, and placed a huge portion of garlic bread on their table. When he realised their napkins were paper, he quickly had them replaced with linen, reserved for his special customers.

Valerie asked for *Il Grigio* and Gabrielle's eyes lit up. He put two fingers to his lips and bellowed, '*Bellissimo!*' The garlic bread dripped butter and they both knew they would still smell of it on Sunday night.

'Kiss me now,' Caz giggled, 'and get it over with!'

They ordered fresh brill and a peppered fillet steak. They were drinking the Chianti Classico Riserva. When the waiter squeezed through to their table, Caz was finishing a conversation. 'No, really, it's official . . . Sneaky fuckers!'

Gabrielle frowned at her. He was a good Catholic. 'Oh no, Gabby!' Caz giggled, already slightly pissed. 'It's scientific fact.'

She stuffed more bread in her mouth, 'I wasn't swearing, 'onest!'

The waiter moved away, obviously disapproving. When she shouted after him for a second bottle of *Il Grigio*, Valerie caught his eye and shook his head, just enough. On Caz's blind side, he flashed his fingers twice. Gabrielle would give them at least ten minutes.

'Bloody Hell!' Caz laughed. 'Look at the *size* of this steak!' Valerie tried to laugh back but felt slightly sad. His brill was magnificent.

The head waiter brought their second bottle of Chianti half-way through their main course. He grinned and spoke Italian to his *bella signora* and, by a sleight of hand, placed the bottle out of her reach inside Valerie's territory. He looked into Valerie with a father's deep appraisal, decided he liked what he saw and then apologised directly, '*Signor*!'

To Caz he spoke quietly, '*Mia Bella Caz*, the cook . . .'

She looked at the waiter, then just as oddly at her escort. Gabrielle turned for the kitchens and she followed, shrugging her palms at their table.

Michael was shaking a huge black skillet, sizzling with butter and onions. She touched his upper arm in a warm hello. '*Ay, bella mia!*' he cried out, clapping a spoon on a saucepan above him. '*Franco, ay, Franco!*' A stream of kitchen Italian brought young Franco running. She understood '*Vitello al funghetto*', and one swear-word.

'We go by the fridges,' Michael said and took her hand gently. 'Mia Caz, you ask me once. About the dead man I tell you, he with a fat man like me?' She had almost forgotten.

'Yes, Michael. I showed you George Burnley's picture.'

'Tonight. The fat man. He is here. I cook for him veal *funghetto*.'

'Oh Michael!' She was sobering up fast. 'Here now? Where?'

He tiptoed conspiratorially ahead of her saying, '*Come stai!*' and led her back through the cast-iron clangs and sizzling garlic. From behind a tall pizza oven he pointed towards the back of a young, fair-haired man.

'See? The man I say? He is sittin' with that pretty man there. I think . . . maybe they are . . . ? I know issis him. He as' for me earlier. He tell me how great I cook 'is veal. This is the man. I know it.'

She left him, breathing deep into her stomach, trying to counteract the wine. By walking past that corner she would be able to see both the young man and the man who had been Burnley's dinner companion. She hadn't decided what to do. As she emerged from the kitchen she could just see Valerie on his own at the table, pouring himself another glass of wine. She waited as he quickly swallowed half and she heard herself think, 'Valerie, you cannot slug *Il Grigio*!'

Valerie seemed deep in his thoughts and did not see her, so she decided to walk back to him, passing the young blond man. She was fighting to remain calm. Normally it would have been easy, but not when she had had so much to drink.

The two men were talking quietly over a flask of wine. The corner was in darkness. The younger man looked beautiful, almost too much so, with a light fresh face and soft lips. He was whispering with a lowered head. Opposite the young man was a small balding man in his mid-fifties. The last time Caz had seen him, he had been in a seventh floor office at Amex house. Then, he had been on the brink of tears. Now Reg Smith sat with orange light shining on the side of his face, a look of soft love in his eyes.

For once she had some self-control and didn't dive in. She decided not to speak to Smith. He only had eyes for the boy opposite and he had not seen her. She knew she could interview him any time in the next week and, anyway, she wasn't sure how quickly she wanted to be told that she had been wrong about George Burnley.

Valerie had caught up by three glasses and now seemed more mellow than she was. He slurred something ending 'Officer!' at her, and she looked away.

'It's what I bloody *do*!' she thought. She waved her glass at him.

'Thorry!' he said. Don't be, she told him, it was all her fault.

By the time they were drinking cream-lipped liqueur coffees made with Italian brandy (over-slugged courtesy of Gabrielle) they were back on the same tipsy track, teasing each other. For a while they skirted round sex but finally Valerie steered them towards the evidently more interesting subject of micro-light flying.

'I bought my micro-light about four years ago for just under four grand. It's a Flash One; a *Gemini* Flash One to be exact, but no one ever calls them that. I thought about buying a Flash Two but they're unforgiving and it was too easy to plough one in. You have to fly them all the time.'

She was looking at him with glazed eyes. She was listening to his voice but had forgotten to pay attention to the words.

'Once you've got a Rotax strapped on . . .' he was saying.

'Rotax?'

'Oops. Didn't I explain? The engine. Four-forty cc. Made in Austria.'

'Oh,' she said.

'Yeah. So there's a Rotax 440 on this one – some have a 462 liquid cooled – and, officially, a two-bladed prop.'

'Officially?'

'Well, there's this crazy CAA ruling that if you modify an engine, say by sticking a more efficient propeller on, you have to get it tested for noise which of course costs you an absolute bomb. So officially we buy a new engine with the three-blade propeller. The maker has already done the tests so we get CAA clearance automatically.'

'So what's "unofficially"?'

'Well, if you bolt a three-blade on your old Rotax you get a nice quiet engine and a smoother ride, so everyone's happy. Forget the rules.'

'So how safe is micro-lighting?' she asked.

'Safer than riding a motor-bike, that's for sure.'

'People do get killed, though?'

'Usually only if they're breaking the rules.'

'Like fitting a three-blade prop?'

'No. Like pushing a craft past where it's designed to go. Putting forces on the wings that they weren't designed to take.'

'And what happens then?'

'They fall off the sky or they fold up. Either way, it's very bad news.'

'Have you ever crashed?'

'Only six or seven times.'

'What!'

'Relax. I was joking. I've had a couple of half-prangs but I was young then, and anyway, they were only little sillies on landing.'

'Is that all?'

'Of course. Why? Don't you believe me?'

'Well, you've got that look in your eyes. I don't know . . .'

'OK,' he said, 'I'll come clean. It's true that I once flew into overhead power lines near Salisbury and wrote off a Flash Two.'

'Tell me you're kidding me.'

'I'm afraid I can't. It was when I'd been flying about three months. I took someone else's "Two" up and I got myself into trouble. Flew straight into the National Grid and blacked out three-quarters of Wiltshire.'

'Oh, my God! Were you OK?'

'I walked away. Nothing hurt but my pride.'

'Oh, bloo-oody hell . . .' She feigned a look of despair. He picked up on the real fear underneath and took her hands in his.

'But that was then and this is now,' he said. 'Caz, look at me. That was *then*. This is *now*. I would never, *never* take the slightest chance with a passenger on board.' He paused, looking at her,

'Caz, I promise you. You're absolutely safe with me.'

She giggled again to relieve the tension, 'Oh, bloody hell!' she said, 'that's what I was afraid of.'

For different reasons they each felt tiredness sweeping over them, and Valerie suggested it was time to go. They waved for the bill and while they waited for Gabrielle, Caz asked to know more about the trip tomorrow.

'Well, if we're away on time, we can be ready to fly as soon as it's light. The field's about twenty miles out of town, just past Storrington.

'If the weather's kind to us, I thought we'd get up twice. How would you fancy taking a look at Seven Sisters from the air? It's wonderful.'

Gabrielle arrived and Caz dropped an Access card on the bill.

Val continued, 'We have to be up at a reasonable height in case we get a problem like a sticky engine. That way we can glide out of trouble.'

'Does that happen often – a "sticky engine"?'

'Fairly often. We get a few problems with dirty fuel or poor ignition but it's no big deal. A micro-light is a powered hang-glider, so, if the engine decides to pack up we just look for somewhere to land.'

'Isn't it dangerous?'

'Not at all,' he said. 'Well, at least not unless you're crossing the Alps or trying to fly to France. We call a no-engine landing a rapid approach or a dead-stick landing even though there's no stick! I've done hundreds without a problem.'

Gabrielle returned with her receipt and, as usual, refused to accept a tip. They said good-night and left. They walked slowly up the hill towards Valerie's flat. When they crossed one road, yobs to their right were threatening trouble outside a club. She logged it mentally but forced herself not to get involved. It was nearly midnight, nearly Sunday, Valerie's day. Outside his house, she picked up her bag from the back seat of his car and smiled as he waved her towards his door. She went up six steps before him.

He had the top-floor flat, up three flights of narrow leg-straining stairs and built into the roof. His estate agent would now sell it as a penthouse but once upon a time it would have been a loft extension. When they finally got to the last quarter-landing, she knew inside would be nice simply by the quality of finish on his front door.

He leaned by and pushed a single key into the lock. As he did so he pecked at her ear. With an open hand he invited her to turn the key. She did and they went in.

She stepped through into a single long flat room probably thirty feet from the door to the far end. Behind her, he clicked a switch, and hidden lights flickered into life, revealing a threepenny-bit ceiling dropping down to a row of Velux windows opposite a plain plastered wall.

In one corner was his desk, a mid-nineteenth-century hall table with an open lap-top on it. By that was a modern office chair that didn't go at all, next to that a wicker bin filled with coloured paper spilling on to the floor. He had no suite, just three unmatched fat chairs squared around three sides of a deep cream rug as if opposite a fire. Instead of a fireplace there was a mirrored firescreen with painted flowers creeping up one side of the glass. The floorboards matched the ceiling, polished pine. Their line led to the tiny kitchen at the room's far end on the right, and a huge dining table of dubious origin on the left. There was no television, but an expensive hi-fi beneath one window fed two four-feet tall Mission speakers with their front covers removed. She was probably meant to say something like 'Wow!' and she wanted to, but she managed to stop herself on principle. Ladies had been here before and they had all said 'Wow!' too.

'Where's the loo?' she said.

'Off the bedroom,' he told her, 'behind the kitchen.'

'Have you really not got a telly?' she asked.

'In the bedroom.'

'I'll be back in a mo',' she said.

He said he'd stick something on the stereo. What did she fancy? She laughed and said that if he could play something she had never heard before her body was his for the night. Then she was gone.

He took the challenge seriously, but decided it was unfair to dig out any old vinyl. He had folk records in there that even *he* hadn't heard of. He thought 'Electric Prunes'? but decided no; 'Incredible String Band'? No again. He heard the flush go. Come on! Come on! Then he saw it, a black and white CD cover, *Ca sonne pas beau, un bidon*??

He'd found something! 'Nagasaki Pour la Vie', 'Bazooka Jo', 'Le Grand Mecano', 'Glorie au Rhino!' This was no contest. He shouted, 'Don't come out yet!!' and grabbed the compact disc. *Percussion Industrielle – Rock Ferrovaire*. Was she getting a fair chance? He did hope not.

The guy in the flat below went to Manchester every weekend to see a girlfriend. The guy on the first floor, he didn't know, but even if he heard the music, he wouldn't be sure where it was coming from. Valerie put the stereo on low to medium which meant bloody loud. Then he let Nagasaki off its leash. Jojo (Chef Tambour) led it away.

She came back into the room in shock, the metal African rhythms almost knocking her down – Dagg-Dagg – Dagg-Dagg-Dagg!! He was grinning even before she began to dance: two steps forward, two back, two forward, one back. There was raw fire in her face and she began to unbutton as she crept towards him. He was so hard he hurt.

They came together for 'Bazooka Jo', naked, still dancing. Her fingers were in his hair as he dropped to his knees, still moving with the drums. He was biting at her, her belly, her thighs.

She danced on to his mouth.

Twenty-four

They were away at six thirty-five and on the way to Storrington in the car when she told him she'd seen Les Tambour du Bronx perform live in Paris. She thought Jojo's lead dancing made Mick Jagger look like a wimp.

'You mean you'd heard them before?' Valerie said. 'I'm shocked.'

The light had still to break when they turned off the main road on to a deeply rutted farm-track. A newly painted sign at the end of the drive said 'Two Trees Farm'. 'We're a bit early,' Valerie said. 'Might as well stay in the car.' He broke out a thermos flask. 'Coffee?'

He explained a little bit more about their aircraft. 'You'll see it soon enough. We'll check it over as soon as it's light. The wings from tip to tip are about thirty feet and the chord, that's the wing measurement of the front-to-back, is eight feet or so. We'll be sitting in the pod and I control the angle and pitch of the wing by moving the A-frame. That's a triangular-shaped thing made out of tubular alloy that hangs above my head.'

She was hunched up around her coffee, nervousness making her cold.

'You'll be nice 'n warm and you'll be able to talk to me over a simple intercom. We wear ear-defenders and mikes. It works quite well.'

She was very quiet and incredibly interested in the plastic rim of her coffee cup. He asked if she was OK.

'U-huh.'

'Good,' he said. 'Now this is what you do if I have a heart-attack.'

They could already hear early-morning birdsong, and now light was cracking over the South Downs. Ahead of the car, the dark silhouette of a barn gradually broke away from the night black.

'Wanna stretch yer legs?' Valerie asked and got out.

They walked round to the other side of the barn, which was open like a giant car-port, dark nine-inch-square timbers supporting the metal roof. Inside smelt of motor-bikes and grimy fingernails. There was a wooden bench fitted with a vice and faded posters suggesting safety. The one she liked best showed a red-haired man looking unsure. Above his head was splashed the notice, 'Don't Presume, Always Check!'

In one corner was a small pointed cab a little larger than a baby's pram, something like the body of James Bond's autogiro. Nearby were stacked wings in washed-out colours. She had been expecting bright day-glo oranges and reds and was slightly disappointed.

'You can give me a hand if you like,' Valerie grunted as he pulled their pod out into the open. He sounded faintly sarcastic. She went to assist but the craft was ludicrously light. 'We need to clip up the wings now,' he said. 'Those yukky-looking brown ones just there . . .'

He was moving quickly and confidently, clipping, tightening, pulling and testing. She stood by hopelessly. Suddenly, the various bits and pieces were beginning to look like an aircraft and she began to realise that this awful thing was about to happen.

'Let's get our flying togs on then, shall we?' he said.

He was sickeningly cheerful.

'Must we?' she answered. She thought the whole affair looked about as strong as a large kite. He laughed and took long strides back into the barn.

He helped her into lovat-green flying dungarees and massive boots. She tried on a helmet over her ear defenders and he passed her large yellow gloves to put on over her thin runner's pair.

'Just the part,' he said, 'you look great!'

He changed quickly. She could see how keen he was to be up there. Then he was leading her out to the 'plane and she was climbing into the rear seat of the pod. He strapped her in and suddenly she wanted to go to the toilet. She knew there would be nowhere to go so she bit her tongue and hoped the sensation would go away. Valerie moved round the aircraft one last time, flicking a few taut wires; then he turned the propellor twice before coming back to her.

She saw him wink, then he climbed into the seat, his back between her legs, the top of his head about her eye-level. She heard the final 'click' of his seat belt then a burrrrp and crackle before she heard the intercom say, 'This is it then, Caz. Too late now!'

The engine didn't start first time and she thought, 'If it doesn't start first time, how do I know it will keep going?' On the second try there was a puff and then it burst into life. She was surprised at its sound, more like a large model aircraft engine than a life-supporting power unit. It bree-eed and it braa-aaed as Valerie revved it through a test. Then she saw his hand held up above him with a gloved 'O' showing and they were moving.

Valerie turned the nose of the micro-light, she had no idea how, and they were bumping down what seemed like an incredibly rough field. She could feel herself bouncing vertically against her straps and by now she had decided that this whole thing was really *very* silly. Shouldn't they be going faster now? Shouldn't they have taken off? She blanched. Were they in trouble?

'. . . Turn into the wind,' she heard Valerie crackle. The engine note changed and the nose swung round. No trouble. Not yet. She took a quick deep breath. She had survived a whole minute!

Valerie's hands were above them both, clenched to the A-frame. They were rolling through the bumpy grass. The engine's whine took on another tone and then they were bouncing across the field, wind whistling in the wires. She looked right and left at trees and bushes, the barn, then forward at Valerie's head, his hands, the twitching nose of the micro-light and the far trees that were quickly getting ever so much closer and larger.

'I trusted you! You bastard!' she hissed to herself. 'Now get me over those bloody trees!' She squeezed her eyes shut for a second, sending out a 'to whom it may concern, please!' on the ether, then the earth gently let them loose. There was a tiny flutter as they unstuck from her grip and suddenly they were floating on the morning above fields glistening gold.

They broke out of the tree-line, then seemed to drop down and sit in the sky. She saw rabbits pecking at the ground and cows in convoy, moving towards a breakfast gate. The sun was now up, fat and lemon over the Downs and early morning wetness shone on the fields and off hedges. Suddenly, she was deliriously pleased with herself. She felt like the girl she once was, on the back of a motor-bike, passing her schoolfriends.

Her intercom crackled, Valerie asking if she was OK.

'Fan-tastic!' she squawked back. 'Yeah!! Great!!'

'I'm making a turn, OK? Back over the field!'

'Yeah! Fine! Anything!'

'OK. Turning now.'

She had been looking right, left, down, out, not wanting to miss a thing. Now she watched Valerie's firm hands on the A-frame as he nudged the micro-light round in the turn. She felt her own weight before she noticed the tilt of the aircraft, and then she thought they were just standing on a wing-tip, hardly moving forward at all. Looking downwards, it felt as though the aircraft would slide left towards the ground at any moment. There was virtually no sensation of movement.

'It's an illusion!' Valerie shouted. 'No frame of reference. Right now we are cornering at fifty miles an hour.'

She heard 'reference' and 'fifty'. She didn't care.

'. . . Up . . . twelve hundred feet . . .'

'Uh-huh!'

'. . . Better view. There's where we took off from . . .'

The barn looked small, like a neatly laid out toy. She could just see their car and another micro-light being pushed out. Valerie looked down. 'Jeff! That'll be Jeff!' he shouted. 'Me mate. He owns this plane!'

They were floating south-east, across the downs, rolling green fields cut by occasional walls or white wooden fences. She could see a thin road wriggling from the A27 through to the A24 and, beyond that, the brown and grey roofs of a town. Valerie anticipated her question. 'Worthing!'

'Right!' she shouted.

Then he told her through the crackle that they would skirt the built-up areas to the north and follow the Downs all the way to beyond Seaford. He was speaking in very short sentences, barking phrases at her.

'. . . Sisters! Far as Beachy Head. Spectacular! Well worth it. Get some more height then come back. Just off the cliffs. What d'you think? OK?'

'It's *brilliant*!' she shouted.

'What?'

'I said, it's brilliant!!'

They were cruising at a steady sixty miles an hour and, after swinging round Brighton, they flew parallel to the coast road until they crossed it at Seaford. Picture-postcard villages dropped behind them as they headed for the sea, then they were sailing above the green bulges of the Seven Sisters, white cliffs dropping away from them and down into a flat, blue-grey sea. She could see Beachy Head lighthouse ahead.

She heard Valerie communicate something about spiralling upwards, and soon afterwards she felt the inward turn of the micro-light. Then her views alternated between Eastbourne, the lighthouse, open sea, Birling Gap, a long dark forest, and then Eastbourne again.

'We climb in a circle,' Valerie called to her. 'We need plenty of height as a safety margin.' She shouted back that it wasn't a problem.

The return trip was a delight, high over a flat sea, reviewing the geology of chalk cliffs and the deposition of beaches. They did not turn inland until after Rottingdean, and she could see where she ran her hard half-miles, high up on the coastal road.

When they skirted back round the top of Brighton for the second time, Valerie pointed out Coldean and then the sprawl of Patcham's council estate and the row of white-distempered cottages on Patcham Hill. It reminded her of Jeremy Avocado, and she went to shout something back until she realised it would mean absolutely nothing to the pilot.

'The cottages look so pretty!' she shouted. 'The colours are so crisp!'

And they were. By now the winter sun was higher and brighter, but not so summer-bright that colours were flattened by glare. Valerie saw them too and she heard him squawk something back. Then they began to drop in an arc towards the Storrington strip.

By now she thought that she was blasé about flying, but when Valerie spiralled in, using a tight turn to lose height quickly, she once more became conscious of her mortality. The open hangar-barn and the more distant farm quickly became large and she gulped. Then they were lined up on the strip and floating downwards across a road.

The landing was almost an anti-climax, just a single bump then a few wobbles, with Valerie struggling with the A-frame. They beetled across the field with a puttering engine, and pulled up with the equivalent of a handbrake turn as the tallish blond figure of Jeff came out with a rag twisted between oily hands.

'You bounced!' he shouted. 'I most definitely saw a bounce!'

'Downdraught!' Valerie countered.

'Yeah, sure!' Jeff said. They began to unclip their belts as the engine sputtered and stopped. Jeff ducked under the wing, blond hair dropping in front of sparkling eyes.

'And this is?' he asked, speaking to Valerie but nodding at Caz.

'Caz Flood!' Valerie said.

'Wing Commander Flood!' Caz explained. As she stepped out, her legs were a little wobbly.

Jeff bowed curtly and they exchanged hand-shakes. He spoke to Valerie.

'So what was it, Sal? The Fairground Special or the Granny Trip?'

'Standard Granny . . .' Valerie said.

'This one looks as if she'd cope with a Special.'

'Not sure,' Valerie shook his head. 'Maybe, maybe not.'

They were walking into the barn. Caz didn't want to ask the obvious but she knew she had to and she knew that Valerie knew. So she didn't. Instead she turned to Jeff. 'You can fly a bit then, Jeff?'

'I taught Valerie everything he knows.'

'Not a lot then?'

'No.'

Inside there was an engine partly broken down. Jeff said it was being cleaned. He offered them tea and when they said yes he turned up the camping gaz underneath a very weather-beaten kettle.

'Ok,' she asked quietly of Jeff, 'so what's the Fairground Special?'

'Hairy!' Jeff answered.

'Dangerous?' she said.

'Not really.'

'So why do you say it's hairy?'

'It looks and feels dodgy. But it's pretty safe with a good pilot.'

'And it is . . . ? What?'

'Low-level stuff, quicker turns, that sort of thing.'

'Just showing off, you mean?'

'Absolutely!' Valerie said as he came over. 'This guy's an amateur. Still never done a Wiltshire Special.' The face Jeff pulled helped her guess.

'Don't tell me, Jeff – that was your Flash Two Valerie electrocuted?'

'I call him Sal,' Jeff explained, 'and yes, that's why I love him so.'

She decided that Val's mate Jeff was all right, so when he suggested they take both micro-lights up together and fly north she was doubly pleased. Jeff was flying a Flash Two. The more stable Valerie was in the sedate Flash One. They left the field at ten-fifteen, almost line abreast, breaking over the trees and heading straight for Midhurst.

Over the wind noise, Valerie was trying to educate her and the various intercom shouts were instructions to look at this, could she see that? By the time they were at a thousand feet she knew how to read the height off the altimeter, and when she saw the A29 heading straight-as-a-die for London she knew it was on a line nor'-nor'-east.

Valerie was being true to his word and would not fly fancy. Jeff wasn't so cautious and she saw him down to their right as he made the hand sign for 'wanker' and dipped his machine towards the ground.

'Just watch this clown!' Valerie shouted to her. 'He *loves* to fly!'

Jeff's 'Two' swooped down into a valley between two roads as they sedately followed down to watch. When the Flash One levelled out it was more than a hundred feet above the road line, and three hundred from the valley floor. The 'Two' kept dropping.

'It looks dangerous,' Valerie shouted (Caz could hear the flutter of excitement in his voice), 'but it's pretty straightforward. The only thing to watch for is power lines!' Caz thought, 'Well, that's *definitely* true.'

Then she asked Val who was the better pilot.

'Don't tell him,' Valerie said, 'but it's Jeff. He's hot when he wants to be.'

'Yeah!' she shouted looking down at the other pilot. It looked like the 'Two' was flying below tree-level.

'Watch him now,' Valerie shouted. 'This is his party trick.' He waved his gloved hand, 'It's a nothing thing but it looks great!'

Jeff's Flash Two scurried along the valley floor, moving gently left and right to sweep past groups of trees or follow the hillside. The busy road followed him except that ahead their paths would cross as the two micro-lights headed for Midhurst. Caz leaned out to look, no longer aware of her own precarious state as Jeff's Two began to climb out of the bowl between the hills and head dangerously for the road that traversed it.

They had dropped to less than a hundred feet above the valley sides and they were now close enough to hear the whine of Jeff's 462LC as he climbed from under the road. Suddenly, he was breaking up through the horizon of the innocent motor travellers, bursting into the sky as they must have thought, at least for a split second, that something horrible had erupted from the earth.

'I just *love* that!' Valerie screamed. 'It's nothing at all but it looks *so* funny!'

'I think I'll have to book him when we land,' Caz said seriously.

'What was that?' the crackling intercom asked. 'Something about a hook and a band? Please repeat, over.'

She muttered something back but was thinking, 'Boys!'

They were back at six hundred feet, passing Midhurst with forests laid out in dark green blocks below them. Jeff's Flash Two blimped up alongside and she could just see Jeff's teeth in a big grin as he dropped into line. She shouted to Valerie, 'Where are we now?

'That's Grigglesham Foster.'

'Where?'

'Almost dead ahead. You want to fly over?'

'It'd be fun!'

'OK. No problem,' Valerie said. She saw him waving at Jeff's machine. There was a brief exchange of signals, some of which, from Jeff, looked rude. Then both Flashes tilted and headed due north. Below, she saw the road they had travelled just nights ago. It felt like a month. That was the night . . .

'Valerie?' she shouted.

'Yeah? What?'

'I – Oh, nothing. Thanks for the ride.'

'My pleasure, Miss.'

The two micro-lights were about ten wingwidths apart, either side of the winding A286. They had dropped to about three hundred feet and farms and small villages rolled out beneath them. Now they were side by side, sailing on the sky towards Grigglesham Foster.

She heard Valerie shout, 'There's Grigglesham Hall. See the grounds. Look at that drive!'

'Looks like a corkscrew!' she shouted back.

'What was that about a screw?'

'I told you before. Don't be dirty!'

'That landscaping must have cost millions!'

'Or a few dead peasants!' she told him.

Valerie dropped the Flash One down through a hundred feet of sky with a slow turn over the village and the manor grounds. Grigglesham Hall was surrounded by a high redbrick wall that ran fifty yards out from the outside turn of the corkscrew drive. Immediately inside the drive was water which, at first glance, looked to be a narrow river, except that it had obviously been shaped artificially to run around the house in a spiral.

The house itself looked like a two-storey copy of Chatsworth and was completely surrounded by the lake. The water was too wide to be seen as a moat, but that was the final effect, the spiralling road turning in to a cream-painted bridge with a metalled roadway crossing.

The overall effect from the sky was of isolation and of solitude. Peaceful walks through manicured wilderness, dripping waterfalls, ducks and moorhens. In spring, it would burst out with parades of daffodils and the semi-rough area along the walls would break out in a flood of bluebells.

'OK, I'll buy it!' Caz shouted. The perfect lawns in front of the house looked longer than John Street! She guessed there would be very little change coming from ten million if the house was ever put up for sale. Valerie didn't answer. He was waving hard towards Jeff's airplane. She glanced the way he was pointing. Though she could hardly hear the other's engine, she could tell the note had changed.

'Jeff's got problems!' Val was shouting. 'He's mis-firing!'

They pulled up and to their right, dropping over Jeff's Two which was now clearly spluttering and puffing blue smoke.

'Jeff's gonna have to put it down straight away!' Valerie told her flatly. 'He's dead stick!' She watched as the Flash headed, nose down, straight towards the house. 'We'll follow him in, make sure he's all right!'

She could sense Valerie's concern as he swooped up over the steeply gliding Flash Two. Jeff was heading in a straight line after one turn which had cost him height, but now he looked to be in complete control as he lined up on the long grass frontage of the main house.

'Nice and easy!' she heard Valerie say as Jeff put down. She had the impression he was willing the other pilot in safely. The Two bounced once after a final flare which cut its ground speed, then it trundled to an easy stop, almost parked, in front of greystone steps leading up to the manor.

They swooped to buzz the downed micro-light, Valerie returning Jeff's earlier 'wanker' greeting as they passed over it. He was laughing and chuckling, whatever words he was actually uttering, lost in the crackle of the intercom and the changing notes of the engine. Now Jeff's Two was safely down, Caz tried to feel relieved, but for some unknown reason she still sensed danger.

'Is he all right?' she shouted. 'Val?'

'No problem!' Valerie shouted back. 'That lawn was built for a Flash.'

Val was turning again, dropping left to run back over the grand house. Caz still felt uneasy. People were moving down the steps from the front doors. They could see Jeff just climbing from his machine. Then she saw the guns, two of the men approaching Jeff with shotguns levelled, a third pointing a barrel upwards and letting go a cartridge.

'What the fuck?' Valerie gasped, pushing full throttle and haring away from the shotgun blast.

'They're not shooting at us!' Caz shouted. 'That was for Jeff's benefit!' Jeff was now out of the Flash. They could not see his face but his hands were very definitely high above his head.

They climbed away, looking for time to think. If they were shot at again they would be as easy to pick off as a hunted duck. Valerie came back over the house, low enough to see Jeff but hopefully where they could drop behind the angle of the roof if weapons were pointed at them.

Caz was charged and frightened but concentrated on seeing Jeff and the armed men. One had already broken his barrel. Then she saw that Jeff had dropped his hands and was talking to the largest of the three. Then an arm shot out and they were shaking hands. She looked again. The big man had a small bald patch on the crown of his red head. It was George Foster, the comedian from the Drunken Preacher.

Jeff was waving them down. They took a chance and swung lower and closer. He was grinning and still waving. They could see his thumbs up sign. 'Seems he's OK,' Valerie shouted. 'He wants us to land.'

There were three guns down there; three gunmen. Caz was trying hard to think. Staying in the air was the safest option and landing was . . . what? There were *shotguns* down there, not Uzis. This was the country so shotguns weren't *that* unusual. But someone had just let loose a warning shot and, for at least a minute, they had thought Jeff was in real danger.

Valerie said he wanted to land. What did she think? She wasn't sure. Tom MacInnes would land, Norman Blackside probably wouldn't. She made her decision.

'Let's land, Val! I could do with stretching me legs.'

Twenty-five

Valerie brought the micro-light in quickly, rather than let it drift down comfortably. He steered the plane in, close to the water line, then dropped it on to the grass as early as he could. All the landing speed was gone in fifty yards and he taxied up to park alongside Jeff's Flash Two. Jeff walked towards them with George Foster. One of the other workers must have taken Foster's gun because he came to them armed only with a huge grin and a proffered hand.

'Sorry about that,' he said loudly. 'We're not used t' people dropping in uninvited. Some of our guests are a bit nervous, you know?'

'Val Thomas,' Valerie said as he climbed out. He turned to help Caz.

'And Wing Commander Flood,' Jeff said. He was surprisingly relaxed.

'Your mate 'ere says 'is engine's broke,' Foster told them. 'Can we offer you a drink?' Valerie said yes please. As they walked towards the steps, he asked quietly of Jeff if everything was all right.

'Yeah, Sal. Dirty fuel, I reckon. It'll need a quick cleaning job, but I don't think it's anything too major.'

'What about our friends?'

'They were just a bit nervous, I think. One of the gardeners set his gun off by accident. I think they're a bit embarrassed. The big guy, Foster, says we're going to be introduced to the lord of the manor as soon as we've had ourselves a cup of tea.'

'You are joking?'

'I don't think so. Some professor and his daughter apparently.'

Foster was obviously listening. 'That'll be Professor Hely,' he explained. They were at the bottom of the steps. 'His daughter is Miss Rachel.'

At the top of the broad steps there was a slightly pink gravel driveway. As they crossed it they could hear their feet crunch on the granite chips. The other estate workers had melted away with their armoury and George Foster was now playing his version of the charming host. The four of them approached a pair of massive oak doors.

'Welcome to Grigg'sham 'All!' George said.

The doors were still open and they stepped through into a grey marbled hall with clinically white walls. It was shaped like a pentagon and had a large dark wood door in each of the other four sides. There was no stair-case. The fliers were wearing rubber-soled boots but George's heels clacked on the stone floor. 'Pretty, d'yer reckon?' he said. Caz was looking at the alarms over the main door.

'Know the history of Grigg'sham 'All d'yer?' George asked cheerfully as he went through the first door. 'About the Grigg'shams and the Fosters?' They were in a short narrow hall carpeted in royal red. 'First Lord Grigg'sham, he fought for Cromwell, Oliver Cromwell, that is. Did real well fer 'isself and got 'isself this big estate, Grigg'sham 'All.'

They were passing through another door, stepping into another hall with a stone staircase leading off. 'Only thing old Grigg'sham never 'ad was an heir. So he set to an' married a village girl called Annie Foster. That's 'ow the village is Grigg'sham Foster see?' He walked ahead. 'She were near twenty year old, Annie, and he were nearer fifty. By all accounts he were a brute with 'er.'

Foster stopped in another white room, bright and airy with long tall windows letting in the winter sun. Huge tassled furniture dominated one end of the room and a long lumpy table the other.

'Take a sit down,' Foster said. He pulled a thick silk cord to summon the help.

'Young Annie Foster never caught pregnant. She started both times but she lost the baby early. The Grigg'sham side reckoned on it were because Annie Foster weren't proper stock, but it got to be a joke in the village pub because the rest of the Fosters bred like rabbits all over the county.'

A girl about twenty clipped into the room. She was dressed in classic black with a white pinafore. Foster told her they would like tea.

'That all right for everyone?' he said to the room. There were nods. 'Four teas then, Bess. And set up some coffee for Miss Rachel and the Professor.' The maid went out.

'Where was I?' He was waving them into seats. 'Anyways, it turns out that Annie had had a childhood sweetheart that everyone thought were dead in the war. That were why she'd took up with Lord Grigg'sham.

'This lad, he was a young buck called Edwin Sly, comes back to the village. When he finds out his sweetheart's married the lord of the manor he gets mighty angry. He wants to go up to the house and take his Annie from Lord Grigg'sham. He's as mad as spit but old heads in the village calm 'im down. Later he gets to be working for Grigg'sham and before you can say "corn dolly" the lady is pregnant.

'There was some talk in the village tavern, but then old Lord Grigg'sham, he starts to be kind and gentle to young Annie. He gives alms to the poor and he lays on fair days for the village folk.'

Caz winked at Valerie.

'Then a second child arrives. It's a boy. Old Grigg'sham gets to be even happier and he lays on a big feast day for the village. They has roast ox, boar and venison from the forest. That's when the old heads from the village take Edwin aside again.

'Edwin marries his cousin, a girl from next village. He still works at the hall and Annie has one more baby. She were thirty when she died. Old man Grigglesham took it really bad, and Edwin was the only one who could get through to him. He told Lord Grigglesham that he had to be strong for the sake of the children.

'Edwin Sly ended up as the lord's bailiff. The old man gave him the gatehouse in perpetuity. When he got older still, he had his bailiff teach the children games on the great lawn while he watched. It were said that, by the end, old Lord Grigglesham died contented. He left Edwin Sly a small farm. There's Slys still live there now.'

Bessie came back in with a drinks tray, clip-clapping towards the table. Caz was amazed to see she wore old-styled black stockings with seams. 'Ah tea!' Foster said, his accent suddenly done, 'thank you, Bessie!'

Caz was curious about the corkscrew drive and the intertwining stream.

'Lord Grigg'sham's love-message,' Foster explained, handing out the teas. 'After the first child was born, he began to landscape the estate for Annie. The water immediately around the house was originally a moat, and what's now the lakes was two linked streams.' He sipped his tea.

'Annie loved the water, and she loved to see water birds. Old Grigg'sham wanted there to be as much water as possible and he made the lakes and the manor drive spiral in and criss-cross. That way you're forever crossing water from the main road right up to the house. The drive is just about four miles long but it's only just over half a mile in a straight line to the main gate.'

'Water?' Caz asked. She noticed Jeff looking past her at the window.

'Water means fertility round these parts,' Foster said quickly. 'Especially crossing it.'

'I thought Grigglesham had cracked fertility!' Valerie said with a light laugh.

'Well there's lots of Fosters and Slys hereabouts,' George answered. He looked at Jeff. 'Are you all right, Jeff?'

'Oh, yeah,' Jeff said absently, 'I'm sorry. I was just thinking . . .

about my micro-light engine. I have to find out what's wrong and get it fixed.'

'Of course. Do you need tools?'

'No. I carry them on the 'plane, but thanks.'

'Well, if we can—'

'Help? Yes, of course. If I need any, I'll ask.' Jeff looked to Valerie. Valerie looked up, but before he could speak George Foster announced loudly, 'Ah, Miss Rachel, Professor Hely!'

Two people entered the room by the servants' door. The first was Rachel Hely, a tall size ten with long legs, blonde, almost white hair and startling green eyes. She was stunning; model-beautiful, a head-turner with an animal presence. Behind Rachel was the professor, even taller, but stooped and somehow slightly bent-kneed, as if trying to hide his height. He was six foot five, six inches taller than his daughter.

Though they were obviously related, where the daughter was bright and open, the father was dark-faced and seemed withdrawn. He had the same white hair but his deep dark eyes were sunk behind round gold glasses. 'Creepy' was the single best word to describe the man now nodding hellos to the room. Valerie would have said 'gorgeous' to type Rachel. With handshakes, they introduced themselves one by one to their hosts.

'Caz Flood.'

'Val Thomas.'

'Jeff Thomas. No relation.' Jeff smiled. 'At least not as far as I know!'

The professor spoke slowly. His voice was tiny, like an animal subdued. 'I am Doctor Samuel Hely. The principal here. May I introduce you to my daughter Rachel? I am glad that we are now showing you real hospitality. I cannot apologise enough for the manner in which we greeted your arrival. Perhaps over lunch we might make things up to you?'

Jeff spoke first. 'That's very kind of you, Doctor Hely. I have some sort of problem with my aircraft.' He pointed in a general way out of the window. 'It might take a while. I'll have to—'

'Excuse yourself? Of course. George will be only too happy to assist you in any way he can.' He turned to Valerie and Caz. 'May I take it that we can offer you both lunch'

'Lunch would be wonderful!' Valerie said quickly.

He looked smitten by the professor's daughter. Caz gave him a sideways glance but smiled her agreement.

Rachel spoke confidently, her eyes flicking over Caz, 'You probably know, but Grigglesham Hall is a research centre and a working maternity clinic. We are busy this morning but we will be finished for one o'clock. We do apologise for not being able to entertain you now but, if you would like it, George will be happy to show you around the house . . .?'

Foster shifted his feet and nodded. There was no negative response, so she continued. 'Fine, then we look forward to sharing our Sunday lunch with you. I believe today we have beef.'

There was a moment's awkward silence, then the professor excused them both and they left. Jeff visibly relaxed and said he was going down to his Flash Two to check out the engine. George Foster directed him through the servants' area, then he turned to the others.

'More tea, is it then, or is it the grand tour?'

They had been sitting in what George now explained was the Grigglesham Hall's east wing. He told them it contained the servants' areas, kitchens, a couple of guest rooms, the computer room and two small laboratories.

'This wing is pretty boring,' he said. 'We'll start off with the west.'

They went back along the short red carpet and into the main entrance hall. George crossed this and opened the far door leading to the opposite wing. This time the carpet was a rich dark blue and the walls were magnolia.

'Most of our guests are lodged in the west wing,' he said. 'We have eight suites, with a drawing room and two bedrooms, each with en-suite bathrooms and a jacuzzi. Four of the suites have a sauna and we have a small gymnasium as well as a heated indoor swimming pool.'

There was a heavy golden key in one door's lock. Foster spoke to them over his shoulder as he turned it to allow them in. 'Obviously we would not show you a room, in fact anywhere in this wing, if we had any guests. Our last visitor recently left us after a successful stay so we can show you round. Please feel free . . .' He pushed open the door.

'Oh, yes.' Caz heard Valerie whisper behind her, '*verrry* nice . . .'

'Not bad,' she said.

Nothing in the room was anything less than perfect. Superb carpet ran wall-to-wall, heavy mahogany-legged furniture was elegantly placed around, and thick curtains were tied back from the narrow french windows. Fresh copies of *Country Life* and *Tatler* were carefully placed on a superbly polished desk in one corner. Limited issue prints hung on the walls.

Valerie was muttering, 'This makes the Brighton Grand look like the Eastbourne Ordinary.' His voice was a mix of jealousy and admiration. Caz smiled. She had a fleeting thought: making love to him on that huge four-poster bed. She paused before replying. 'It *is* nice,' she said.

'This is a very exclusive maternity clinic,' Foster was explaining. 'Our clients are the wives of the rich and famous,' He was looking at Caz. 'Even this luxury would seem very ordinary to the wife of a head-of-state.'

'I didn't realise—'

'That we had such precious clients? Oh yes.'

'What about security?' she asked vaguely, hoping she sounded suitably dumb blonde. Foster smiled and said that was dealt with. She suddenly realised that to him she was just a hitch-hiker who had dropped in.

Lunch was served in the guest room of the east wing. Professor Hely sat at the head of the table, his daughter beside him, opposite

Caz. She was smiling. Jeff was outside, eating hot beef sandwiches and striking up some sort of relationship with Bessie and a carburettor. When she glanced across, Caz thought Jeff looked well in, as if he had known Bessie for years.

The meal was classic English fare: roast beef, Yorkshire pudding, boiled potatoes, cabbage and peas. The gravy had been made with animal fat, browning and cabbage juice. Rachel explained their preference for the food of their adopted country. 'We left the land of the bland many years ago. We like the English Sunday, to us it's like Thanksgiving once a week.'

'I think my daughter is a chameleon,' Professor Hely said lightly. 'She blends in wherever she abides. I'm sure that if we were in Berlin now she would be swearing her allegiance to *bratwurst and sauerkraut!*'

'I quite like American food,' Valerie said. 'Give me a nice Mac any time.'

'Wait until you've had them for decades,' Rachel replied. 'Wait until all your corner-shop chippies are gone and there is just one chain. It will probably be called MacFish! Every portion will be the same size, cooked identically and dipped in internationally standardised batter. Oh no! I'm for differences, diversity, the fuel of change, of growth.'

'How about Burger King then?' Valerie asked facetiously. Caz felt a little flicker of annoyance. She couldn't believe that Valerie could be so trivial. Then she realised he was nervous and excused him.

'It's a bit like the Holiday Inn syndrome,' she said to Rachel. 'Wake up jet-lagged in one of their hotels and it's impossible to tell where in the world you are.'

'I agree,' Rachel said, quickly smiling at Caz. 'The endless drive for efficiency creates homogeneity. International standardisation leads to individual blandness.' Caz felt a flicker of something pass between them.

'Automobiles are another good example,' the professor said. 'In their drive towards ever more efficient designs being produced, with less and less redundant material, car designs are converging. There was a time when a General Motors automobile and a Ford looked totally different. Now it is hard to distinguish them, their shapes have come together like the shark's and the dolphin's. Despite totally different evolutionary starting points, they are dangerously similar.'

'Well actually,' Rachel countered, 'the shark and the dolphin are not good examples; they may *look* the same due to convergence, because they are coping with a single environment, but they are still at heart – in their genetic make-up – fundamentally different creatures. The shark is a fairly primitive fish, the dolphin is a mammal. The problem with automobiles is they are *fundamentally* converging. Where is the variety of approach that pre-adapts for future change?'

'This metaphor is no good,' her father realised flatly. 'Engineers can respond to demands far more quickly than God can organise evolution.'

'Oh, don't get Caz started on "evolution",' Valerie joked. 'If you start talking to her about heredity she's like a dog with a bone!'

'Oh really?' Rachel said to Caz. Her interest was obvious. 'What was your major in?' Then she corrected herself, 'What was your degree subject?'

'Psychology,' Caz said, 'and animal behaviour. I did my subsidiaries in genetics and evolution. My third-year project was in sociobiology.'

'Then you should be interested in our work here,' the professor said.

'Oh, I'm sure.'

'George Foster showed you round the complex?'

'Yes,' she said. 'We saw the West Wing and the hospital area. We didn't go in the theatre. George felt it was unnecessary. As you know, we avoided the labs as you were working in there.'

'Do you understand what we do here?'

'Not exactly. Just that this is a clinic but that covers a multitude of sins.'

'Sins?' Hely asked.

'It's an English saying,' Caz said. His face pulled into a thin smile.

Rachel spoke. 'Grigglesham Clinic is primarily a convalescent home and/or a very exclusive hospital. We cater for only very special female clients, those who require the treatments developed by my father.'

'Which are?'

'Fecundity Management Techniques,' Hely said.

'Fecundity?' Valerie half asked.

'Fertility,' Caz replied without looking at him.

'Yes,' Rachel continued. 'We deal with infertility, particularly the kind caused by psychological stresses. We treat our members' complete body-soul systems. We bring them to a peak of "receptivity" by making them as rounded and as fit and happy as we can. Very often that is all that is required for them to become pregnant.' When she said 'pregnant' her eyes locked on to Caz for a brief but definite moment.

'It sounds like the fatted calf,' Valerie said.

Rachel answered him. 'That's partly true, Mr Thomas. Thinness itself is sometimes a problem. In those societies where being slim is considered attractive, female fertility can drop markedly. The natural level of fat in a woman has a major effect on the production of hormones. Anorexics and runners—'

'I'm a runner,' Caz blurted.

Rachel paused but smiled at her.

'—are often amenorrhoeal; their periods stop.'

'I wish!' sighed Caz. Rachel shared another smile. 'This is due to insufficient fat levels in the body. The hormonal balances are lost and various body rhythms –' she glanced up at Caz's face – 'however tiresome, are thrown out of sync'.'

The women were sharing something to the exclusion of the men. Caz was nodding. Valerie and Professor Hely were mere onlookers and Caz had the distinct impression that Val wasn't happy. Caz could feel Rachel's real interest in her, not sure if it was social, intellectual or something else.

'There are still societies where the fuller figure is preferred by men,' Rachel continued, 'but even in countries where previously it was not the case, women are now to be seen seeking an ideal which is far from normal.' The conversation was now just between the two of them.

'When our guests arrive,' she said, 'we first try to ensure that they are genuinely healthy, free of serious drug use, reasonably calm, reasonably happy. The surroundings to the house are very therapeutic, particularly in the spring and summer. It is important that they are able to truly relax.'

Caz was thinking that if stress made a woman infertile, why was she on the pill?

'Only when we are happy that our guests have distanced themselves from the rigours of their normal life do we consider any further treatments. Fecundity management can be stressful, especially when you remember that our guests have come to us because they dearly want to be pregnant. You must remember also that our guests are partners to some of the world's richest men. They would not wish to have their needs openly discussed in the public domain. Theirs is therefore an even more stressful situation. They need privacy and discretion as only the British can offer. That is why the clinic is here and not, say, in the United States. Here our visitors are anonymous and we never address them formally. They choose a simple first name like Rose or Emily, and that is who they are for the duration of their stay. We supply loose casual clothes for them and once they have changed from their everyday clothing into ours they are able to throw away many of their burdens and simply become women again. Most love the sense of freedom we offer. We have many guests who return here to enjoy being anonymous for a while.'

Professor Hely finally broke in on them, 'We try to be very

discreet. We try hard to keep the press away. That's why our staff live in. They are paid very well for their loyalty and more specifically their bonuses are based on no information ever reaching the press.' He used a little hand-bell to call the staff. Bessie was immediately present with a little cough.

'Now that you both know what we do here – who our guests are – I am sure you understand our nervousness when you and your friend simply dropped in. You gave us quite a shock.' Valerie looked away towards Jeff's micro-light. Caz was vaguely uncomfortable.

'But we would like to make things up to you if you will let us. We have a sort of open house this weekend. Friends and colleagues, a few ex-staff are popping in. For two days the house will buzz again. We would dearly like you to join us. Will you?'

Caz said 'yes' too quickly. Valerie suddenly remembered his friend.

'Look,' he said, 'Jeff's been quite a while. Would you mind if . . . ? I think I'd better pop out and see if he's all right . . .' He left without looking back, his ears faintly pink.

'Caz,' Rachel said, more softly now, 'I think your friend Valerie is still a little unhappy with us. Will you be able to make our peace with him? We would, I would, really like to have you here this next weekend.'

'I'll talk to him,' Caz answered, 'but I can't say that I feel massively confident. I don't think he's very happy with anyone right at this moment.'

'Oh dear,' Rachel sighed, 'Will you come if . . .'

'I've already accepted, Rachel. Thank you, I would love to come.'

If Valerie had his bum in a sling for some reason, that was his problem. She wasn't going to let his little-boy petulance affect her.

'Oh, *good*,' Rachel said. There was a light of faint pleasure in her eyes.

'Then we can look forward to some stimulating conversations,' Professor Hely said, 'that will cheer Rachel up. And perhaps also we will have an opportunity to show you a little bit more of the complex?'

'That would be fascinating, Professor. Thank you very much,' Caz said back. God, Flood! she thought, you're beginning to sound just like them!

Rachel moved to stand, suggesting they left the table now to have coffee. As they all got up, Caz moved to the window, looking out and down at Jeff and Valerie. Jeff appeared to be describing some particularly hairy flight, his arms out like wings. Valerie was laughing. When she saw him punch Jeff lightly on the cheek she guessed he had loosened up. 'I think Valerie might come after all,' she said. 'Can Jeffrey come too?'

They flew out just before four o'clock. Their Flash One first, slashing a straight line across the double-helix of stone and water, then banking to wait for Jeff's Two to take off. He came away smoothly, his 462 running sweetly now, and drifted up alongside them as they headed south-east.

The edge was gone off the day's sun, distant thin clouds hiding its power. They cruised uneventfully, with Jeff alongside. Despite glorious views, Valerie had nothing to say. He had told her before take-off that they would be at the field for four-thirty and home for six. He did not speak again.

They came in to the airfield routinely and bumped towards the barn. When they stopped, he was curt but courteous. She came close to biting back but she stopped herself. First, she knew she should be grateful for the flights; second, somehow, once again, her work-life had intruded on them, and third, the day had not been without its trauma.

Jeff's Two landed effortlessly, without the slightest bump. He taxied up to them and jumped out. 'Bit of a day, eh?' he said. He was beaming, totally unfazed.

'I have had less eventful ones,' Valerie said to him. He spoke so evenly that Caz couldn't even try to sense what he meant.

It took less than twenty minutes to wheel away the micro-lights and break them down. When she finally got out of her flying gear,

Caz felt lighter, the weight removed. She decided she was a little musky and began to look forward to a bath. Valerie tossed her the keys to the Daimler, saying he would follow in a moment. She went ahead. As she clipped the door open, she watched him with Jeff. Their closeness was palpable; it couldn't be hidden. She envied them their deep friendship. They were shaking hands, bashing each other's shoulders as only men do, then they broke. Jeff appeared to be walking to his car but then he turned quickly, as if outwitting Valerie, running quickly to her side of the car. Her window was wide open and he kissed her full on the mouth.

'Nearly fergot t' say g'bye,' he said. He was grinning like a schoolboy as he shouted, 'See yer, mate!' to Valerie.

'Up yours!' Valerie shouted after him.

As he got in the car Valerie kissed Caz briefly on the cheek. 'Sorry!' he said.

'For what?'

'For being a pain,' he said as he started the car. They watched Jeff pull away in an old Cortina Mark Two. It was a 1600E. He'd had the car since his seventeenth birthday, Valerie told her, and he still loved it. 'It's his sex substitute, I reckon.'

'Well you should know,' Caz said.

They drove down into the city, talking inconsequentially but at least they were talking. As they turned along the front towards Brighton, Valerie said that he would be in Portugal over Christmas, hang-gliding with Jeff. 'This'll be our third time there. Do you want to think about coming?'

She had no idea why, but at that moment she felt achingly sad. She said she'd think about it. The idea of some sun on her back sounded nice but she wasn't sure if she could get away.

'I'm very tight on leave,' she said. 'Let me check.'

'Well, you know,' Valerie said, 'whatever . . .'

She told Valerie she had to go to the flat, at least briefly. She really wanted him to say something about tonight's sleeping arrangements: one part of her needed to be cuddled to sleep; the other needed space. She cared though, and was caring enough not to want to say the wrong thing.

'Need some company tonight?' Valerie said gently. It was as though he could sense her confusion. It was so sweet, she felt like crying.

'Oh, please,' she said. She felt about ten years old.

'Just company?'

'Yes, love.'

'That's good,' Valerie said. He was just a little lighter. ''Cos if you'd wanted much else I'd've taken a rain-check. I'm knackered.'

'I could cook,' she offered.

'Is that a good idea?'

'Sod off! I'll have you know I've got a GCE in Home Economics!'

'Oh, that's all right then,' he said. They were being trivial but Caz felt something dark leave quietly from between them.

They parked in a space at the bottom of the street and walked up it, past the place where George Burnley had been ripped to pieces, past where she had touched a bloodied head and seen a grey staring face.

Inside the flat she asked him to hold her tight and, when she began to cry, he said sorry. She told him it was nothing to do with him. She cried herself out, bathed, cooked them pasta. They drank Rioja with it and she listened to Frank Sinatra with him. Then she took him to bed. In the end, they did make love.

Afterwards, she cried again.

Twenty-six

Monday. For the first time in months Caz had skipped her early morning run. When she arrived at John Street, instead of her normal sensation of sharpness, she felt heavy and lethargic. She put it down to poor sleep.

Blackside had called a briefing for oh-eight-thirty in the War Room. She wasn't sure, but she got the impression there were even more faces in the squad. The hard core from Brighton were outnumbered now by some seconded plain-clothes and some drafted-in uniforms, four of which had come from Woking.

Brown was away, no one said where, and MacInnes and Blackside came in together. The Chief Super loomed over the DI as he walked behind him.

MacInnes went on to the stage first. Caz could almost sense the tension in his shoulders and feel the prickle on his neck as Blackside followed.

'OK! OK!' Blackside bawled. The room went instantly quiet. 'Nar then, we're not doin' too well, are we, lads?'

There were exactly one hundred and fifty-eight door-to-door returns still outstanding. They had no direct witnesses commenting on Beecham whatever. They had failed to firm up on the young man or woman seen outside Burnley's flat and the only formal connection between Burnley and Green – which didn't impress Blackside very much at all – was the tenuous one via Jeremy Avocado.

'I am *not* impressed. I am not impressed at all,' he boomed.

'It's about time you bunch of tossers got it together. What are you, girl guides?'

There was a bit of forensic back. Written confirmation that sample B, for Boyfriend, was in Beecham's bed as well as inside Beecham, and a positive report that two hair samples, both light brown or blond, connected Beecham with Burnley. Otherwise, if you discounted the victims' own detritus, the murder scenes were almost spotless. Blackside finished and nodded to MacInnes. The DI stepped forward into the light.

'We've got one possible new lead, courtesy of DC Flood.' He looked up into the room to see her face. 'Seems at least one other sudden death can be linked to the decorator, Avocado. The name came in from Avocado himself and he's now come up clean twice, but we need to know a bit more about our man, Jeremy, anyways, just t' be on the safe side.

'Ah know the coroner, and ah've got me a copy of the inquest on the guy, name of Davies, picked up Sunday. There's not much doubt that our man was well pissed when he fell off his balcony but his sister's statement said the lad never drank heavy. We're gonna need t' look at this case again and ah've put Sergeant Reid on that.'

DCS Blackside stepped forward. His mood was no better. 'Now get me *information*, you tarts! Stop pissing about! For starters we'll have fresh statements from everybody connected with the Davies death like yesterday. I've told you I don't have a lot of time. That means *you* don't have any time at all! Now get out there and catch me villains.'

Caz moved more slowly than the rest. She didn't have as far to go. The double doors were still flapping as she sat down at the computer. Billy Tingle and Moira Dibben came in together. Caz was sure there was something different about Billy but she couldn't put her finger on it. There were plenty of reports to type. She took more than half of the files and set her finger–brain links on to automatic. The others were laughing quietly and took a while to settle.

She was thinking about Reg Smith. When she had interviewed him at Amex House he had looked so feeble, so depressed. He had nearly cried – she remembered that. It was when she had actually told him that George Burnley had been murdered that he perked up. She tried to recall his face that day but she couldn't. At the time she had been so focused on Burnley and the receipts and distracted by Valerie . . .

But the old man had lied to her. Or at least he hadn't told her the full truth. If he had eaten with George Burnley at Armando's, why did he not mention it? Was there something about their relationship that Smith was worried about? Could he be a suspect? Even if Burnley was gay – and she still could not believe that – even if they had something going, or not, that she found very hard to believe, why hide it? Why?

At least Valerie had been open. He had come armed with files, with his computer, with a predisposition to flirt and be helpful. She'd responded and . . . they had . . . her stomach suddenly fluttered. They had been to Grigglesham Foster together, they had ended up at the Hall together. They had been to Armando's together. And Valerie knew Burnley and Smith.

Her fingers were still moving over the keyboard but there was a fat fist of heat in her stomach. Her world moved slower and slower. Suddenly she could feel her finger-tips and see them flicking left and right.

She was trying so hard to remember. What had she said when she first telephoned American Express? Thomas had been ready with his files and his computer; in fact, everything he had on George Burnley. What had she told him? Everything had been so efficient, so quick. He had been so helpful with his Paradox database. 'Everything unofficial', she had said. And Valerie had given her just what she had asked for. It had all been very pat. She had asked Valerie to take her for a drive to Grigglesham Foster – or had she? Again she couldn't quite remember. She had said something about driving to Midhurst, or was it Haslemere? She was thinking about going to the village but who had mentioned it first? And hadn't Valerie been easy to persuade? Wasn't he too easy?

She felt physically ill. It got worse. Was their flight over Grigglesham pre-arranged? Did Jeff's Flash Two *really* have to put down? Could a pilot fake a missing engine? And if he could, and if Jeff did, then Jeff . . .

She rushed out, feeling sick, stumbling, knocking files from a table next to Moira. The ladies' toilets were down a floor but a single gents' was forty yards away along the corridor. She burst in there.

She was looking down into the bottom of a blue-veined white urinal dotted with cigarette ends. She wanted to vomit. She tried, but when she retched nothing came up. She groaned but it was not for her and Valerie; it was because she had made a mistake. In the end, it wouldn't matter whether Valerie turned out to be involved or not; she had been exposed. Wanting Valerie had blinded her and she had put her career at risk.

The white china stank, adding to her misery. It made her think of Jim Green. She stared into the bowl. One of the cigarette ends was fraying, gradually seeping tobacco towards the drain. A deep rage was welling up inside her, dark and nasty. She was furious at her own stupidity. She couldn't make herself pull away. Then the automatic flush burst into life, breaking the spell.

She turned to a sink and opened the cold tap. The water ran with a spray flying from it, gradually wetting her front. She dipped her head towards the swirl round the plug and splashed liquid into her face. With a wet hand she combed back her hair from her forehead. Then she looked up at the mirror. She saw her face deep in the glass, much further back and smaller than she expected. She stared at herself.

'Oh, Flood!' she whispered, 'Oh, Flood you stupid, stupid . . .' Everything she had ever wanted was wrapped up in this building, in the force, in being a good copper. A moment of weakness and it had all so nearly fallen apart. How could she have let herself be so naive? So stupid? More importantly, now that she had been, what would she do now? There was nothing to be done but to go through and see Tom MacInnes. Before that she needed to whip herself into shape. Staring at the mirror, she undid her pony-tail and pulled her hair back tightly until her scalp strained. Then she re-tied the hair-band. In the mirror she saw some of her hardness returning via the pain. She slapped her face twice. Be angry!

She went back into the computer room. Moira was laughing and Billy made some sort of silly remark. She barked at them. 'Try getting some work done, Billy! You want to be a PC all your bloody life?' His mouth dropped open. Moira looked shocked. 'That's right, Moira! There's more to life than four lagers, a quick Chinese and a hand up yer knickers!' Caz's cool was gone and she knew it. She grabbed her bag, and stormed out, leaving Moira and Billy exchanging bewildered glances.

She walked out quickly through the war room and out into the hall, crashing the paired doors out of her way. Heads turned and she thought she heard some DC say 'PMT'. She almost turned, wanting to smack him in the mouth, but all the men in the room saw was her step falter and her head tilt upward.

She went downstairs and along a corridor to MacInnes' office. As she approached, her fists were stiffly clenched. At the last moment, instead of knocking his door she strode past.

She needed time to think. Would DI MacInnes have come clean? 'Kiss some arse', he had said. Well, she was already doing that. 'Keep your head down', he had said. Well going to the DI, worse, going to the Chief Super, was definitely not that. She could not fall over. She would not fall over. She kept walking.

She passed through doors, making a circuit of the nick, fighting down the sensation of panic and anger and slowly replacing it with resolve. Since her first day as a DC she had been steadily chalking up points, just as she knew she would. The Jones incident was a bonus: that had put a little light behind her. Saint, Greavsie, even Bob Moore, had to admit she was doing all right. DI MacInnes was already making noises. Even DCS Blackside, gross as he was, knew she had done well in Southampton.

She was due time out for psychological rest. After finding a couple of dead bodies she could get away with almost anything. DCS Blackside had already told her to get some counselling. If she walked away now, if she dropped out of sight, took a few days leave, she left them while still covered in the good news. A short sick leave was absolutely standard; no one could mark her down for that. All she might be missing was the collar for the murders. She wanted to be there for that – she might still be – but right now she needed to recover, to lick the wounds no one knew she had. And anyway, as Tom MacInnes had said, she didn't have to stop thinking while she was out. She felt better. Once more she could hear police noises; offices loud and alive with ribaldry. Her face was bright again, the green eyes piercing and certain. The smell of the place came back to her. She could almost feel her nostrils flare like a vampire sensing blood. She could get away with it . . .

She went down to the canteen It was almost empty except for a couple of traffic wardens and a young PC. She grabbed a tray and began to make coffees for the army. When she had made twenty, she grabbed two handfuls of sugar packets, put those on the tray, and went upstairs. The activity had done its job. Now she was cool and calm. When she got to the war room she had to kick hard at the door to get someone to open it. A fit-looking DC from Woking came to her aid and made some remark about tea-ladies. She laughed at him like it was the funniest thing she had ever heard. The DC shouted 'coffee up!' and the lads descended on her like vultures before she had time to put the tray down. She squealed to order and called them all bastards as hot liquid splashed into the tray then, with an artistry that surprised her, she dipped away from the last few sets of hands retaining three cups.

'Tough!' she said perkily to the two unlucky DCs, 'these are for the workers!' She was grinning as she went into the computer room. Moira and Billy were leaned towards each other as she walked through. They were bowing low, whispering across an aisle.

'Peace offering!' she said, gesturing with the tray. Moira looked at her and Caz flicked her eyes downwards towards her own stomach. It was almost imperceptible and just for the instant it took for Moira to think she understood. 'I was bang out of order just now,' Caz said, 'I'm sorry. I'm just a little bit tetchy at the moment.' Then, just so Billy could chalk up a point, she added, 'You know how it is with us girls . . .'

By the time they had finished their coffees she was once again deep into entering data into Holmes. It was mindless and, she was convinced, useless too. She waited for the hour she had decided was about right, and then she said she was going down to see MacInnes. 'I'm feeling a little bit . . .' She groaned, 'I'm gonna take ten.' This time when she left, her shoulders were lower and she tried to look pathetic. The Woking DC said hello to her by name and she smiled weakly back at him. Then she left the war room.

She knocked the DI's door. He snapped a gruff 'Yes?' and she went in. He lit up for half an instant before looking sharper.

'Ah, DC Flood!' he clipped brightly, 'how's it going?' His head moved about an eighth of an inch towards his right and the light on his face changed.

'OK, thank you, Sir!' Caz said. She made it sound as if she was faking brightness. 'I wanted to update you, Sir. About information I picked up this weekend.' He shook his head slightly and glanced right. 'We'll talk about that in a minute. You say you're all right but that's not what your face says.' He was waving her to sit down. 'Take a seat.' His eyes looked at the chair then rolled top right towards the next office. She grinned faintly and gave a tiny nod.

'Now then, gal,' he said, relaxing. 'What can we do for you?'

'I think maybe I need a couple of days off, Sir. Things seem to be catching up on me. I'm not sleeping and . . .'

'Tell her about George Foster, Tom!' It was Blackside, shouting through from next door. MacInnes shrugged at her.

'We did a sweep on the immediate area round Grigglesham

Foster. We were looking for a reason for Green and Burnley's visits.' She was pale.

'There's nothing there except Grigglesham Hall. You know the hall?'

'Yes, Sir, that's why I came—'

'To talk to me? Have you booked with Counselling yet, Caz?'

'I was about to, Sir. But I came in and there was so much for Holmes . . .'

'Forget Holmes,' MacInnes said. 'You're due some time out. It's not a problem. You've had a rough ten days and you need a break. Take some time. Step off the treadmill before you fall off.'

'But, Sir . . .' They both hoped the protest sounded right.

'Flood!'

'Sir?'

'You take seven days off, starting now, OK? Get your appointment with Counselling and, before you leave, confirm it with me. Now go off and run yourself silly or something.'

'I'm half-way through some data-entry, Sir. Is it OK if I wrap that up?'

'Finish what you're doing, Flood, then come back here no later th'n twelve. Ah'll tek y'home m'self.'

'Sir?'

He rolled the eyes again towards the office next door. 'I understand you met George Foster this weekend. That right?'

'Yes, Sir!' she said. 'My boyfriend and I, we had to—'

Blackside was in the doorway. 'Had to drop a bloody aeroplane into the middle of an investigation!'

Caz flinched but stood her ground. 'We didn't have much choice, Sir. It was an emergency! The fact it was Grigglesham Hall where we landed was just pure coincidence.'

'Well, Flood, you rang alarm bells over half the country, dropping in like that, including John Street. Do you know what Grigglesham Hall is?'

'Yes, Sir. It's a maternity place and they do some fertility research there. I met the clinic's director and his daughter.'

'Rachel Hely,' the DI said.

'Yes, Sir, but—'

Blackside cut in sharply, his voice at its most intimidating. 'Shut up and listen, Flood. When Holmes came up with Grigglesham Hall it also told us that Professor Hely and his daughter were being looked after by our own. You say you met George Foster?'

'Yes, Sir. I think he owns a garage in the village, but he was working at the hall. It looked as if he was a manager or the gamekeeper or something.'

'Try Special Branch!' Blackside said.

'What!'

'Yer gamekeeper, Flood. He is *Sergeant* Foster, Special Branch. And he picked up on you straight away. He asked me if you might fancy a job at the hall.'

'A job, Sir? Doing what?'

'What young Elizabeth Lowndes is doing now . . .'

'I'm sorry, Sir, now you've completely lost me.'

'Bessie Lowndes? She's the help there. She's a little go-getter from the Met. Got a BSc in criminology and works for George. She's due to leave in four or five weeks. George asked if you'd be interested.'

MacInnes came in quickly, 'I told him you were too important to me.'

'Thank you, Sir!'

'Thanks, nothing. Do you realise what you dropped into up there?'

'Not exactly, Sir. They told me they get a few distinguished lady guests. I guess it's a bit of a security nightmare for the locals and Special Branch.'

Blackside turned away. 'It could be,' MacInnes said, 'but they keep a very low profile. They fly their heavy-duty guests in the back way by helicopter. According to George, the locals don't even know some of the serious people who've stopped there. Anyway, the Branch have put a lid on everything. Unless one of our victims has actually been to the Clinic we're out of there. Have you got that? Grigglesham Hall is clean, OK?'

She heard herself saying OK to the DI, but by now felt as if she was gibbering. Maybe she really did need a break. She thought about the clinic, George Foster, the professor, Rachel. Whatever went on there, she didn't think it was sinister. She didn't know why, but she was certain that everything Rachel Hely had told her was true. She agreed with the DI. Grigglesham Hall was clean.

'Well, piss off then!' MacInnes said. There was a huge grin on his face. As she went out from the office, he shouted to her not to forget to call Counselling. She raised a hand to indicate she had heard but she was striding away with the pink back in her cheeks.

When she got back upstairs there was a dripping bacon buttie on her desk next to her keyboard. She looked up and Billy was waving his. He had butter dribbling down his chin and there was a silly twinkle in his eyes. 'Lots of iron!' he spluttered. Moira gave him a little dig.

'Why, Billy,' she said heavily, 'I am deeply touched. Thank you.' He looked like he might actually go red. Caz stared lovingly into his eyes.

'Billy,' she said, 'does this mean we're engaged?'

It took little time for Caz to finish off the two files she had outstanding, then she saved, exited data-entry mode, and started asking Holmes a few questions. The first print-out started with an intrusive craarrrrppp!! and Billy quickly closed the lid of the printer's acoustic hood.

Paper mounted up on the floor, line after line of grey type, page after A3 page of courier twelve, folding and stacking itself into a neat two-foot-by one block, inches deep. 'The fruits of yer labours!' she said, pantomiming to the others. 'Cor bloody blimey! Makes yer feel proud!' The printer stopped, clicked, then spattered a few more words. She leaned across to the machine. It smelt hot. 'You finished?' she said. Suddenly it sparked and produced another two lines.

To the others, she explained that the print-out was for DI MacInnes. It was hardly a lie. She looked up at the clock. It was ten-to twelve. She put the block of computer paper near the door. On top she put her bag and her Goretex jacket before leaving to go to the loo. She spoke to Billy Tingle.

'Small favour, Billy . . .' she was smiling, 'look after that little lot would you? Five minutes?' Billy said yes, no problem. Then she said, 'If for any reason you manage to lose the stuff, Billy . . .'

'Yes?' he asked.

'Smack your face into a wall and rip off one of your testicles.' He gawped. She smiled. 'It'll just save me some time when I get back.'

When she came back, she picked up her gear and left with the DI for the Grapes of Wrath. She was forceful, striding out in trainers. MacInnes tipper-tappered alongside, staying with her.

They used the lounge again, and again MacInnes bought them whiskies, this time both doubles and without asking. When he came back to the table his cough sounded raspingly worse. She had taken the folded Holmes print-out from her jacket and now she was sitting on it. Blackside's words, 'The killer has signed every murder', made her feel strange. If he was right, she was sitting on the murderer's name and address.

Tom MacInnes sat down opposite her. Every time she saw him she thought he looked smaller. Now even his eyes looked small. If she had disliked him, words like 'ferret' or 'weasel' might have come to her easily, but she didn't dislike him, she really liked him. He was the same as her; he was sharp and intelligent and hated criminals. Like her he was obsessive and he felt some instinct that took him into the mind of the men he sought.

Unlike me, she suddenly thought, you're ill. She had no idea where the thought had come from but it hit her like a blow in the gut. She knew she was right. He was fading away almost as she watched. He *was* getting smaller. She wondered when he would tell her what was wrong. 'You should get that cough checked out, Sir,' she said quietly.

MacInnes said that if she wanted to be his nurse she should call him Tom.

'I don't think I can yet, Sir. I don't think I deserve it.'

'Maybe not, lass,' the DI said, 'but you're getting close.' He suddenly swigged his double in one throw. As he stood he said, 'Another?' She said no, but he went to the bar and brought back two doubles anyway. When she shook her head at them he told her not to mind, he had room enough.

'So you're going t'get counselling like a good girl, Caz?'

'I guess I have to, Sir.'

'Yes, you do, lass, and it won't hurt you.'

'But it makes me feel like I can't take it, Sir. That I'm not as strong as one of the blokes. Like you maybe, or Greavsie or Saint.'

'Bullshit!' MacInnes said.

'I'll do what I'm told, Sir, just to keep out of grief, but I really—'

'Get counselled, Caz,' the DI said sharply.

She nodded and drank her whisky.

'So what d'yer think y'll do with all that information then?' MacInnes said after he had downed his second Bell's.

'I don't know yet, Sir. I just thought I'd . . .'

'Thought you'd take a complete break from the case . . .'

'I don't think I can do that, Sir.'

'Why not?'

'Because it's personal, Sir. Like I told you before. Because it came so close. And I think because . . .' she faltered.

MacInnes asked, 'Because what?'

'Well, Sir, because there was something at Burnley's flat that . . . Well I don't know really. I think maybe I know the killer. No, I don't mean that. I don't mean I know *who* the killer is, but I feel I will know him, that is, understand him, something about him. Sometimes I think that I can *feel* him out there. Sometimes I think he knows I'm coming.'

Tom MacInnes was looking at her; weighing up what she was saying. Behind him she saw Norman Blackside's head as he entered the bar. For a second she thought she could hear Sergeant Moore's permanently sarcastic voice. MacInnes was talking but the words weren't registering.

'*Flood*?' It was a little too loud. She twitched.

'Sir?'

'I was asking. Have you thought? If the killer knows you're coming . . . ?'

'What, Sir?

'He might be looking for you.'

'Why?'

'You said sometimes you think he knows you're coming.'

'Yes but that was just—'

'Melodramatic crap?' MacInnes suggested.

'No, Sir!'

'Then *what*, Flood? You said it first. What exactly *did* you mean?' She saw DCS Blackside moving away from the bar. He was with someone but from where she was sitting she could only see him.

She was not paying attention. MacInnes snapped her name at her. She shook her head and her eyes flashed angrily. Her fists were white. '*Don't* you bully me!' she said. It was absolute. 'I'm not Bob Moore!' She suddenly snatched the second whisky and downed it. 'You bloody well know *exactly* what I'm talking about! Sometimes I can feel things before I know them. That's why I've never wanted to be anything other than a detective. You *know* that. Because I am just like you.' There was a long pause before she said a low but definite 'Sir.'

MacInnes sat quietly. His face was pointed at her but he was looking a long, long, way away. Then she saw the focus come back to their table and he smiled very slowly at her face. She could read respect and affection and something else in his eyes. It was neither joy nor sadness. It was oddly dark brown and ambiguous, like the bitter-sweet memory of a true love.

Someone dropped a tray of drinks in the other bar. There was a man's roar of laughter and glasses banging on tables to applaud the misfortune. MacInnes ignored the racket. His soft voice cut through the noise.

'Flood,' he said gently, 'you need to go carefully out there.'

'I will, Sir,' she said. There was a rugby club cheer from next door.

MacInnes made sure that she knew how to contact him. He made her memorise his home phone number. He promised to talk to her every day. He made *her* promise that she would talk to *him* and he got her to say she would take some real days out.

'Trust me, Caz, you'll be better for it. You never know when you might have to be sharp. Take a day off. Go back t'bed after your morning run.'

'I didn't know you knew I ran in the morning, Sir.'

'Ah've seen yer,' he said. He saw the question in her face.

'You run past my place, usually about an 'our and a quarter before you turn into work.'

'That's about right,' she said.

'Aye,' he said, 'so ah know exactly where you are every mornin' . . .'

She looked at him. There was still more to come. 'And anyone else might be watchin' you as well, Caz. Mightn't they?'

MacInnes did not give her the promised lift home. He had had three good whiskies by the time they finished and, though he was prepared to drive, she wouldn't let him. He had offered to get her a taxi home but she said no. She told him she wanted to go for a walk down on the beach.

They parted outside the Grapes of Wrath. She walked down towards the sea and he walked the short uphill to the station. As they said goodbye he touched her hand and a brief electric something passed between them.

Twenty-seven

The afternoon was flat, grey and ordinary, not much wind, not too cold, not actually raining. It was very 'British winter', very 'Brighton'. The reflecting shops on the hill were just ticking over, white-coated assistants in slow-frame passing soft bread rolls in paper bags to solitary customers. Doors opened with pinging bells. A car puttered slowly up the road. The town was pale and pastel, relaxing, breathing in short, shallow breaths, trying to conserve its body-fat while it waited for the spring.

Perversely, Caz liked Brighton like this. The real colour of individual people had more chance of breaking through in winter when the town was at its rest. Once winter gave way and spring-green started to shine through again, the town's blue-and-white gleaming personality would re-emerge and dominate. Mere people would be ants again, teeming its streets.

She found herself near the Palace Pier and wandered on to it to stare at the sea. Her mind wandered and a thought intruded of those people who stand on motorway bridges and watch cars shllapp past, car-top after car-top after car-top. The cold grey-green of the water was depressing her and she broke away. Then she decided she should wander the Lanes and waste some money.

She finally found herself in Armando's Ristorante. It was half-empty and two waiters were arguing loudly just off-stage. She heard Gabrielle's voice boom briefly and the argument fizzled out with one catty remark to each side. Then Gabrielle came through to see his *mia cara*. She told him she wanted to get drunk and he twinkled as he went to get her a bottle of *Il Grigio*. When Gabrielle came back he brought two glasses. He suggested that she had the Dover sole as it was very fresh and *bellissimo!* She smiled a 'yes' and he told her it was already being prepared. He had guessed right again, he said, and the wine was his present for her. '*Mia cara*, Caz,' he said warmly in his deep brown voice. She thought he sounded incredibly seductive. 'You are not a little bit un'appy?'

No, she told him, she was OK. It was just a little bit of man trouble.

'This is your friend? He is new? The man who speak good Italian?'

'Sì.'

'I think he is probably a good man. I know him from before. He come in here a few times in the summer but, you know, it is very busy then.'

'Yes,' she said. Then she asked was Valerie with a woman?

'Sì. Sometimes. But I see him also with the fat man Michael talk about. The fat man you jus' find out sometimes eat with the dead man.'

'Reg Smith,' Caz said darkly. 'The dead man was George Burnley.'

'Sì. I did not know Mr Burnley. Did not know fat man, Reg Smith, had been with him. Reg Smith, I see him a few times with other men 'aving a meal and I see him too when he eat with your friend.'

Caz must have looked awful. She felt betrayed but, instead of anger, she felt resignation. '*Mia* Caz?' Gabrielle asked, '*Mia* Caz?

She switched her face back on. 'Oh, I'm sorry, Gabrielle! I was thinking about something.' She sipped the wine and savoured it. It was wonderful, rich and round. 'I'm fine. I'm much better now,' she said. 'Come on, let's have a drink! Gabby! *Ciao!*'

When the grilled Dover sole came it was fat, with deep soft white flesh. She ate it with freshly cooked *sformato* potatoes and garlicky courgettes.

Caz left Armando's about five o'clock. The street-lights were already on. Her afternoon had rolled back softly as she ate with her rotund friend. There had been a little too much *Il Grigio* and she'd managed a *tiramisu*. She had thought of the calories for a moment but then, what the hell, she thought, I'm on holiday! Gabrielle had a wife to go to. Caz decided to risk the weather and walk home. She thought it would clear her head a bit.

Cars fllummed by her as she strolled slowly back. The folded print-out was inside her jacket, protected against the first spots of impending rain. She felt peculiarly good; too drunk to be sensible but not drunk enough to be ill when she finally got to the flat. She was even too pissed to care right now about Valerie Thomas or Reginald Smith. They could go to hell.

She passed the Brighton Centre and the cream-fronted Grand Hotel. The night was quickly blacker and the rain began to sweep at the buildings from the sea. She hunched forward, her eyes on the pavement six feet in front of her. The thick folds of paper felt uncomfortable against her ribs and she shifted them slightly, cursing her luck. If she hadn't had a liqueur coffee she'd've been home ten minutes ago and would've missed getting wet.

Ah, but hadn't Gabrielle charmed her so delightfully? God, he must've been devastating when he was just a few years younger. The old Romeo! Absent-mindedly she wondered what sort of lover he would have made.

Then she was at the bottom of her street. Yuch! it was foul now; she ducked her head even lower. Someone was running down towards the sea trying to avoid the rain. She saw the light-coloured coat and some dark instinct flashed through her. But it was too late.

It did not hurt, but something heavy hit her face. The shock was strange and slow, like being aware of an oncoming car as it bore down on her.

She felt the back of her head hit a railing as she fell. She was spinning sideways and the painted black of the metal uprights came to her crystally clear. This clarity, she thought, how pleasant; this is a life moment.

She felt something cold touch her face then move away. Then she saw the long shine of a wicked blade moving upwards through the yellow fuzz of a distant street-lamp. Her world was grey and stuttering, held up by the dull shocks to her head. She felt a thought, almost academic, telling her to react, but she couldn't, some spark she needed simply wasn't there.

A red flash of something that felt like sexual excitement passed through her and she realised she was about to die. It felt not evenly remotely bad. The world was a black circle coming to a point. As the circle closed, she felt the sudden thump of the knife hammering at her chest. She wanted to smile but instead she went to sleep.

Winter rain rolled over her in the empty street.

Twenty-eight

From the absolute blackness first came something dark blue that pulsed. Then there was deep red and a thudding, terrifying ache. The shower had been too hot but now it was too cold. And she couldn't reach the control.

Her father was shouting that she should come in now, out of the rain. She shouted back that her chest was hurting. He said he didn't care and turned away. It was too dark to stay outside and she felt very, very cold. She thought it would be a good idea to go in anyway.

She woke with the rain lining her face. The wet touched her lightly like a gentle lover. She was lying on her back and felt foolish, so she decided to get up and go into the flat. When she tried to move, her head throbbed and she let out a whimper of pain. She moved an arm. It was almost under control and her hand came slowly into view. It *was* hers but it danced spastically like a puppet with no master. I am, she thought, then amber lights swept over her, hurting her eyes. The hand dropped to protect her. Then she heard water. She heard rubber. She saw silver spikes.

She wanted to wake up properly and have a nice bath. She heard her priest say something about her mum. Then she was being lifted up and her head was no longer against something hard. It was still very cold and it was very, very wet and she wanted to go inside now. Someone was looking at her and he was wet too. He called her Caz and she tried to tell him not to because her mum said her name was Katherine.

The man was nice. He carried her out of the rain.

She was on her bed and everything was wet. She asked the man to get her handbag and he said it was all right, he had picked it up. He said his name was Valerie. Her hair felt sticky. Valerie told her she had cut herself.

'Christ, Caz,' the man was saying, 'you frightened me to death. How much have you had to drink? You've ripped your jacket.'

She hurt but she asked him to sit her up. 'I want a bath,' she said.

'Shushhh!' Valerie said. 'Shushh. Just lie still, I'll sort things out.'

He dabbed her face dry with a big white towel. The towel was warm. When he touched one part of her head it hurt a lot. He said it was still bleeding. He said they should go to the hospital. She said, oh please, not yet, could she have a bath? He sounded very worried and he went quiet. Then he said OK. Then he undid her shoes.

'I'm cold,' she said.

The man began to undress her. Her shoes were pulled away and her wet socks left her feet. Then he pulled her body forward and held her while he tried to remove her jacket. He couldn't get it over her head. Then he was cutting the cloth and she complained. He told her it was ruined anyway. Then there was paper everywhere. It smelt and some of it was pink. Then Valerie said 'Oh my Jesus!' and laid her back on the pillow.

She managed to speak. Slowly she said, 'Valerie, please. I'm not dying. Don't ring anyone. Please. Just help me . . . please . . . ? Help me undress.' He said there was a cut on her neck and there was a cut on her head. She needed to go to hospital. She begged him again and she said please. She said she would explain. 'Please,' she said. 'Please, Valerie.'

Her eyes were concussively dull but a fire inside was making them sharper. He looked deep at her, trying to decide. Then she saw his finger on his lips and a yes in his face. She relaxed and he began to cut away her shirt. Her neck was stinging.

Then she saw his cheeks pale as he said, 'God!'

He looked behind him. She felt the sudden rush of his fear. He touched her, pressing her down gently, then he went quickly out of the bedroom. She heard him shout, 'Hello?'then she heard the front door slam shut.

Seconds passed, perhaps a minute. She heard nothing except the deep thud of her own chest. She forced breath down. Then he was at the door. He had a meat hammer in one hand, a long bread-knife in the other. She could still see fear crawling. There was a darkness across his eyes. He whispered, very softly, 'Caz, are you OK?' She nodded with a tiny gasp.

He waved, then he moved away again. She saw him tentatively push the bathroom door. Then there was a silence again. Every second of the silence blupped; terrifyingly slow, like dripping blood. Her breath was cold and it caught in her upper chest. She could taste the acid of vomit.

Now she could hear the electric breath buzzing from her bedside clock. Valerie appeared, backing away from the bathroom and into the bedroom. He was looking into the hall. She realised he was in his working clothes, a charcoal suit. His neck was freshly shaved. The back was drum-skin taut. His ears were pricked. She called his name. He turned round.

'It's all right,' he said. His finger was light on her lips and he was trying to smile. 'I was stupid. Whoever it was . . . I didn't realise until . . . I hadn't shut the door . . . I suddenly realised that . . .'

He was lifting dirty wet hair from her forehead. Then he tilted her head slightly as if to look at her head wound.

She heard him whisper, 'Oh, Caz,' just to himself. Then he managed to brighten up. He smiled, eyes as well. His hand cupped her head.

'But everything's all right now,' he said softly, 'there's no one in the house except you and me.'

He bathed her in soft pink water. She was laid back, her head resting on a sponge and her long legs stretched towards the taps. His voice was soft and soothing as he gently cupped water over her shoulders and her arms. Points of dark blue surrounded by blossoming red peppered her upper chest. A thin red line slashed from the muscle of her shoulder in a diagonal towards her sternum. It was broken at the hollow of her collar-bone which was painted with the brown of crusting blood.

'How many . . . ?' she asked weakly. She was staring at the yellow of a plastic duck.

'Seven,' Valerie said. He was dabbing gently at the cut with cotton wool, 'And your neck. Oh, babe, it—'

'Is it deep?'

'No, love, it's not.'

'Is it bleeding?'

'No.'

Then she asked, 'My face. Valerie, is my face cut?' She remembered the cold of something touching her skin.

'No,' he said. 'You've got a nice wallop on your cheek, but no cuts.' He smiled for the first time. 'But you're still beautiful, Caz. Bruised but definitely beautiful.'

'My chest is sore,' she said.

'You surprise me,' he said back. The humour didn't work.

She grimaced at him. 'I know all about surprises,' she said.

She was more alive now and she asked for tea. He hesitated, so she sat up sharply to show she was with it. 'Make us a cuppa, eh?' she said.

The bath was cooling down and she leaned forward to run some more hot water. She winced with the pain and wondered if she might have cracked a rib. She opened the tap slightly, just enough to let the heat bloom near the plug and slowly crawl up her legs, then she gently eased herself backwards until she was resting her head again.

As a policeman, she began to assess the attack. The chances of it being random were millions to one, and she had seen the cream coat. She was angry that she had been drinking. It could have cost her her life. It *had* cost her an accurate witness report. The blow to her head had been peculiar; more a thudding softness than a sharp crack. After that she remembered nothing until she was in her bedroom and Valerie was undressing her.

Her attacker had touched her face. It had been cold. Was it the blade of a knife? Had he been checking her identity? She had been stabbed at, not slashed, and her assailant had struck at least eight times, each time hammering the weapon into the accidental folds of the Holmes print-out.

The one cut was probably the incidental edge of the weapon as it struck downwards, perhaps as she was falling. It had been half a degree or a tenth of a second from killing her. If, instead of brushing the outside of her collar bone, it had been inside, it would have been steered deep down, into her lung.

The weapon? Probably not sharp-edged, not a knife for cutting. Her Goretex jacket had been ruined by punctures and rips, not slashes. The millimetre-deep cut to her shoulder and upper chest had been caused by the edge of the weapon so it was not blunt. But neither had it been particularly sharp. If it had been, she would have opened up like a gutted fish. She shivered slightly.

Valerie was coming back. 'Hello, soldier!' he said. He looked brighter now that she was more alert. He had two mugs of tea with him. 'Where d'you want these?' he said.

She said she'd get out of the bath and get dried. 'Would you look at my body?'she asked.

'You didn't just say that, did you?' Valerie laughed.

'This is business, not pleasure.'

'I'm sorry. What?'

'What shape are the bruises?'

'They're just bruises. You know. Little blue blobs.'

'Valerie!' she snapped. 'Are they round?'

'Are they round? Yeah, more or less.'

'Is that they *are* round or they aren't round?'

'They're round,' Valerie decided. He had sat on the loo and she was standing in front of him. He reached out a hand and touched one mark. She stiffened. 'Oops, sorry!' he said. Then he decided that the middle of the bruise was oval-ish or . . . 'I guess it might be a diamond shape.'

'So the bruises are round oval diamonds, is that right?'

'Yes,' he said brightly. 'D'you think I'll ever make a good copper?'

'If you rephrase the question,' she said, 'the answer is definitely no.'

'I thought as much,' he said. Then he added that he didn't like navy blue anyway.

He pulled a big white towel round her. It crossed her shoulders and dropped to her calves. With another towel he dabbed at her feet and her lower leg. He spoke. His head was down near her knees and the sound was deep, almost an echo.

Valerie dried between her legs. 'This is very embarrassing,' he said. 'But I am quite definitely getting horny. What can I say except apologise?'

'You apologise,' Caz said, 'and if I let you lie on top of me inside four weeks, I promise you it'll be a miracle.'

'You on top?' he asked.

'Three months!' she said.

He kissed each thigh lightly and said something sweet.

She was faintly annoyed at him. The damn man was too nice! She threw him out so she could use the loo.

Twenty-nine

When she came out of the bathroom she could hear Valerie working in the kitchen. Popping her head round the door she saw that he was cleaning. She thought, 'Tension-reducing displacement activity', and smiled.

It was necessary to feel pampered, so she sprinkled talcum where she could and gently smoothed it down her front and over her thighs. Then she pulled on fresh underwear and white cushioned socks. From a drawer she took a large light-grey Russell Athletic jogging suit, dressed in that and then padded through to see the cleaner.

Micropore surgical tape covered the faint gash on her shoulder and this was beneath the soft inner fleece of her Russell top. All that was left was the mess on her head and the growing bruise on her cheek. She kissed Valerie and asked him to put music on. She told him 'something meaty'. Then she went back into the bathroom to clean up.

Valerie had chosen the Rolling Stones. She heard 'Jumpin' Jack Flash' as she brushed out the blood from her hair, and 'Street Fighting Man' as she carefully pinked out her bruise with make up. She dropped Optrex into her eyes while she listened to 'Sympathy for the Devil' and prayed a thank you that she wasn't developing a black eye. When she came into the room, 'Honky Tonk Woman' was playing and she looked great.

She told Valerie she would contact DI MacInnes. 'We'll need at least an hour to talk, Val. Would you . . . ?'

'I could nip round to my place,' Valerie said, 'and grab a few things, but don't ask me to leave you before your boss has got here.' He stared at her from the kitchen doorway. 'I'm not leaving you alone.'

She smiled at him and picked up the 'phone. It was five-to seven, so she tried the nick first. MacInnes was still there. He said he would be with her by quarter-past. She turned to Valerie. 'My DI says he'll be here at ten-past seven. Now I'm going to need a big favour from you.'

'What's that?'

'I want you to go now and give me ten minutes alone.'

'That's stupid. There's a maniac out there. I'm not leaving you alone.'

'Valerie,' she said softly, 'I *need* this, please.'

'I'll go as soon as your boss gets here.'

'No, Val, you'll go now. Please. This is important to me. I can lock the door behind you but I want to have ten minutes to myself. Please, Val.' He stared at her. He looked more angry than worried. She thought he might still say no.

She spoke firmly, much more loudly. 'Valerie, you cannot be here when my DI arrives.'

'Why not?' he said.

'Please don't make me fight you, Val.'

'Why can't I stay?'

'Because it might be bad for my career,' she said. He glowered at her. 'Because I think you might be a material witness in the Burnley case.'

She knew he would be enraged and right now there was nothing she could do about it. She knew she could easily be in love with Valerie but love, she thought, well it can come and go. It was better for Valerie to go now, better for both of them but especially for her.

'Valerie, I . . .'

'Don't bother with any more explanations!' he snapped.

'Will you be back?'

'Ring me when your boss is due to leave.'

'Is that a yes?' she asked.

He looked with something quite close to hate in his eyes but said it was. As he left she touched his stiff back. He didn't turn round. She closed the door softly behind him and bolted it top and bottom.

The DI didn't arrive until seven-thirty. Caz had let the Rolling Stones CD run its course and then had sat in the silence to think. When the press of the call buzzer broke into her quiet, she flinched. The sudden flush of adrenaline made her feel faintly sick. 'It's Tom MacInnes!' the speaker said. It sounded just like him.

'What's your favourite whisky?' she asked.

'Bell's, Flood. Now stop pissing about. D'yer want t'see me or not?'

'Come on up, Sir!'

'Gidd!' he said. She thought she heard him mutter something.

When he knocked on her flat door she opened it as far as the chain would allow. He was light on the balls of his feet and on edge, his hands behind his back, tension all over his face. She let him in.

'Christ, Flood!' he said. 'You nervous or somethin'?' She told him no, it was just habit. He gave her a thinnish smile. 'Ah suppose it's only good sense fer a girl these days.'

'Just like the police videos, Sir.'

She sat him down and offered him a drink. He took a White & Mackay. She poured a dribble for herself, drowned it in dry ginger, then sat on the far end of the sofa with her legs pulled up under her. He waited.

'Sir . . .' she faltered then took a deep breath. 'Sir, I'm concerned I might have put myself in a compromising position by becoming involved with a potential witness.'

'Who is?'

'Valerie Thomas, Sir; personnel manager at American Express.'

'Why do you think he's a potential witness?'

'He knew Burnley, Sir. I know he's eaten with Burnley's boss. I've been in his flat as well, Sir. He's got a very expensive hi-fi. I checked the back. He bought it at Pearson's Audio so he might well have known Beecham.'

'Is that it?'

'No, Sir. I interviewed Reginald Smith, Burnley's boss. It was just a routine chat. I don't think I logged anything about it. I saw him Saturday night, Sir, eating in Armando's with a young man. And I have a witness who has put Smith with Burnley at the restaurant.'

'Let me get this straight, Flood, you now know that Burnley ate out with his boss and you know that two managers, Smith and Thomas, also ate together? Why's that unusual?'

'Maybe it's not, Sir, but neither of them thought to tell me about it.'

'So?'

'And I think maybe Reg Smith is gay, Sir.'

'Oh, and why is that?'

'Saturday night, Sir. He was with a young man, very pretty . . . I think they call them chickens. He just looked as if—'

'As if he was bent, Flood? A queer? As if he was a queen? A woofter? 'Christ, girl, yer beginnin' to sound like Bob Moore.'

'I'm sorry, Sir, I just thought . . .'

'Thought *what*, girl?'

'Well, Smith, Sir. He looked like . . . when he was with this boy . . . well he looked like there was love in his eyes when I saw him.'

'Really?'

'Yes, Sir. I do think we should talk to him in a bit more detail.'

'You do, huh?'

'Yes, Sir.'

MacInnes finished the drink and ran a nail-bitten finger round the top of the glass. He seemed to be thinking hard. Then he spoke. 'Young lady, I think your radar is on the blink at the moment. I can tell you who the young man is. His name is Smith, first names Adrian John. He's at London University studying English. We never asked him if he was gay; we saw no need. He was down fr'm college for the weekend visiting his father.' Caz looked pale but swung the bottle of White & Mackay towards him.

'Reg Smith has been checked out. He's no alibi for the night Burnley and Green died but he was in Birmingham at a conference when Beecham was killed.' He poured a deeper chunk of whisky. 'But as for Mister Thomas . . .'

She pushed her glass towards him. He poured as he spoke. 'Seems Holmes got to him about the same time as you.'

She could feel bile rising in her throat but MacInnes hadn't finished.

'They fed the beast today. Gave it all Green's clients. One was Thomas. When they gave it Beecham's customers it gave us a long list. If you cross both lists you don't get so many names, but you do get Green and Burnley. You also get Valerie Thomas. He bought a stereo for cash last year.'

'Valerie couldn't be a suspect, Sir! That's ridiculous!' She heard herself talking but she was remembering all those small doubts.

'The connections are there. Why didn't he mention them?'

'Well he did, Sir. He was fairly open about George Burnley.'

'And Green?'

'Well no, Sir, but how long ago did he buy his flat?'

'Eighteen months. And he forgot his building society contact right?'

'Well yes, Sir.'

'Who's yours, Flood?'

'It's a lady, Sir. Her name is Emma Pilbeam. But I've been trained, Sir. I'm a copper. I make a point of remembering things.'

'OK, so what about Peter Beecham? We know that Thomas dealt directly with him at Pearsons.'

'I don't know, Sir. We don't talk about the killings. Valerie thinks the job gets in the way of our love life. The only time I mentioned the third victim, I didn't even use the name.'

'But he must've found out. He'll read the papers.'

'I guess so, Sir.'

'But he's never discussed knowing these men with you? Do you think he should have?'

'Possibly, Sir. But you're making his behaviour out to be suspicious. If he was innocent he really might not have made the connections.' She had a sudden thought and asked the DI what the new papers had said Beecham did for a living.

'He was working at the airport.'

'Well, Valerie could easily have missed the name then, couldn't he?'

'Does the defence wish to call any other witnesses?' MacInnes said.

'No, Sir.'

'OK, but we'll be popping round to see him again. Just in case.'

She could feel her ribs pulsing with a dull pain and she had a mother and a father of a headache. She wanted to be drunk again but she had already decided that wouldn't happen until this case was closed. There was a problem with later. What should she do? How should she behave?

'Sir?' She spoke slowly; ideas were still sorting themselves out in her head. 'Do you think Thomas is a real suspect? Do we know anything else that points to him? What's your gut feeling?'

'We're talking about detecting and not computing?'

'Yes, Sir.'

'Then he never done it.' It wasn't quite final.

'But?'

'Well, it would be nice to ask him just where he was at the time of the deaths, wouldn't it? It would be worth knowing if he did realise about either Peter Beecham or Jim Green.'

'Valerie is supposed to be coming back here later, Sir.'

'When?'

'I was going to ring him when you were due to leave.'

'I thought you said you might be compromised.'

'Yes, Sir, I might be, but I already am now. I'm on sick leave. If you or one of the lads visits him at work I can be kept out of it, can't I?'

'But, Flood, if . . .'

'If he's the killer?'

'Yes.'

'But he's not, Sir.'

'You might be betting your life on it, Flood.'

'I already have and I'm coming out even.'

'What does that mean?'

'Well, Sir. I've met him without anyone knowing where I was going. I've been to remote sites with just him. He's been here in the flat overnight and I've stopped at his place. Don't you think if he was going to do something drastic to me, he already would have?'

'Not necessarily,' MacInnes countered. 'He might be using you to keep an eye on what we're doing.'

'But I don't discuss the case at all, Sir!'

'Are you sure? Are you sure you don't say odd little things about who's on the case, about meetings?'

'Nothing sensitive, Sir, I'm sure of that.'

MacInnes sighed, very slowly and very deeply. He seemed resigned. He had decided to follow his protégé's instincts but worry nagged him.

'I don't think Valerie Thomas is our man, Caz,' he said heavily, 'but something about him, something that's around him, worries me. Now this *is* instinct, but it's as real as it gets.'

'Like me thinking I already know or know of the killer?'

'I guess so, but *you* worry me, Caz.' He was pouring more drink.

'How, Sir?'

'That's the problem. I'm not sure I know. It's as though you attract . . .'

He wasn't going to say it, so she said it for him, 'Death?'

He tried to laugh and said, 'No, trouble.'

'You mean death,' she said.

'No, I don't,' he tried to say but she dived in, 'What am I? A witch?'

'Are you getting drunk?' he said.

'No,' she said, 'but I was earlier tonight.'

'What?'

'It doesn't matter.'

'What doesn't matter?'

'Earlier tonight. I was pissed. I fell over.'

'You mean this *afternoon* you were pissed.'

'Well, yes,' she said, 'sort of. I was upset this morning. I was worried about Valerie Thomas and a bit worried about Reg Smith. Blackside had already told me to get some counselling and you wanted me to take time out. I was upset that no one thought I was man enough for the job.'

'Why d'you think you've got to be a man?'

'I don't, Sir. But if the squad does. If you do and Sergeant Moore does and DCS Blackside does, what chance have I got?'

'You're doing all right, Caz.'

'Yeah,' she said, 'that's why I'm in with Billy Tingle and Moira Dibben playing Space Invaders'

'Don't be so touchy, Flood. The Chief Super wanted a detective in the computer room. Someone who might notice things, instead of blindly typing. First off, I thought he'd picked you simply because you're new and a woman but I think he might've been giving you a back-handed compliment.'

'Felt like it!'

'Now don't be bitchy, Flood. Just take it from me that yer doin' all right.'

'I'm going to put a kettle on,' she said.

From the kitchen she shouted through to the lounge. 'You know, Sir, being out of it has got me thinking . . .' She came back into view at the door. 'There are two loose ends that vaguely worry me.'

He was having another White & Mackay.

'When we picked up Trevor Jones it was because he knew both Green and Burnley and he had a bit of form.'

'Uh-huh. When I jumped the gun a bit . . .'

'But his common-law wife, Sir, Jenny Wilkinson. There's just as much evidence against her. One, she would be connected to both Green and Burnley. Two, she could have been very unhappy about losing her flat. Three, she could be just as anti-gay as Trevor Jones – it was her fellah who was cut up. She might have been having an affair with Burnley or something and there was a woman seen with him just before he was murdered.'

'Hang on a minute!' MacInnes said with a grin. 'Burnley and Green were killed by a *man*. Whether they were homosexual, and whether or not the killer was, hardly matters if we're deciding the *sex* of the killer. There was seminal fluid all over the place, including *in* both Green and Beecham.'

'That's *strong* evidence . . .'

'It's *conclusive* evidence, Flood.'

'With respect, Sir. It's not. What do they say: never presume, always check? We know that semen was present at all three sites and we've *presumed* that the killing was sexually motivated. For all I know, Wilkinson could've killed them all, and some nutty boyfriend could have done his weird whatever to them after they were dead.'

'Oh, fer Christ's sake!'

'I don't actually think that, Sir. What I'm trying to say is that we seem to be so set on seeing these murders as sexual. I've already said that I don't think George Burnley was gay. I'm virtually certain of it.'

'Only virtually?'

'OK, I'm certain.'

The DI sat up a little more and looked with grey eyes as if trying to decide what all this was really about. 'All right, Caz. Let's just say that George Burnley was one hundred per cent heterosexual. Where does that leave us? There's no question at all that a man committed the murders, is there?'

'There's no question that a man was there and ejaculated at some point in the proceedings. But that's not direct evidence that he killed, is it?'

'Never let the best be the enemy of the good,' MacInnes said.

'What, Sir?'

'We don't wait around for the neatest, most perfect explanation of every single fact. If things appear to fit we follow that road until evidence is produced to the contrary. It *appears* that these killings were done by a man. It's a very rare woman who could be so gruesomely vindictive. The victims *appear* to be gay. One positively was, the other two lived alone and may have been. I feel pretty confident that the killer was a gay man.'

'But am I right in saying that we've produced no evidence that Burnley or Beecham was a known homosexual? I presume we've hit every club at least twice by now, and the posters around town have given us no joy. Wouldn't the gay community be keen to clear this thing up? If Burnley and Beecham were gay, shouldn't we have found out by now?'

'OK, Flood, I'll run with you. So we've got what – a psychopathic rapist who attacks men and then kills them?'

'Male rape is not unknown.'

'It's a bit extreme, isn't it?'

'These are extreme killings, Sir.'

'I hadn't noticed . . .' MacInnes said.

'Sir, look. Oh hell, can I call you Tom – you're drinking all my whisky?' He grinned. 'Tom, we've still got these cash amounts, what were they for? Both Jim Green and George Burnley went to Grigglesham Foster – why? I think we should chase the connections through and wait and see on the killer. If we find the link we might find out why the men died.'

'Can *I* speak now?' MacInnes said.

'Sorry, Sir.'

'It's Tom, remember?'

She nodded. MacInnes spoke again. 'We've followed up the Davies death, you know? The guy who fell off his balcony?'

'Yes?'

'There's no argument that he was tipsy. His blood-alchohol was the equivalent of about five pints. His sister told Sergeant Reid that he rarely drank more than a couple of pints, but when pushed a bit she said he'd had four or five at Christmas.'

'He wasn't gay?'

'We don't think so. He lived on his own but he had a regular girl-friend. She told Reid that they had a pretty good sex-life.'

'He had wanted to spend cash-money, same as the rest?'

'According to Avocado.'

'So do we think he was helped over the balcony?'

'He might've been, but we'll never know for sure.'

Caz waited, thinking out loud, 'But if Davies was pushed, and it is something to do with this money, and he wasn't gay, and he wasn't sexually attacked, then . . .'

'Then what?' MacInnes said. 'That's the trouble.'

'Then the sexual element of the three recent deaths may not be the key to finding the killer. It may be incidental or coincidental. It could even be a smokescreen.'

'Oh come *on*, Caz, you're not serious.'

'I'm perfectly serious, Tom. I can give you at least two reasons for someone doing this.'

'I'm all ears.'

'When I was doing my degree, one of my third-year courses was in abnormal psychology. My lecturer once explained how, if he ever had to murder someone, he would cut off their head, wrap it up, and post it to the prime minister.'

'What!'

'Let me finish. Say you decide to kill for practical reasons, access to money or whatever. If you get caught you get life, a minimum of seven years, more likely twelve or more and permanent parole.'

'You're telling *me* that?'

'But if you make the killing "abnormal", by hacking the victim to bits and, as I said, you post the head to the PM. *If* you get caught, then they know you're mad. You end up in Broadmoor or in Park Lane.'

'And that's better?'

'It *is* if you're sane. It *is* if year on year you pass every test they give you. It is if you convince your assessment board that it was an aberration due to drugs or something else. It is if you show a miraculous recovery, spend a few years as a trusty and then get out.'

'Are you sure you're not cracking up yourself?'

'Of course, I'm cracking up! And hacking up a body for reasons of expedience is *not* sick. It might be gruesome and we may imagine all sorts of things, but if it's the difference between being caught and not being caught, then it's common sense. It's all a matter of perspective really.'

'Remind me never to walk down a dark alley with you, Detective!'

'I'm serious, Sir. It *is* a matter of perspective. If someone went around cutting the throats of animals every day we would put him down as a nutter, wouldn't we? But if he was working in a Hal-al butcher's we could justify the behaviour because of its context.'

'Not if he was jumping about and screaming.'

'No comment.'

MacInnes picked up the whisky bottle again, a look on his face that was either exasperation or admiration, maybe both. Caz thought he was going to pour a good measure but then he sighed and put the bottle back down. 'You said there were two reasons?'

'Did I? Oh yes. The other's a smokescreen, like I said.'

'And I said you can*not* be *ser*ious.' His John McEnroe impersonation was awful.

'Don't you find it interesting, Sir, that the one victim that was a known gay *wasn't* savagely attacked about the rectum? Say we'd found him first – ah-hah, a gay killing! Then we find Burnley, similar MO, and he's been brutally attacked so bad that, what was it you said at the time? "We can't even *tell* if he's had anal intercourse!" And Peter Beecham "looked as if a JCB had been driven up his Jacksie". I take it we can't prove that *he* ever had anal sex either.'

'All this because you liked Burnley's flat, Flood?'

'No, Sir! I was lucky if you like. Because I started off with the feeling that George Burnley was interesting to me, that is sexually interesting, I saw a murder but not automatically a gay one. Perspective again.'

'Do you really believe that a straight person could do that sort of thing to another man? And if there wasn't a sexual motive, why the semen stains?'

'I don't know, Tom. I'd have to know what other drives were affecting the killer's behaviour.'

'Like what?'

'I haven't the faintest idea – but soldiers at war have been known to mutilate the enemy's dead and wounded, even castrate them. One form of Zulu execution was to slowly force a spike into the anus! No one has suggested that that was meant to be sexual. It was done to instil fear into the living warriors.'

'OK, OK, let's say I'm impressed. Now tell me where all this gets us.'

'Nowhere, Sir, Tom, but it might stop us going down the wrong route. It might stop us going down the dead-end road that the killer has chosen for us.'

'And go where instead?'

'I'm not sure, but this cash link is peculiar to say the least. If Davies was murdered – if we've got four deaths . . .'

'And he wasn't gay . . .'

'Then maybe whoever our killer is . . .'

'. . . Needed to eliminate people in a hurry and didn't have time to arrange three convenient accidents.'

'So he makes the killings look like something else . . .'

'. . . Like sex attacks,' MacInnes said finally. 'Jesus!'

Caz finally stopped talking long enough to realise she had never finished making the tea. She excused herself, but when she offered the DI a cup he said no, he really ought to go. Her headache came rushing back to pulse across her scalp. 'Thanks for coming round, Tom,' she said as she came back into the room. 'Could I ask you one more thing?'

'Fire away, lass.'

'It's Avocado. Could he have come back from the States in the middle of his holiday?'

'Yes, he could quite easily, but it would be logged on computer by the US Immigration Service. They have a check-in and check-out system, so if he did, his movements would be on record.'

'Then he wouldn't have done that, would he?'

'What?'

'Set up a great alibi – in the States on holiday. He wouldn't have nipped back here, killed Green and Burnley, then nipped back over there?'

'No, unless he's a fool.'

'False passport?'

'When you fly back out you have to be on record as having arrived!'

'So no way?'

'It'll be checked out.'

'Thank you, Sir.'

'No problem,' MacInnes said smiling. 'Can I go now?'

She smiled back from the kitchen doorway. The light that hadn't been there in her eyes when he arrived had come sparkling back. He realised quite suddenly just how pretty she was. She showed him to her door.

Thirty

As soon as Tom MacInnes had gone, Caz went through to the bathroom to check herself in the mirror. When she touched her cheek she could feel its puffiness, but it looked OK, only noticeable if you were looking for it. Her ribs were still sore but she decided they weren't cracked. Only her head really ached. She went back into the kitchen to grab a couple of paracetamols and her tea. Then she called Valerie. There was no answer.

She cursed, but only lightly. Then she redialled the number. A distant brrr-brrr repeated in her ear. No answer. She decided to allow it twenty rings. While the far-off double tone continued, she flicked on the stereo and pressed 'go'. The Stones' CD was still in the machine and the heavy blues guitars of 'Jumping Jack Flash' pumped out at her. Still no answer. *Now* she was annoyed. The remains of the whisky looked at her. She thought about it, but grabbed her hot drink instead. Then the phone rang.

'Valerie?' she said, a flutter of relief in her voice. There was no answer. 'Is that you Valerie? I just rang and...' The silence was hot, fat and black.

'Valerie?'

'*No, Cunt!*' the voice said. There was nothing else. Nothing. She could feel the cold steel of a knife coming up into her. No breathing. Nothing. Just blood-red silence, something animal out there. She expected to feel weak and terrified.

Instead, someone who was vaguely her retaliated. '*Fuck you, Wanker!*' she shouted. 'What's wrong? Can't you get it up?'

The phone went dead. She dialled a number straightaway.

This time, when she connected with Valerie's flat, the line was engaged. She replaced the receiver. She felt cold and sick. Then very angry.

The phone rang again. She watched it as if it throbbed. She stood up and looked at the two fat bolts on the inside of her front door. She took a deep breath. Ready. She picked up the receiver but did not speak.

'Caz? Hello?' It was Valerie's voice, slightly breathless. 'Caz? Caz?'

She put the telephone down. Eleven seconds later it rang again. This time when Valerie spoke her name she said, 'Oh hi, Val, there must've been something wrong with the line. I was speaking, but you couldn't hear me.'

'Christ! For a minute there, you had me worried,' Valerie said. 'I was imagining all sorts of things. Are you all right?'

'I'm fine, Val. Why shouldn't I be?'

'I'm sorry,' he said, 'Jeff came round. I went for a quick pint with him.'

'That must've been nice for you.'

'You said you wanted an hour and I did say I was sorry.'

'Yeah, you did.'

'I'll come round now. Was that you ringing me?'

'When?'

'A couple of minutes ago. I could hear the phone going and I belted up the stairs but it rang off just as I got to it.'

'No, it wasn't.'

'Oh well, is your inspector still with you? Is it OK to come round now?'

'Yes, Valerie, you can come out now,' she said.

'What?'

'You can come round now. I'll cook.'

'I'll be there in six minutes.'

'Goodbye, Valerie.'

'Six minutes,' he said.

Valerie could not see her slightly strange smile as she went through to the kitchen. As he was driving towards her flat he did not see her savagely butchering an onion with a large vegetable knife. She was skinning and flattening a garlic bulb as he drove the length of the promenade and she was pounding the life from some steak as his Jaguar pulled up outside.

She had prepared for him, and by the time he stepped through the unbolted front door she was actually smiling, her whole face pink and bright.

'You're looking better!' he said spontaneously.

Caz smiled back, 'I know.' She still had the knife in her hands. There was a glint of pure joy in her eyes.

He went into her parlour. He didn't notice but she had taken the phone just off the hook.

She made a light stroganoff with yoghurt and twice the normal amount of mushrooms. The boiled rice she served with it was light and fluffy. Valerie seemed pleased with the meal as if it was a carefully cooked peace offering. He didn't notice that the wine, Don Darias, was about a third the price of his girlfriend's usual serving. Caz had decided that a more expensive wine might be a waste tonight.

The look in her eye was different now, somehow harder, but ill defined, as though her words, her thoughts and her actions weren't truly parallel. Right now it seemed she was apologising.

'...and it's all I ever really wanted to do. My dad was a

Sweeney, in the Flying Squad. He got crippled by a blagger during a bank raid, a guy called McKay. Dad was half a second in front of the rest of the team and McKay cut him down with a sawn-off shotgun. Because my dad still had his revolver McKay shot him a second time, in the back. He never walked again.'

Valerie mumbled, as if commiserating, but she ignored it. 'McKay was hit by rounds from five Smith & Wessons. He died more or less instantly. When Dad came out of Stoke Mandeville hospital they offered him a desk job and he tried it for six months. He packed it in because he was too near to the action and he still wanted to catch villains. He said it hurt him too much. I was nearly sixteen then, just about to do my O-levels. He came home in his converted mini one evening and just said he was never going back.'

'What about your mum?' Valerie said.

'Mam and Dad had split up when I was about six. She married a chap called Graham and I lived with them after the divorce. She died four years later in a car crash and I went back to live with my dad when I was eleven.'

Val raised his eyebrows. He knew how unusual that was.

'I won't bore you with all the details. There was a time when they weren't going to let Dad look after me, but he fought like hell. Eventually I was allowed home, but we had to have a female live-in so that there was always someone there when I got home from school.'

'And who was that?'

'Oh, we had hundreds. My dad was almost impossible to live with and I was very independent. I think the longest one of them ever lasted was about three months. Then Dad managed to persuade his sister to move in upstairs and the courts forgot about us.

'All we ever talked about was policing, and all I ever wanted to do was be a copper. Dad never tried to dissuade me, but he did make me promise to get a qualification that I could use elsewhere. I thought a psychology degree was a good compromise.

'Dad knew one thing. If they are committed, coppers nearly always have miserable love lives. I think that's why he wanted me to have a second string to my bow. It's very hard to maintain a good relationship with lousy hours, the danger and the stress.'

'Are you trying to tell me something?' Valerie asked heavily.

'If you mean is this a kiss-off, no,' Caz said back, 'but if you mean there will be times like tonight, times when the job, *my* job, my career comes first, then the answer is "probably".'

Valerie said he could live with 'probably'.

'OK then, how about definitely?' she asked.

'I'll let you know,' he said.

They picked at their food and drank steadily. Valerie asked what her father was doing now. She told him. He did a bit of work as a consultant, advising banks on security and he was trying to write a book about the Sweeney. Caz forgot her resolution and about the price of wine. When the Spanish red was finished, she sent Valerie through to the bedroom for a bottle of *Il Grigio*. While he was gone, she grabbed two fresh glasses, turned down the lights and went through into the lounge.

They sat at opposite ends of the big sofa listening to sombre cello music from one or other of the Webbers. Both of them had their feet up off the floor and they touched in the middle, toe-to-toe in a tiny competition.

'So what time did Jeff call you?' Caz asked casually. She felt sure he would sense the edge in her throat.

'He didn't,' Valerie said innocently, 'he was waiting for me when I got home from here. What was that? About seven, I suppose.'

'Did you have a nice pint? Where d'you go?'

'Just up the road from the flat. There's a pub called the Grapes. You probably know it. It's an old-fashioned drinker.'

'I know it,' she said. 'What did you talk about?'

'What? Oh, lots of things. We talked a bit about micro-lighting and about our trip to Portugal. I think we talked a bit about women but not much. He asked after you. I said you'd got yourself pissed this afternoon and had had a bit of an accident. I don't usually keep secrets from Jeff, but I didn't tell him about you being attacked. When he asked after you he made me feel guilty. I shouldn't have left you, no matter what you said.'

'Well you did.'

'I know I did!' he said firmly. 'You got me to go because your Chief Inspector was coming. You pretty damn well threw me out! Do you think I *wanted* to go? Do you? How do you think I *felt* right then?'

'I don't know, Val. So why *did* you go?'

'Because you asked me to. Because your boss was coming. Because you said it was important.' He stiffened. She could feel guilt tinged with anger building right through his body, 'I went because you wanted me to go!'

'I'm sorry, Valerie. And I'm grateful. Really, I am. I think more of you because you went. Most men would have wanted to be macho and stay, but you trusted me. I'm grateful for that. Can we drop it? You were saying, you and Jeff? You said you were talking about women . . . ?'

'More or less. Jeff knows about most of my relationships over the years. I'm not exactly the luckiest bloke in love. Jeff doesn't seem to do all that well with the ladies either, though God knows why, he's good looking enough! Every girlfriend I've ever had seems to take an interest in him.'

'*Every* girlfriend?' Caz said. 'How long have you two been mates, then?'

'About for ever, I reckon. Jeff and I go back right to secondary school in Liverpool. We played in the same soccer team. I played as centre-forward and Jeff played on the wing. He was *very* good you know; some lads reckoned he could have gone professional. Me, I was just a decent park player. Every game Jeff would say, "I'll give you two goals today but you're not having three, it'll go to your head." He really was that good. He could walk the ball in on his own but he got more of a kick laying goals on for me.' Their feet were touching. She could feel him relaxing a little.

'It must be nice to have friends like that.'

'Maybe,' Valerie said, thinking. 'Jeff would hang out with me all the time if he had half a chance. It's great when I'm between girl-friends and on a downer – and that's a bit more often than I'd like – but there are times when a man wants to be on his own, you know, like now.'

'On his own?'

'You know what I mean, Caz.' He smiled for the first time that night.

'But I became a man, I put away childish things,' Caz said.

'Men never *quite* do that,' Valerie smiled again, 'we just exchange our cheaper toys for fast motor cars and water-skis; in mine and Jeff's case we swapped our Dinkies for a couple of micro-lights.'

'You both had micro-lights, yeah? You bought them at the same time?'

'Not to start with. Jeff was a bit richer than me, family

money. We trained to fly together and, when we'd qualified, he bought a Flash Two. You can double up in one of them. We used to go up together.'

'And then you crashed it for him?'

'Yep.'

'I'm amazed he ever forgave you.'

'Well, it's a long story. At the time I was really into a girl called Debbie, who worked as a research student at Southampton University. She was my first serious relationship after Kathy. We'd met in a pub in Salisbury when Jeff and I were out intending to get badly pissed. I managed to get her telephone number before we disappeared on our pub crawl.'

'We *are* still talking about your crash?'

'Yes. I told you it was a long story.'

She pouted to order.

'Anyway, at the time, Jeff and me were doing just about everything together. Apart from a few one-night stands, I'd hardly bothered with women. But Debbie was different and I fell really bad for her. I wouldn't like to say now if it was love or not, but it was definitely heavy.'

'So what happened?'

'Well, this is weird. Debbie started getting roses sent to her every day. First off, she thought it was me being a romantic and she quite liked it. When I said I hadn't sent them she thought I was being coy.'

'But you weren't sending them?'

'No. I couldn't afford to now, and then, by comparison, I was a pauper.'

'So who was sending them?'

'We never found out, but Deb was totally convinced it was me. Every day these flowers kept turning up where she worked and, instead of being something lovely, she started seeing them as sinister. Debbie got madder and madder and then one day she called in the police.'

'What happened then?'

'Not a lot, basically. They gave me a hard time but I told them that if I was rich, I *would* be sending her flowers, but I couldn't because I didn't have any money.

'The next thing I knew, Debbie wouldn't see me at all. I rang her, I wrote to her, but she ignored everything I did. I just wanted to tell her it wasn't me. I was going crazy. By now I was convinced that I loved her and that there was this almighty conspiracy to keep us apart.'

'Let me guess the next bit. You went to see her at her home?'

'Almost. I went to see her where she worked. At the university. Next thing I knew two heavy security guards were bundling me out of the building and a couple of days later she got a court injunction stating that I couldn't contact her or go within half a mile of her.'

'Wow!'

'The worst bit was Deborah herself. When she turned on me, she was like a wild-cat, spitting and snarling at me. I was heart-broken. When I got the injunction I was almost suicidal. Jeff came round and slapped a bit of sense into me. She was only a woman and all that – you know – plenty of fish in the sea, that sort of thing. Then he persuaded me to go micro-lighting for the weekend near Salisbury. He said I could use his Flash Two.'

'And this was the weekend you crashed?'

'I didn't exactly *crash*. Well, OK, I did. But it was a bit more complicated than that. What happened was that I was turning quite hard, pushing the Flash Two to the limit, a bit stupid, but actually still inside the envelope, as they say. I had just turned quite tightly to drop under these wires when there was a crack and I lost control. I didn't drop quickly enough, and instead of flying underneath these electrical cables I ploughed straight into them.'

'Oh my God!'

'Oh, it wasn't that bad. I wasn't scared. More like acutely embarrassed. There was a huge bang, a blue flash and a lot of smoke. Then I was sitting on the ground with a few bits of the Flash Two and I smelt a bit funny.'

'You weren't hurt at all?'

'My hair was burnt a bit, that was about it.'

'Did Jeff not go mad?'

'Nope. He told me it was all his fault. He said that I was distraught over Deborah and he should never have let me take the micro-light up. He knew he was a better pilot than I was and Flash Twos are definitely harder to fly. I remember I was still sitting there when he got to me and he asked me to forgive him. I quite literally pissed myself laughing.

'Anyway, Jeff got the bulk of the insurance money and he got himself another Flash Two. A year or so later I got myself a Flash One and we got a fair bit of flying in. About two years ago I had the chance of the Jag and I needed to sell the plane. Jeff gave me market price and he still lets me fly it whenever I want.'

'Doesn't that surprise you?'

'Not really. I'm the best friend Jeff's ever had. We go back a long, long way. As teenagers we were *very* close. I think he figured that if I wasn't able to fly any more we'd see each other less. No, it doesn't surprise me.'

Caz was lost. Her face pointed at him but her eyes were somewhere else, focused on a distant thought. She leaned forward slightly, putting her arms round his lower legs, then she pulled him towards her. Valerie slipped awkwardly down the sofa's arms before sitting up, then he was upright and they were eye-to-eye. She held his gaze. She waited, breathing calmly.

Then she asked him if he had alibis for the murder nights.

Thirty-one

His face never changed. She had been prepared for any kind of indignant outburst but not the sudden look, only in his eyes, of almost pure hatred. The darkness was gone as quickly as it had come, but it was as if something that had bound them together had instantaneously and irrevocably snapped. He smiled almost maniacally as he answered her.

'Why would I need an alibi, Caz?'

She began to lie. 'My DI has linked you to all three victims. I told him he was mad but I think they will be coming to see you tomorrow.'

'And you were only thinking of me, right?'

'Yes.'

'You lie like a cheap watch . . .' he said, looking away.

She saw misery waiting for her on the next corner.

'I'm telling you the *truth*, Valerie! You knew Burnley and you knew Green. And you bought your fancy stereo from Peter Beecham!'

'What d'you mean, I knew Green? I've never ever met the guy!'

'Who did you get your mortgage from?'

'You obviously know, so why are you asking me?'

'According to DI MacInnes, you got the mortgage on your flat from the Nationwide Building Society and you dealt with Jim Green. According to records you were interviewed by him when you first applied and just before you finally had your offer.'

'That's crap!' He was sitting up now, bristling. 'I don't know the guy!'

'It's on record, Val.'

'I don't give a *shit* what's on bloody record!' He swung his feet to the floor. 'I'm telling you; I have never met anyone called Jim Green!'

Valerie stood up. Caz looked at him, trying to stay calm. She felt beneath the sofa for the kitchen knife.

'If we showed you a picture, would that help?'

'We? We?' He was spinning with frustration. 'I thought *you* were worried about what your *boss* thought!'

'I meant we as in "the police", Val. I'm still a copper, you know.'

'Oh, I *do* know that!' He glowered at her, his anger making him look less than pleasant. She asked him very softly to sit back down.

'Why the *fuck* should I sit down?' he spat back at her. 'I don't *want* to sit down!'

'You're frightening me, Val.'

'Tough!' he said coldly. 'Me, I feel just dandy!'

'I'm sorry, Val. Please?' She gestured towards his end of the settee but he strode quickly away as if about to go somewhere important. Then he turned and rushed back towards her. His hands were flying about him, rage and frustration threatening to burst out uncontrollably.

'Jesus, Caz! I picked you up from the pavement just a few hours ago. How could you even *suspect* me of killing three blokes?'

'*I* don't, Valerie,' she said. She was talking very calmly, still tapping the cushion. 'And I don't think my DI does either. He's concerned that you had a connection with the three victims and you never mentioned it.'

'I didn't bloody *know*!'

'You said. You'll just have to tell the DI that as well.'

'You're not sure, are you?' he said slowly. 'You think that you might have slept with a maniac, don't you? You're not convinced it wasn't me!'

She could feel the cold steel of the blade, the black bone of the handle. 'You've read the papers, Valerie. The men were killed by a homosexual maniac.' She tried to flutter her eyelashes, 'You forget I know you.'

'Oh, you mean that because I screwed you a few times I'm off the hook? That won't be good enough for your DI. I could be AC-DC, couldn't I, putting up a good show for you just to keep up appearances and getting my real kicks from knocking blokes off?'

'I can't believe that, Valerie. I just can't. If I thought that I wouldn't be here with you now. I wouldn't be alone with you.'

'Am I really in trouble?' he asked. 'If I didn't do it? Will I be all right?'

He collapsed on to the sofa. Without anger's adrenaline he looked wasted.

'You'll be OK,' she said, 'I guarantee it.'

'But how can you be so sure? The police still make mistakes.'

'We can be sure, Val. There are ways. When we catch our man we can be absolutely certain about his guilt. Just as if you wanted to we could totally eliminate you from suspicion.'

'How?'

She realised she couldn't say, so she blustered, 'By providing us with your alibis for a start . . .' There was a pause. '. . . And there are other ways, technical ways to clear someone or to confirm guilt.'

'You mean like fingerprints, that sort of thing?'

'Yes, Val,' she said, calm again, 'fingerprints, that sort of thing.'

He looked a little older, grey and definitely unhappy. She uncurled and got up, leaving the knife under the settee. As she stood, she touched him lightly, trying to regain contact but he was cold and detached.

She went through to the kitchen and came back with two tumblers of gold liquid. Hanging from her fingers was a large plastic bottle of coke. 'Your favourite,' she said, offering him a glass, 'Southern Comfort.'

'I thought you hated it,' he said, waking up.

'No, I said it tasted like cough mixture. I *love* cough mixture.'

'Where's the bottle?' he said. She nodded towards the kitchen.

'Please don't get pissed,' she said.

'Why not?'

'Because you're here to look after me, remember?'

'And you really need that, right?'

She didn't answer. He poured a little coke into his glass and a lot into hers. She tried to find his eyes but he was still hurt. She whispered his name more than once, but he appeared not to hear her.

'You want that?' he said after a while, nodding at her drink.

'Not as much as you,' she said.

She knelt at his feet and put her head in his lap. Eventually he put his hand on the nape of her neck. She was bare and open to him, her neck exposed, like a defeated dog with its offered throat. His fingers moved beneath her hair, first stroking gently, then kneading, seeking out the tensions around her medulla. She could feel his strength as she closed her eyes, and she groaned a peculiar bliss as he found the spot. She begged him not to stop.

He began to talk softly as he worked at her neck. His fingers and thumbs reached either side as far as the hollows behind her ears. The first time she tried to speak he pushed gently down to stop her interrupting.

'When all that happened with Deborah –' he pressed on the borderline between pain and ecstasy – 'I was frightened as well as hurt . . .' She moved slightly, the top of her head against his abdomen. 'What really freaked me out was the sensation of being totally unable to prove that I hadn't done anything. I was being swept along by a tide and I could do nothing about it.' His fingers continued. 'A bloke can't cope with that. Blokes need to be able to bring their problems into the light and face them. It was as if . . .' He stopped. She felt his grip on her neck as it changed.

'I haven't got an alibi for that Friday night, so I could've killed George Burnley. Jeff and I were supposed to be going to South Wales. He rang me to say he had car trouble and he'd be there at about ten. The bother turned out to be worse than he expected. He didn't arrive until midnight. I was alone at home all evening and I can't prove it.'

Caz had guessed right. He had no alibi. She climbed on to the sofa and lay down with her head in his lap, turning her head towards him, face up, exposing her white throat. Valerie ran his manicured fingers lightly up and down her presented neck. Despite her injuries, and the aches that rolled regularly through her, his gentle touch was gradually arousing her. The peculiar dangers she had placed herself in aroused her too. She could speak now. 'I suppose . . . the night Beecham died?'

'You'll love this,' Val sighed, 'but I was stopping in the Gatwick Hilton. A two-day personnel managers' conference with an overnight stop.'

'Witnesses?'

'Plenty. And plenty to say that I went off to bed early. What time did they say Beecham died?'

'Two in the morning.'

'Well, I might have been at an all night card-game but I wasn't.'

She let the resulting silence grow until it was a heavy presence in the room. A hopeful idea came to her. 'You go to Portugal every Christmas, don't you? For how long?'

'A couple of weeks.'

'Exactly? When do you normally get back?'

'It varies. This year we started back at work on the sixth of January, so the fifth I guess.'

'Are you sure, Val?'

'I started back on the Monday. We flew back on the Sunday. Yes, I'm sure.'

'Well, this is a hard one for you. Have you any idea what you did that night – the evening of your first day back?'

'I know exactly!' His voice was fractionally lighter. 'I ate out with Jeff early on. We talked about the holiday. Jeff lived in Midhurst then, so he stopped over at my place rather than drive back. We had a meal in Le Chanteclere, that little french bistro in the Lanes. Then we came back here and had a few drinks.'

'So you were together all evening?'

'Yep. I was dead tired. I'd fancied getting pissed with me mate but I was out like a light not long after we got back. I woke up in the morning slumped in one of the chairs opposite Jeff. I remember, I ached all day.'

'And Jeff could vouch for you?'

'Of course! I said – we were together all night.'

He held her for another hour, her face cupped in his hands. She drifted into sleep and when she stirred, still in his lap, she was aware again of her aches and pains. Her groan woke him. It was late enough for bed and, as he creaked into life he said he'd make her a drink.

She went ahead, grateful for Valerie's help and for his simply being there. She wished the night's interrogation had never happened, but consoled herself with the fact that Jeff could provide an alibi for the night Davies had died. It was only when she was eventually in her bed that she realised that they still didn't know if that death was a murder.

When he stripped for bed she watched his hard body reveal itself. It was crazy, but even half-hospitalised she wanted him. He slipped into the bed beside her and kissed her softly on the lips. She decided to try.

She raised a hand to gently pull his face on to hers. She could sense him walking on glass as he pecked tenderly at her face. He was supporting himself on one arm, too afraid to let any passion go. She chased his mouth with a tiny, eager, tongue until he began to respond. Finally he did. His mouth was warm and tasted of chocolate.

She rolled away from him and pulled his arm over her body, pushing herself back towards him. He kissed her behind the ear and, as he moved, she felt a sharp pain in one rib. She buried the cry and willed him to take her from behind. She wanted to say 'I love you', but she thought that if she did, he would get up from the bed and leave her alone.

His position changed slightly, and she felt a hand gently lift her thigh. Then he was between her legs, not inside her, but clamped into the deep wetness of her. He hardly moved, barely rocking. She held a hand against it all, directing the friction, and his tiny movements began to warm her like soft, growing music.

The waves of pleasure grew in her, washing up from her sex and down from her shoulders, meeting somewhere in her stomach and sprinkling heat in all directions. She could feel his right hand, the fingernails on her shoulders, tracing across the strong muscle there. She had become so sensitive, his nails were like electrodes passing over her.

She reached down to unceremoniously push him inside. They hadn't said a single word and now she heard him gasp. His hand was in front of her and she began to lightly bite the fingers. Then, with the words masked by his hand, she told him not to wait.

Every time she moved at all her ribs screamed, but as he began to make a growling noise and push harder, she pushed towards him, drawing herself tightly closed with her eyes clamped firmly shut against the pain. Then she could sense his control going. She heard his breath change and felt his teeth on her back before he called her name from deep down in his gut. She felt the hot milky pulse of his release filling her up and heard him cry out. Then he began to weep, softly, as if he was trying hard not to be heard. They fell asleep like that, the awkward mess of loving forgotten until, some time deep in the night their bodies slipped apart, like a petal dropping from a flower.

She woke in the morning to the fawn smell of the night before and red-brown blood dust colouring her pillowcase. Valerie's left arm was around her, heavy and protective, and she kissed his wrist lightly before slipping underneath him and away. She was grinning when she began to move but was taken up short by the needling pain still present from one rib. She escaped to the bathroom.

Her hair was a mess, its straw marked by overnight brown blood and a tiny core of seeping bright red. The micropore bandage covering her shoulder wound was gone and the light knife-marks, though crusted, had also bled in the night.

Even her face had betrayed her, the make-up now rubbed away and the start of half a shiner, purple-green, was faintly visible below one eye. She stared at the mirror then poked her tongue out with a half-serious 'urgh!' at herself. A bath was running beside her and as it filled she took aim at the day.

When she emerged half an hour later she looked five years younger and ten years fitter. Valerie, typically male, had slept through everything.

She made toast and coffee, put 'Bat Out of Hell' on loud and waited for him to wake. When he padded through she pointed him at a bubbling pot of Kenco and cursed him for looking so human. He grinned and told her it was clean-living wot done it fer 'im. Then he leaned back in from the kitchen and added, 'Oh, and lots of sex!'

'Who with?' she said.

For the second time in her life love threatened her.

Thirty-two

Valerie left her at seven-thirty with a parting kiss, light enough not to excite, and a hug soft enough to spare her ribs. As soon as he was walking down the stairs she closed her door and rebolted it top and bottom. The secure brogues of early morning Radio Four came thickly through from the bedroom as she went back into the small kitchen to make some more toast. It was her racing breakfast, two rounds of wholemeal, no fat, spread with honey. Then she lay quietly on the soft sofa to eat, rest and think.

The telephone rang at seven forty-five. She had drifted into near-sleep and didn't respond to it until the third ring. She rolled from her rest by the fifth and picked it up on the sixth. Whoever had dialled her had just rung off. She looked into the phone as if to see right down the line, then shrugged and shuffled back to her warm cushions. As she relaxed into the sofa's softness, the phone rang again. She grinned and got back up, reaching the receiver by the third ring. This time she was quick enough to hear the electronic clunk of the caller disconnecting.

Her mood was still placid. Smiling at the grey plastic, she picked it up, trailing the cord across the room as she went back to lie down once more on the sofa. She lay back for the third time, now with the phone on her stomach, her hand ready on the handset. This time she was made to wait for minutes. On the first half-ring she snatched at the plastic and quickly said, 'Hello?' She was speaking to silence. She thought of wires laid in clay, lines that swept across streets, fingers passing through switches and relays leading from something out there to here. Someone lurking darkly. Something, someone, able to reach out into her home and touch her.

She left the phone off its hook, not interested in playing the caller's game. Then she finished the remains of her toast and went looking for her purse. Patrick Tomlinson's number was in a small black notebook. She replaced the receiver briefly then dialled him. His phone rang seven or eight times before being picked up and then a drugged voice said, 'Hello?'

'Is that Patrick Tomlinson? It's DC Flood.'

'DC Oo?' the other voice said. 'Bloody 'ell! What time is it?'

'It's eight o'clock.'

'Well, it feels like six o'clock. Give a bloke a break, eh? I 'ad a real skinful last night. My mouth is like the bottom of a bird-cage . . .'

She interrupted, 'You said to ring, Mr Tomlinson.'

'Yeah, I know. Look, I've only just gorrup. Give us yer number and I'll ring you back in ten minutes.'

She didn't fall for it. 'It's OK,' she said, 'I'll ring you at ten-past.'

She put down the phone. No way was a creep like Tomlinson getting her telephone number! There was time for another coffee, so she nipped through to the kitchen to flick the kettle back on. She thought about Pat Tomlinson, what a low-life! If he had her number she might never get rid of him. That was why she had always been ex-directory. She was *very* choosy about who had her number.

She was tea-spooning coffee into a fresh mug when she thought, the caller – the sick bastard last night, and this same idiot this morning – was it a random-dialling sicko or had someone chosen her, *specifically* her?

But to do that they had to have her home telephone number. In six months she had only given two people that. Tom MacInnes. And Valerie.

When she rang Tomlinson again she had a hard cast to her mouth that he was lucky he couldn't see. This time he was wide-awake.

'Hell-ohh there,' he drawled, a long drawn-out medallion-man's hello.

'Good morning, Patrick!' Caz said smartly. 'I trust that you have now cleaned your teeth?'

'What? Oh, yeah.'

'About these appointments . . . ?'

'No problem,' he said. 'Two tonight and the third one tomorrer.'

'Excellent. What time shall I meet you?'

'The first appointment is over in Hove at seven o'clock. Where do you live? I can pick you up say half-six, quarter-to seven.'

She had to give him marks for persistence! 'No, that's OK. I'll be with my boss in Hove this afternoon. I'll meet you at six forty-five in Church Road, outside the tourist information place.'

'The other appointment is in Peacehaven at nine.'

'We'll talk about that tonight.'

'Suit yerself,' he said.

'Thanks, I will. And thank you for your help, Patrick.'

'No probs, duck! Do us a small favour tonight, would you?'

'Which is?'

'Wear something *really* short? I don't care, but the punters love it.'

'Six forty-five,' she said.

She put the phone down. He was so thick-skinned and arrogant she almost liked it. Presumably, somewhere in his life, his strategy worked.

At nine she rang Grigglesham Hall. She wanted to confirm she would be taking up Rachel Hely's invitation to stay the weekend. When she had first dialled the number she hadn't thought about it, but as the telephone's distant burr–burr buzzed back at her she realised she would really like to say good morning to Rachel Hely.

Last night, Tom MacInnes had said that the clinic was clean. She believed him and she instinctively knew that he was right. So why did she feel such a desire to be there?

She got through to a secretary who said that neither Rachel nor the professor were available, but would she care to leave a message?

'When will they be free?' Caz asked.

'They are working in the laboratory wing until about twelve o'clock. Shall I say you'll call them back at twelve-thirty?'

'That's ideal, thank you.'

'And it's . . . ?'

'I am sorry,' Caz said, 'I do apologise. It's Detective Constable Flood, Caz Flood.'

She was thinking about George Foster and Special Branch warning them off.

'Oh!'

Caz heard the flutter in the voice and quickly corrected herself, 'Oh, I do apologise. I should have said. This is a social call. I'm supposed to be spending next weekend at the hall with Rachel.'

The tone of the second 'Oh' was totally different. Caz continued. 'I wonder if you could mention it to Rachel? I've suddenly found myself free on Thursday and Friday. My friend will be travelling for the weekend and he will arrive separately, but I would quite like to take up the offer she made of a little extra rehabilitation. I could do with beefing up.'

'Are you unwell?' the voice said professionally.

'Not exactly,' Caz said.

'But you are a little thin?'

'Not really.'

'Our guests usually choose to dress in our casual clothing. Will you be . . . ?'

'Please, yes. I'm a size ten, very occasionally an eight.'

'So, just a *little* thin,' Caz sensed the scribbling at the other end. She was probably a size fourteen.

'And your height, Miss Flood?'

'I'm five feet seven.'

'Hair colour?'

'What?'

'Could I have your hair colour?'

'It's blonde,' Caz said, faintly bemused. Then she thought, maybe they need a description for security reasons.

'Eyes?'

She said 'what?' and immediately, 'Green.' She interrupted before the other end could ask for her weight and date of birth. 'Excuse me, but is all this necessary? I'm stopping with you as a house guest, not a patient.'

'Miss Flood,' the tone was of an unleashed hospital receptionist, 'I *do* apologise. We never have patients, *everyone* who stops here is a guest. We like to allocate rooms to our friends according to certain criteria . . .' The secretary left her superior knowledge hanging in the air. 'I will make the arrangements for your stay now, arriving Thursday morning.'

'Thank you,' Caz said.

'And if you'll ring Miss Rachel at twelve-thirty . . .'

'I'll be glad to.'

The secretary spoke again. 'My name is Mrs Oakley. If you ring again you will probably get me. If you don't come directly through to me, please ask for Margaret in the office. Now, there are just a few other small points . . .'

'OK,' Caz said, then she said impulsively, 'Margaret, I know it's a funny question, but do you have a sister, Annie, early thirties? I met a lady in the Drunken Preacher last week. She sounded very much like you and she said she had a sister working at Grigglesham Hall . . .'

'That's our Annie.'

'Annie Oakley!'

'She used to be. Her name is Lewis now. Her husband is Teddy Lewis. They live in the village. He's the local handyman and joiner. Nice bloke.'

Caz laughed lightly, 'Well, Margaret, I feel as if I already know you.' There was a little laugh back, then they got back down to business.

'These other few questions, Miss Flood? Could I?'

'Of course,' Caz said.

'First off, is blonde your natural hair colour?'

Thirty-three

When Caz rang John Street, DI MacInnes was on a lead and not expected back before eleven o'clock. Bob Moore was unavailable. When she queried the desk, the WPC she was speaking to told her his board actually said 'unavailable until further notice'. She left a message for the DI to contact her as soon as possible.

She could feel her chest bruises again, so took a couple of Nurofen with a slick of milk. Then she began to pace the floor waiting for the drug to work. The lounge curtains were still closed and she moved to draw them back. Without really choosing to, she found herself looking down and scanning the street below for strange cars or waiting people. It was cool and overcast outside and the street was empty. She heard a toppling milk bottle and felt her ears prick up. If he was out there, she looked forward to meeting him. She decided on a short walk.

She was wearing her near-regulation Levi 501s when she came from the bedroom, but her trainers were sensibly replaced with low-heeled black shoes. Her chest had been doused with a cold anaesthetic spray, powdery, stinging and white, and the marks were now covered with a man's singlet underneath her favoured Russell Athletic sweat-top. Her money and keys were in a small leather wallet which hung from her belt, and the black-diamonded riding crop was strapped to her left forearm by a single turn of Micropore tape. Enough of the leather grip protuded for the whip to be grabbed quickly. Enough was hidden, she hoped, so that she still looked defenceless.

Her room looked quiet and dusty, faint winter light diagonal across the floor. She looked around once and felt satisfied. Vincent and her other piggies were stacked in one corner, staring at her with beady eyes.

She undid both top and bottom bolt on the door, turned the knob on the inside of the Yale lock and pulled. Her very being bristled with expectation as she faced an empty hall. She took a breath and went for it. Without looking left or right she stepped out and walked straight down the crimson stairs. At the bottom, envelopes were scattered on the brown hall tiles.

She went out and gasped at the cool day. Sun was almost breaking through and the street was streaked with gold. Steps and railings glistened with dew-damp. Despite everything, something made her feel good. She took a deep breath against her protesting ribs.

At the bottom of her steps she glanced up the hill at the gardens which created a cul-de-sac of the road. She turned left to walk down the slope towards the front. Cars cruised both ways every fifteen or so seconds. Beyond them the sea was grey and broken.

She lowered her head as if ducked against a biting wind but her eyes were turned to the horizontal, sharp and wary. Without a band tying back her hair it hung below shoulder length, lifting gently in the light wind and dropping occasionally across her powdered face. A strange excitement made her feel half an inch taller. Her shoulders felt more powerful and she imagined sharp claws on the ends of her fingers instead of her neatly cut, half-mooned nails.

She walked steadily but less than purposefully. Compared to the lithe animal she was when she ran, she seemed to lack power and looked both ordinary and vulnerable. The morning light was quickly changing, the sun flitting furtively behind wispy clouds like eyes in the bushes. The cars that passed meant nothing to her, eyeless cocoons, mere background as she walked.

She was drifting towards town and crossed the road in a gap between the cars before pausing, then climbing down on to the beach. The sea's stink welled up against her: seaweed, seagulls and nose-flaring salt. She wished that she was running, energised by red-blooded glory rather than walking, stoked up by this cross between lust and fear.

Slumping her shoulders she trudged across the shingle, heading almost miserably for the rusting West Pier. Without actually seeing it, from the corner of her awareness she thought she sensed a dark figure up on the promenade, walking slowly towards Hove. As she stooped to pick up pebbles, the figure paused imperceptibly and, as she turned to whip the stones across the water, it moved on again, the stutter in its passage hardly noticeable.

The back of her head buzzed like sunburnt skin. She willed something to confront her now, something absolute, something deadly. She needed the gory finality of facing up to the danger. She walked slowly, the realisation that this lumbering fear was somehow faintly pleasurable almost making her cock her head in surprise.

Salten sea-damp slithered away through the pebbles as she moved, and she bent to take up some before throwing them, one by one, on to the water, making them skip in threes and four before they dived to their own little oblivion in the sea. She waited there.

Minutes passed, but nobody crunched through the shingle towards her. Casually, she turned away from the waves, a gust fluffing spray up round her ears. In either direction she saw no one, and no one walked up on the road. She felt like spitting in disgust.

While she walked she touched her scalp where yesterday something had struck her. The bump was long and thin from two inches above her ear right to the front edge of her hairline. It rose like a fat pillow from her skull, smooth and swollen but with a subtle dip along its long axis. Nothing she could imagine could cause such a welt. Thinking about it reminded it to throb and, with that, she felt her aching ribs again.

The water's edge chased her feet, grey froth breaking over her shoes. Briefly, she danced out of trouble, the lowest of giggles reminding her that, inside she was still a girl. She looked up at the dark underneath of the old pier and out along it towards the heavier green waves breaking on the rusty steel to seaward. Flashing back along its criss-crosses of stained grey ironwork, her eyes darted into the narrow darkness where the water didn't reach and where she would soon be walking. She saw nothing there except echoing black.

She turned and walked for a few moments perpendicular to the water's edge. Then she scrambled up a short, steep, shaly bank, wet with salt. The eight or so feet were awkward and her stumbles caused her to stretch, reaching agonisingly between her ribs and tearing red-hot at the short inter-costal muscles there. Her eyes were wet with the waves of pain.

Swelling fear threatened to overwhelm her senses, her scalp crawling as she approached the rectangle of blackness. Pausing, she took in three belly-deep breaths through her nose, searching for control, still tense and expectant, calling on a sixth sense to see her through the dark.

Behind her was nothing except faceless beach, to her right was cold sea. To the left was a moss-covered, unclimbable wall and, just beyond, the steady stream of cars that might as well be space-ships. In front was just forty to fifty feet of sunless dripping dark, brown with the slow march of rust and green with the creeping slime of lichen. Crumpled coke tins, brown-stained syringes and spent condoms were scattered about at the edge of the darkness, their seediness matching her mood. In the gloom, two riveted pillars stretched upward from the sea-level waste towards the underbelly of the pier's planked walkway.

Caz walked in. She was so tightly wound up now she was sure that if she was confronted she would hiss and bare fangs. Her feet crunched in the shingle, the left's foot-fall a few decibels louder than the right, each pebble-dashed step rebounding from the sea wall. She could feel the blood move in her head, pulsing in her ears, pushing at the back of her eyes. He should be here, she thought, you should be here. But she felt nothing except the cold wrap of the darkness.

'You feeble shit!' she mouthed, quieter than the sea. 'I was here, you knew I would be. Where are you?' She spun quickly, ice in her bowels but whatever she expected was not there. Then she stepped through into the sunlight. Immediately she heard birds, cars, the tinkle of people.

She climbed up spray-wet steps, away from the beach. After the gloom beneath the pier, the mid-bright shine of the morning took her full in the face and was startlingly sharp. She came out opposite a square and on a whim she started to walk round it. The homes were still majestic, four-storey buildings, white and cream, with round hooded windows and semi-circular balconies above white pillared doorways. In the middle, a multi-floored concrete car park loomed over everything, a crude thank-you from town planners forced to respond to the demands of the car.

Despite the depression that had waved over her, she was no longer prepared to slink around as a victim. Her eyes flashed and her walk stiffened. She had licked her wounds and now she was Caz Flood again. Caz the Runner. Caz the Winner. Detective Constable Flood.

Now she was a little brighter, she thought about DI MacInnes. It was nearly half-past-ten and he could be ringing her any time after eleven o'clock. She picked up the pace to get round the square a little quicker, keeping the shadows of the car park to her left. Defensively alert, her senses patrolled the area to both sides as she walked, but with each step she became less convinced she was about to be confronted. Just once did she feel the cold prickle of apprehension, as two levels above her, on one of the car park's slitted walkways, she thought, just for a moment, that the darkness moved. When she looked again, the animal shadow had shifted inconclusively. She came out of the square and turned away from town. If someone had been in the car park she had seventy yards on him. No quick footsteps came after her but she remained acutely aware. The one time she turned round, nothing was there.

Inkerman Terrace had the depopulated calm of six a.m. At the top of her steps, Caz tensed and waited as if she were sniffing the air in expectation. She opened the front door wide enough to light the hall and, once satisfied, stepped inside on to its clear polished tiles. With a glance down the street she closed the door and went quickly up the stairs. She was half-way to her room when she remembered the mail and was just about to turn when she saw it stacked neatly against her flat door. At first she was surprised – there was no other tenant in the building to pick up the letters – then a cold surge of fear raced up from her gut and up into her throat. Suddenly her skin hummed with the electricity of anxiety. She could feel the touch of cold wet fingers as they ran down her spine. Anger raged up in her. The bastard. He had been here.

She rammed her key into the lock, cracked round its tumblers, slapped open the door and stormed into her home. Inside, she slammed the wood back hard, closing herself in with a bang.

She wanted this pig so badly now that she could taste it. She dearly wanted him to be waiting for her but she knew absolutely now that he would not be there. She no longer expected some direct and honourable clash. This creep was a coward, someone slithering, crawling in the night. Even the knife attack surprised her. That must have taken *some* balls.

'You're not here, you shit!' she shouted. 'You wouldn't have the guts!' Nevertheless, she rushed from room to room, throwing back the doors and declaring herself noisily. She was white with fury and adrenaline was making her heart flutter wildly. She had ripped the crop from her forearm and desperately wanted to whip it into the face of this animal. For herself she wanted to cut him, to mark him, to make him bloody. For every other frightened woman she wanted to break his flesh, to see him cry out in pain.

The telephone rang. It was loud, a sudden, jarring shock. She stared at it, transfixed. Once it had been something ordinary, something benign. Now it had become threatening. The receiver had been inanimate, grey and flat, but now, somehow, it had its own life. It would feel hot. It would pulse. It would breathe. If she picked it up and it was him he could bombard her with silence. He could whisper her dangerous affection. He could curse her with the foulest of mouths. He could rape her with words. But if she *didn't* pick it up he would be winning, trapping her, making her cower, showing her that he was her master.

She glanced at the clock; ten-fifty-five. The phone had rung six times. After a deep, readying breath she picked it up. She thought she heard '. . . oment', then there was the burr of silence. She wanted to scream.

'It's me,' the voice said softly. There was no menace at all.

'Hello, Valerie,' she said flatly.

'Are you all right, baby? You sound a bit—'

'I'm fine,' Caz said, 'what do you want?' She was far too short.

'I was just saying hello, love, what's yer problem? Jeff been on the phone to me. I've just finished talking to him. He was asking me about the weekend and I wasn't exactly sure what we'd finally arranged . . .'

'Arranged?'

'About the weekend. Are we going up to the hall?'

'*I* am,' she said.

'OK. So I'll tell Jeff. Are we going Friday night or Saturday?' For some reason she was finding his voice grating. 'Whatever you like,' she said, 'I'll already be there. I'm going up on Thursday morning for an extra couple of days being pampered.'

'I'll miss you,' Valerie said softly. Then he said would she ring Jeff?

'I'm just about to go into a meeting; if you could it'd be a great help.'

She sounded resigned but said yes. Valerie spelt out a Shoreham number.

'And he'll be there now?' Caz asked.

'Yes,' Valerie said, 'he's only just put the phone down on me. Tell him we'll be going up on Friday night. He can meet me at my flat at half-five.'

'Anything else?' Caz said. 'Shirts needing ironing, that sort of thing?'

'Oops!' Valerie came back at her, 'Maybe I should call at another time. And there's me thinking we were falling in love. I suppose lunch is out of the question?'

'What time?'

'One o'clock.'

Caz said she'd be there.

Jeff's phone trilled when she rang it and he answered fourth ring, saying, 'Thomas' and the number, surprisingly formal. She suddenly realised she did not have a clue what he did for a living.

She said hello. 'Valerie said to give you a call.'

'How are you?' Jeff replied. 'Val said you'd had a bit of an accident.'

'You could say that!' she said. She pretended to laugh, 'Didn't take enough water with it. I ended up taking a flier and landing on me 'ead!'

'You OK now?'

'So-so. I'm recovering fast.' She was thinking about the night before and the line yawned empty, buzzing faintly. It was Jeff who eventually broke the silence.

'Er, you rang me . . . ?'

'Oh yes, I'm sorry, Jeff. Grigglesham Hall. I'm going to go up on Thursday morning. Valerie said to tell you to meet him at his flat, five-thirty Friday afternoon. He said you can go straight from there.'

'Can't miss another night away from you, eh?' Jeff said.

'Well, that's understandable isn't it?' she fired back.

'*Touché*,' Jeff said. 'And thanks for calling.'

Before she could say anything else, he had rung off. She looked at the phone in her hand and spoke wryly into the mouthpiece. She sat back to wait for Tom MacInnes to call. When he rang, the DI had news. He had been with DS Reid following up on the John Davies accident and though they were no closer to finally deciding cause of death, they had a sheaf of photographs of him.

'Davies was a bit of a singer. Worked part time in night clubs. He'd had publicity shots done; some really good quality black-and-whites. His sister gave us a couple of very good ones. They're being copied now.'

'What about Peter Beecham? What's new there?'

'George Lindsell went back to Pearson's Audio but none of the new staff knew anything about him. His boss at Gatwick said nothing significant except that he was a bit bland and boring.'

'I take it there's nothing new on the, er, preferences, of our bodies.'

'No.'

'Then we're still on, boss?'

'Just about, lass, just about.' She felt a little thrill.

She explained her appointment with the book rep, Tomlinson. The DI was noncommittal. Then she told him she was spending four days at Grigglesham Hall at the invitation of her new friend. He didn't bite. 'I had a bit of a tumble yesterday, Tom, and took a nasty crack on the head. A few days' rest should do me a lot of good.'

'And of course, you've booked up with Counselling?'

'I rang them, Sir. I explained I was away until after the weekend. They said to ring Monday and they'd sort me out then.'

'I'll let the DCS know.'

'Thank you, Sir. I appreciate that.'

'You ought to, Caz.'

'Tom?'

'Constable?'

'I was hoping I could get a little favour . . .'

'Oh yes?'

'My print-out, Sir? From Holmes? It got a fair bit damaged yesterday when I fell over. It got torn and bit too wet. I was wondering if there was any chance of getting a fresh one.'

'No,' MacInnes said. It was short and final. She dropped it straight away.

'A set of photographs?'

'If you speak to Saint or Greaves, they'll let you have them.'

'I'd like one of John Davies, Sir.'

'That shouldn't be a problem. Ring after one o'clock and you should be able to pick up the full set.'

'Anything else, Sir? Anything on Grigglesham Foster?'

'DCs West and O'Leary have been door-knocking the village for the last two days. The villagers don't seem to be that easy to catch. There's not been a positive ID yet on any of the three bodies.'

'They should try Annie Lewis, Sir. Waitress at the Drunken Preacher.'

'Your receipt lady?'

'Yes, Sir. And her sister Margaret works at the Grigglesham Clinic as a secretary. Margaret has waitressed a few odd times in the village pubs. I've reason to believe she may have served one or more of our targets.'

'Is that logged?'

'No, Sir. I've only just realised. I thought I had a handwriting match between two of the receipts we found. The writing *was* very similar but once I had a real match it was obvious that it wasn't the same. Then I thought, two sisters, same school, wouldn't their writing be quite close?'

'And you're going to Grigglesham Hall for a *break*?'

'Yes, Sir.'

'In that case, maybe you shouldn't interview the sister.'

'Sir?'

'You should let one of the male DCs do it. Let them do it as part of their door-to-door enquiries. If you start asking questions as soon as you get there you won't find out much. No, let the boys handle it. You just see what you can pick up from simply being around.'

It made sense. She said OK without a quarrel.

'Flood?' the DI said.

'Yes, Sir?'

'You really should take that break. Drop all this for a day or two.'

'I can't, Sir. You know I can't.'

'You've been warned, girl. Let it drop. If you don't, it might drop you.'

'OK, Sir,' she promised, 'I'll try not to push it when I'm at the Hall. I won't actually switch off, but I'll not force anything either, how's that?'

Before ringing Rachel Hely, Caz went through to the bedroom. The ripped, stained print-out was in there, pushed underneath a bedside locker. It was less than twenty hours since it had probably saved her life, but for all that it looked decidedly ordinary and smelt of stale water and rotting paper.

When she sniffed at it, it made her wrinkle her nose. She sat on the bed and partly opened the layers like a two-hundred-yard map. The edges were bloodstained. She touched her neck. Only in one place had the point of the attacker's blade passed right through to touch her skin.

It was then that she felt as if she had a guardian angel, as if she had been spared by the gods while they waited for her to learn. A vision came back to her from deep down in her long-term memory. She was being pulled from a wrecked patrol car after a joy-rider chase had gone badly wrong. Someone had held her while they tried to rescue Bob Murray's body from the flame-flickering car. It had exploded in a ball of flame driving them back. She had had a bloody nose.

She had read once that a hundred thin things were stronger than one thick. Every page of the computer print-out was a small but singular challenge to the knife, each one falling, pushed aside, until, bit by bit, the power of the blows had been wasted.

She had the paper pages in her hand, trailing a sprinkle of brown and pink snow as she went back towards the phone. She was thinking about the police computer. Holmes could produce but it could only work with the information it had been given. She suddenly had an idea.

She dialled John Street. MacInnes was in with DCS Blackside. She decided to ask if they could be interrupted. As soon as the phone was picked up she blurted, 'I've just had a thought, Sir. We should put Davies into Holmes as murdered and see what he gives us back. It's a completely different type of killing. If it *is* our man it might open the investigation right up.'

'Go on.' He sounded odd.

'Well, Sir. You know how I feel about how we may be getting directed into one way of thinking by the killer. If we presume for the time being that Davies *was* a murder victim, Holmes will look for all the connections and might give us a totally new line of enquiry. We can play what-if, Sir.'

'Very good, Flood. And this is what you call sick leave, is it?' It was DCS Blackside. Oh, shit! She tried to mumble something back.

'I'm speaking with the DI at this moment, Constable. He has just suggested the same thing. We will be looking at the possibility this afternoon.'

'I'm sorry, Sir.'

'In the end you probably will be, unless you knuckle under.'

'Knuckle *under*, Sir?'

'Learn to do as you're told, Flood! We were all bright young coppers once. Remember, Dick Tracey was *outside* the police force.'

'I understand, Sir.' She said it subtly so Blackside heard a little girl giving way to the huge and dominant male.

'Don't blow a good start, Flood. Learn to pace yourself.'

'Yes, Sir. Thank you, Sir.'

She was about to ring off, but Blackside spoke again. 'It's taken your DI and myself this long to come round to this idea, Flood, so give yerself a little pat on the back.'

'Sir!'

'But do it on *holiday*, right?'

'Yes, *Sir*!'

'One last thing, Flood. DI MacInnes says could you ring DC Greaves in the war room before one. Greaves has some personal effects of yours he wants to get to you.'

'Yes, Sir. Thank you, Sir. Would you thank the DI for me.'

'Go away, Flood.' The phone went dead.

She still had time to ring Rachel Hely. She got through to Margaret Oakley who now said a very bright 'Hello!' before putting her through. Caz confirmed her Thursday arrival and Rachel suggested they ate together that same evening.

Before she left for lunch with Valerie, she rang Jim Greaves. She had the silly thought that with all these calls she might as well go into work for a rest. Greavsie was his usual flippant self, but he did tell her he had an envelope of photographs for her. Then he said that they'd just had orders to stick John Davies on to the computer as a murder.

'Billy Tingle will be thrilled,' he said. 'Did you know he's trying to give up smoking? The lads are convinced he's trying to get into Moira Dibben's knickers!'

'You've a lovely way with words, Greavsie!'

'I know,' he said. 'It took years to perfect.'

Caz arranged to pick the photographs up straightaway, on her way to see Valerie. 'I don't suppose there'd be any chance of me getting a print-out from Sherlock once Davies is logged on?' She held her breath.

'About the same chance as you spending a weekend of passion with me,' Greaves said wistfully. Oh yeah, Caz said, where did he plan on taking her? Greavsie laughed and said he'd do his best.

'Jim?' Caz said seriously. He said what? 'I really appreciate this, mate. I know I owe you one.'

'But you're not going to give me one, are you?' Greaves said.

'Oh, please!' Caz said with mock anxiety. 'I'd never cope, you know.'

'Ring Billy after three o'clock,' Greaves said.

She put the phone down. It was time to go see Valerie. As she stood, she grabbed the whip from the sofa and held it in its ribbed middle, the handle up. It was fat and dark, non-lethal but devastating for all that. She slapped the thick end into a solid palm.

Definitely time to go.

Thirty-four

Caz went out without any conscious attempt to be on her guard. Somehow she knew that now was not to be the time. The weather had brightened considerably since her morning walk and with it her mood was hiked up a couple of notches. Her head felt OK unless she touched it, and the pain in her ribs had narrowed itself down to one severe sharp-pointed bruise close to her heart.

She went through the small park into the next street and her lock-up garage. Perhaps the sunshine was making her careless, but she hardly looked around her as she walked. At the garage she stopped to find a key then clicked open the padlock before throwing back the doors.

Her MGB GT was called Frederika and probably needed a crooked MOT to be still on the road. Once upon a time it had been white, and bits of it still were. She had promised herself that one day she would renovate Frederika, but work kept intruding and she still looked like the old banger she was when Caz had bought her for a pittance.

She walked into the garage's gloom and opened Frederika's door. Then she climbed into the car's red leather inside and started her up. Frederika boomed and roared into life, then she settled down into an EEC-challenging throb: totally meaty. Whenever the car started up, Caz thought that really 'she' should be a 'he'. The car was wonderfully, hornily powerful. One day she would have a Mazda MX5, British Racing Green, fresh, sporty and spanking brand-new. She lusted for her MX, but she knew that no newcomer, however spirited, would ever quite be old Frederika.

She floated the sports car down the street, turned it into the Kingsway and throated along it at a blubbering thirty. It occurred to her that Valerie might like to bring Frederika back to life. She wondered about the cost and made a mental note to ask him about it over lunch.

Going to the nick was convenient as it allowed her somewhere to park. She dropped down the ramp and left her rust-trap next to a spotless panda. Then she went in to see Greavsie.

MacInnes was as good as his word but, better, Greavsie had arranged with Billy Tingle to rip-off a print-out for her and drop it round her place after work. The Post-it note he had left warned her that the Davies data might take a little while to process and not to expect Billy much before nine p.m.

She popped her head into the computer room and said Hello! to Moira. To Billy she winked and said, 'See you tonight, luv!' She left as he began to blush and Moira was in the act of leaning forward to begin grilling him. If Moira was interested in Billy, Caz thought, she must be mad; looking like she did, she ought to have the pick of the nick. Even better, she could actually go out with a guy who *didn't* take *Police Review*.

She arrived at the Amex building just as a distant clock was chiming the hour. Valerie came through the smoked-glass doors as she strode up towards them. He was wearing a single-breasted charcoal suit, a white shirt and an unassuming blue tie with tiny yellow micro-lights flying across it. His shoes were polished dark brown, breaking the rules. As they met, they kissed the way people who are sure of each other kiss, and then he said, 'Fancy a pizza?' Caz took Valerie's arm as they walked down towards the Old Steine. He took her into a tiny Italian with only forty or so covers. As they entered, a waiter flashed teeth at them, and Valerie introduced him as Pepe Strologo, the rudest Italian in England. The little man nodded.

'*Sì! Sì!* It is true. But what does this peasant know, uh?'

Valerie said, 'See what I mean?'

'You 'ave booked, yes? If you 'aven't booked you bugger off? I have no places, you can see.' Pepe swung his arms to reveal at least four empty tables. 'You see, not a spare seat in the 'ouse. Now tell me, you book?'

Valerie *had* booked. Minutes later there really weren't any seats spare and they were squashed in between couples, the men all in suits. Valerie asked her to play a game; who did she think was with his wife, who was with a colleague and who was eating out with his mistress? She turned round pointedly and quickly scanned the room, first with a policeman's eye, then with a psychologist's. Lastly, she tried gut feeling. Excluding themselves, she said, they were all innocent. A man was sitting in the far corner of the restaurant, facing the room and his female companion.

'Except him,' she said. She pointed cheekily. 'He's as guilty as sin.'

'Why do you think that?' Valerie asked.

'He's facing the room which is good, that can be protective, but every time the door opens he shrinks slightly, as if he's trying to hide.'

'He might be taking too long at lunch and be feeling guilty.'

'Oh, yeah, I'm sure,' Caz said. 'And she's reaching out more than him, look, into his space, past the half-way line of the table. He's responding, but his touch looks less than certain. I'd say he wants her like hell but he's terrified of getting caught. I reckon they've never been away together. If they've done it yet, it's been quick and furtive and she wants a bit more.'

'And you got all that from a few nuances?'

'You don't believe me?' Caz asked. 'I'm making it up as I go along, is that what you think? Well, I'm not. I'm reading his body language. I can't prove it, but if I had to bet my life on it, that's exactly what I'd say.'

'Body language! You're not into that, are you?'

'And why not? Before we had language we had gestures and postures. We've been around for a couple of million years. We may have had language for only thousands. It's real, all right, but forget the popular books about it, they over-simplify it and cheat like hell.'

'So what's my body language like?' Valerie said.

'Open, assured, loving, and seductive.'

'Oh, that's too easy,' Val countered. 'You know I'm open and you also know that, being a reasonably successful manager, I'm fairly self-assured.'

'Yes, and you've been loving to me and subtly seductive, even when you consciously chose not to jump into my bed.'

'Well, I'm a Rock 'n Roll Sex God, aren't I?'

'Of course you are, Valerie.' Caz decided to run a little experiment on him. She moved very slightly, changing her sitting position. The waiter came and they ordered a round of garlic bread between them, plus a couple of large ham and mushroom pizzas. Instead of house red, they ordered a litre of mineral water. She looked at Valerie. He seemed faintly aggrieved.

'Are you all right, Caz?' Val said. She said she was fine and leaned back slightly.

'You sure?' he said. She told him she was really pleased to be lunching with him and crossed her arms.

'It's just that . . . well . . .' he stuttered. She was looking past and above him, avoiding his eyes. 'Just that you seem a bit . . .'

'Hostile?' Caz suggested, 'or perhaps you mean frosty?'

'Well, yeah.'

'Well, I'm not. There is nowhere else on earth that I'd rather be right now than here with you. I mean that, Valerie. I really do.' She rubbed her nose and coughed lightly.

'Forget it then,' Valerie said. 'It's just me.'

She picked up the salt cellar and put it down again, slightly inside his half of the table. They started talking about flying. While he spoke, she toyed with her glass and moved it slightly towards him.

She sat up slightly and cocked her face haughtily as she picked up her knife. While she asked a question about learning to fly she pushed her plate forward and put her elbows on the table.

'You *are* in a bad mood,' Valerie said, slightly uncool. 'Have I done something? Why do I feel as if you're pissed off with me and I'm under pressure?' Caz smiled, and even tried to flutter at him sensuously. When she put down her knife it was across her plate, parallel with his side of the table. She dropped the pepper pot just inside his territory. 'Valerie, I promise you. I am *not* pissed off with you. You make me happy. I'm glad to be here. Honestly, there is nothing wrong.'

'I'm going to have a glass of wine,' he said quickly, 'I feel . . .'

She dropped her shoulders suddenly, took his stiffening hand, looked him in the eyes and leaned lower, towards the table. 'You know, Valerie, maybe there *is* something about this body language thing. I've even heard it said that by unobtrusively taking more than your allotted portion of a meal-table, you can put your eating partner right off lunch.' She watched the penny rolling down through the mechanisms of his brain. She almost heard it clunk as it finally neared his knowledge basement. When he grinned and sat back with his arms crossed, she knew it had actually dropped. There was a rush of exasperated love in his eyes and he waved a fist at her, but before anything else could be said, Pepe parted them with two steaming portions of garlic bread.

'So, Mr Thom-*as*, you are so bloody poor now. *I* buy the lady some garlic bread. Me myself I do. And we 'ave Barclaycard 'ere. American Express not do so bloody well nicely, all right thank you.'

Valerie smiled, 'Well thank *you*, Mister Strologo.' It was said with a ludicrous syrupy voice. 'It is *such* a pleasure to eat here with you.'

'I am too kind,' Pepe said. Then he said he had to go and talk to some real customers. As he clip-clopped away his hands were waving, some mad conversation continuing.

'Well, eat yer bread then!' Valerie said quickly to Caz. She was looking at him with wet eyes. 'This is good stuff. It'll put hairs on yer chest!'

It was a pizza base, sprinkled with herbs and lashed with butter. There was so much garlic, little bits of the cloves could still be seen.

'Do you realise,' Val said, 'that there hasn't been a vampire in Brighton for six hundred years? Do you know why?'

With bright eyes, she waved her dripping bread at him and cocked her head. He looked at her and said, 'Well done, *madame.* Yours in one!'

Her face drained, 'What did you just say?'

'I said, well done, yours in one.'

'What did you say, Valerie? *Exactly*?'

'I don't know!'

'You said, Well done, *madame.* Yours in one!'

'Did I?'

'Yes, you did, Valerie.' She stared at him, 'Why did you say that?'

'I don't know, I just said it. Why's it important?'

'Believe me, it's important, Valerie.'

'Well, not to me, it's ridiculous. I think you're being silly.' His voice was raised but he still had humour in it. He tilted his head and looked like he was trying to recall something. 'Nope!' he finally said, 'can't remember.'

'Valerie! *Think* damn you!' She regretted it before she'd said it.

His face changed. She saw it darken. Anywhere else and he would have gone through the roof. Instead he spoke quietly, in short, hissed phrases. But he was angry. Deeply angry. 'Caz, look, I do not know why I said what I just said, OK. Why is grass green? I thought I was having lunch with my friend, not some manic bloody copper. Now listen. If you tell me what your problem is I'll help but never, *never* try to grill me again. If you want to interrogate me in the future, make it official. Take me to the station.'

'Valerie, I . . .' she reached out a hand on to his. He simply looked at it.

'You're like two people, Caz. One minute you're sweet and sexy, the next minute you're some probing, hard-faced police bitch. If this case is causing us a problem, what do you say we split until it's all wrapped up? Would that be better? Is that what you want?'

She could only shake her head.

He snatched at his glass and swigged down some mineral water, trying to let some of the anger go. She decided to speak. She did so slowly.

'Valerie, you used an odd phrase that I've only ever heard one other person use. That person is strongly linked to three murders.' He went to say something but she held up her hand. 'The police are aware that you knew all three dead men, even if you say you don't remember meeting them. Now you've just dropped another little clue on me. I feel disturbed .'

'So what d'you expect me to say?' Valerie replied.

'I don't really expect you to say anything, Val. Just understand that I'm in love with a man who is not yet off the police suspect list. I'm upset. I don't think you're a murderer, Val. I think that's crazy, but the dead men were linked and you are linked in the same way. For God's sake! For all I know you might be the next target!'

'You're putting me off my pizza!'

'I'm sorry,' Caz said. 'I *am* a hard-faced police bitch. All of the murder squad are like it. We're trying to stop someone before he kills again. I know you're not the someone, Val, but if you're not, you just might be the key to finding out who is.'

He had stopped eating.

'Look,' Caz added, 'I'm not treating you like a suspect, but there are things that you might know which could help us out. Like, do you know a chap called Jeremy Avocado? He's an interior designer. Has he ever done work for you? And you bought your hi-fi system for cash. Why?'

'This is what you call *not* interrogating me?'

'Please, Valerie. Can you help me?'

He took a deep breath and began to speak calmly. 'The stereo thing is easy. I always buy my things for cash. It's a discipline I learned while I was at university. If you pay for things with pound notes it makes you realise exactly what you're doing. It's funny, me being a manager at Amex and never using charge cards, but I don't. I'm just not disciplined enough. The thing about plastic is that it distances you from the pain, the *real* cost of purchases. I'm sure that if you have my bank account checked you'll see that I drew out cash just before I bought my hi-fi.

'As for Jeremy thingy, the name vaguely rings a bell but I don't think I've ever met him. About a year ago, I was looking for some work to be done on my flat. I rang round quite a few decorators then. If he's in the book then maybe I rang him. I really can't remember.'

'He's the one who said, "Yours in one, *madame*."'

'Well, I don't know him. At least not as Jeremy Avocado.'

'Thank you, Valerie. So do you think you could have heard the phrase somewhere, maybe on the radio or something?'

'I might've.'

'Or from a friend or an acquaintance?'

'Perhaps. But I really don't know. I simply can't remember. I'm afraid you'll just have to take my word for it.'

She knew it was time to let it drop, so she asked Val if he would think a little harder about it over the next few days. Would he try to remember when and where he had picked up the phrase? He said OK, and would *she* try to remember when she was off-duty?

'*Touché!*' she said. It made her think of Jeff.

They picked at the rest of their meal, neither of them really happy, both of them thinking that DC Flood had managed to spoil things again. Caz let the meal taper off, hoping that whatever they had between them was strong enough to rise above their problems. She asked Valerie what would be her chances of learning to fly with him. She added that she really meant flying as in aeroplanes, as with wings, et cetera, as in up in the sky.

Valerie said he could teach her a little but in the end, if she got serious, she would have to be taught by a professional. Then he said that among his many other talents, Jeff was a fully qualified instructor and could teach her. That brought up Jeff's job and Caz asked what he did for a living.

'Jeff? Anything and everything! Whatever pays a bob or two. Jeff says he's a bit of a fixer. He did his degree in biology and biochemistry, got a good two-one and started out life intending to be a researcher. He did a couple of years of a PhD at Leicester but then he changed his mind.

'After that he qualified as a state-registered nurse. I reckon Jeff's done just about everything in his time. He's sold double-glazing, done bar-work, and traded in antiques. He made a bit of money as a male model not long after university, and he's worked as a courier.'

'He's had a bit of a varied career then!'

'Oh yeah, Jeff's done just about everything, been everywhere – India, South America, Russia, North Africa, the Middle East – but he always ends up back home, usually just down the road from me. Whenever I fall over, he has the knack of being around just in time to pick up the pieces.'

'He sounds like a good mate.'

'He is. Every time I've had some sort of disaster he's turned up to bale me out. I've not been picked up for smuggling drugs yet, but if ever I was, I think Jeffrey would tunnel in from outside and rescue me!'

'And would you do the same thing for him?' Caz asked.

'Of course!'

'You would?'

'Yeah, more or less.'

'You're not just saying yes?'

'No. I once had a girlfriend who said that if any one of her friends was in trouble she would go to them immediately, no matter where she was, no matter what she was doing or who she was with. When she said it, she sounded like Mother Teresa. At first I thought it was really generous but afterwards, I wasn't so sure.

'Why not?'

'Well, it's a bit obsessive, isn't it? Me and Jeff go right back to our early teens, and I'd do almost anything for him. If he was in trouble I'd want to go and try to dig him out. I'd go right to the wall for him, but we all have to recognise that there are still times when we have to let our friends struggle through on their own. It's like a mother having to let a toddler take a few tumbles so it can learn. Ankle supports may take away the pain, but in the end the joint is weaker.'

'What does not kill me makes me stronger,' Caz said.

Valerie smiled.

Thirty-five

Most of the rest of the afternoon was spent soaking in a hot bath and reading. Caz finished her Krebs & Davis with a mug of coffee perched on the bath's edge, then she leaned out from the frothy water to grab a copy of Joseph Wambaugh's *The Blooding* from the loo top and, from a sink filled with ice cubes, her last bottle of Auslese: disgustingly amber, cold, dripping and deliciously sweet.

Before she had left Valerie after lunch she had finally discovered that he and Jeff had gone to Leicester University after both taking a year out. Valerie had only scraped his upper second in business studies because, in his words, 'One month into year one I found out what my willy was for.' And Jeff, was he the same, she had asked? Valerie had smiled and shook his head. But apparently, he said, Jeff had learned to water-ski well.

She enjoyed Wambaugh's clean, straightforward prose as he tried to paint a picture of life in rural Leicestershire for an American-International audience. For a Yank, he did OK. At least he didn't portray every local as a mindless yokel. She ran more hot water in and added bubble-bath. The thick wine drooled down her. Her pains were melting away.

When she finally dressed she had a problem. Most boyfriends made do with her in 501s and some sort of leather top. For the once or twice a year formal 'do' she had the 'little black dress' cocktail job, but what she hardly had at all was something in between. In the end she had to settle for work gear, a smart blue suit, the kind she would wear for testifying in court.

She arrived in Hove early, making sure that Pat Tomlinson would have no reason to complain. He also was early, arriving in an E-reg BMW. As he pulled up, she got out of her car, walked across to his and opened the passenger door. She spoke first, eager to set the tone of the evening.

'Good evening, Mr Tomlinson, Patrick. Thank you for being prompt.'

'What? Oh yeah? Get in then,' Tomlinson grunted.

They were quite close to the Harvey address, another tall terrace, a little more up-market than Onderman Road. A woman answered the door and introduced herself as Mrs Harvey telling them both that Brian had only just got home from work and would be down in a few minutes. 'He just wants to have a quick swill and to change his shirt.'

Jennifer Harvey sat them down and made them tea while her husband changed. They were in a green-gold chintzy room with a white fireplace, flocked wallpaper and soft Persian rugs. They could hear Mrs Harvey calling out something cheerful and clattering around her kitchen. Then her husband came into the lounge through one door at the same time as she returned through the other. She carried a formal tea service on a large enscribed silver tray.

'There!' she said, primly putting the tray down on the largest table from a nest. 'Just right! Milk? Sugar?' She had an affable, totally innocent face.

They took delicate china in their hands and Tomlinson began to talk. Caz had to watch uncomfortably as he crawled obsequiously to his clients, admiring a carpet here, complimenting them on their taste there. She felt certain that he was so outrageously sycophantic that they must notice, but Brian and Jennifer Harvey obviously didn't. They loved him.

The Harveys bought two yearbooks and seemed very happy with the special offer price. Brian insisted they went through and see his fitted office, complete with its rows of leather-bound volumes.

'This study is my favourite room,' he said, 'do you like it?' It was rich, dark and mahogany. Caz told him it was lovely because it was. He smiled proudly at her. She introduced herself properly.

'My name is Katherine Waters, Mr Harvey. I survey sales patterns for the Britannica organisation. May I ask, you paid by cheque for these books today, but last year you paid in cash?'

'That's right, it was nineteen hundred pounds.'

'Would you mind awfully? I was wondering. Cash payments like yours are quite unusual . . .'

Harvey replied, 'Oh, I know. It was coincidence really. I had just sold Jennifer's Escort that evening, just before the representative arrived, and the chap had paid me in small notes. I would have had to go to the bank in the morning, so it was just as easy to pay for the encyclopaedias with the money. That was the most cash I had ever had in my hand.'

As the pleasantries continued, she decided this was strike one. Her instincts told her that Harvey would be of no interest to them. He was too old and had spent significantly more than a thousand.

And he was alive.

Tomlinson got them out quickly and smoothly, his excuse being that they needed to get to their next appointment. It never occurred to him to open Caz's door before his own. They drove back to her car after he suggested that she could follow him to the Brighton appointment. She took a copy of the address as a precaution.

'Unless you want me to follow you back to your place?' he suggested.

'Fergerrit!' Caz said, flashing teeth.

Arthur Dunn lived in a large semi-detached with a mock Tudor front. He was small and slight with thick glasses. He wore corduroy trousers and a knitted cardigan over a check shirt. He looked like a train-spotter.

He invited them in to a room set out like a single bed-sitter complete with a bed, a tiny formica-topped table, a small television and a single armchair. In one corner was a small bookcase that looked as if it was designed for the set of encyclopedias it contained. A curtain hung behind the door and Dunn pulled it across.

'Saves on heat,' the little man said. They sat on the bed opposite him.

Eventually he explained. 'Everything cash. I never use banks. I bought my Reliant Robin for cash and I pay all my bills with cash.' Suddenly he looked furtive and made a big act, 'Of course, I *never* keep my money here. That wouldn't be sensible would it? Oh no, I've got a safety deposit box in the high street.' He sniffed.

She looked at the little man. If he had a safe deposit box in town then she fancied Patrick Tomlinson. And she didn't. Strike two.

They left the little feller just after nine o'clock. Patrick had one more try for a drink. She told him she had a regular boyfriend and that she was meeting him at ten o'clock. Thanks for the offer and all that but . . . Then on an impulse she said all right, they just had time for a quick half. He grinned.

The so-called quick drink was like a fencing match. For some reason Patrick Tomlinson thought that after he'd received a certain number of metaphorical smacks in the mouth Caz would be too tired to keep doing it. He was wrong and he got nowhere. At the end of twenty minutes of bliss he told her that the visit scheduled for the next night had been cancelled.

'I made the appointment with *Mrs* Small. I thought her old man was out. She rang the office today to cancel. Apparently her husband did a runner last year, two weeks after they'd bought the books. She was cracked up. She said he'd come into some money, decided to spend it on encyclopaedias for the kids and then a fortnight later, he just pissed off, no note, nothing. She hasn't heard a dicky-bird from 'im since.'

'What was the order value?'

'Ten-fifty.'

'Can I have the address?' Caz said. He passed her some paperwork and held her hand for a second too long. She smiled coolly at him.

'That means we've got tomorrow night free,' he said. 'We could—'

'Thanks, but no thanks, Pat. But God you're a trier!'

'No offence meant, eh?' he said.

'None taken, Patrick.' She touched his arm and left.

Before she had got to the door, Tomlinson had shrugged his shoulders, forgotten all about her and gone to the bar.

Caz hadn't forgotten that Billy Tingle was coming round to the flat, but she had given him a lowish priority. For a start, when a copper said 'not before nine', he probably meant nearer to midnight, and secondly, and this made her feel not even slightly guilty, it was only Billy Tingle. He'd wait.

She had a couple of miles to drive, and was back in the street for five-to ten. It was as dark as death, and only three street-lights fought the night. She drove slowly up the street, looking into the shadows, and five-point-turned the car at the top of the cul-de-sac before driving the length of the street again. Satisfied, she did an illegal U-turn on the Strand and came back up the street. A few bay-windows showed cracks of light.

It was only after she parked the car that she realised Billy was already waiting, sitting on the low wall outside her front door, resting his head against the wall, thoroughly bored. *Now* she felt guilty; he was doing her a favour and she was back late. She vowed to make it up to him. She wouldn't take the piss out of him for a month. That was about fair.

'Sorry I'm so late, Billy. Had a puncture. One of those things.' She was shouting this over her shoulder as she locked the car. Billy was so pissed off he didn't even bother to reply. 'Hey, Billy!' She was at the bottom of the steps. 'Sorry, mate. I just said, did you hear . . . ? I 'ad a puncture . . .'

Billy ignored her. No he didn't. He wasn't hearing her. The sod had fallen asleep. 'Billy, you little bugger. Have you been tomming it with Moira?'

She stopped. Billy was too still. Then she saw the little line of blood that seeped from his scalp and down his cheek. She felt the cold come rushing back; the fear and then the anger. 'Oh shit! Billy!'

Thirty-six

She dropped her bag near Billy's feet and felt at his neck for a pulse, praying. It was there. It was definite and regular. She gulped air in relief.

Billy was in civvies under a dark grey mac. She felt in his pockets and came out with his radio. She called the incident in and asked the desk to let DCS Blackside and DI MacInnes know *now*, no matter where they were or what they were doing. 'And we'll need an ambulance for PC Tingle,' she added.

Either Billy was very lucky or someone had jumped the queue for a copper down. She had barely started basic first aid when she heard the siren and saw the lights flashing into the street. By the time the yellow-jacketed paramedics had opened the ambulance doors, the first panda had screamed into the street; and by the time they had unstrapped a stretcher, there were three more parked, still with their lights bleeping blue.

Billy was just coming round. She hadn't stopped talking to him for a single second since she'd found him, keeping him in contact, making sure he didn't slip too far away. Even when she'd called in the incident she did it as though she was chatting directly to him. She felt as guilty as hell.

She had been stroking his hair as she talked. His eyelids fluttered and he mumbled, 'Will whoever it is stop stroking my bloody 'ead.'

Her laugh was nervous and very short. She continued. 'And anyway, Billy, from what I hear, you and Moira Dee-Bee look more and more like becoming an item. Now you've given up smoking you'll soon be a new man. Us girls are all dead impressed with you.'

He groaned, 'Oh God, Caz, you're so full of shit.'

She realised that she was still holding Billy's hand even as the paramedics were tending to him. One had flashed a light into his eyes and nodded satisfaction. Another stuck a flap of yellow-gunked plaster on to his head-wound. The lad was much more with it now, and before the brass arrived she asked him if he knew what had happened. He spoke slightly more slowly than normal but he was sharp enough.

'Not exactly, Caz. I reckon I got here at ten-to ten, yeah. I'd just got to the top of the steps. There was a light on upstairs so I thought you were in. Just as I went to ring the bell the front door opened and someone shoved me back against the wall. I was so bloody surprised I didn't do anything. I probably swore or something, then this bloke whacked me.'

'You said a bloke. Are you sure? Did you see his face?'

'No, I didn't. I think he must've switched the hall light on or shone a torch in my face or something. I couldn't see. It was a bit of a shock.'

'But you're sure it was a man, Billy?'

'Pretty sure.'

'You've done brilliant, mate. I could kiss you. Thanks.'

'Does this mean we're engaged?' he said.

'You weren't *that* brilliant,' Caz said.

They were ready to take him away. As they lifted him up his other hand had something in it: black plastic.

'What's that, Billy?' she asked.

'What?'

'*That*, in your hand?'

Billy looked at his fist as if it belonged to somebody else. In it was a circular piece of black plastic or vinyl, but harder, almost like Bakelite. Caz watched him as he turned it over and it passed his face. It was obvious that he didn't have a clue what it was or how he had come to be holding it. She took it and dropped it into her bag. The paramedics stumbled down the steps with the stretcher and Billy was slipped into the rear of the ambulance. A gleaming black Scorpio had just pulled up across the street. DS Reid climbed out from the driver's seat, then DCS Blackside's huge frame appeared on the passenger side. She could feel her career sliding away, out of control.

The ambulance pulled slowly away, squeezing out past the blue and whites, one of which needed to back up to let it out. DS Reid was speaking to one of the drivers who nodded, got into his panda and left.

Caz looked out across the street, straight into Norman Blackside's face. Even over that distance and in the poor light of a Victorian street-lamp she could see him taking stock and making decisions. Seeing the DCS made her think of the print-out Billy was supposed to have brought her, yet more evidence of her being a loose cannon. She glanced around, trying to find it. The porchway was clear.

As casually as she could, she sat on the wall where Billy had been and glanced down into the basement. It was down there, yards of paper in a long chain of A3 sheets like a giant tapeworm. She turned back to face front and pretended the print-out wasn't there, praying that it wouldn't rain in the next couple of hours. Blackside walked towards her.

The Chief Super came up her steps in two bounds. She was surprised by the agility in such a huge man. She wondered if he'd ever done athletics. 'This is your place, Flood, right?' She nodded. 'OK, we'll chat inside.' He pointed at the front door and she got out her keys.

As they went through into the hall, another car pulled up with a tiny toot as if saying, 'I'm here.' She prayed that it would be Tom MacInnes. She dearly wanted to turn round, but Blackside's bulk was behind her, forcing her up the stairs. She could hear a loud conversation down in the street.

It came to her that the last guy to walk up these stairs behind her like this was Valerie, and she felt suddenly awkward as she remembered that night. She got to her flat door and could feel the Chief Super looming over her impatiently. She began to get flustered and started fumbling with her keys. She apologised painfully, like a sixteen year old. He was silent. She found the key and turned the lock. She was trying to think of something to say, desperately trying to find her feet in quicksand. As she opened the door she spoke, 'I could make some tea, Sir, if you—' Then she stopped, stunned.

'Flood?' The DCS pushed roughly past her. His roughness brought her to the brink of tears. 'Holy Fuck!' she heard him say. Inside, she was crying but she had learned. The tears were internal. They didn't show.

Once, when she had been in uniform, some woman victim of a burglar had told her she felt as if she'd been raped. She had felt violated; unclean. Now Caz knew exactly what she meant. This was happening to her.

It wasn't the mess. The place had been wrecked, but that could be mended. The flat could be put back together again. It wasn't the financial loss; in the end her insurance would cover that. What upset her deeply, what sickened her to her core, was that someone had entered a part of her that was secret. He had touched her insides. Someone black and faceless now knew her. She could never forgive that.

Blackside was talking to her but she wasn't listening. She was looking up at the wall above the fireplace where red spray paint screamed SLUT! at her. He shouted down to the pandas and she heard bootsteps coming. She was looking at her little piggies. They had been butchered, ripped up their backs. The floor was scattered with kapok, feathers and red-stained straw. Tiny polystyrene balls littered the floor. Even their eyes had been ripped out. 'Why?' she said. 'Why the piggies?'

She went through to her bedroom, walking limply, almost in shock. SLUT! had been scribbled there too, in pink lipstick across her bathroom mirror. A picture from a pornographic magazine was pinned to the top of her bedside cabinet by some sort of pointed tool, a grinning witch-like woman with a square chair-leg shoved into her vagina. Caz looked at her bed. The duvet had been pulled back and her underwear was thrown all over the sheets. She could smell the sharpness of semen and the items were wet. The bastard had masturbated all over her clothing. She wanted to be sick.

She heard Tom MacInnes' voice talking to a PC in the other room. He came into the bedroom and barked a gruff, 'Hello, Norman', to the DCS.

'Hello, Tom,' Blackside said. 'Flood has had a visit from a burglar. Some sickie with a weird sense of humour. The guy took a bit of a swipe at PC Tingle on his way out. The lad's gone to hospital but he should be all right.'

'Are you OK?' MacInnes said to Caz.

'Yes, Sir, I'm fine. I've no home but I'm not damaged.'

'What the hell was Tingle doin' here ennyweh?' MacInnes said, his accent roaring back with a vengeance.

Blackside answered the DI before Caz could. 'Delivering a print-out from Holmes, I suspect. One of the uniforms has just picked it up from the basement garden.'

'Fer fuck's sake, Flood!' MacInnes said. She felt she had let him down.

'I know, Sir. But don't blame the lad. I told him I had your authority.'

'But you did have, Flood. You know that. That's not the problem. I was complaining about you dragging a young PC round here late at night. He'd only just finished a bloody fourteen-hour shift!'

'I'm sorry, Sir.'

'Good!' he said. It came out 'gidd'.

She felt suddenly legless and tired and went to sit on the bed. Then she realised with disgust what it was like and leaned against a wall instead.

'Sir, I've got something to say,' she looked at MacInnes, then turned to fix Blackside with her strongest stare. 'Sir, last night I was attacked just outside in the street. I was struck on the head and then my assailant attacked my upper body repeatedly.'

'*What!*' Both officers spoke together.

'I had fallen to the ground. My assailant aimed a number of blows at my upper torso with some sort of pointed weapon. These blows failed to do serious damage because I had taken a print-out from Holmes and it was down inside my jacket. The wad of paper absorbed most of the force.'

She glanced at the DI who stared back at her oddly. In part he looked betrayed, but at the same time he looked almost loving, like a man discovering his daughter is on drugs.

'The bruises suggested a sharp-ended weapon but not a pointed one. The end will be oval-shaped, as I believe that weapon over there will be. I have reason to believe that Billy Tingle might have saved my life tonight.'

'Fer fuck's sake, Flood!' This was Blackside. 'If you were *trying* to fuck up you wouldn't be as stupid as this. What is it with you? Do you like being in uniform or something? Christ!'

'I do not, Sir. I think my excuse must be Post Traumatic Stress Disorder. You know that I am a keen officer. My record will tell you that. A series of bizarre things has happened to me over the last three weeks and I believe that I have begun to behave irrationally as a result. I suspect that the Police Doctor will confirm this.'

'And when are you seeing *him*?' Blackside said.

'I was taking a five-day break starting tomorrow, Sir. I'd arranged to have a long chat Monday next.'

'No fuckin' weh!' MacInnes suddenly snapped. 'Now you lissen, Flood. You're in ma offiss fust thing tomorrer morning. Ah'll bell the quack m'self. Y'see him before y'go on holiday – an' that, that's 'n order!'

'But, Sir!'

'But, Sir, Fuck! Ah've had it now Flood. Do it, or expect yussel' t'be on a formal charge. I don't give a toss about "stress disorders" but when one of my coppers gets hurt . . .' His face was red. His clenched fists were at waist level. Gradually he lowered them to his sides, slowly uncurled them and turned to Blackside. 'Thank you, Sir, fer gettin' here so quickly. I accept full responsibility for DC Flood's behaviour. Can we talk about it in the morning?'

The DCS grunted a yes and suggested ten o'clock.

Caz sat on a corner of her bed, away from the mess. She was certain that her career was in ruins. She sat dully, her shoulders aching. Video images of her days as a copper floated through her consciousness as the two senior detectives moved round, examining the room. She could see Bob Murray's body enveloped in flames in the crashed 'traffic' – the hand of the dying little girl trapped in the wreck of a family car.

MacInnes and Blackside stood at the head of the bed. The DI was trying to pull the stabbing tool from the cabinet top. When he failed and swore, Blackside stepped in and wrenched the blade from the wood.

'It's a knack,' he said. MacInnes grunted.

Blackside excused himself and left. As he went, he nodded to Flood with an ambiguous eye-contact. She had absolutely no energy. It was as if she had just fought off the attacker herself. She was empty and wasted.

'OK, Flood,' Tom MacInnes said quietly. He gestured for them to leave the bedroom. 'Now let's work out what's really been happening.'

She got up and followed his back. Once they were in the lounge he steered her to the sofa and pressed her shoulders, making her sit down. He took command. 'Fust off, where y'goin' t' sleep tonight?'

'I can't . . . I don't know, Sir.' She looked around her, feeling wretched.

'How about yer new boyfriend? Can y'stop at his place?'

'I think you'll find he's not there, Sir.'

'And you don't have a key?'

'No, Sir.'

'Are you sure he's not in, Flood?'

'More or less, Sir. If he is there, then he's only just got home.'

'Ring him.'

'I'd rather not, Sir. I wouldn't want to stay there anyway. Not now.'

'Not now?'

He left it. He thought for a minute then went through to the kitchen. He shouted through, 'You do *have* some whisky, Flood?'

She told him no; he'd drunk it all.

'There's plenty at my place,' he said.

They left in his car and drove the short distance along the front to his flat in Grand Junction Road. From his lounge window she could see the Palace Pier and, up to her left, Marine Parade running along high above the sea. On the way there she had been quiet, her face turned to the pavement, the reflection of her face coming and going in the changing light.

MacInnes warned her that his place was not much. In size, that was true, but it was carefully filled with sombre dark furniture, the newest of which was late Victorian, and recessed bookcases that were filled with old books on law and crime. The floor was polished floorboard scattered with rugs, and on one wall was an oil of what looked like Derby Day circa 1850.

The whole smelt of beeswax polish and fading book-leaves. On a bright summer day, she imagined, with the tall curtains drawn back and light streaming through the rectangular Georgian panes, it would look rich and deep, but now, in mid-winter grey and at night, it felt gloomily sad.

'Whisky?' he said. He had poured while she had been dreaming. She nodded. It came in old crystal tumblers. 'Sit down, lass,' he said.

She sat on the floor next to a red-buttoned leather chesterfield, her legs folded away and her arm resting on the cushions. It was an old habit but it threw MacInnes temporarily. He asked her where did they think they should go from here. She swallowed his good malt and sighed.

'I think we'll be forced to arrest Valerie Thomas, Sir.'

Thirty-seven

When she said it, finally said it, there was a kind of relief that burst out of her, tinged with sadness and something that she wasn't able to identify. MacInnes sensed her pain and swung the decanter towards her. Without thinking, she dropped a good belt of whisky into her glass.

'Valerie is connected to the first three killings, Sir. He has no alibi for any of the three murders and was staying in a hotel less than five miles from Beecham's house the night that Beecham died. In some way, I know he's connected to Jeremy Avocado and he has only half an alibi for the night John Davies fell or was pushed from his balcony.'

MacInnes was sitting in a high-backed winged chair. His whisky glass was held in front of him with both hands. He leaned forward, listening.

'The night I was attacked, Sir, Valerie Thomas was there almost immediately. I was dazed, probably in shock. He picked me up and took me inside. When I wouldn't go to the hospital he made efforts to make me but he wasn't really convincing. Then later, after he left, I got some funny phone calls. When I rang him he was engaged.' She paused.

'Go on.'

'I just think that everything points to Valerie, Sir. No alibis; he's placed at or near the scene on at least two occasions; he's connected to two other people whose names have come up in the investigation, and he's the right age as far as Holmes is concerned . . .'

'It's all very vague, Caz. You have no real evidence.'

'I know, Sir. But it's an accumulation of things, tiny things, pin-pricks that keep adding up. For example, when I first met Valerie Thomas, he was exceedingly helpful about George Burnley, almost too helpful. It was Thomas who firmed us up on Grigglesham Foster. He said then that he didn't know where it was. About a week later I said I fancied a drive out past Midhurst and he knew that would take us near Grigglesham.'

'Maybe by then he'd found out.'

'Maybe.'

'Why *exactly* should we arrest him, Caz?'

'Specifically, I don't know, Sir. I just know that you'll have to.'

MacInnes shifted even further forward, 'Woman's intuition is all very fine, Caz, but don't you think I'll need a little bit more when I go to Blackside?'

'I'm not talking about intuition, Tom, I'm talking about evidence. When Thomas is arrested I'll talk to you about intuition.'

'What the hell does *that* mean?' MacInnes said.

'I'm not sure I can explain right now, Sir.'

'Well, I bloody well know we need a bit more than gut-feelings, little pin-pricks and coincidences in order to arrest a man for murder!'

'I know that, Sir. When I said I thought we would have to bring him in eventually, I think I said we'd be *forced* to. I think the evidence will just appear and will be un-contestable. Maybe we'll find his fingerprints on the weapon at my flat or something.'

'But *why*?' MacInnes said. 'You have to justify what you're saying!'

'I know that, Sir, but as yet I can't.'

'We still have no motive, Caz.'

'It's worse than that, isn't it, Sir? We're still looking for a homosexual psychopath I presume? Despite the simple fact that we have little or no evidence that more than one of the victims was gay and no evidence at all to suggest that John Davies was anything but straight.'

'Yes and no,' MacInnes said.

'Sir?'

'You might have noticed that Bob Moore's not been around recently? Well he's been up at the Home Office Forensic Labs at Aldermaston talking with the scientists there. Keeping it simple, when someone's alive it's quite easy to tell if they take it up the bum. The characteristics of the sphincter muscle alter. With someone who's dead it's still easy enough to see certain tissue changes.

'Our victims were all brutally savaged about the anus. Two of the attacks were particularly vicious, and that sort of attack can almost destroy the sphincter tissue. We were so damn certain that the attacks were homosexual that our original brief to the labs was to do DQ-Alpha testing on the semen, to try to work out what kind of weapon was used and to ascertain the actual cause and time of death.

'Scene of Crimes put the three murders in the same frame. They could hardly do otherwise; the DQ-Alphas matched, the MOs matched and, in the case of the first two, the killings were close in time. It was only because you were being so obnoxious that I told DCS Blackside and he sent Bob Moore to Aldermaston.

'We've finally got back the post-mortem tissue analysis on Beecham, Green and Burnley. We already knew that Green was homosexual. He was a regular receptive passive. Philip Beecham and George Burnley weren't.'

She went to speak, but he stopped her. 'That does *not* mean, Flood. That does *not* mean they weren't homosexual or that they weren't murdered by a homosexual. All we know is that they weren't previously active receptives. There's more than one way to skin a cat; you can screw or be screwed or do both. They could have gone in for oral sex or mutual masturbation; that's common enough in teenage boys even basically heterosexual ones.'

'But it does make . . .'

'Yes, it does make the smokescreen idea *slightly* more plausible. But for Christ's sake, Caz, what we're saying *then* is that someone killed three men and wanked all over them or even screwed them either before or after they were killed to cover up something else?'

'Yes, Sir.'

'But *what*, for Christ's sake? We have to have motive.'

'Try looking at it like this, Sir. Maybe the men are linked some other way – through Grigglesham, because of this cash, or through Jeremy Avocado. If, just for a minute, we presume that John Davies was murdered and that someone made it look like an accident, maybe whoever it was came under time pressure and had to get rid of the other three quicker. So he landed on this idea – a burst of killing from a gay nutter who then disappears.'

'OK,' MacInnes said, 'even if I go along that far with you . . . We still have absolutely nothing to suggest why all this should occur.'

'I know that, Sir. But the answer has to be something to do with this money and probably has something to do with Grigglesham Foster. I've been to the fertility clinic at Grigglesham Hall, Sir. We know it's fairly high-powered there and it's pretty secure. If Special Branch is in there, it almost certainly is clean; but that doesn't mean that something there or something in the village might not give us the reason for the deaths. If we can place any or all of the victims in the Grigglesham Foster area or, better still, actually at the clinic, then we'll be a lot closer to the answer.'

'West and O'Leary have drawn a blank up there so far.'

'Have they managed to speak to everyone in the village? Have they interviewed the staff at the hall? There's a gardener there called Tom who mentioned youngish men coming to the hall one Sunday.'

'West and O'Leary are still working the village. I can get some more feet up there in the morning to go round with pictures. Special Branch have already said they don't want us trampling all over the hall unless we have probable cause, so I'll have to speak to George Foster before we start disturbing the natives.'

He sat up and stared momentarily into the fireplace. 'I don't know,' he said slowly, 'there's something not quite right about all this. Thomas and Avocado are the two people who have been most helpful to us, yet they're the two you suspect!'

'I didn't say I suspected Valerie Thomas, Sir. I said the evidence will force us to pick him up.' She rushed on quickly. 'And Avocado, Sir. Have we found out whether he could've got back into the UK secretly?'

'Yes, and he could have. The US Immigration Service has a special card and computer system to log individuals landing in Florida. When you land it's recorded and a card is clipped into your passport. When you leave they use the card to sign you back out via the computer. So our man would be logged in and out. If he had done it, we would know.'

'But there are other ways, legal ways, of dodging that system?'

'Avocado said he went to Miami and the Keys right?'

'Yes, Sir.'

'Well, these are major cruise centres for Mexico, the Bahamas, and so on. You can get cruises from Port Canaveral, from Fort Lauderdale, Miami or Key West. The cruise companies do all sorts of different runs; quick weekenders to Nassau or round-robins taking in the Keys, Mexico, the Bahamas, The Virgin Islands and points east.'

She topped up his drink.

MacInnes continued, 'So. You board a cruise, say at Miami. Say you're with your family, real bucket 'n spade, Mum, Dad and a couple of kids. You go through passport control as you go on to the ship then you cruise overnight to Nassau. That's independent, ex-British. You skip the ship when it docks and island-hop from there, then fly back to England from some non-US territory like the British Virgin Islands or Antigua. You get back to the UK, do what you have to do, jump back on another plane, and then, when you're back in warmer climes you island-hop again, meet up with the family at some other pit-stop and walk back on board. If you know your cruises you'll know that they don't count them all out and count them all back. You'll be missing at meal-times but that's an easy one to lie your way out of.'

'So it could be done.'

'Definitely. Bob Moore's already been talking to the airlines. We've had Saint and Greaves doing the rounds of the travel agents, but we've already figured that our man wouldn't have booked the flights locally.'

'Can I just say, Sir? I know you hate these "tiny pin-pricks", but you remember that Avocado was originally contacted by us?'

'He came to Onderman Terrace.'

'Yes, Sir. Well, he sprang the Burnley–Green connection on us and he said something a little odd at the time, a funny little phrase I'd never heard.'

'So?'

'Well, Valerie Thomas used the same phrase earlier today.'

'What was the phrase?'

'Well done, *madame*. Yours in one.'

'So what are you saying, Caz?'

'I'm not really sure, Sir. Valerie Thomas seemed to have no idea where he'd picked up the phrase. He didn't seem to think it could possibly be important. I just find it too coincidental that two men can be linked to the same three dead bodies and maybe to each other.'

'You don't seem to realise, Caz. What you keep coming up with is not even innuendo. We need to tie these people together in some way. We need to find a *reason* for them to do these things.'

'We could eliminate them from the enquiry quite easily, Sir.'

'How?'

'Blood-type them, Sir. If they come out clear on DQ-Alpha then they're clear. If they don't, we could then go to DNA fingerprints.'

'But what justification have we got for asking them to do the test?'

'We could explain we were clearing the decks, Sir, eliminating as many people as possible, like at Narboro.'

'Do you know how much DNA testing *costs*, Caz?'

'Yes, Sir, two hundred pounds per sample.'

'Right, Caz, and that's per sample, not per incident. If we ask for DNA profiles on three samples from, say, a victim and a couple more from the victim's bed, that's a thousand quid and usually three to four weeks.'

'But the DNA Profiles on the victims have already been called down, Sir. We're only looking for DQ-Alphas on Avocado and Thomas. If they come out positive on DQ-Alpha there's only a one-in-fifty chance that it's by accident. We'll be justified in spending the two hundred then, surely?'

'OK. I'll give you a "probably".'

'I've been thinking, Sir. I don't know what the law is on this, but we could run DQ-Alphas on my bed.'

'You mean the semen from the burglary tonight? The guy who made a mess of your underwear?'

'Yes, Sir. And some older samples. If there are stains in the bed . . .' She lowered her head. 'If there are other stains, Sir, well, I know their origin.'

'Christ!'

'Well, either way, Sir, it solves a problem . . .'

'And creates none, Caz?'

'What do you mean?'

'If the test comes out positive what does that mean to you? You'll have been sleeping with a killer. How will that make you feel?'

'And if it would have been positive and we don't do it, is that better?'

'No. But if it's negative . . . How will you deal with the distrust?'

'I'll deal with it, Sir. Valerie once said that there are times when you need to remove doubt. I'm happy to do it. I want to do it.'

MacInnes went quieter. His silence made her think again. There was a subtle change in her face as she shifted position. He saw her pour more whisky for them both and drink a mouthful. When she looked up, she saw him looking into her face.

'Your decision,' he said.

Caz slept on the chesterfield sofa, her head rested on a golden felt cushion. MacInnes explained that he was too set in his ways to give up his bed. She expected to struggle to find sleep, but was gone almost as soon as the lights were out. In the morning when she woke it was to the smell of frying bacon and she rolled out ready to kill for some.

'Good morning, Tom!' she called brightly.

'How'd'you like yer eggs?' he replied from the kitchen. 'You can pull the curtains if you like.'

When she swept back the long green drapes it was to reveal a morning still dark and lit by spray-sparkled street-lamps. The sea glittered near the pier. Below, early morning cars drifted by, silent, the other side of solid french doors. 'This place is lovely, Tom!' she shouted to her DI.

He appeared in the doorway with two plates. 'It's outside. It's the *view* that's lovely,' he said sadly. 'The flat is empty. Remember that, Caz.'

Thirty-eight

Over breakfast Caz told Tom MacInnes about Ted Small's disappearance. As yet, everything was third hand from Patrick Tomlinson but once again, something in her was ringing alarm bells. She repeated what Tomlinson had told her.

'If Small didn't run off, Sir. If he has disappeared, perhaps murdered, then we're up to five suspicious events: two together in January this year and the three clear-cut cases in November.'

MacInnes nodded, 'And the Small and Davies cases would support the idea of the killer having more time. They didn't look like murders.'

He promised to check out 'Missing Persons' and to talk to the wife. Ten months down the line they both knew that looking for Small, or his body, would be very difficult. They were eating toast when the DI switched the conversation back to the events of the previous night. He had already rung the hospital and Billy Tingle was fine.

'You think the burglar was your attacker?' he asked his DC.

'Yes, Sir.'

'And the murderer?'

'I'm not sure, Sir, but I doubt it. Up to now, the murderer has been extremely efficient. In my case the culprit hasn't been. Either he's had a few off days or it's someone else.'

'Or, for some reason, the killer has come under extreme pressure and now he's beginning to make mistakes.'

Caz picked up her bag, suddenly remembering. After fumbling for a moment she came out with the plastic cap. 'Last night, Sir, Billy Tingle had this in his hand. He gave it to me. I haven't a clue what it is. It might be a cap or something but there's no thread on the inside.' She passed it to the DI. He turned it over in his hands.

'I agree' he said.

'What, Sir?'

'It might be a cap or something but there's no thread on the inside.'

'Great!'

'We know anything about it?' MacInnes said. 'What did Tingle say?'

'Nothing, Sir. He didn't even realise he had it in his hand.'

'So it might have come from anywhere.'

'Including my burglar.'

'Well, it means nowt to me,' MacInnes said. 'Take it in to the station and we'll see if anyone else has any ideas.' She slipped it back in her bag.

It was out of the way, but on the way to John Street they dropped in to say hello to Billy Tingle. There were no visiting restrictions for damaged bobbies, and when they entered Billy's private room they were surprised to find it was full of flowers. He already had company. Moira Dibben!

'Oh, hi-yer, Caz!' Moira said nervously. She half rose, then she saw the DI. 'Oh, good morning, Sir. I was just . . . PC Tingle . . . bringing him a few things . . . he . . . um . . . I was just off, Sir . . . to John Street . . .'

'Good morning!' MacInnes said, particularly brightly. 'Good t'see mates mucking in.'

'Yes, Sir, well . . .' Moira said. She rose to leave touching Billy's hand.

As soon as Moira was gone, MacInnes started into Billy. 'You look all right, lad. Ah tek it they'll be booking you out later today?'

'I don't know, Sir,' Billy said.

'You tell 'em y'want outta here, Billy, strong lad like you . . .'

'I'll do my best, Sir.'

MacInnes gently punched the PC's shoulder. 'Anyway, laddie, I didna come to see after yer health. Mind, I'm glad t' see yer recoverin'. Ah came to talk t'yer about last night. Are yer up to talking now, laddie?'

'Yes, Sir.'

'Tell me what happened then.'

'Well, Sir. Not a lot really. I went to see Caz – DC Flood and I saw her light on. It was nearly ten o'clock. I saw her light on. I'd said I'd be there sometime after nine.'

'Aye.'

'Well, Sir. I'd just got to the front door. I was like tidying myself up before I rang the bell, when suddenly the front door burst open and I couldn't see very well. Somebody pushed me backwards then hit me with something while I was on the floor.'

'And what time would y'reckon it was then?'

'Between quarter-to and ten-to, Sir.'

MacInnes turned to Caz, 'What time did you arrive, Flood?'

'Almost exactly ten o'clock, Sir.'

'So our man had between ten and fifteen minutes to do whatever he wanted to do and still vacate the scene . . .'

Caz interrupted. 'More or less, Sir. But he had to avoid me and I'd driven up and down the street before I stopped.'

'What?'

'I was checking the street, Sir, I was a bit nervous.'

'OK, so we're talking a maximum of seven or eight minutes.'

'Not even that, Sir, unless the guy has terrific nerve. If he was expecting me he'd've realised that I'd see Billy and not go into the building.'

'Probably,' MacInnes said. He turned back to Billy. 'OK, laddie. Now what else can y'remember?'

But Billy wasn't a great witness. The DI began with humour, moved on to cajoling and finished off with bullying, but the PC still recalled nothing more. In a last ditch defence he offered, 'It was a bloke, Sir.'

Caz touched her DI's arm, 'Sir, could I just . . . ?'

The pair moved away from the bed. MacInnes nodded. Caz went back to Billy. She began to speak slowly. 'PC Tingle, I'm DC Flood. Billy, I'm Caz.' She sat on the bed. 'OK, Billy. No more questions, mate. What I'm going to get you to do is to run a semi-conscious "walk-through" of the events. All you've got to do is relax. Lie back and think of England.'

She took hold of his hand.

Billy closed his eyes when she told him to. There was a look of vague pleasure on his face. She told him to relax absolutely and to try to go to sleep. She began to talk softly to him. Her voice was sensuous.

'OK. Billy? You're in the nick working on Holmes. You're nearly finished. Is Moira still there?'

'No, she finished at half-eight. She's playing badminton tonight.'

'Look at the clock, Billy. Time is knocking on.'

'It's five past nine.'

'When are you going to finish, Billy?'

'I'm off downstairs to change. Holmes is printing out. I'm just off for a quick wash.'

'Great, Billy. Now you're back upstairs. Holmes has finished?'

'Yes. I'm going down to the car park. I've got to drive over to Caz's.'

'OK, you're in the car.'

'Yeah. Down the hill, into the Old Steine. Driving along the front.'

'Can you see the Grand Hotel?'

'Yep. It's all lit up with floodlights.'

'You're at Inkerman Terrace. You're driving up the street.'

'The road's pretty full. There's a couple of Sierras, a Cortina, a Cavalier, a BMW, two 205s parked nose-to-tail. There's not a lot of parking spaces.'

'Park the car, Billy.'

'I can get in next to a Mercedes.'

'Good. Car into neutral and handbrake on?'

'I'm getting out of the car. There's an old dear looking at me out of her window. No one in the street. Here's Caz's. I'm going up the steps to the flat. Caz is in. I can see her lights are on. Her call button is the one in the middle. It says C. Flood on it. I'm pressing it. There's no answer. I press again. I tidy up my hair, well . . . The front door clicks. Hi, Caz! I say. It's bright. It must be a torch. This bloke calls me a cunt and shoves me. He's got something under his arm. I try to get up. The end of this thing has a black bit on it. Then something whacks me. Then . . .'

'Billy, you're beautiful,' Caz said. 'Now let's do it again. Keep your eyes closed, Billy. Relax a bit more. OK, now you're driving up the street.' She was still holding his hand. Now he sounded sleepy.

'I'm in my motor. It's a bit noisy. The street's full of cars. Not a lot of room to park. I squeeze in between a Mercedes and an old Volvo. I go across the street to Caz's flat. A woman pulls her curtain back. She looks pretty old with white hair. The curtains move in Caz's upstairs. I see Caz wave. I go up the steps and ring her bell. When the door opens there's a bloke, just for a second, then a light flashes in my face. I'm on the floor before I know it. I try to get up and catch hold of this bloke's arm. He's wearing a raincoat. I'm not quite with it. I grab hold of this thing under his arm. Then my lights go out. Then my lights just go out.'

'Billy, you're doing fantastic. Just stay relaxed. Billy, you open the door and there's someone there. Can you see him? What does he look like?'

'You. He looks like you.' Billy sounded anxious.

'OK, Billy. He looked like me. Was his hair the same?'

'Yes.'

'Blond?'

'Yes or light brown. He had good teeth. He was smiling.'

'How tall, Billy?' He tried to sit up. 'No, Billy, close your eyes.'

'About my height, maybe shorter. Five-eight or nine, five-eleven.'

'I'm five-seven, Billy. Was he taller than me?'

'I think so. I'd say five feet ten.'

'Billy, do you remember . . .? The man that hit you, did you see his eyes?'

'His eyes? No. Yes! They're wide open. He's staring. He's grinning.' Billy tried again to sit up. Caz pushed gently down. She leaned over him and whispered something quietly in his ear. Then she sat back up. 'Stay under, Billy. Stay under. We're nearly done, mate, nearly done. Now, the thing under his arm. Look at it. Can you see it, Billy?'

'It's just a thing. It's silver. It's black on the end.'

'Is the black end the cap, Billy?'

'What cap?'

'Shit!' Caz said quietly. 'Billy, just relax a minute. Don't open your eyes. Now, think yourself awake. Open your eyes slowly. Put your hands up, so you can see your fingers. Wiggle them. OK? Good. Now sit up, Billy.' She was holding the cap.

'That's it!' Billy said. 'It was on the end of the canister, the silver thing.' He took the cap, turning it over in his hand. 'I must've pulled it off just as the twat 'it me!'

'Thanks, Billy. See, you remembered more than you thought you did.'

''old me 'and again,' he said, 'I might remember some more.'

'Another time, mate. And anyway, what would Moira say, eh?'

'She's all right, isn't she?' Billy said.

On the way back down to the station MacInnes quizzed her over the interview as he drove. 'That was impressive, Caz, but what the hell was it?'

'Absolutely nothing, Sir. If I was on the stage I'd call it hypnosis, but really all it was was what I said it was, a semi-conscious walk-through of the events last night.'

'Well if that's hypnosis, I'm impressed.'

'There's really no such thing, Tom. Everything that's been done under so-called hypnosis has been done by simple relaxation. I'm not knocking the idea. As an *idea* hypnosis can be very powerful. For example, when a victim of rape can't bring herself to talk about the incident, being "hypnotised" relieves her of the guilt of saying bad things.

'Billy Tingle was in the process of post-event justification. His mind was busy tidying up the events and slotting them into more logical pigeon-holes. It's only half-conscious. We try to be helpful and we end up distorting what really happened. The idea of relaxing Billy – hypnotising him if you go through all the associated bullshit – was to remove him from this process of tidying up and release his *real* memories out.'

'Well, I'm still impressed.'

'Thank you, Sir.'

'And your visitor looks a lot like the unknown man or woman seen at George Burnley's on the night of the murder. Raincoat, blond hair, the right height. Why didn't you ask about the colour?'

'That was a mistake, Tom. When Billy said "raincoat" I automatically heard "cream".'

Thirty-nine

Once they were back in the nick with its familiar smells and its echoing corridors, Caz could feel herself coming alive again. No counsellor was ever going to take this from her. She clipped through to the DI's office with her mind racing, trying to work out the best scheme for conning the psychiatrist. She knew enough to know it could be done.

MacInnes didn't even bother to sit down. They arrived at five to eight and by twenty-past he had arranged for a sergeant and another DC to go door-knocking in Grigglesham and the surrounds with West and O'Leary. In the same time he had arranged for the sheets to be lifted from Caz's bed and brought to the station. She agreed that half would be retained under dry conditions while the second half was sent by squad car to the Home Office Forensic Labs at Aldermaston. It didn't worry her that she had lost an item from her home. No matter how well they were laundered, she found it hard to imagine she could ever have used the sheets again.

At eight forty-five MacInnes rang Aldermaston and called in a favour. At eight forty-six he turned to Caz. 'Normal DNA-profiling will take too long for us. There's a chap at Aldermaston Forensics owes me a big favour. We can get DQ-Alpha back on the stains by ten o'clock tomorrow, and there's a new digital system of DNA-profiling under trial that takes just two-and-a-half days. I don't want to pay for a DNA profile until we've got a positive on DQ-Alpha, but if we do get a hit, we could have our answer by Saturday.'

'I'll be at Grigglesham Hall then, Sir. I'm spending the weekend with Rachel Hely. And unless I stop Valerie Thomas, he'll be there with me.'

'That's not the greatest of ideas.'

'What, Sir?'

'Going to the fertility clinic.'

'I was *invited*, Sir. Rachel Hely says I can recharge my batteries there.'

'George Foster will go ape-shit if he thinks we're crawling around.'

'Well I won't be, Sir. I'm on sick leave, remember? I'm off the case!'

MacInnes looked resigned. 'Well, I can't say I'm crazy about you going, Caz, and I'm even less happy about Thomas being there with you.'

'That's how it is, Sir. Unless we're going to pick him up.'

'We can't, Flood. Not yet.'

'Exactly, Sir.'

She sat down opposite his desk as a PC brought two teas. 'I suppose at least we'll know where he is,' MacInnes decided. 'I guess we'll just have to let things go on as if everything is normal.' He finally used his chair. He spoke to Caz as he picked up the phone.

'I wish I felt better about this. You be bloody careful, Caz.'

Caz thought for a moment, trying to imagine Valerie as a killer. It was impossible. Even if she was his arresting officer she wouldn't believe it.

'Would it be a good idea for me to ring in, Sir? Maybe once a day?'

'It would be, Flood, if you didn't need this break.'

'A *break*, Sir! Are you being funny? Until this case is resolved I'm going to go closer and closer to going off my trolley. It's only being active that's keeping me sane. I'm only going to stay up at Grigglesham Hall because I think the answer is there. You must know that.'

There was a cough from the next office. MacInnes put his fingers to his lips. The number he had dialled had finally responded.

'DI MacInnes, John Street,' Caz heard him bark. 'Yes. Is Doctor Leng available? Two days! What?' There was a long pause as he listened.

'OK,' he said finally, 'can't be helped. Thanks anyway.'

'No joy, Sir?' Caz said.

'It depends what y'mean, Flood. There's no counselling today, if that's what you're asking. Ah suggest you get what you need from home and piss off for your break. Take someone with you when you go to the flat.'

She was gone at nine, bumming a lift with Harry Deans. When they turned into Inkerman Terrace she felt a little shiver. Harry came into the building with her and stood guard while she scurried through her flat.

The bedroom smelt stale and damp. Her stomach churned as she looked at her bed. How could someone be so sick? She and Harry had passed a pile of items stacked near her flat door: the classic burglar's MO. The stack included her Sony TV, her stereo, a clock and her CD collection. Despite all this, she knew it hadn't been a burglary. Her visitor had had deeper intent.

She grabbed a sports bag from a cupboard and threw in some T-shirts, Lycra running tights, socks and two pairs of trainers. All her underwear had been strewn on the bed. Even though some of the pieces looked untouched, she couldn't bear the idea of sorting through them. Instead she folded the sheet towards the centre, hiding the insult, and placed the whole into a plastic carrier-bag. She asked Harry to radio in and tell DI MacInnes that she would deliver it later.

There was a Frank Shorter Goretex suit drip-drying in the bathroom. Caz took that down and rolled it up before putting it in with the rest. The bag full, she looked round the flat. Her piggies had been pushed back into a corner and someone had laid a black bin-bag over them as if they were real. Of all the things done to her, this felt the worst.

She looked round what had been her home and realised she would never ever be happy there again. The sadness was terrible. The blackness and the anger made everything good that had ever happened in her home seem somehow cheap and sullied. The real and deep cost of burglary now hit her with a vengeance. It made her think of Trevor Jones and their moment of decision when she'd faced him in the excavation. Now she wished he had made a move to pass her so, at least once, the people could have fought back.

She shook her head and kept up the anger. There were no tears. 'Come on, Harry!' she said. 'Time to fuck off.'

Margaret Oakley was brilliant when she rang her. Yes, she said, Caz could come a day early. No, she said, it would not be a problem. Yes, she told Caz, she would inform Miss Rachel and no, she wouldn't have a problem with security. She promised.

'And what time do you expect to arrive, Miss Flood?'

'After one o'clock and before five. Is that OK?'

'That'll be fine. We look forward to seeing you.'

She knew MacInnes would have to bollock her and that Blackside would probably go spare, but she took the carrier bag into the nick herself, hoping for one last fix before she went into cold turkey for four and a half days. As she approached the DI's office she could hear her senior officers deep in loud conversation, but she was beyond caring and she knocked anyway.

'*Yes!*' This was Blackside. She strutted in, pelvis forward.

'Good morning, Sir, Chief. Samples as requested.' She held out the bag.

'That your sheets, Flood?' Blackside said.

'Yes, Sir.'

'Well, get the desk sergeant to log it in, girl, and then bugger off out of here before you wind me up any more.'

'Yes, Sir!' she clipped back, then she said, 'Could I just ask the

DI, Sir? Is there anything back from Sergeant Moore on the air flights?'

'Not yet, Flood,' MacInnes snapped. 'Now go away!'

Caz left the MGB parked underneath the nick and walked down into town to buy some clothes. From Marks & Spencer she bought a dozen pairs of briefs and a couple of bras then, unleashed, she went into some serious shopping, buying expensive underwear, a kimono and a pair of silk trousers. She needed pampering and she knew it. She went into a tiny café in the Lanes for coffee, and the high-caloried cream bun she bought to finish off was arguably medicinal. It worked. This was now the fourth consecutive day that she hadn't run and she knew that tomorrow she'd be a pound heavier. Her aches had subsided into niggles now and the bump on her head no longer hurt. What did hurt was thinking of Valerie. It hurt so much that she stopped doing it. She decided what would be, would be.

Forty

Caz drove moderately as she slipped away from Brighton. Determined to feel things again, she had the MGB's top down so kept her speed between thirty and forty to stop herself freezing to death. She had time to spare, so wandered the map, aiming at villages with cute, silly names, then trying to reach a landmark town from there. She puttered the car through the villages of Washington and Storrington, then swung on to roads with twists and turns, lost signposts, hump-back bridges and blind corners. She found West Chiltington and Nutbourne and a tiny place called Gay Street. Then she managed to get lost for a while and had to seek out a more major road.

She was heading south again, on the A29, thinking about Gay Street. It was strange how a word like gay could quickly move in a generation; how use of a word could change so dramatically. 'Happy and gay' had given way to 'happy to be gay'; more than once she had heard people one generation older than her own use terms like, 'I feel gay', and then find themselves apologising that of course they didn't mean . . . It was then that the more primitive prejudices slipped out. It was then that she realised just how powerful a force conformity was.

And now gay was death; gayness was supposed to be a killer. She was talking to herself as hedges rippled by. 'So happy is death; happiness is a killer!' It was sad. She wondered if she had ever been innocent. Had there ever been a time when she didn't test, didn't check, didn't assess?

She was driving the way the micro-lights had flown barely a week before. To her left was the river Rother and, further, the South Downs Way. She had forsaken names like Barlavington, Fittleworth, Cocking and Bepton. They echoed a slower life, one of romance, but she knew, deep down, that those places, like Narboro, had dark memories just like everywhere else, no matter how harsh or romantic their name. She gunned the engine. Now she was back to the job in hand. Would she weigh every handshake and measure every smile? Why couldn't she just stop for a while, relax and soak up comfort?

She was the right side of Midhurst now, brub-ubbing the MGB slowly into Grigglesham Foster's main street. She glanced down at her watch. It was just half-past twelve. Half-twelve on a Wednesday, she thought, yeah, that should be pretty quiet. She had time to stop for a quiet drink.

Trying hard to be in a non-investigative mode, she closed her eyes to the scattering of cars outside the Drunken Preacher. As she crossed the car park, she concentrated on the front door and the sign which indicated the licensee. Inside, she ordered dry white wine, then went to sit by a window with her back to the light. With her eyes closed, a sip of wine held in her mouth, she tried to relax, from her scalp, through her ears, right down to her toes. She pushed the wine through her teeth and felt it tingle against her lips and gums. Now warm, she let it slip down. Her shoulders were strung like piano strings. MacInnes and Blackside were right, she needed this break. Her body was just about to give up on her.

She fancied something to eat.

'Well, well, well, if it ain't Modesty Blaise! Looks like our luck's in, lads. The Queen of Crime is here to help us out.' It was West and O'Leary; West was talking. 'Well, well, Cazzer,' he said. 'Fancy seeing you here. You come along to help us out, have yer?'

The DCs were towering over her as she huddled into the window-seat. She really did not want this. 'I'm on sick leave, John. Don't you know anything? It happens that I've got a friend living near here and I'm not due to arrive until after two, OK?'

'It's OK by us,' West said. 'Isn't it, Frank?' He looked at O'Leary who nodded. He had a grin like a schoolboy slashing his face. She resigned herself to her fate and waved her hands to the bench seats either side of her. 'Looks like I'm cornered,' she said, 'take a pew.'

They came either side of her and O'Leary spilt some of his beer as he sat down, side-swiping in against her, thigh against thigh. 'This is cosy!' he grinned. She groaned and swigged her wine.

'I suppose you're going to tell me how well the investigation is going, are you, boys? You're so up on it all that you've retired here to discuss who's going to arrest the killer?'

'Something like that,' West said.

'So who did it?'

'We all reckon it was you, Flood,' O'Leary said. 'Every time you open a door there's another body. We just haven't worked out how you did the Horsham guy in yet.'

'Grow up, Frank!' she said, not even bothering to look at him.

'All right,' O'Leary said. 'We keep fergettin' that you're a weak little girl. D'you wanna know what we got or don't you?' She glowered at him.

'She wants to know, Frank,' West said.

Before he laid it all out for DC Flood, John West went back to the bar, returning with two pints of 'Local' and a double whisky and ginger. Caz pointed a finger at her glass, a question mark on her face.

'Oh, the lads know what Tom MacInnes feeds yer,' West said.

She left it. There was no response she could think of that would help. 'Tell me what you've found out then,' she said sweetly. She took a sip of her drink.

'Oh, right!' West said. 'I think you're gonna like this.'

'Not a lot,' O'Leary said, 'but you're gonna . . .'

'Shut up, Frank,' Caz said.

'We've been punting these pictures around.' West explained,

'We've got the three stiffs, Burnley, Beecham and Green, and another picture of a guy called Davies, the singer whose death is a bit iffy.'

'I know about Davies,' Caz said.

'Yeah, OK. Anyway, we struck oil this morning. The DI rang us and suggested we interview some old codger called Tom Dobson and a bird that works in 'ere called Lewis.'

'Annie Lewis.'

'Right. Anyway, we struck gold. Hits on the lot of 'em!'

'All four?'

'Yep. And dates, well, thereabouts.'

Frank O'Leary chimed in. 'Burnley and Green were here together some time in July, Annie Lewis remembered them. Said they sat together once. She thought they were brothers. The old codger reckons he saw both of them late July. One of them asked him where Grigglesham Hall was.'

Caz was spreading the photographs out. The sources were different and the quality of the shots went from OK to brilliant, but what she had not seen until this moment was how similar they all looked. Beecham, Green and Burnley could have been triplets. Only Davies looked different, he was dark and Celtic with thick black eyebrows.

'This old bloke's all right. Says a few young men have been to the hall over the years. He thought they were there for interviews. Placed Davies there late last year, Novemberish. Said he came there with his brother.'

'Another look-alike?'

'Sounds that way.'

'This is good stuff, lads. When are you ringing in?'

'Half an hour ago,' West said with a laugh, 'but you know how it is, we're "stuck on a difficult interview".'

'Well, speak to Tom MacInnes when you do ring in,' Caz said. 'There's another "iffy", some "missing person" called Ted Small from Peacehaven. DI MacInnes knows all about him. We need a description and a photograph as soon as poss. I've a feeling Small will look the absolute spit of John Davies.'

'I may be thick,' West said, 'but what the fuck's going on?'

'I haven't got the faintest idea,' Caz replied.

She wasn't sure if she was lying or not.

Caz had managed to get John West moderately excited and he left to ring in. While he was gone she clarified the situation with Frank O'Leary. The two DCs would probably be going up to the hall after lunch to question the staff. Westy was just clearing things with the DCS back at base.

'Well, do me a favour, Frank,' Caz said quietly. 'When you get to the hall I'll be there. I'm stopping as a guest for five days or so. Don't give me a hard time and don't be too familiar. They know I'm a copper but I'm on holiday. I'm not on this case, all right?'

'No problem,' Frank said.

West came back, 'Small was twenty-nine, dark-haired, good-looking. DS Reid interviewed the wife this morning. The only picture she had was crap but Reid says he does look a bit like Davies.'

'In that case it must be my round,' Caz said.

Forty-one

It was a couple of minutes in the MGB through the village to the estate. The huge iron gates were open but as she turned in, a large man stepped into the road in front of her. He was about six foot two and wore a lovat shooting jacket with shotgun cartridges like medals across his chest.

'Miss Flood, is it?' he said broadly. She said yes.

'Drive on up to the hall then, Miss. There's only one road. Take it steady, though. Them sleepin' policemen we got are a bit high.'

The gravel driveway swept away to the left, following the red-brick wall. On both sides, the grass was short. After six hundred metres the road swung into the beginning of a spiral and she saw the colourless water of the man-shaped river to her right. She was doing about fifteen miles an hour but the first bump in the road still whacked the suspension. She dropped her speed even more. Now the road crossed a bridge and the water was to her left, now to her right again. It was very pretty. In the warm green months it must have been wonderful.

When she saw the hall it looked crisp and English, echoing its history. As she approached across the last bridge she saw a side door open and the huge frame of George Foster appearing briefly. Then Rachel Hely walked out on to the pink gravel in front of the building. She was dressed smartly in a skirt and white blouse and her hair barely moved in the breeze. 'Miss Flood! How nice of you to come. And a day early, too! Welcome!'

The MGB rolled to a halt, the crunch of gravel sounding peculiarly rich. Caz stepped out to a handshake and a delicately light peck from Rachel on her cheek.

Rachel led her in to the building, taking her elbow lightly and telling her how pleased they were that she had decided to visit with them. As they approached the building, George Foster reappeared with a smallish man who scurried passed them to retrieve her bag from the car.

'Would you like tea or coffee, Caz?' Rachel said. 'There's coffee perked, but tea will only take two or three minutes.' Caz said coffee would be fine.

They stepped inside and Rachel spoke again. 'Mr Foster has told us that you are a police officer. We were a little surprised. I hope you are off duty. We're expecting a visit from a few of your colleagues this afternoon.'

'I know,' Caz said heavily, 'but it's really nothing to do with me now. I've been taken off the investigation and sent on leave. I've had a few terrible weeks and I've been told to rest. Really I'm glad to be off the case. You know about it? The killings in Brighton? Not really my cup of tea . . .'

'Or coffee?' Rachel smiled.

'I just want to rest for at least a month.'

'Well, Caz, if that's true then I would say you've come to the perfect place. We know one thing here, and that is how to bring back a woman to her essential self.'

'It sounds lovely,' Caz said.

'It is,' Rachel said sweetly. 'Believe me, it is . . .'

Caz smiled.

'But first we need to get you to your suite,' Rachel added briskly. 'We have booked you the very best room. You have your own jacuzzi and sauna and a direct door to the swimming pool. You'll find some comfortable clothing in the wardrobes. The rooms are splendid. They are my favourite. Their last occupant was an Indonesian Princess.'

'Thank you,' Caz said, genuinely grateful. 'It sounds wonderful.'

They went via the pentagonal main hall into the main guest area. Caz could smell the superb scent of almond polish and the gentle aroma of some pot pourri that was different somehow from the norm, almost fruity.

The heavy door to her room was marked 'Mango' and the interior was based on the colour, a cross between magnolia and pink. There were three large chairs and something that looked like a *chaise-longue*, all heavy with fluted legs painted gold. Furniture was one of Caz's blind-spots, but she thought it all looked like late eighteenth- or early nineteenth-century French – Louis and a big number following. The one oil painting on the wall looked Turnerish but wasn't and the soft red carpet was deep enough to hide in. She wanted to kick off her shoes and paddle barefoot.

It was two-thirty. Rachel left her after opening wardrobes and drawers to show what had been prepared for her guest. The wardrobe hung with three different coloured track-suits, all the same loose shape and softly lined. Caz was uncertain about the material, but they felt expensive and were smooth to the touch.

She did the tour. The changing room was just as luxurious as the rest, with a long white and gold dressing table and the same rich red carpet. The bathroom was about the size of her Brighton flat, beautifully white, with gorgeous replica Victorian Vernon Tutbury sanitary ware and golden taps. Even the few bath-oils and salts displayed on a short glass shelf were the sort she only ever dreamed about as presents. The little noise she made was one of sensuous delight.

She ran a steaming bath, water exploding from the taps to fill it. She poured in a mauve liquid from a tall glass jar, watched it swirl, then stepped in. Once submerged, she surrendered herself to the luxury and felt herself folding away blissfully. Her hands ran over the faint blue marks on her front. Only if she directly pressed one of them did they feel remotely painful. She closed her eyes, trying to melt into the water.

At three she crawled out and rubbed herself down with a huge rough white towel. Once dry, she dressed quickly in one of the fleecy track-suits over new underwear torn from their cellophane packs. Her socks were new; Ultramax, extra soft, padded and splashed with a red logo. Physically she felt like a pampered cat. She should be nibbling chocolates now or sipping Tia Maria in front of an open log fire. Before she went back to the other wing she slipped into canvas beach shoes. Then she left.

She had been asked by her host to buzz when she was coming through. They met in the central hall, where Rachel told her that the police had arrived. 'Two constables, West and O'Leary. Do you know them?'

'To nod to, yes,' Caz said, 'but not particularly well.'

They walked through to the guest lounge where John West and Frank O'Leary waited. Rachel suggested Caz might stay. 'Mr Foster will want to be around as well. He can be a bit heavy-handed at times. I thought you might be a useful counter. Would you mind? We would be most grateful.'

John West was sitting formally behind a table. Frank O'Leary sat to the end more casually, with his hands together, the fingers entwined. His nose was resting on his fingers and he peered out as though a superior overseeing a protégé. George Foster was standing by a window, his bulk blocking the light. He was speaking softly into a Motorola Micro-Tac cellular phone.

West spoke first. 'Miss Hely. Thank you for being so prompt. We would like to speak to all the staff here and we would be grateful if you could answer a few questions as well.'

Rachel gestured Caz into a large leather chair and replied to West, 'What do you require of me, Officer? Would you like me to sit here?'

'Please,' West said. He waved at the chair opposite. 'We are aware that these gentlemen were in Grigglesham Foster earlier this year. We think it possible that they visited your clinic.' He spread four black-and-white photographs in front of him. 'Can you tell us if you recognise any of them? Could they have visited here?'

Rachel leaned forward, apparently studying each photograph in turn. One she picked up and studied more carefully, turning it in the window-light.

'This one,' she said, 'very handsome, very dark. He seems vaguely familiar but I cannot honestly say where I have seen him.'

'His name is Davies,' West said, 'John Davies. If he came here it would have been about this time last year.'

'I do not deal with the hire of domestic help, Mr West. That is the province of George Foster. If he came here I might have glimpsed him briefly and registered his face unconsciously.'

'You're quite positive that you've never met any of these men?'

'Absolutely. I have told you so. I may have seen this John Davies fellow. The others, never.' She moved to a chair near Caz.

West asked if he could now see Margaret Oakley. Moments later, the secretary came into the room, slightly bowed, nodding to all present. West introduced himself and she sat down.

'Miss Oakley, I'd like you to look at some pictures.' He wafted them under her face.

The secretary took the sheaf and began to study the top photograph minutely, pushing back her glasses every few seconds. Eventually she said, 'This is Peter Burnley.' She looked at the second photograph, 'And this is Peter Beecham. Sorry, the other one, this first one, is George Burnley, I meant *George* Burnley.' She continued. 'This man's name is James Green and this chap is called Davies, I'd have to look up his first name. He was here late last year.'

Frank O'Leary muttered 'Jesus!' West gave him a shut-up look.

'That's extremely helpful, Miss Oakley . . .'

'It's Margaret.'

'That's extremely helpful, Margaret. Could you tell me why these men came to Grigglesham Hall?' By the window, Foster shifted.

'Miss Oakley, could you tell me why they came to the clinic?'

'For Sunday lunch,' Margaret said. 'They came for lunch.'

'I'm sorry,' West said. He looked bemused. 'Would you repeat that?'

'They came here for lunch. One of our big lunches.'

'I'd be grateful if you would explain, Miss Oakley.'

'Margaret, it's Margaret.' He gave her a thin smile.

'We have guests here quite often, Inspector.' Frank O'Leary choked a laugh.

'These gentlemen were our guests sometime in the summer.'

'Your guests? But why these men? And wouldn't Miss Hely be present at these lunches?'

'Oh yes, of course.'

West leaned past Margaret Oakley to speak to Rachel, 'Are you *sure* you haven't met these men before, Miss Hely?'

'Quite sure, Detective,' Rachel said.

'Could I just . . .' Margaret Oakley was rifling through a small notebook. 'Yes . . . Burnley, Green and Beecham came to lunch on June the twenty-eighth. Professor Hely was present and so was Mr Foster. Some of our female clients attended as well. Miss Rachel was away, however, taking a long weekend break. In the Cotswolds, I believe.'

Rachel explained, 'I stopped with an old girlfriend, a television producer. She has a second home in East Leach, not far from Broadway, in the Cotswolds.'

'May I have the lady's name?' DC West said.

'No, you most definitely may not!' Rachel replied.

West went faintly pink. He spoke again to Margaret Oakley. 'These lunches? Your male guests. How are they selected?'

'I can't tell you that I'm afraid. You'll have to speak to Miss Rachel.'

There was a flicker of annoyance on John West's face then he recovered to smile at Margaret. He thanked her for her help and she asked if she could go now? When he said yes she stood up and gave him a little nod then turned to see where George Foster was before she left the room.

DC West scribbled into his notebook. When he spoke again, he did so without looking up from his writing. 'Miss Hely? Do I get an explanation?'

'Of what?' Rachel said from her chair.

'Your gentleman guests, Miss Hely. Would you tell me how they were chosen. For what particular reason were they here?'

'I'm not sure that I can tell you that.' She glanced at George Foster.

'She's right,' Foster said. He was dialling a number. 'Can't tell you. Have to take it on advisement.'

'Ad*vise*ment!' West said. 'What are you talking about?'

'Give me a second,' Foster said.

Foster turned away towards the long window, barking short sharp sentences into the phone. He was fired up with adrenaline and couldn't stand still. 'Yes, Blackside, DCS, now. Matter of urgency!'

He spun round, looking for something to burn fuel, then he shouted, 'Margaret! Any chance of drinks in 'ere?' Then he was responding to the voice in his ear. He stepped back into the window-light, muttering as he looked at the others. 'Yes. Critical. Twenty-four hours. Yes. Good idea. Thank you.'

He passed the phone to West. 'Your DCS wants a word.'

Foster took a couple of strides towards John West who stood to take the phone in his fingertips. He looked at it before placing it to his ear then he listened. He was nodding vigorously and briefly appearing to protest before the voice in his ear barked him into submission. 'Yes, Sir. DC West, Sir. About five-thirty.'

West returned the Micro-Tac to George Foster and didn't even bother to sit back down at the table. Foster flipped the cellular phone closed, ending the connection and West closed his pad, explaining to all in the room that a far more urgent line of enquiry required that the detectives leave immediately. They were thanked for their courtesy.

'We may need to come and see you again some time in the next seventy-two hours,' West said. 'I trust you will all be available?'

He turned to O'Leary. 'Come on, Frank. We're wanted in Brighton.'

They got away quickly with George Foster accompanying them. At the door, Foster laid his arm on O'Leary's shoulder then shook West's hand. When he turned to face the room it was as if they had never been there.

Caz looked up. She was amazed that she had kept her own counsel, but now she was desperate to be told something. Foster caught her eye. 'Brighton are pulling in a prime suspect about now. Some chap called Avocado. DCS Blackside wants his lads back there now.'

'They've pulled Avocado?' Caz asked. 'On what grounds?'

'I didn't ask,' Foster said, 'but the word is that the guy is bang to rights.'

Caz sat there. She was stunned by Foster's matter-of-fact revelation and was almost nailed to her chair. One part of her fell back into the upholstery while another wanted to rush around headless making phone calls and asking questions. Avocado!

She calmed herself down, breathing deeply and silently through her nose, telling herself to relax. There was an awkward silence as Caz tried to think of the right thing to say. She struggled until Margaret Oakley tiptoed into the room with a tray of drinks and Rachel finally spoke.

'An arrest! I presume you are pleased, Caz?'

She replied, distracted. She had been thinking about Valerie. 'What? Oh yes.' Gradually she focused on the room and on the speaker. She was sharper now. 'Yes, I'm very pleased.' She could hear the chink of china. 'Tea please,' she said, anticipating the secretary's question. 'White, no sugar, thank you.'

'Are you all right?' Rachel asked.

'Um? Yes, I think so. There was so much tension while I was on the case . . . and now I'm off the case . . . and then this. It feels strange.'

'Well, now you can forget all about it,' Rachel said brightly. 'You can take it easy and enjoy yourself. Recharge your batteries. Relax today. Have a swim and a sauna. Tomorrow, if you like, I can show you the laboratories and we could walk the gardens in the afternoon. Would you like that?'

'Oh yes,' Caz said softly. 'I'd like that very much.'

In theory, the rest of the afternoon was called relaxing. Caz had excused herself and drifted back along the corridors to her room, passing doors that were solid and immaculately decorated, each with a different motif and name. Before she reached Mango, her room, she passed Vermont, Penang and *Col legno*. She had at least heard of the first two and she had eaten mango but who, what, or where *Col legno* was, she had not the faintest idea. It was impossible to resist the unlocked door, and she pushed with electric fingertips against its rich finish. Inside, the room was stunning; a deep brown polished courtyard that led seamlessly from fitted mahogany office through a music room into a salon that looked stolen from a gentleman's club, with deep green buttoned leather chairs and old crusty oils on the walls. On the margin of music room and office, a gleaming fat cello stood with its point on the parquet floor. All around, from hidden speakers, dark brown music was coming from the same instrument. The overall effect was one of security; of an all-enveloping richness and solidity. Where her own room was light, bright, airy and uplifting, *Col legno* was deep, reassuring and protective, like an ageing white-haired father.

Caz sucked it all in. The contrasts could hardly have been greater. She was amazed at the different emotions she could feel simply by standing in the different room. She thought briefly about the psychology of the chosen decors, then she speculated about the craftsmen who had created the rooms; their designers, interior decorators. People like Jeremy Avocado. She thought of the same man now, sitting in front of a bare table in a cream and green interview room. He would be with Sergeant Moore and either Saint or Greaves, and Tom MacInnes would be showering now, getting ready to dress in his blue suit.

She stopped herself looking into the other rooms, creeping away from the bass notes of *Col legno* and walking softly to her own door. She guessed Penang to be golden and bright, with soft whites and pale blues, maybe with the sound of breaking waves tumbling across a sandy carpet that wriggled between the toes of its barefoot guest. Vermont would be rustic, with stretching dark greens and a sense of openness. She was fascinated. Profoundly, she wondered whether a fundamental her would merely react differently to each room, or would she actually *become* different, depending which room she was in. Trains and hotels had always made her feel sexy, but these rooms made her think in terms of sensuality rather than sex. They made her think of her body. She had the perverse realisation that the manner of love-making in each of these different rooms would somehow take on the personality of the surroundings. Then she knew for certain that she would be different people in the different rooms. There couldn't possibly be one, but she wondered what the hard-rock, red-and-black, great-room-to-bonk-in would look like.

She was smiling as she went into her room, and only gradually did the ongoing drama at John Street drift back to her higher consciousness. A part of her desperately wanted to ring the nick immediately but she surprised herself by keeping her hands away from the phone. She was like a wavering abstainer staring at an open bottle, so she stripped for the gym and went through to work out before a swim. After ten minutes she was glowing with warmth, her muscles coming alive, and after forty more she was sated, tensile and elastic, ready to loosely swim in the pastel blue pool. She felt brilliant. Avocado was nicked and she was on 'oliday.

Forty-two

As she swam, pale yellow lights lit her back while the afternoon gave way to a dark November evening. The water was noticeably warm and the pool length only fifteen metres, so she didn't swim for fitness, but merely drifted along in a lazy crawl. The gym session had been deliciously hard and she had got back in contact with herself, emerging hot and wet with good sweat, feeling lithe and athletic.

When Caz bathed – in a gorgeous oily water smelling of fruit – she decided that she had died and gone to heaven. After fifteen decadent minutes she had perfected control of the hot tap with her toes and she allowed herself another six hundred seconds' immersion with the water hot to the edge of pain. When she finally rose to towel down, the deep pink of her body had swollen to surround the last bruise on her heart. She felt she had finally passed through the darkness and was now back in sunlight.

Her blonde hair was looser and fluffier once it had dried, and when she saw herself in the mirror she thought she looked less sophisticated, slightly less hard. 'A country lass,' she thought, and smiled at her reflection. The bed-cover had been turned back, revealing a soft, off-white blanket, and she threw herself at it face down, squirming into its fibres, her knees moving up and down against the bed as she pushed deeper. She felt wholly animal; filled out, red and glowing. Valerie was forty-eight hours and a world away. Groaning with comical frustration, she pushed harder towards the floor, her hands above her on the pillow's white, fistfuls of linen and feather squeezed between her fingers.

It was twenty-past seven when she finally dressed, in soft white, underneath an equally soft, light grey sweat-suit. She had slept so soundly that she needed to splash cold water in her face to bring her brain back into gear. She had the urge to grin. Her eyes sparkled.

She didn't bother with make-up and simply fluffed her hair away from her collar. When she left to walk along the silent corridors, she did so in her socks, feeling vaguely naughty, like a schoolgirl slipping out of the dorm. Far off, she thought she could hear the clap of dinner plates, and a delicious smell wafted by her tantalisingly before she lost it. Suddenly, she felt desperately hungry and was aware of her empty stomach. She had arranged to meet Rachel at seven-thirty for dinner at eight, and the meal now seemed a long way off. Though she was looking forward to good wine, pleasant company and stimulating conversation, she thought she would need a sandwich just to survive the next half-hour.

'Right on time!' Rachel said brightly as Caz paused at the door. 'It must be your police training!' She was smiling at her with real affection.

'A fluke, I'm afraid,' Caz said, 'I fell asleep.'

Rachel glanced towards the white-stockinged feet of her guest and laughed, 'Well, I see you are already entering into the holiday spirit!'

'What?' Caz looked down. 'Oh, I see. It's an old habit. I pad around all the time at home and this place feels so good and so warm . . .'

'I know,' Rachel said quickly, 'it was designed that way. Come and have something to drink. We have most things. What would you like?'

Thinking of her blood sugar, Caz asked for Southern Comfort and Coke. Rachel approved and made up two identical drinks in tall, heavy-bottomed tumblers, each half-filled with ice cubes, topped up with amber liqueur and dashed with a suggestion of Coke: 'It must be Coke, not diet, not Pepsi,' Rachel told Caz. After the first mouthful, Caz replied that the mixer's pedigree hardly mattered, so little was present it barely suggested itself. 'I would try it neat, but they say it's a man's drink,' Rachel said. 'What do you think?'

'That's nonsense,' Caz said through her first sip. 'Typical male bull.'

'You are right, of course,' Rachel said slowly, as though making a momentous decision, 'I think, from now on, I'll forget the cola!' She was smiling and gestured Caz towards the nearby chairs. They moved to sit down.

'We have perhaps five minutes before the men arrive, what shall we talk about?'

'Oh, this place,' Caz said, 'those wonderful guest rooms, the grounds, everything . . . You were absolutely right about what happens to a woman here. I feel totally different and I've been here less than six hours.'

Rachel's face lit up with pride. 'You really like it?'

'Oh God, yes. I feel indulged, pampered; like I'm rediscovering . . .'

'Your womanhood?'

'I don't know if I'd call it my "womanhood". What did you say this afternoon – you could help me find my essential self? Well, it's something like that. I can feel all the bitter layers of my everyday life falling away and I'm back in touch with the core me, not just what I think *about* things, but *how* I think; who I see in the mirror, who I really am.'

'And fundamentally you are a woman, not a policewoman. Is that not right? At your core you are a potential mother before a Chief Inspector.'

'What do you mean?'

'Women know *how* to be women, lovers, mothers. Very simplistically, it comes to us naturally. You, Caz; in one sense you can close your eyes and fall into your biological role without trying too hard. But if you choose a route through life involving other things like a career, you will never quite rid yourself of the sensation of striving. It will always be work.'

'Fighting male prejudices.'

'Well, yes, but that's too easy to say.' Rachel's tone was suddenly different, altogether firmer, sharpening up for some debate. 'None of us *chooses* to be prejudiced, Caz. We assimilate bigotry, but that is not my point. Even if the football field was truly level, if there was no male bias at all, we would still struggle to succeed, as it were outside our bodies, or perhaps I should say, *despite* our bodies.'

Caz let out a short, forced laugh, 'Oh, Rachel, if you were a man, now I'd expect you to say that a woman's place was in the home.'

'That's completely unfair,' Rachel fired back, 'I am not saying that at all. I think you know that I am not. I am saying that, exclusive of cultural differences, we are predisposed by our biology to be mothers. Without making any value judgements about worth, I'm saying that we, as females, when we strive to do the things that men have always done, are condemned to swim forever upstream, against the flood-tide of our hormones. Even without the inequalities that come from living in a man's world, we are fighting the way we are built.'

'What are you saying – that women shouldn't want careers, that men should remain as the masters of privilege and power?'

'Not at all! Our biological imperatives don't dictate our lives, but they do give us a certain bias. Motherhood is a massive disruption to a woman's career, whereas fatherhood hardly need cause a stutter to a man. Men light the blue touch-paper and retire, but women are confined.'

'This is pretty standard stuff.'

'Yes, I'm sorry. It is not really what I wanted to say. I mean that, because there are biological and psychological differences in women, differences pre-written to accommodate them to breeding, to nurture, that when they choose a "male" life-pattern – male as we see it now, at least – they take on an inner stress which may or may not ever be conscious.'

'So women shouldn't have full-time careers?'

'Of course they should! If they wish to. I would say that both you and I seem to be doing well enough. We simply need to be aware that we are generating conflicts within ourselves that can create both dark and light.'

She glanced towards the door, 'The men are coming.'

Professor Hely and George Foster stepped into the room, finishing what looked like an animated discussion. Foster had just said, 'One month', and the professor barked back, 'Please deal with it, George.' As they entered the room and saw Caz, their faces changed from hard to soft in an instant. Professor Hely smiled broadly at his guest while Foster simply nodded.

'I trust my daughter has kept you entertained, Miss Flood?' Hely said as he crossed the room. 'Does she have you debating yet? Be warned, my little girl has a fiery temper when unleashed!'

The men were dressed casually, George Foster in dark cords and a white Arran sweater, Professor Hely in light grey billowing slacks and an open-necked lumberjack's shirt. Dressed more softly, both of them seemed milder and less threatening.

Rachel had another Southern Comfort, this time without the Coke. Caz had a smaller one. A clock struck eight and Rachel gasped, 'Ah, dinner! Shall we go through?'

They sat down at a circular table, in the middle of which was a flowered tureen containing the soup, a mouth-watering creamed watercress. Professor Hely did the honours, spooning its rich green deftly into simple white bowls. With the soup they ate thick, black-edged, crusty bread that reminded Caz of long cherished holidays on her grandmother's farm. She had to restrain herself in order to leave room for the main course: steak and kidney pie.

'It's so strange to eat "proper" English food,' she said as she picked a flake of bread-crust from her lips, 'I hadn't realised how much my diet had changed over the years. Now it's pizzas, burgers, and Chinese and Indian meals. I get an English breakfast about once a year!'

The professor smiled. 'The menu here varies considerably, depending on our guests, but whenever we can we eat classic British fare.'

'Oh, please,' Caz protested, 'not tripe.'

'But tripe and onions is *wonderful*!' Rachel crooned.

Caz shook her head. 'I draw the line at tripe.'

'How about haggis?' Rachel asked. 'Is haggis all right?'

'No tripe, no haggis.'

'Have you ever actually *eaten* haggis?' Rachel enquired. 'Or tripe?'

'No . . .'

'Ah-hah!' Rachel said victoriously. 'Then surely you see what I mean by prejudices, Caz. Have you any idea when you decided you wouldn't like either of them? Could you not be wrong?'

Caz grimaced. 'I'd rather not take the test if that's all right with you, Rachel!'

Professor Hely spoke to ask if she was happy with her room. 'I believe you are in Mango. Is that correct?'

'Yes, thank you. The room is delightful. The gym is quite excellent and the pool is very pleasant. You really do pamper your guests, Professor.' She paused. 'There was another room, er . . . *Col legno*. That was beautiful too, all rich dark woods with fitted bookcases and things.'

Rachel explained, 'Every room is different, the brief to the decorators was to create certain moods. Some are bright, some are soft and pastel. I believe *Col legno* was meant to be "solid, safe and paternal".' She smiled at Caz, 'We all need different things.'

'Did one designer create all the guest rooms?' Caz asked the professor.

'No. We interviewed ten and chose four a few months before George Foster came to us. Each designer was responsible for just two of the suites. We have Penang, Vermont, Mango, Downs, *Col legno*, and er . . .'

Rachel stepped in, 'Kerry, Oasis and Taj Mahal.'

'Can you spot the room pairs?' Caz asked lightly. 'Does the designer's signature show through despite the different colours and furniture?'

'I'm not sure,' Rachel said. 'What do you think, Father?'

'It has never occurred to me before,' Hely answered. 'I did not see the rooms while they were being decorated, but I did see them soon after they had been transformed. It would be amusing to try to discover the pairs. Perhaps you and Miss Flood could try after dinner.' He turned to Foster. 'George, presumably we have records in the office? Invoices, estimates?'

'I'll get whatever paperwork there is later,' Foster said.

The rest of the dinner passed by pleasantly. The red wine was light and a little too easy to drink. The professor held court, retelling stories about his days as a research student, surprising Caz with a mischievous sense of humour.

The change in him was remarkable, and Caz thought it was incredible that she could once have cast him as 'creepy'.

The professor eventually excused himself, and George Foster used the moment to leave to find the decorator's paperwork. Earlier he had told Caz about Bessie leaving, and that he had asked Tom MacInnes whether his DC might be interested in a job. 'He told me you was a good 'un,' Foster said loudly. Then with a chuckle he said, 'And I told him I'd get you working here!'

'After a few hours in Mango,' Caz laughed, 'I think you may be right!'

'Perhaps you could talk to Mr Foster about it in the morning?' Rachel suggested. 'Right now, shall we tour the bedrooms?'

The women left just after the men. Caz shuffled silently with woollen steps while Rachel's heels echoed with a business-like clip whenever she stepped off carpet. They began with Penang, the first room in the residential wing, and it was close to how Caz had imagined it; bright lightweight blues, white woodwork, pastel furniture and the occasional splash of colour making the whole like a three-dimensional Hockney picture. The carpet was white.

'Let's say this one was done by "Arty",' Caz said.

She had expected Vermont to be bare and open. In fact it was panelled with pink-and-lilac finely-flowered wallpaper between cedar borders.

'I love this room,' Rachel sighed, 'and it's Bessie's favourite. I quite like Bessie. It's a shame she will be leaving us soon.'

Caz was looking at the oversized American furniture. 'I can't believe Arty did this room,' she said. 'I shall say this one was done by "Ronald", as in Reagan.'

They walked across to *Col legno*. As soon as the door was open they both saw it was another 'Reagan'. Rachel spoke first. 'The same author as Vermont, yes?'

'I think so,' Caz agreed. Then, as they walked towards Mango, she asked how Bessie would be replaced.

'That's Mr Foster's area,' Rachel said. 'Because our work is sensitive, Mr Foster has to interview every job applicant. Anyone who works here has to sign some British Government thing which guarantees they will not jeopardise the clinic's confidentiality.'

'The Official Secrets Act,' Caz said matter-of-factly. 'I signed it years ago.'

'That's it. The professor and I have the final veto, but George will usually suggest the replacement.' She paused at the door. 'Why do you ask?' They stepped into Caz's room.

'Sorry about the mess,' Caz said, 'I left in a hurry for dinner.'

'Could this suite be another one of Art's?' Rachel suggested weakly. 'It is very simple, but somehow I do not think it is quite the same.'

'I agree,' Caz said. 'It's *too* simple, I reckon, and the carpet colouring is a bit strong for Arty's taste.' She sat for a moment on her bed, then, as if making a decision, she took a breath and asked, 'Rachel?'

'What?'

'Could *I* qualify for the job? – as Bessie's replacement?'

'You?'

'Yes,' Caz said. 'I do have valid reasons.'

'I am really not certain, Caz, but I would suspect so. We require a woman who has been police-trained; who is well educated and is able to converse well. I am not sure what Mr Foster's further requirements might be, but we could find out soon enough. Most importantly, if *we* wanted you, you would be very close.'

'Six months?' Caz suggested.

'The secondment is usually for a year.'

'I could live with that,' Caz said. She moved to leave. 'Shall we get on?'

'And who should we say designed Mango?' Rachel asked.

'Oh, hell, um. Well, compared to the others it's um . . . a bit . . .'

'Simple?' Rachel suggested.

'That's it. Designed by Sid Simple.' Caz laughed, 'What's the next one?'

'Kerry is on the left, Oasis is on the right.'

'Well, if we're running true to form, Kerry should have low-beamed ceilings, a huge fat brass bedstead and an old patchwork quilt. The floor will bend, the pillows will be Irish linen, and there will be a Bible beside the bed on an old pine-pot cupboard. How am I doing?'

'Terrible!' Rachel teased. 'You go in first.'

The ceilings were not lowered, but a picture-rail, only seven foot from the floor, split the walls into two; the lower half was precisely the Irish cottage bedroom she'd imagined. 'Rachel,' Caz said softly, 'I think I would consider working here. Would you and your father represent me to George Foster?'

'Really, Caz? You said you would find it hard to leave after the weekend but I presumed that you were just being polite.'

'Oh, I was, but I am serious. I feel attracted to this place. If I came here I would still be working as a policewoman but I would be dealing with and helping other women. And I think the change would do me good.' She could hear herself talking, not sure if she liked herself.

'I will talk to my father,' Rachel said. She pointed at the door. As they walked out and across to the next room she added, 'If it means anything, Caz, *I* will strongly recommend you. I have a good instinct about you.'

'Thanks,' Caz said brightly. 'Now let's go into Valentino's tent.'

She was as right about Taj Mahal as she had been about Oasis, but she thought that, to be fair, from their names they were both a little too easy. They were obviously both by the same decorator. With only Downs left, two of the three rooms still unassigned had to make up a pair, but Rachel suggested that the last room might solve the conundrum.

'This is Downs,' she said. 'My favourite room. It's so exciting.'

The room had a tiny entrance hall, perhaps twelve feet by six. Along both walls was a thick, brightly-whited dado rail, below which was pink-striped high-quality wallpaper, and above was rag-rolled cream with a hint of rose. The carpet was grey-blue, leading to a solid, brass-handled Georgian door, so deeply finished that the white almost pulsed. A vaguely familiar watercolour of rolling Sussex countryside completed the scene.

They stepped through from the hall, into a single room about sixty by thirty feet. In its centre was a six-inch-deep solid black block more than four feet square serving as a low table. From the high ceiling to three feet above this hung a heavy light, its shade shiny black and shaped like a pyramid. The cast of its illumination fitted the square of the table like the tight beam of a focused torch.

On one wall was a black, gimmick-free hi-fi, which appeared to be built into the wall furniture, all of which was black and solid. Behind a sliding door, which moved away automatically when Rachel touched it, was a wide-screen Nokia television fed by a compatible VCR. Another segment had a squared window through which amazingly beautiful fractal images could be seen, blossoming on a computer screen. The black wood gleamed. There wasn't a speck of dust.

'What do you think?' Rachel said. Caz had just sat on the floor against a huge black and grey cushion.

'I think those speakers are a bit small,' Caz answered, lightly. 'If I stood on tiptoe I'd be able to see the tops of them – definitely a bit of a let-down.'

'They *sound* fantastic!' Rachel said breathlessly. 'I sneak in here and play my Pink Floyd and Cream records when I need to be cheered up.'

'Pink Floyd? Really?'

'Yes,' Rachel said, raising her eyebrows. 'Why, does that surprise you?'

'Er no,' Caz lied. She was still staring at the dark opulence of that side of the room. It looked like it cost as much as her house.

'Shall I put some music on?' Rachel asked.

'Please,' Caz said, 'something a bit dangerous.'

'How about Hendrix?'

'That'll be fine.' Good *grief* she was serious!

'What do you think of the memorabilia wall?' Rachel asked. 'The coat is actually one of Jimi's; that's one of his Fenders. The posters are all signed originals. The other guitar is an Eric Clapton from his Cream days.'

Caz hadn't even seen the wall. She was still staring at another revelation, a display of compact discs that covered forty square feet of wall, four feet wide and from floor to ceiling. 'Good God! Rachel. How do you find anything?'

'I just ask the wall,' Rachel laughed. She pointed, 'Speak to the grille.'

Caz uncurled from the floor and went to stand by Rachel. 'This thing?'

'Yes. Speak directly into it. Say anything you like.'

Caz spoke to the wall. She said hello, feeling faintly silly.

'Now watch,' Rachel said.

Another black panel slid silently back, and a small computer screen was revealed, displaying 'CD Choice' on a bright blue background. Rachel leaned past Caz and whispered, 'Hendrix.' There was a flicker on the screen and a Jimi Hendrix picture appeared. Then it shrank to a small window while a list of albums scrolled down the right of the screen.

'Experienced,' Rachel ordered. There was a faint whirr and a compact disc moved forward half an inch from the rest. She took it from the wall.

'Will this do?' she said.

'Gobsmacked is the word,' Caz replied.

They sat on a long grey sofa, exactly central between the two speakers. Rachel leaned forward and reached underneath, opening a drawer and asking if Caz would like a drink. She selected one bottle from a range and said that she would be having Tia Maria. 'Good choice,' Caz said.

They drank their first glass of the coffee liqueur quickly, excited by the raunchy music, then they sipped at their second. The lights were low, the suite lit only by the hanging lamp and the soft glow of the wall equipment. Caz asked if a room like this would be out of bounds to staff. Rachel said, usually, yes. 'But when *I* come in here, my friends can always join me.' She smiled and offered up her drink towards Caz. They clinked glasses. 'So what d'you think?' Rachel said again. 'How do you like the room?'

'It's very different from the others but I think it's more me.'

'You don't think it is a man's room?'

'No. It's masculine perhaps, but no. It feels right for me.'

'It's sexy?'

'Oh God, yes!'

'That's what I think. I've never brought anyone back with me to the hall but, if I did, I think we would have to hide ourselves away in here.'

'I don't suppose that . . .'

'You and Mr Thomas? We can stick him in here. That's no problem.'

They moved on to their third and fourth liqueur. Caz persuaded Rachel to play Pink Floyd's 'Dark Side of the Moon', then she sat down with Rachel to watch the bleeding colours of the fractals as they chased the music. Rachel was talking about her days as a research student, and slowly her speech became less formal. She told Caz that she had done research at MIT and at a couple of universities in the UK. 'My father's name helped, but I was pretty damn good myself. After my doctorate, I did a lot of good work on fertility, right down at the level of the human cell, but gradually I found myself drifting towards working more directly with women and I ended up here.'

They were still drinking steadily and when Caz asked about the rest of the tour she was promised a special treat in the morning. She appeared to be between mellow and drunk and giggled softly, 'Did you never fancy one of those lunch guests, Rach? Some of them were a bit tasty.'

'It's always the mind I go for, Caz. A face is just a face and so is a body.'

'I think with me,' Caz said, 'it's the heart or the soul that's important. It's nice if a chap is bright and good-looking, but first off I think I need him to be decent. I want to feel warm when he's around. Oh, and I prefer them fit.'

'Are you being rude?' Rachel said. She was beginning to sound drunk.

'No, I mean . . . what do I mean? Well, because I run every day I'm quite worked out. I don't think I'd be comfortable living with a podge.'

'We have to select *our* men very carefully,' Rachel mumbled, almost to herself. Caz looked up, a lot less drunk than she thought. 'Our donors, the men. We always select them with above average IQs; men with good physiques and fairly good-looking. We never go for the very small or the very tall; it's usual for us to look for Mr Slightly-Better-Than-Average.' Caz poured more liqueur. 'Hey, Caz Flood, I do hope you come to work here. Me and you, I think we'd really get on well together, don't you?' Caz said yes and passed Rachel her glass. 'So how about it, Caz? You get to meet some of the lunch guests and they're always not bad, you know? They're blood-typed of course, and we check them out pretty thoroughly. And we store all their physical details on computer. So you tell me what kind of man you fancy and I'll tap it into the ol' Compaq Desktop and Bingo! What d'you say? Good idea, huh?'

She took more of her drink. 'We use their DNA profile as an Identifier. I'm the only person capable of putting names to donors. When we use one, only I know who he is.'

DC Flood was suddenly wide awake. Rachel's eyes had slightly lost their focus, but the accumulated alcohol had loosened her and she was enjoying herself.

'Men, they are so–' Rachel paused while she sat up straighter – 'so fucking *pompous*! And the richer and more powerful they get, the more, the more fucking . . . the more pompous they get.' She obviously swore rarely and was enjoying each oath.

'Our guests, look, Caz, our guests, they, they're all *won*derful women. They are some of the most beautiful women in the world.' She hiccupped. 'Oh, I am sorry.' She sipped her glass again. 'What was I? Oh, yeah . . . They're the most . . . Oh, I said that. These women, when they want babies . . . they're married to tyrants most of them, powerful men, even dangerous.'

'Dangerous?'

'Caz, there's nothing more dangerous than a man with too much pride.'

'I doan . . .' Caz slurred dramatically. 'I doan un'erstan'.'

'Come 'ere,' Rachel said. She leaned comically towards Caz. 'Don't fink – I mean don't *think* – that all our ladies are at fault. Some of them are so fertile that if they kissed someone they'd fall pregnant with twins.' She laughed at her own joke. 'It's their husbands. It's their inflated egoed all-important history-making zero sperm-count spouses!'

Caz stared.

'Imagine you are Mrs Gadaffi or Mrs Saddam Hussein and you do it but babies just won't happen for you. What do you do? Everything's *bound* to be your fault. What do you do – you go to the friendly local obstetrician and he tells you that you've got burgeoning ovaries, there's absolutely nothing wrong with you. You realise that the problem is with the old man, he's firing blanks.' She was now so drunk that her breath came in odd gasps and her voice waved from whispers through to an embarrassing shout. She took Caz's hand.

'Now are you, or the doctor, going to tell him? Would you be brave enough to do that? Or would you come here?'

'Here?'

'To "cure" your infertility.'

'Oh, Christ!'

'We have an amazing success rate. Our guests love it here.'

'You don't mean that the men actually . . .'

'The men? Oh no, Caz, hardly.' Rachel giggled, 'We use many techniques here, *in vitro* fertilisation, egg donation and the like. The one technique which isn't advertised is sperm donation. There are leaders in some parts of the world who would *never* accept that they are anything other than all-powerful and that obviously includes their fertility. Their wives could never come here openly. We're here, Caz, *I'm* here, for all those women.'

'Your donors, Rachel. Aren't they a potential source of–' Caz grinned, almost breaking out into a giggle – 'I was going to say leaks.'

Rachel smiled, 'We get our "donations" at a separate place. There is a man who arranges our collections and he liaises with Mr Foster. We don't want our donors to come to the Hall. Normally they wouldn't come within twenty miles of Grigglesham. They are all paid for their, er, emissions, on the understanding that these are for research purposes. Only very, very occasionally have we had people here, again, as far as they are concerned, for "research".

They take lunch with us. It gives our female guests the chance to, as it were, evaluate the goods.'

'Bloody hell!' Caz said, louder than she expected.

'We tell the men, we need regular donations for research and they are here for assessment. We get at least one test sample. Then we send them a nice letter saying they're not suitable. They are paid off through an agent, the same person who finds the types we are looking for. That's George's province. We never see them again. As far as our lunch guests are concerned, they had a nice day out and a meal with the staff. They didn't get the job but they were well paid.'

'I know I'm changing the subject,' Caz said, 'but did we decide who designed this room? Or are we too drunk to make the decision?'

'Don't you want to talk about all this procreation any more?'

'I think we're too drunk, Rach. No more secrets tonight.'

'We're friends, aren't we?' Rachel said with a wink. 'An' I'm not dwunk.'

'Nor me,' Caz said. 'Yes, we're friends. So what's the answer?'

'Well, this room is hard and black and sexy. Kerry is a bit too . . .'

'Twee?'

'I thought Mango and Penang had similarities,' Rachel said. She was lying back with closed eyes, 'But when I imagine them they don't *feel* as if they came from the same hand. I think Kerry goes with Penang.'

'Leaving Mango and this room with the same author. D'you really think so? One so dark and masculine, the other so pink and soft?'

'Two sides of the same coin,' Rachel said. 'Definitely! Why not?' She closed her eyes again and sighed. 'I'm too tired to think any more. We can find out in the morning. I think I'd better go to . . .'

'Bed,' Caz said.

'That's what I meant. Go to b—'

Rachel struggled to her feet, almost falling back, then she stiffened and shook her head haughtily, her nose tilted slightly upward. Caz rose from the sofa and offered an arm for support.

'S'no need f'that,' Rachel mumbled. 'I'm OK, y' c'n walk me 's far as y'room.' She wobbled, then walked deliberately out into the corridor, Caz following. As they reached Mango she stopped, kissed her fingers, and touched them gently to Caz's lips. 'G'night, Caz,' she said dreamily, 'iss been a really good evening. I like you. Iss good t'have someone t' talk to. Sleep tight.'

She walked away, laughing.

Forty-three

She woke at seven-thirty, seriously late for DC Flood but OK for plain Caz. She stretched in bed then talked herself into getting up. Her room had no window looking directly outside, so she stepped through into the pool area and looked out through the glass roof to assess the morning. Drizzle. She shuddered. The water of the pool was a still turquoise.

She muttered to herself about masochism, but managed to coax herself into her running gear. In ten minutes she was dressed and walking in trainers down the red carpet towards the central hall. She hadn't been as drunk as Rachel the night before but, nevertheless, a well-deserved hangover thudded behind her eyes. The best cure was this steady run. The lousy weather was merely extra Hail-Mary's.

At the front door she paused for a second, wondering if she would set off alarms by leaving without notice. Then she decided to go for it anyway and see what happened. She pulled back a heavy brass bolt, then turned the fat handle, pulling back the weight of the magnificent door and opening up the early day. The pink granite forecourt was cobwebbed and damp, the grass beyond dark and slippery. For a second she didn't want to go, then she kicked herself out into the cold. She could smell winter England. Dark trees beckoned and she gasped. In her head she tossed a coin and, when it landed, she began by jogging down the steps towards the water. The rain was like mist. It caressed her face. Parallel with the front of the house the lake's edge was manicured, a neat border between turf and water. The further she got from the steps the more natural the border became and, half a mile from the house, she had to step carefully to avoid boggy patches that led to reeds.

She jogged. Her pace was a sedate eight minutes a mile and she was simply glad to be out. The fine drizzle had worked its way through her and now she was chilled at the edges; her ears, the tip of her nose, her fingertips. To avoid wet feet she had been criss-crossing the road and using the delicate bridges. She arrived near to the gatehouse and readied herself to turn back but, as she swung in an elaborate curve rather than stop and restart, there was a sudden click! and a large man with a shotgun stepped in front of her, rainwater dripping from his face.

A rush of cold went through her, but her eyes met the man's and his were neutral. He touched a hand to his wet forehead in acknowledgement of her and he let the gun's butt drop away, swinging it towards the floor like a pendulum, the barrel's end held in his massive fist. She managed to squeak out a breathless, 'Good Morning!' then she was past him as he shouted, 'You must be quite daft, Miss. Yer'll catch yer death out 'ere!' She waved but quickened her pace and raced back along the circular road. The real world surged back at her and she felt her stomach flutter. She began to wonder if maybe she was losing it. She would need to ring Tom MacInnes and find out about the decorator. Had he been charged?

She stopped at the steps. The run hadn't even been enough to make up for the alcohol from the previous night. Her head still screamed.

Once in her room, she threw off her wet things and padded naked into the bathroom. She ran a bath, washed in minutes, dried quickly and hurried through to the dining room to scrounge some breakfast. She had been close to ringing Brighton but a supreme effort had stopped her. Secretly she was hoping that the DI would ring *her*.

A long table carried the breakfast and her worst fears had been realised, silver-covered dishes there reeked with calories. As she walked in, George Foster said hello. He was sitting at a small table ıear the window and tapped a spare chair. She nodded to him and ifted a cover . . . Argghh!! There was bacon, pork and beef ausages, white spotted black pudding, mushrooms that ached with ıbsorbed fat, fried bread, sautéed potatoes and three different ypes of egg. She groaned with illicit pleasure. Oh, just the once, she old herself. To the right were grapefruits, figs, muesli and bran-ɔased cereals. She looked the other way and took an extra egg.

'Mornin', Detective,' Foster said as she sat down, 'that you out unning this morning, was it?' She nodded. 'You're even keener han I thought.'

'I'll have to run twice a day if I'm going to eat this stuff!' she said.

'It's a bit like waking up in a sweet shop isn't it?' Foster smiled. You get used to it, though.' He waved at his place setting, fresh ruit and a small helping of All-Bran. 'I put on a stone in my first nonth here, but I've got it under control now. I have a cooked ɔreakfast once a week.'

'I wish,' Caz grinned. 'I think this'll have to be a one-off. You now I'm a serious runner? Well, I've got a figure and my ranking to vorry about.'

'I'll get some coffees in,' Foster said.

As soon as he came back, George Foster began speaking. Caz ıad egg yolk on her lips. 'Miss Rachel tells me you fancy Bessie's ob, that true?' She was eating and simply nodded. 'Know what it ntails, d'yer?'

'Not exactly, George.'

'Well, it looks Girl-Friday stuff and, initially, very little police vork but don't let that fool you. The cover is maid or cook, omething like that.'

'Doing what?'

'Security. Checking out visitors. Keeping the lid on leaks. It's lelicate and very important work. Have you had firearms training? Ever used a gun in anger?'

'I'm qualified for hand gun.'

'Ever used one in the field. Even had to carry?'

'I thought you'd pulled my record, George. You must know I wa in an armed patrol car for six months.'

'I didn't pull your record. I just made a phone call.'

'I've never had to fire in anger, Sergeant. But I did well on th range and on situation simulations. I've got a good arrest recor including a few nutters.'

'I heard about that Southampton guy. The word was you did ver well.'

'I really fancy the job, George. I've got an instinct about thi place. Now that the Brighton murders are sorted I could really g for it.'

'You've only just become a DC.'

'I know that, George, but opportunities like this don't com along very often and I'm a great believer in fate. A secondment t Special Branch wouldn't look exactly bad on my record.'

'What team are you on at John Street?'

'On this last case I was with DI MacInnes and Sergeant Moore but that was just a one-off. DCS Blackside was IC, but he' supposed to be moving up to the Yard for the New Year.'

'He's going to the Branch, isn't he?' Foster said.

'Far as I know, yeah.'

'So, you won't miss your colleagues. Your DI?'

'Wrong question, George. Tom MacInnes is a bloody goo copper and he's helped me out, but I've not been with him ther long enough.'

'No loyalty then?'

'Bollocks, Sergeant. You know that's not true. I'm a bright, fi young copper and I'm well educated. I'm going places. I have t take my opportunities when they arise. Special Branch this early i one of those opportunities.'

'Just testing, Flood.' The Sergeant paused long enough to drin half his coffee. 'So what's the connection between these Brighto killings and Grigglesham?'

'I'm not sure, George. I had a bit of a hard time at the beginnin of the case and then I managed to get myself attacked a few days ago. The DCS pulled me out for my own good. We knew two of the victims had been to the village. It was just another lead. Then we found out that they'd all been here at the clinic.'

'And this Avocado guy. What's the connection there?'

'I think Avocado did work here. If you sorted out the paperwork on the interior design work, you should know that. Avocado Design?'

'Not according to the papers. All the decorating firms were from inside the M-25; two were in London. There was no Avocado Design.'

'But I was sure. One of the suites, Downs, it's got the same trademark as the first victim's place, George Burnley's. The wallpaper is the same, the choice of pictures, even the black furniture and striped cushions.'

'According to the invoices, these suites each cost more than a few thousand quid each to do. What kind of place did Burnley live in?'

'Nice, but not in that league. The finish, the quality of the furniture here is streets ahead of Burnley's place but the style – I can't believe it's not Avocado, I just can't.'

'I've got the papers through there but, if I remember rightly, the bill for Downs was paid to a company called Grace Jeremy Ltd. Their address is in the East End. Whitechapel, if I remember rightly.'

'That's it then!' Caz said. 'Avocado's first name is Jeremy and his wife is called Grace. Their business is split into two now; Grace Interiors and Avocado Design. Either they folded the other company or Avocado has it hidden away, maybe as a tax fiddle. But that's him. Definitely.'

'So what's it all about?'

'I don't know, is the answer, George. I'm off the case, remember? But they've pulled him and he's connected to Grigglesham and the victims. It's only a matter of time. The forensic evidence should bury him.'

'And motive?'

'Don't know on that one, George. As I said, I'm off the case. I' quite like to find out though . . .'

'Avocado was picked up yesterday, right? About lunch-time They should have got somewhere by now. Who d'you reckon will d the interview?'

'Tom MacInnes.'

'I'll bell them then and find out the score. How's that sound Flood?'

'Absolutely brilliant!' Caz said. She grinned and bit into forbidden hunk of fried bread.

Foster took a slim cellular phone from his inside pocket, th Micro-Tac he had used the day before. 'Magic little things, these he said as he dialled. He smiled and raised his chin at Caz while h waited to get through. 'Ah!' he suddenly said, 'Sergeant Foster Grigglesham. Speak to DI MacInnes?' There was a wait then h raised his eyebrows, listening. Caz braced herself to listen to on end of a conversation.

'Yes, Tom. Aye, it's George Foster!

'Aye. The Flood lass is here. Wondered how the case was goin'. There was a pause. 'Why not?

'He *volunteered* . . . ?

'D'y'have the results . . . ?

'Shee-it . . . !

'So why did the bastard sneak back to England . . . ?

'He won't fuckin' *say*? Who's his brief . . . ?

'McDonnough! Fuck. The one they call Jesus Christ . . . ? I'll rin yer back, Tom, thanks.' There was a longer pause then he turned t speak to Caz. Caz looked bewildered, her mouth half-open ready t crunch her fried bread. She was staring at Foster, her eyes wide waiting. He clipped his phone shut. 'You ain't gonna like thi much,' he said, 'but it looks like yer man's out of it. They haven' charged him.'

'What! Why the hell not? You said yesterday he was bang to rights!'

'Don't shout at *me*, Flood. It's not *my* bloody fault. Tom MacInnes says that they pulled Avocado when they discovered he'd sneaked back to the UK from some holiday. They thought they had him dead to rights because he had originally offered them the alibi.'

'I interviewed him. He said he was in Florida and could prove it.'

'Well, apparently he was back in England for thirty-six hours when he shouldn't have been and he won't explain why. It's bloody suspicious but he's simply refusing to speak. His brief is as hard as nails.'

'I presume that he was here for the crucial thirty-six hours,' Caz said hopefully. 'We can hold him until we get some other evidence, can't we?'

'Nope. Apparently this Avocado says he can't tell MacInnes why he came back to the UK on the Q-T but he insists that he's clean. He asked if there was some other way he could prove his innocence and MacInnes asked him to take a blood test.'

'Then we've got him.'

'No, we haven't. Avocado has a different blood group to the murderer. MacInnes wouldn't let him go. He insisted on waiting for a DQ-Alpha but Avocado was still clean. They had to let him go.'

'Oh, Christ!' She was white and Foster asked if she was all right.

'I don't know, I was so sure. If it's not Avocado then we're back to . . .'

'Square One.'

'Yes,' Caz said, 'and I don't like it there.' She felt faint. Square One was Valerie. She became quiet and Foster went to get two more coffees. She had her eyes closed, trying to think hard. There was no way that Avocado could not be involved. She could prove that he knew at least three of the men, he had lied about his holiday alibi, and now she knew that he had been to Grigglesham Hall as a decorator. Such a string of coincidences *had* to implicate him. She didn't *care* that Avocado had the wrong blood group. She knew he was a liar and now she was convinced he was the killer. She had the frightening, sickening sensation that the proof was terribly close to her, in front of her but unseen. She was stupid. Somehow this was all her fault.

'Caz?' She heard George Foster's voice. 'Caz, don't take it to heart. You're off the case. Let Tom MacInnes and his boys worry about it now.'

She looked up at him. He looked benign. 'You're absolutely right!' she said. 'Fuck it, I'm on holiday!'

'Look, I've got to be off now, Flood,' he said, 'I'll think about Bessie's replacement today. I'll give it some thought and talk to you tonight.'

'Thanks, George.'

'Go for a swim, lass. Let yer hair down. You're off the case, remember?'

He touched Caz's shoulder as he left her. She stared down into her cup. She desperately wanted to go to her room, lie down and close her eyes but, if she did, she thought she would sleep for ever. She was acutely depressed, still trying to read George Foster and worried about Valerie.

There was no time to dwell on the problems as Rachel then decided to appear at the door, bright-eyed and alive, raring to take a run at the day. 'Good grief, Rachel,' Caz said, despite herself, 'how can you possibly be so bushy-tailed after last night?'

'Practice!' Rachel said.

Caz stopped thinking. Valerie would be there tomorrow.

Forty-four

Rachel had arranged for them to do the tour of the scientific section of the hall, the wing containing the offices and the main clinic areas. She was chattering and explaining the basic principles that governed how the clinic worked. 'Well over seventy per cent of our lady guests need only to loosen up and relax to become pregnant. Their day-to-day lives are highly stressed and this pressure often sublimates their womanhood.'

They walked down a white corridor. 'Of the rest, we find that a high proportion can be helped by hormonal treatments and perhaps ten per cent by minor surgery. In rare cases we use egg donation and I believe last night' – she coughed to indicate faint embarrassment – 'I told you about our other donors.'

They came to a door marked 'CLINIC'. Rachel used a swatch card, then typed a pass-number to gain access.

'We have had just two impossible cases, both guests with congenital abnormalities that prevented conception. I always feel anguish when we finally have to admit defeat. We contract to the world's greatest surgeons, but even they occasionally fail. For those women that desire children, the inability to conceive is the greatest tragedy.'

The clinic's record section was uncluttered and simple. There were four pine desks, each with swivel chairs, two lockable cupboards, and a filing cabinet with a hefty steel bar locking it closed. Three of the desks had computers, the other was spread with scientific papers.

'We keep our client details on this Compaq 386,' Rachel said, waving at one desk. 'Obviously they are highly confidential. All the databases are password-protected and encrypted, so even if a hacker could break into the system, the information would look like garbage.'

She pointed to another desk. 'This is my territory. I have information on our visiting surgeons, our male and female donors and the treatment for every client. On this machine each client is known by her code name, so there is no easy link between what happens here and their full name and details. But it is all passworded just in case.'

They moved again. 'This machine contains some standard software. On it we have word-processing, spreadsheets and accounts programs. There is also a hidden file which tells me which client has which pseudonym. We're very tight on security, here. If, say, Lady Di, the Princess of Wales was our guest, she might be known around the place as Betty, but on that computer, over there, she would be yet another name, known only to me and my father.

'A few years ago, before security was tightened up, we had a burglary here. The intruders gained access to the laboratories, the stores and to this office. We are scientists, Caz, not policemen. We hadn't made sufficient allowance for security but we learned a good lesson. We became more concerned about our information. After we contacted the authorities for advice, they gave us George Foster. Now we have computer access logs and the system boxes are bolted to the desks. When they broke in, our intruders could have stolen the computers, but they didn't. Now it would be impossible and if they tried to look at our data we would know.'

The room was well lit, with fresh, light furniture and non-distracting plain cream walls. Caz had been in there for five minutes before she realised there were no conventional windows. On one wall, high up, there was a length of non-opening glass, and this cast a light across to the far wall and a series of SASCO boards marked with the years from 1985 to the current one. It was far less gloomy than there, but it reminded her of the lecture room at John Street. It made her think of Norman Blackside.

There was something strange about the light, but she couldn't think what. She glanced up just as Rachel explained, 'I see you are wondering about the lighting. It is not standard. It matches the spectrum of natural light. All the lights in the building do. My father used to suffer from SAD, Seasonal Affective Disorder: he needs lots of sunshine.'

'And I suspect it enhances the mood of the guests too?'

'Of course,' Rachel said. 'We try to think of everything here.'

There was a noise behind them, and Rachel turned as Professor Hely entered. He looked worse than Caz felt. She was surprised because he had drunk little at dinner. 'Good morning, my dear,' he said with affection, 'and good morning to you, Miss Flood. I trust you are well?'

'I've felt better, Sir, but thank you.'

'Out again last night, Daddy?' Rachel asked quietly. There was a flicker of tension, as if the question had been asked before.'

Hely nodded, his eyes narrowing. He went to his desk. 'Where is the mail?' he said briskly. 'Where is Margaret?'

'Oh, Father, you gave Margaret the day off, remember? The boy from the village? The funeral is today.' She paused, then she asked if he was feeling tired. He looked up coldly then turned to his papers.

'Shall we get on, Caz?' Rachel said quickly. 'Would you like to see the laboratories?' She moved away, turning the question into a command.

'Professor Hely,' Caz said formally and followed. The bent head made a noncommittal grunt.

'Don't take too much notice of my father,' Rachel said as she swatched another door. 'When he goes out, he is often like this. He's a creature of the night but without the biological predisposition. If he enjoys himself he pays for it in the morning. I've gotten quite used to it by now.'

Caz mumbled something and Rachel continued, 'Through here are the laboratories, the cold room, our test area and the two operating theatres. I'll show you the labs first.'

They went left through a pale green door with a small wired window and into Laboratory One. It was nothing like Caz might have presumed; her expectations were somewhere between a school-chemistry lab and Dr Frankenstein's cellar but instead of gothicly dark benches, gloomy corners and the odour of formaldehyde she entered something bright and cheerful, ultra-modern and crisp. She could hear music. It was Strauss's *Alpine Concerto*.

There was only one workbench and this was surprisingly deep, coming out nearly six feet from the wall. The fitments looked more like an expensive kitchen and the surface much like a marbled kitchen top.

Light from outside beamed in through windows that ran the full length of the wall, and through the glass was a rewarding view of the grounds. Caz noted the high-quality locks on each opening light.

The floor was ceramic tiles, grey-white shapes interlocking to form an illusion of crosses. To one side was a clinically white L-shaped desk with a large Sun workstation on the return surface. The computer was on and a screen-saving device showed a peculiar coloured cartoon where fish ate fish and bigger fish ate them. Nearby was a high graphic artist's drawing board with a tall stool before it. On one wall were three light-boxes; the kind Caz suspected were used for looking at X-rays.

'This is the heart of Grigglesham Clinic,' Rachel said succinctly. Caz was looking at the light-boxes and didn't respond. Presumably, Rachel had been looking away. Now she said, 'These are sighting displays. We use them for a number of functions but the main one is to view DNA Profiles.' Caz failed to respond. Her brain raced with thought, running ahead of her volition. She heard herself say, 'What?'

'My, you *are* far away!' Rachel said softly. She touched Caz's arm gently. 'I said, these devices on the wall, they are similar to light boxes that are used in hospitals for viewing X-ray photographs. We use them for viewing DNA prints.'

'Tell me about it,' Caz said slowly.

'How about coffee?' Rachel said, smiling again. Caz nodded as she sat down, staring at the cold empty plastic of the wall. Rachel was saying something. 'And sugar, Caz? Don't you runners load up with carbohydrates?'

Caz still stared blankly. She spoke from far off with a different, lifeless voice. 'Only for big races or winter training runs. Only for . . .'

'White without then!' Rachel said brightly. Caz heard the mugs chink.

'You want to know about our DNA profiling system?' Rachel said. 'You're sure you won't be bored?'

'I won't be bored,' Caz said.

'How's your biology?' Rachel asked, mug in hand.

'Rusty.'

'OK, I'll take it easy . . . Drink up your coffee.'

Caz picked up her mug and thought about a sip. Her throat was dry.

'Right!' Rachel said, 'DNA, deoxyribo-nucleic acid. In simple terms, it is the genetic code which lays down the rules that guide how each of us develops.'

'I can remember that much.'

Rachel continued. 'Well, things have moved an awful long way since Mister Watson and Mister Crick. We know now how the DNA message is made up from just four amino acids. Fifteen years ago a scientist could win a Nobel prize for discovering the tiniest sequence of a protein; now, for a PhD, you almost have to discover the meaning of life.' She sipped her coffee and glanced up at Caz.

Caz said, 'Adenine, Guanine, Cytosine and Thymine.'

'A-G-C-T,' Rachel responded. 'As always go with Ts, Cs with Gs.'

'Uh-huh.'

'Well, the complete human blueprint comes on twenty-six

chromosomes. Chromosomes are made up of genes, genes are made up from strings of DNA, DNA is sequenced with the four acids.'

'I'm hanging in there,' Caz said.

'If we took your complete chromosome blueprint we would find that it was made up from a combination of your mother's and father's genes. The chromosomes in every cell – except the sex cells – come in pairs, one paternal, one more or less maternal. The sex cells are single-sided, eggs needing sperm and vice versa. To make things more interesting, at conception we get cross-over from one parental gene to another.

'You are your genes and, theoretically, if we could lay out the complete sequence and photograph it we could describe you. As yet science only knows a small number of tiny sequences of genes that specifically create adult characteristics; most are hidden because a *number* of genes combine to create the phenotype. How are we doing?'

Caz said OK.

'In the early eighties a British scientist at Leicester University found a way to take a snapshot of DNA. To put it crudely, you squidge up the cell nucleus to make alphabet soup, then add lots of radioactive A-G-C-T. The new letters faithfully recombine with the ones in the soup, and you get clumps of radioactive rebuilt DNA. We stick the gunk in gel and apply a small electrical charge at one end. The bits of gunk move away at different rates dependent on their make-up and settle into stripes. Stick an X-ray film above the gel and you have a photograph of an individual's DNA, lots of stripes, like a bar-code on groceries.'

'I know what it looks like but I didn't know how it was achieved.'

'Well now you do,' Rachel said. 'Newer schemes use light-sensitive amino-acids instead of radioactivity and the very latest techniques will produce strings of numbers on a computer rather than a rough black-and-white photograph which has to be interpreted.'

'And every DNA profile is absolutely distinct? Like a fingerprint?'

'Yes and no – that's one of the myths,' Rachel said. 'You are roughly half like your father, half your mother. At the level of sophistication that can now be achieved, we can see your inheritance, but DNA profiling takes only *portions* of DNA and results from closely related persons can be very similar. DNA profiling that produces just a few bands can produce prints that look equivalent from two different people. The more bands, the more diversity. For example, if DNA-profiling was to distinguish between suspects in the same family, the scientists would need to aim for a larger number of bands.'

Caz straightened up slightly, looking up at the light-boxes. 'So you can identify all your donors by their DNA profile?'

'Yup,' Rachel said playfully. 'All our guests, donors of eggs and our gentlemen . . .'

'Could you show me?'

'Of course. But I should explain that I cannot just say, this is John Doe. The security system prevents that.'

'I'd like to see, anyway. Before today all this was just been theory to me.'

'No problem!' Rachel said, 'I'll call something up on the Sun.'

Rachel swung a chair towards the computer keyboard, pressed a single key to blank the screen, then tapped something quickly with a typist's speed. A brightly coloured query form appeared and she typed in a number. 'Here's one for you,' she said. 'White male, aged twenty-nine. His code number is Q829-136A.'

'Q for male and twenty-nine his age?' Caz offered.

'Nope,' Rachel said. 'A reasonable shot, though. This means that the gentleman was our thirty-sixth donor in quarter two of 1989. The "A" means we used him.'

'I don't quite understand. Why do you have the light-boxes if you can display the profiles on the computer?'

'Safety, to begin with,' Rachel explained. 'We start with a standard film and then this is scanned and saved on the computer disc. With a bit of effort I can eventually produce a name to go with that code number, but it can't be done over land-lines, you have to walk between terminals and carry data back and forth. Security again. For every entry on the Sun there should be a corresponding film in the fridge room. You know what they say about the difference between an amateur and a professional?'

'Tell me,' Caz said.

'An amateur practises until he gets it right,' Rachel said formally. 'A professional trains until he cannot get it wrong.'

'Am I right in saying that we could look at any guest's profile if we took the time to do it?'

'Yes, of course,' Rachel said patiently, 'but I think you should understand a little bit more about how we work and the trust we have been honoured with. There are, of course, things that I would not and could not tell you.'

Caz was smiling. 'Of course not, Rachel, that I understand completely.'

'If that's understood then?' She looked at Caz who was nodding, 'Well, first, you would need to know the individual's code name. To get that you would need to know the combination on the safe in the office and know which file to read.'

'OK,' Caz said, 'we've done that.'

'Then you would need to know which computer held the individual's in-house name so that you could know his or her pseudonym.'

'Right.'

'And on another computer you would need to search to find the code number belonging to that pseudonym.'

'But we've done that.'

'And if the individual is a donor or the individual is a guest who has used a donor they are further coded so the combination is anonymous.'

'But we could find out? You could find out?'

'Yes. Provided we have the first paper file from the safe and we know all the passwords for the various databases . It takes time but that is deliberate. Our work here is *very* sensitive. Our information would be devastating in the wrong hands.'

'Just one more question,' Caz said. 'It's something that occurred to me yesterday when the detectives were asking about Burnley and Green . . .'

' Yes?'

'You said that donors – er – produce elsewhere and they rarely come here. Is that right? Well, would they have already – um – made their donation at this other place, or would they be discreetly asked to perform here?'

'Ah, it could be either or both. It really depends on the situation. I think I told you that, very occasionally, one of our lady guests wants to see her potential donors. If she selects a male donor we have a code gesture to indicate which one.'

'Which is?'

'What?'

'How would the lady indicate the required man?'

'Oh, it varies. The ladies themselves arrange it with either myself or the professor. They can have a wicked sense of humour. One lady offered her gentleman caviar saying, "Would you like my eggs?"'
Now Rachel was smiling. Without wanting to, Caz burst into a grin.

'We could take a look in the fridge room now,' Rachel said. 'It's quite cold in there but we'll be in and out. These track-suits are quite warm . . .'

Caz almost had time to say yes. Instead she twitched as the phone rang. 'Wow, that's loud!' she gasped.

Rachel laughed and picked it up. After seconds she said, 'It's for you, Caz. Detective Inspector MacInnes . . .'

Forty-five

Caz took the phone, trying to slowly take a deep breath and remain calm. Her buzzing brain threatened her, but she forced herself to remain cool. 'Tom,' she said, 'nice to hear from you. To what do I owe the honour?'

'Are you alone, Flood.'

'No.'

'You OK?'

'Fine, Sir. I'm with Rachel Hely. You caught me right in a middle of a tour of Grigglesham Hall. It's a fascinating place.'

'There's a surprise visitor arriving there this morning for you.'

'What?'

'Valerie. He's arriving early. He rang the hall and George Foster has just rung me. They've given him permission to micro-light in there with some mate called Jeff.'

'Jeff Thomas, Sir. They go back a long way.'

'Well, I was just letting you know, lass. You heard about Avocado?'

'Yes, Sir.'

'Slick bastard. He never stopped smiling. He may not be *the* man but the bastard is definitely bent in some way. We're keeping an eye on 'im but of course he'll expect that.'

'And Valerie, Sir?'

'No news, except that there was just one blood group on your bits.'

'Oh . . .'

'Hang on, gal. That means nowt. A third of the population is A-secretor.'

'I wish the DQ-Alpha would hurry up.'

'Same here, lass. Just stay nice 'n public from now on, OK?'

'Yes, Sir. I'm having a lovely break. Thank you, Sir.'

She put the phone down and smiled softly at Rachel. 'My man's arriving a day and a half early. I can't wait! You were going to show me the freezer?'

'Follow me!' Rachel said.

The cold room was through a short passageway marked with small green arrows on the floor. As they walked, Rachel explained things. 'The room itself is quite cold but not desperately so. We have a large number of samples in there and they are individually stored; those that require it in deep-freeze canisters. The room itself is kept at minus two degrees Celsius but, because it is dry, still air, it doesn't feel that cold.'

'Why two layers of cold storage?'

'When we take a male donation from its deep storage we want the rate of defrost to be very slow. Properly defrosted semen is indistinguishable from fresh but quick thawing is detrimental to the potency of the product, and sperm motility is reduced. Also we have other samples that require cold storage of a less severe nature.'

'So you've got cold, very cold and bloody cold,' Caz said.

'Absolutely!' Rachel said. They stopped at a red door.

'Well this is the place!' Rachel said brightly. 'We call it the Cold Room.'

They went in, Caz leading. She had expected something the equivalent of a meat cold-store with hoar-frost everywhere, grey-white on dull steel. Instead, the room was more clinical; white formica and small white cupboards stretching along a cold white wall. It was as bitter as a winter's cross-country meeting but without the wind.

'All these cupboards?' Caz said slowly.

'Sperm donors,' Rachel said bluntly.

'And these?'

'Sperm donors.'

'And the cupboards at the end?'

They said it together: 'Sperm donors.'

Caz said she didn't understand, so Rachel explained. 'So far analytical science has taken us into blood-grouping and tissue-typing. Genetic analysis, we are getting slowly there, but our methods still need some development. My father has been collecting and storing samples for eleven years now and, rather than try to isolate gene patterns and relate these to adult characteristics, we have employed a cruder empirical method which just happens to work.'

'A crude method of what?'

'Matching DNA to appearance. It's my father's main research. Rather than attempting to break down DNA into small chains which stubbornly refuse to be related to say, eye colour, we have taken a completely different approach. For years my father collected semen samples from volunteers, mainly university students, even before DNA-typing had reached the literature. He decided to categorise the samples by an attribute, like the colour of eyes, or perhaps height, or IQ or sporting ability. He was recruiting samples for years before he had a way of assessing them. In the early days he was looking at the correlations between blood groupings and various phenotypical attributes, but now DNA profiling has given his research a massive boost. We are very well funded by both your own government and that of the US.'

'So what are you saying – you're looking for the bar-code for blue eyes?'

'Roughly, yes, but it is a little bit too crude and we need a very serious computer. Daddy says that a Cray would be nice. Recently, a new DNA-profiling system has been developed which allows a signature to be produced digitally, just a string of numbers. We are hoping that we can get a large mainframe computer to run the correlations between our donors' number-profiles and their characteristics. It's all very exciting.'

'What about the clinic? What about your work on infertility?'

'That's really my work; my baby. I'm sorry for the pun. Everything seems to knit so well. Our clients pay the earth to achieve their aims, and the money they provide goes to help run the hall. Meanwhile I can choose the characteristics of my donors from many thousands of volunteers. All the samples have been carefully logged on the computer for more than three hundred attributes each. You must realise that the donor and the foster-father cannot be too dissimilar in their characteristics.'

'One in three children born is Chinese,' Caz chuckled, 'but I don't suppose Saddam Hussein would be happy if his son was one of them!'

'Then you get my point,' Rachel said. She said it just as their eardrums told them that the cold-room door had closed.

Rachel spun round. 'That can't happen!' she said. Her face flickered with anxiety. 'The door cannot close by itself,' she repeated slowly. 'It is weighted carefully to prevent accidents.' She reached for a telephone. 'This is a spur from the telephone in the laboratory. We can speak to my father and get him to come and open up.'

She lifted the receiver, put it to her ear, listened, replaced it, then picked it up and listened again. 'I'm afraid the phone in the lab is off the hook,' she said flatly. Her face drained and she dropped the receiver, slumping against the wall. Caz caught the swinging lead.

'OK, Rachel,' Caz said, 'tell me about the systems in here. Where are the temperature controls? Is there an alarm? Is there an emergency exit?'

'No,' Rachel said. 'All controls are outside the door. There is no alarm, we would normally use the telephone. The only exit is the door through which we entered .'

'Sprinklers? We could set them off.'

'Not in here.'

'OK, OK. Where is the thermometer?'

Rachel straightened up. She pointed, 'Over there.' It was minus four degrees.

'It's too cold to stand still,' Caz decided. 'Walk while you think.'

'I'm hopeless with the cold,' Rachel said weakly, 'and I think I'm a bit claustrophobic.'

'Not any more you're not!' Caz snapped at her. 'We've both got to think if we are going to get out of here. Right?' Rachel's eyes suddenly gleamed gratitude. She wanted to follow not lead. She would do what she was told.

'Right. What's in the cupboards?' Caz said sharply.

'Steel canisters containing liquid nitrogen. Donors' semen. They keep semen at very low temperature.'

'Anything else?'

'Paperwork, that's all.'

Caz was now starting to feel the cold in her eyes. 'How does the refrigeration system work? Can we disable it?'

'Just like a domestic fridge,' Rachel said. 'Fluid is pumped round a circuit of pipes. When the fluid is compressed it absorbs heat, when it expands again it gives heat off. The compression is inside the room. The expansion occurs outside, removing heat energy from the interior.'

'Where are the pipes?'

'There are three in each wall behind those grilles.' Caz went to one. 'But they are bolted on,' Rachel said, 'you need tools to remove them.'

'Great!' Caz said, she was swearing under her breath. They had stopped to look at the grilles and she was beginning to notice the cold.

'Look at the temperature gauge!' she ordered Rachel. 'What is it?'

'Minus five!'

'Shit, then this *is* for real.' If it was getting colder the setting had been changed outside. She decided not to tell Rachel. She began to jog up and down between the white cupboards. Rachel was depressed and listless. Caz screeched at her. 'Rachel! At least *walk*!' Rachel began to shuffle. 'The professor! When are you supposed to see your father next?'

'At eleven o'clock. We have a little work. I said you and I would be finished well before then.'

'What time is it?' The thermometer read minus six degrees centigrade.

'Nine-thirty.'

Shit. She could stay alive but she didn't think Rachel could. What to do, what to do? 'Is there any clothing in here? Anything?' She was shouting slightly.

Rachel moved, chastised. 'No, there's nothing, just paper hats and polythene gloves.'

'Get them!' Caz barked. 'All of them. Get them now!'

Caz took off her sweat-top and fought to pull the arms away from the trunk. They were too well made and refused to tear. She opened a small door to reveal a sharp edged corner. She stretched the sleeve over its point until it burst through. Maniacally she tore at the arm and it came away. The second one she did with her teeth. She passed the waistcoat to Rachel.

'Put this on under yours, Rachel! Do it now and *don't stand still*!' Rachel looked as if she was about to start crying but she began shuffling. Caz sat down on the freezing floor, undid her trainers and removed her trousers. 'Get these on as well. Pull them over the other pair. Get a hat on. Give me a few. Stuff the rest down between your tops. How many gloves have you got?'

'Fifty-sixty. There're an awful lot.'

'OK, put a pair on.' Rachel obeyed. 'Now another pair. And another.'

Caz grabbed a hat. It was shaped like a shower cap but made of crinkled paper like a shell-suit. She bit at the outer edge until she could rip elastic from the head-band, then she grabbed Rachel's arm, took her hand and blew into the gloves. She swore when she realised her idea wasn't working too well, but wrapped the elastic band round Rachel's wrist anyway, trapping a little of her warm breath.

'You do the other one the same!' she shouted. 'Put the elastic on first then stretch it while you blow into the gloves!' She was beginning to get dangerously cold and began to jog more systematically. She had knickers, T-shirt and her own metabolism to keep her warm but she was banking on being found in less than three hours. That was the longest steady run she'd ever done. But then she had been dressed in a Helly Hansen thermal top and running tights. Then she had been running in a dark green forest on a crisp January day trying to get solid enough to run a marathon.

But this was different.

Now she was running for her life.

Once upon a time, when Caz couldn't swim so well, Caz had told a friend that swimming was monotonous. He had replied that running was boring and that jogging was mindless. She had told him he didn't know what he was talking about. Had he never felt that surge of glory with blood pulsing through his muscles as he kicked to the finish line or up a challenging hill? No, he said. Now she knew exactly what he'd meant.

She trogged, she shuffled, she jogged, she tiptoed, she heel-landed, she tootled, she scrubbed along but she kept going. Her head was covered with the ludicrous shower cap, retaining vital warmth, her ankles by her Ultramax socks, her wrists and hands by the arms torn from the sweat-top. She was trying to pace it just right. She had to move fast enough to generate the heat to keep herself alive, but she was trying to go slow enough that she could keep going. If she stopped, she would probably die.

Rachel was fairly well wrapped up but she still needed to keep moving enough to generate heat. Twice Caz had screamed at her as she went to sit down. Rachel had complained about having had no breakfast and feeling sick. 'Good,' Caz had bellowed, venom in her voice, 'as long as you're feeling you're alive!'

After an hour she realised they needed to make noise. In a moment of sanity, Rachel suggested one of the nitrogen containers and every fourth return Caz picked this up and banged the door three times. She began shouting as well but decided that the effort was wasted. Now she was plodding and only banging the door when she remembered. Step, step, step, she felt giddy with its numbing monotony.

She fantasised about Valerie, how her arms could climb up him, how she could lower herself on to him, how they would gently rock together, how waves of heat would pass between them. She was concentrating on a point at each end of the room as she trudged, and she began counting laps as she repeatedly passed Rachel's slower shuffle. Her own pace was slipping slowly backwards from nine minutes a mile, and Rachel was now barely moving. The last time she had looked at the gauge, the temperature had been minus ten degrees Celcius and the last time she had asked for the time it was ten twenty-five.

Somehow she was combining gorgeous sexual fantasies with an April trudge round the London marathon. She had blisters now and her nipples were bleeding where her T-shirt rubbed, but the pain was not winning. She was passing the *Cutty Sark*, waving at the overhead cameras, but Valerie's hard body refused to disappear and her disembodied hands moved up and down his abdomen, into his pubic hair and lightly over his balls. She thought of a huge phallus again as she picked up the container and banged away at the door, letting the metal drop against the inner skin, pathetically tinking as it struck a ridge. Far away she thought she heard a voice and then she dropped the canister and jogged back to Rachel who had stopped again. 'Wassatime?' she said and pulled at Rachel's arm. The gloves and the watch were covered in frost.

She rubbed at it. Quarter-to-one. She pushed at Rachel in disgust and roared, 'Fer fuck's sake! What is it with you Helys? All you gorradoo is keep walkin' and where's yer fuckin' Dad, eh? The old tosser!'

She had the urge to sit down and go to sleep, but Rachel hadn't given in yet. They went together to the door and they were both giggling as they tried to pick up the canister. Rachel was mumbling that she couldn't get a grip and Caz was trying to tell her to take her hands off Valerie's cock.

'You are so *pissed*!' she said instead, and she pushed Rachel into one last walk down the room.

Caz wasn't feeling cold any more. She knew that meant she was about to give up. She started getting angry with herself and called to Rachel. She lifted the canister again. This time it stuck to her hands. She lifted the tube. When she went to strike the door its cream rectangle moved backwards and away from her. Like a mannequin, she slowly fell forwards and rolled on to a shoulder with the steel tube still in her hands. She looked up at legs.

'What time d'yer call this?' she said.

She fancied having a little cry but her eyes felt too heavy and sore. 'Could someone gemmee a blanket?' she said. Then she forced herself to her feet. A hand touched her shoulder to help her from the ground but she snarled at it, baring her teeth. 'Fuck off!' she screeched. 'Jess gemmee a blanket!'

Then she closed her eyes, just for a second.

Forty-six

She was running down the Mall. Spectators were pressing in from the left. There were no more water-stations now. Lots of runners were struggling but she felt strong. Her feet hurt and she had jogger's nipple but now she was turning into Birdcage Walk, Buck House on her right. If she'd done a bit more training she could've done a bit better, but now she would be lucky to break her three-hour target. She could see Big Ben. She could see Westminster Bridge. Then she saw the clock above the finish line: 2:57:47. Another runner had stopped with just two hundred yards to go. If she helped her she might not crack the three after all. It was a woman in a track-suit. She stopped. She couldn't believe it. 'For God's sake, mate!' she gasped at her. 'How can you run a marathon in a track-suit?'

The runner looked up at her with dull white eyes. 'Practice,' she said. They started again, both wobbling a little. She held Rachel's hand as they crossed the line. They were both laughing. That was when a vicious cramp hit her left hamstring and she screamed, lifting from the bed, snot dripping from her face, red hot agony making her rigid. 'Stretch it!' she screamed, 'stretch!'

Feet came running. She was trying to sit up to stretch the muscle but the pain was throwing her backwards. 'Get me up!' she hissed. Arms took her from both sides and her head came up. She reached for her left foot, flexed it towards the ceiling and leaned on to her knee. The pain peaked then fell quickly away. She could feel heat in her eyes but she wasn't sweating. 'I'm dehydrated,' she thought, 'I need a drinks-station.' They lowered her gently back on to the bed.

Tom MacInnes said, 'Thanks for that, Jeff.'

She thought she was made of layers. She felt she had stripes. Her skin was cold but her muscles were warm. Deep inside her was angry heat but she felt herself chilled bone-deep. She would not go back to sleep, it was too dark there. 'How is Rachel?' she said quietly.

'Rachel is fine,' a voice said. Professor Hely loomed over her. 'She was still walking when we brought her out. She told us what you did for her. Thank you.' There were tears in his eyes.

'How? Where is she?' Caz asked.

'Next door. There's a policewoman with her.'

'Moira Dibben,' MacInnes said.

Caz put a crooked finger in her mouth and bit down hard focusing on the pain. She sat up, then she bit herself again working on her anger. Her bed was piled high with duvets and someone at some time had dressed her in yet another of the designer sweat-suits. She thought for a moment and decided that she wasn't cold but her joints ached. The tip of her nose throbbed with pain. She remembered wet shoes and deep instinct made her etch the vision until it was safe. Now she had time to be immeasurably sad. She looked for Jeff and reached out her arm.

'Tell me what happened, Jeff. Everything.'

He took her hand. 'I don't know what to say, Caz. They've arrested Valerie.'

'I know that,' she said. She patted his hand like a mother. 'Just tell me about this morning. I need to know.'

'I wanted to go with him to Brighton but he asked me to stay with you. He never said a word, you know. He just said, "Take care of Caz for me".'

'Did you fly here?'

'Yes, in the Flash Two. That was Val's idea. He rang me last night. Said he'd wangled some extra time off and did I fancy using the micro-light to come up here?'

'Tell me about this morning. Right from the beginning, Jeff.'

'There's not much to tell. We were just going to drop in without permission but, after the last time, Valerie decided it wasn't such a good idea. At the last minute we rang up the hall and they said it would be OK.'

'Who did you speak to?'

'The Foster bloke.'

'What happened then?'

'We took off from Storrington with some extra fuel, came up the valley and just flew straight in. I think we touched down about nine-fifteen.'

'Then what?'

'Foster met us. No shotguns this time. He took us to the dining-room. We were hoping to surprise you, Val was. You weren't there, so Foster took us to your room. You weren't there either so we had a coffee while Foster buzzed the prof.'

'What happened then?'

'When Foster contacted the professor he said you were in the labs but you wouldn't be there for long. We went through to some offices with Foster then the professor took us into the labs. We didn't find you. We looked everywhere, even in the operating theatres. Eventually we decided that you and Rachel had probably gone out for a walk, so we went for another coffee while we waited for you to come back.'

'Then what?'

'Valerie was like a cat on a hot tin roof. He wanted to see you. He went out into the grounds to find you. He came back half an hour later and said you weren't anywhere to be seen. He said that he found two blokes in the grounds and neither of them reckoned you were out there. One bloke said you'd been out running really early in the morning.'

'Before eight,' Caz said.

'Valerie came back in. He was wet and really agitated. He said he thought you were in some kind of trouble. He didn't know what. We called George Foster and he had the staff scour the grounds again. It took a while to be sure you weren't outside and the bloke on the gate insisted you hadn't gone out so we looked in the hall again. Then I said maybe you and Rachel were playing some kind of joke on us. Maybe you'd seen us land and were hiding. Valerie said there was no way you would do anything like that.

'We decided to try the labs again. It was well gone eleven by now and Professor Hely said that Rachel had work to do with him and was late. We weren't really worried, it was just Valerie who was worried, but he was stirring everybody else up. Then he asked George Foster to ring your boss at Brighton. Foster asked what he was supposed to say and Valerie said to just tell him that Caz Flood was missing.'

'Who found me?'

'Me and the professor, I guess. We'd been in the laboratory maybe three or four times and it was pretty obvious you weren't in there. I'd been up to the cold-room door but it was locked. Then Valerie came in to the lab and picked up the phone. He said did no one realise it was off the hook? Professor Hely said something about the fridge and I rushed through just in front of him. You were banging the door when we opened it.'

'What about earlier? When you came to look for us in the beginning? When you arrived?'

'What do you mean?'

'Were you all together?'

'I think so. As far as I can remember. Yes. As far as I can recall Valerie and I just followed the professor. We were more or less all together.'

'So could Valerie have slipped away, even for a second?'

'Not really. Why should he? We were just looking for you. Why would he want to go sneaking off?'

'Did you come into the lab?'

'Of course we did. If I remember we even looked through to the cold room. Oh, and the professor was a bit annoyed because there was a computer booted up and there was data on the screen. It didn't mean much to me but the professor wasn't pleased.'

'Then you left?'

'Then we left.'

MacInnes interrupted, asking if Caz was all right.

'I'm fine, Tom,' she said, 'I'm just a bit knackered. I've been running all morning.' She thought it was funny and gave out a little laugh. She swung her legs out of bed. There were a pair of 'Toasties' on her feet. 'Whose idea were those?' she asked. Hely touched his chest.

They were in the professor's personal quarters: Caz had been in his bed.

'I'm getting up,' she said. She shuffled next door. Rachel was fast asleep. Moira Dibben was at the bedside and she turned to smile warmly at Caz.

'Hi, Mo,' Caz said gently. 'How is Billy?' Moira made a circle with her finger and thumb and grinned. 'Good on yer, mate!' Caz said gently and left.

They went downstairs, through to Foster's office. The others had been spirited away and she was just with Tom MacInnes. He waited until she had sat down and he had organised a large hot toddy for her. Then he told her.

'Caz, your bed was all A-secretor, we knew that yesterday. We got the detailed DQ-Alpha results back at ten o'clock this morning. All the stains were the same.'

'I know,' Caz said.

'All the stains, in and on your bed were the same.'

'I know,' Caz said. 'They were bound to be.'

'And they match the DQ-Alphas for the murderer.'

'Of course,' Caz said.

'When Valerie Thomas asked Foster to ring us, we were already on our way to arrest him. We arrived half-way through the search and he was collared straight away. Bob Moore, DS Reid and DC Greaves have taken him to John Street. He's not been charged yet.'

'But he will be?'

'Yes.'

'So why aren't you in Brighton, Tom?'

'I wanted to talk to you.'

'What's up, Sir? Feeling sorry for me, are yer? Going soft?'

'No, Caz. I'm worried about you but I'm still worried about Avocado.'

'Oh, you want to know the connection between Avocado and Valerie, is that it? Well, presumably Avocado killed them, then Valerie fucked 'em. What d'you think? Is that sordid enough for you?'

'That's not what happened.'

' Of course it's not what happened!'

'So what happened, Caz. What do we know?'

'Can I have another one of these?' she said. She waved her empty glass at her DI. MacInnes took it, touching her hand, but then he paused, as if disapproving. Caz spoke quickly biting back tears. 'And don't say it's bad for me. You can't put enough whisky in.'

She stood and went to the window, throwing away the travel rug from her shoulders. Her fists were clenched. She looked at the dark grass and down to Jeff's khaki and orange Flash two, staring, trying to finally work it all out. She thought of Valerie and knew she was crying.

Tom MacInnes touched her shoulder. She didn't turn round. He put the drink down on a low table and whispered, 'When you're ready, lass.'

'Thanks, Tom,' she said.

She waited until the tears stopped before she turned round.

She took a deep breath and stiffened. 'OK, Sir. Say he did it. Say

Valerie Thomas killed all of them. Why? Why would he kill five men but only screw three and why are all five men connected to this place?'

'I don't know,' MacInnes said.

'Why do people kill, Tom?'

'Sex, money, power, revenge,' MacInnes said, 'or they're sick.'

'Valerie is not sick, Tom. He's not a psychopath. A psychopath may appear to perform normally but it's a veneer, there's no depth. Whatever Valerie is he's not that. He's been *inside* me. I *know* him.'

'You could be wrong, Caz.'

'All the victims have been here, Tom. That means they were possible donors of sperm. That means they have seen the wife of some powerful man and they may have impregnated her. What if the wife became frightened? What if the fertility fraud came into the public domain?'

'What are you talking about, Flood?'

'This place, Tom. As well as their public face they have a private one. When the wives of the rich can't tell their husbands it's *their* fault they're not conceiving, they come to the clinic and Rachel Hely works her magic. That fridge contains the answer. Avocado has been here. He's involved.'

MacInnes went to speak but she stopped him. 'Exactly how did it come about that Avocado was given a blood test, Tom? His brief knows we can't force him. What exactly was said?'

'He was superior,' MacInnes said. 'He just kept smiling. I felt in my guts that he was our man but he just kept insisting that he couldn't tell us why he sneaked back into the country. I remember, he leaned forward and said that surely there must be *some* way he could prove he was innocent? Then he looked at McDonnough.'

'His solicitor?'

'Yes.'

'It was McDonnough who suggested a blood test? But that means they already knew there was forensic evidence!'

'No, it doesn't, Caz. I lost my rag early on in the interview. Th smug shit had got my goat up. I was annoyed because the bastar wouldn't stop smiling and I said something about him fucking dea men.'

'That's a bit slack for you, Tom.'

'I know, lass. I guess I'm getting older.' He paused. 'An anyway . . .'

'Anyway what, Sir?'

'Ah wuzz upset about what he'd done t'you.'

Caz thought for a second, staring at her glass. Then she aske about the sample. MacInnes said they had taken both blood an sperm. 'Avocado thought it was hilarious. He asked if we could loa him a young policewoman. I told him to shut the fuck up then h turned on the camp personality and said, "OK, you'll have to do." Then I really lost my rag. I wanted to smack him in the mouth.'

'Where were the samples tested?'

'The Home Office labs at Aldermaston. I pulled a favour.'

'And you just did blood-type and DQ-Alpha?'

'Yes and no. My friend there whacked out the two quick blood tests first. I'd already asked him to run a digital DNA-profile. I wa certain Avocado was our man. I expected it to match the sample from the murder victims.'

'We need to talk to Professor Hely,' Caz decided. 'If my guess i right, the same woman was here last December and again in Jul this year. If I'm right, all the potential donors met her here, the ended up dead.'

'Jesus!' MacInnes whispered. 'Then . . .'

They rang Professor Hely. He came through with George Foster Jeff was in his suite. MacInnes explained quickly what he needed t know. Hely nodded. Foster protested that the information wa classified.

Caz stepped in. 'I've seen the computer records, George, an they're coded. We don't need to know *who* was here twice, just i someone was.'

Foster began to argue but Professor Hely interrupted him. He spoke very calmly. 'Miss Flood, Inspector, you may come with me to check the files now. I do not care about official secrets. I care about Rachel. If looking at our files will help my daughter, then so be it.'

'I can't let you do this, Professor,' Foster said, standing.

'Don't be a nonce, Geaarge!' MacInnes said.

Hely laughed and suggested George shoot him and the others now.

The four of them went through to the lab office. The Professor switched on one of the Compaq computers. 'What dates do we need to check?' he asked. He was tapping entry codes.

'July twenty-eighth,' Caz said, 'and I'll need Margaret's diaries.'

The professor pointed to a desk as he called up the database. Caz went to it.

'We have three ladies here for that date. There were three male guests. One was an A. George Foster and myself were present.'

'The other date you need is twenty-second December,' Caz said.

He tapped keys. 'Two ladies and three guests. Rachel and myself were present.'

'And the ladies, Professor? Was one of them at *both* lunches?'

The professor looked up at each of them in turn. 'Yes,' he said, 'do you need her name?'

She was known as Soraya, Light of Behaddi. He was Prince Fai, a direct descendant of God, the Perfect Incarnation. Their fiefdom in the Middle East was tiny but floated on a sea of oil. Its borders were protected by a small, highly trained army, bolstered by a division of ex-guardsmen and thirty seconded members of the SAS. Prince Fai had studied at Oxford and even looked western. 'Much loved' by his people, he ruled with a firm hand. He had had two brothers, a sister and an uncle, but all had died tragically. Now Soraya was blessed and carried their child. Thanks be to God.

MacInnes rang Brighton with the name of the sixth man. They came back to him within five minutes. 'Ian Austin, architect, aged thirty. Died Christmas Day. Drunk driver. Hit and run.'

'And Valerie was hang-gliding in Portugal with Jeff,' Caz said.

'There was no need to set him up for that one,' MacInnes said calmly. 'It wasn't supposed to be a murder.'

'Or for Davies,' Caz added. 'Davies just got drunk and fell off a balcony.'

Foster spoke. 'The Branch keeps tabs on all "As" since the project began. We had one death by natural causes a year back, then the Austin death. George Burnley was an "A". It was only then that alarm bells started ringing. You can forget about Prince Fai or his lovely woman. You can't extradite the leader of a country and the country is far, far too important to us anyway. This *has* to stop here. It was Soraya. We thought she was using one of their own people. We would have stopped her but, by the time we knew what was going on, Burnley, Green and Beecham were dead. It was too late.'

'But what about the staff?' MacInnes asked. 'If Soraya is terrified that her husband might find out about her surrogacy, won't she have to send someone to silence the workers, too? The Professor, Rachel? You, Bessie, Margaret Oakley?'

'No,' Foster said, 'Princess Soraya is no longer a problem. As soon as we understood what was going on, we arranged for our ambassador to have tea with the Princess at her Royal Palace. The staff's safety has now been guaranteed absolutely. This was after the ambassador impressed on her what information would be leaked if the clinic suffered in any way. I can assure you, the princess understands.'

'And George Burnley lives on,' said the Professor. 'His is the ultimate success. His child is to be born into great wealth and power. He is safe and he is protected. His genes will move slowly through the blood-lines of the richest and most powerful families in the world. And the good Princess Soraya will never say anything. Her prince has proved himself.

'She could never tell him there was a cuckoo in their nest.'

Forty-seven

Foster had used his Micro-Tac to talk to his people. MacInnes had used a land-line to speak to Norman Blackside, and a couple of cars were sent to arrest Jeremy Avocado. The DCS was concerned that they still had no real proof. If Avocado was a professional, he would be hard to convict.

In the morning, Caz went with the professor to see Rachel. She was sitting up in her bed reading a Jilly Cooper. They shared tea while Caz explained everything. Then Rachel told her that she had donated her own eggs four times and that three of her progeny were secreted away in the homes of the privileged.

'Why not?' she asked. 'I've given them damn good stock, intelligence, a good bone structure, and, after yesterday, a fair bit of stamina!'

Her father had been slightly less prolific, she said. He existed by proxy as a late extension of an Irish-American political family, and also as the first son of a prominent Afrikaner. They wondered did Caz want to invest her genes with them? She said that she would think about it.

She went to find Jeff. He was in the pool, swimming economically with a precise crawl. She went in and sat on the pool's edge with her feet in the water. He turned at one end and saw her, waving acknowledgement. She smiled warmly at him and said would it be all right to join him?

'Be my guest,' he said, smiling back.

She said she had no costume but would he mind? Before he could reply she undressed and slipped naked into the water. He stroked away up the pool. She followed a little less gracefully, feeling the water rippling under her belly. She stopped as he turned and waited for him. He swam past. 'Take me flying?' she shouted. 'Now?'

Jeff turned back to her and stopped close to her face; she could smell his breath. 'Don't you care about Valerie?' he said, a flicker of fire in his eyes, 'even a little?'

'No,' she said. She licked her lips and showed her teeth. 'Do you have any idea how sexy it is to cheat death? I have.'

'I'll take you flying,' he said coldly. 'Get out and get dressed.'

'You're sure you want me to get dressed?' she said from the water.

'Ten minutes!' Jeff snarled. 'Outside!'

She was there in eight minutes. She wore two Helly Hansen tops and two pairs of thermal bottoms. He threw her a flight suit and a pair of boots. 'They're Valerie's,' he said, 'get them on.'

He strapped her into the rear seat and pulled the straps tighter than safety demanded. She glared back through her visor and pushed a gloved hand into her pocket. He went behind her and turned the prop, then he was strapping himself in, the engine was puttering and they were turning on the short runway. 'You want to fly?' he shouted over the intercom, '*then fly*!' He opened up the engine, far more violently than Valerie had ever done. The microlight lurched forward, twitched, then rolled quickly towards the water. At the last second it swept from the ground.

'Did Valerie tell you how good I was?' Jeff shouted over the wind.

'In this or in bed?' she shouted back.

'Oh, very good,' Jeff said. The aeroplane dropped suddenly left and swooped over trees. Caz sucked in air. 'Valerie will get life on each murder,' she shouted. 'They may be able to charge him with six. I think he'll probably get Broadmoor. He'll never get out of there as long as he denies he did it.'

'Denies?' Jeff squawked, 'denies what?'

'The murders. Do you think he locked us in the fridge yesterday?'

'Do you?'

'No, I think you did, Jeff, but I was hoping you'd tell me why.'

The micro-light was climbing steadily. The fields were dropping away and shrinking into pastel patterns split by the near-black of pine forests.

'We were lovers once,' Jeff said.

'Tell me something I don't know,' she said back.

'When we were fourteen. He said it was experimenting. It didn't last long. He soon started with girls, he loved girls. I said it was all right. I wasn't gay either. But I still wanted him. He betrayed me. He loved me, then he dumped me. I might have been different if Valerie and I hadn't . . .'

'You wish,' Caz spat.

'I promised myself one day I'd make him pay. I got rid of his bloody fiancée and I saw off a few others. You were harder. I started out just meaning to frighten you but you weren't like them. You fought back. You made me feel so dirty. I thought I'd killed you that afternoon. I was so happy.'

'How did you set up Valerie?' she shouted. 'How could you be so sure that he would never have an alibi?'

'Oh, piss off! That was easy. If he wasn't with me he was waiting for me. I always made sure he had no escape route. He *worried* about me.'

'Did you kill Burnley and the others?'

'Christ! I thought you knew. Of course not. It was Jeremy. I just helped him out a bit. Jeremy was under time pressure. He needed a patsy and I offered him Val. I gave him the idea of planting semen. We'd shared each other's body fluids often enough. He came to the clinic when I worked in the lab. We were lovers for quite a while. That's how I found out what he *really* did for a living. I still slept with him now and again. He excited me you see, he's so *dangerous*.'

'How did you know what to do?'

'You're kidding me. You're talking to an expert. I was going to do my PhD knee-deep in sperm. I worked under Jeffries at Leicester for a year. Then I got pissed off with it all. Dear Valerie used to give me a sample a week. We used to call it his weekly wank. I lifted a couple of canisters when I left – my own little funny souvenir. Did you know, Valerie always made his donation Fridays? Always on Fridays. He said it made him last longer if he got his leg over on the weekend. He's very bright, you know, but he fucked himself silly at University.'

'I know. He told me.'

'Does he love you?'

'Yes.'

'It's a shame then.'

'What is?'

'Me having to kill you.'

'Don't worry about it,' Caz crackled to him, 'I presumed you would.'

They were at eight thousand feet; the Two's engine purred behind them. 'Don't you mind?' the pilot shouted to her. 'Aren't you scared?'

'No, Jeff,' Caz radioed back, 'I'm just tired. I've done a few things that I'm not too crazy about recently and well . . . No, it's all right.'

'D'you want to fly first? I mean really fly?'

'Please,' she said.

Jeff croaked something over the crackle of the line, then they began to spiral down in a tighter and tighter circle. His arms stretched above him and she could see the muscles of his wrists as he strained at the bar. The circle seemed complete and she felt the wind and gravity tear at them. Her inner ear felt strange and at points she thought her eyes were bulging. They dropped thousands of feet then he suddenly levelled the plane.

'Hey,' he shouted, 'when did you know? Did I foul up, what?'

'Not really,' she said back; she felt badly sick. 'The single biggest thing was that I believed in Valerie. I just kept thinking "what-if it only *seems* to be him?"'

'But you're just a junior copper and it was only a feeling.'

'I know. Somehow I knew the forensic evidence against him would be overwhelming. But when I was trapped in the cold room, I took a deep-freeze canister to bang on the door. The cap was just like the one Billy Tingle took from you. At least I knew how Valerie's semen came to be at every crime-scene. I gave the cap to my DI.'

'That's it? That's how I fucked up?'

'You really lucked out when the clinic's computer gave us six names. Five were dead and one was missing, presumed. The first guy died while you two were in Portugal.'

'So?'

'So then I thought, it's not Valerie, it's Avocado. But it can't be Avocado who locked us in the fridge, he's not around. And if it's neither of them, who is it? The other thing was, you kept calling it the cold room. It says fridge room on the door. "Cold room" was what Rachel and the Professor called it. I thought maybe you had been at the clinic before. I guessed maybe you supplied the donors. Valerie said you did all sorts of jobs. You worked there, right?'

'Nine months. I left to set up the donor procurement.'

'Which is why George Foster knew you but said nothing.'

'Foster and the Prof still think I'm one of the good guys.'

'When you attacked me, Jeff, when you stabbed me that afternoon, I saw your shoes. I hadn't remembered. When I came through the cold-room door and I fell on the floor, I saw them again. They could have been Valerie's but then they told me he'd already been taken away. That left you, Jeff. They were *your* shoes.'

They were climbing slowly, extra power humming from the engine.

'Valerie was always so protective of your name. He thought the world of you. You always seemed to be there just after his biggest crises but he never once connected you to them. I just thought there were too many coincidences. Did you fix the micro-light that day when he crashed?'

'I thought in a simpler fashion then.'

'Maybe you should have called it quits when he got up and walked away. Valerie's a good man. Didn't you realise God was on his side?'

'Why? Is God a heterosexual?'

'She might be,' Caz said. 'Oh, and there was one more thing, Jeff.'

'What?'

'We never had the sexual exchange.'

'The what?'

'When we met, we never had what I call "the sexual exchange". It happens automatically when boy meets girl. If you really fancy someone you notice it, otherwise you only notice when it *doesn't* happen. I never got it from you. I guessed you might be gay. Earlier, in the pool, you were dead to me. Then I knew.' She looked at the sky. She looked out to the sea. She looked down at the greens, the browns and the yellows of the Downs. Far off she could see Brighton.

'How are you going to kill me?' she said.

She didn't so much want to die but she was too tired to fight to stay alive. Everything about her was heavy and languid. She was resigned.

'I wasn't going to kill you,' Jeff said, 'I was going to kill myself, but you, in the pool, you made me angry again. I hadn't thought how, exactly, but I had decided my next time up in my micro-light would be my last. These things crash all the time. I just figured, what's one more?'

'Valerie needs me,' she said. Wind noise almost drowned her voice.

'What did you say?' Jeff called back.

'Valerie, Jeff. He needs me.'

She heard him shout, 'I know that, you bitch!' then his arms let go of the bar above them. She felt him move as he unclipped his harness and there was an electric pop in her ears as he switched off the intercom. Jeff said nothing more as he pulled the radio lead from his helmet. Then he stood, waited for a second, and launched himself wordlessly into space. She watched him fall, a beautiful, floating cross that moved behind her, sailing on the wind until she could no longer see him. She felt in her pocket for the tape recorder and fumbled for the 'off' button. The Flash Two was stable but it was climbing steadily. She thought of Valerie.

'Micro-lights fly themselves,' he'd said, 'but Twos are twitchy. They're not like conventional aeroplanes. To climb, you use extra power, to fall, you power back. Power back slowly and let the micro fly itself.'

She couldn't reach Jeff's foot throttle, but hers was to her right: a straight, black-handled stick. She moved it gently and the engine's whine became deeper. She waited, breathing deeply, leaning forward to look at the instrument panel. The altimeter arm stopped moving clockwise, then it steadied, then it slowly began to move the other way. Tentatively she reached forward for the control-bar. At full stretch she touched it and rested her fingertips on the cold metal. She could feel the 'plane slowly dropping though the sky. Now she looked up. She was heading diagonally towards the coast and then out to sea. She found it faintly amusing. Another touch on the throttle and she could hear the putter of the engine. The micro-light was dropping fast enough to make her feel sick.

Brighton was just a little to her left and she was about to pass over the shingle of the beach. She was way too high and she guessed she would be miles out before she touched the water. She listened for Valerie again. 'Just pull the bar down on one side, gently, gently. You'll turn towards the pull and lose height at the same time. Just spiral, take your time.'

The micro-light curved gracefully back from above the white-capped sea, curling down slowly and swinging in towards the roof of the Grand Hotel. Faces appeared and arms pointed but Caz simply sat there, unable to change direction and praying that it wouldn't hurt too much. Then she was over the grey-sloped roof still curling, still falling, skimming down towards the white of the pier. She dropped the tape-recorder as she crossed the road and failed to see it as it bounced on to the beach. For some unknown reason she was not scared. As she hit the water she called out Valerie's name.

Cold grey rushed to envelop her. The sea roared and slapped into her face. She was dizzy with the perversity of it all as she struggled to undo her harness. She found it oddly pleasant as the cold came over her head. She wasn't sure, but she thought she had undone the buckle. Then it was darker. Then there was nothing, not even Valerie.

Epilogue

It was pissing down. Pissing down and freezing. Flood squeezed in among the bodies trying to stay warm. The cross-country course was a three-lapper, knee-deep in mud and it had a pig of a hill. Lordshill's Sue Dilnot was running, so everyone was fighting for second place. There were a couple of fast Basingstoke girls, Kathryn Bailey from New Forest Runners, and two fairly good veteran runners, one from Team Solent, the other going for Totton. Caz reckoned on coming sixth. *If* she had a good race. God! how she loved winter-league racing!

She started fast but kept her head down, looking at the floor to keep clear of divots and other people's feet. Kath Bailey and Sue Dilnot went away quickly and once the idiots and optimists had dropped out of the way, she was in a comfortable fourth place. She didn't feel too bad all things considered.

Kathryn and Sue were sixty metres ahead by the end of the first lap and Caz was fifth, tucked in just behind the Totton vet. The Totton woman was like a metronome, thung, thung, thung; not a lot of leg speed but more stamina than a team of huskies. On the hill, second time round, Caz went past her, driving through the mud, but as they passed the finish with a lap to go, thung, thung, thung, the vet came back alongside. She had light brown hair cut like Peter Pan and she grinned at Caz.

'Aren't you Caz Flood?' she said. 'D'you think you ought to be running?'

'Why not?' Caz grunted.

The vet said her name was Janice and she went on ahead. Fifth, Caz could live with. She kept working hard, but four hundred yards from the finish, the second Basingstoke girl went sweeping by her.

'All right,' Caz thought, 'all right! *Sixth* I can live with.'

Valerie was waiting with her sweat-top at the finish. She took it as soon as she could lift her head. When she started coughing she swore she could taste sea water. 'I've seen yer lookin' better, Flood!' he said.